PRAISE FOR DAVID MORRELL'S

Ruler of the Night

AND THE THOMAS DE QUINCEY TRILOGY

SELECTED BY *SUSPENSE MAGAZINE*
AS A BEST BOOK OF THE YEAR

"Masterful....Evokes 1854 London with such finesse that you'll hear the hooves clattering on cobblestones."

—*Entertainment Weekly*

"Stellar....Real historical figures mix with the heroes, and the thriller elements are both terrifying and grotesque."

—Jeff Ayers, Associated Press

"I love this series. *Ruler of the Night* actually made me believe I'd stepped into Victorian London. It's an exciting blend of high-thriller and Dickens, with parallels to our own time that are both fascinating and unsettling. I've been a Morrell fan for years, and *Ruler of the Night* is as gripping as anything he's done."

—John Sandford, author of *Extreme Prey*

"Riveting!...With this mesmerizing series, David Morrell doesn't just delve into the world of Victorian England—he delves into the heart of evil."

—Lisa Gardner, author of *Right Behind You*

"A joy to read....Morrell expertly immerses us in another country and another time, while delivering characters so real they could be living next door to us right now."

—Betty Webb, *Mystery Scene*

"The De Quincey series has been among the best works Morrell has produced since bursting onto the literary scene with his debut novel, *First Blood*....Morrell has been called the 'master of the thriller' for many years, but what he really has mastered is well-paced storytelling, weaving in real events with breathtaking and imaginative fiction."

—J. R. Ogden, *Cedar Rapids Gazette*

"Spectacular....The narrative builds to a powerful but bitter-sweet ending."

—*Publishers Weekly*

"Morrell's deft hand with thriller plotting provides copious chills and procedural satisfaction, but it is his mastery of character, shrewd exploitation of Victorian details and attitudes, and tonal sophistication that seduce and delight....Richly detailed and engrossing; Morrell animates the Victorian era and delivers genre thrills with rare style and panache."

—*Kirkus Reviews*

"A complex, top-notch mystery....Philosophical, uncannily perceptive De Quincey competes well with Sherlock Holmes for brilliance....You don't have to read this series in order, but you'll want to read every volume."

—Jen Baker, *Booklist*

"Morrell excels at constructing historically accurate mysteries with enough melodrama to satisfy any lover of Victorian novels. His protagonists are fascinating and entertaining; aficionados of the trilogy are going to miss De Quincey and company."

—Barbara Clark-Greene, *Library Journal*

Ruler of the Night

ALSO BY DAVID MORRELL

NOVELS

First Blood

Testament

Last Reveille

The Totem

Blood Oath

The Brotherhood of the Rose

The Fraternity of the Stone

Rambo (First Blood Part II)

The League of Night and Fog

Rambo III

The Fifth Profession

The Covenant of the Flame

Assumed Identity

Desperate Measures

The Totem (Complete and Unaltered)

Extreme Denial

Double Image

Burnt Sienna

Long Lost

The Protector

Creepers

Scavenger

The Spy Who Came for Christmas

The Shimmer

The Naked Edge

Murder as a Fine Art

Inspector of the Dead

SHORT FICTION

The Hundred-Year Christmas

Black Evening

Nightscape

ILLUSTRATED FICTION

Captain America: The Chosen

NONFICTION

John Barth: An Introduction

Fireflies: A Father's Tale of Love and Loss

The Successful Novelist: A Lifetime of Lessons about Writing and Publishing

Stars in My Eyes: My Love Affair with Books, Movies, and Music

EDITED BY

American Fiction, American Myth: Essays by Philip Young
edited by David Morrell and Sandra Spanier

Tesseracts Thirteen: Chilling Tales from the Great White North
edited by Nancy Kilpatrick and David Morrell

Thrillers: 100 Must-Reads
edited by David Morrell and Hank Wagner

Ruler of the Night

DAVID MORRELL

MULHOLLAND BOOKS

Little, Brown and Company

New York Boston London

Copyright © 2016 by Morrell Enterprises, Inc.

Mulholland Books / Little, Brown and Company
Hachette Book Group
1290 Avenue of the Americas, New York, NY 10104
mulhollandbooks.com

Originally published in hardcover by Mulholland Books, November 2016
First Mulholland Books paperback edition, November 2017

Mulholland Books is an imprint of Little, Brown and Company, a division of Hachette Book Group, Inc. The Mulholland Books name and logo are trademarks of Hachette Book Group, Inc.

The publisher is not responsible for websites (or their content) that are not owned by the publisher.

The Hachette Speakers Bureau provides a wide range of authors for speaking events. To find out more, go to hachettespeakersbureau.com or call (866) 376-6591.

Library of Congress Control Number: 2016945301
ISBN 978-0-316-30790-1 (hc) / 978-0-316-30791-8 (pb)

10 9 8 7 6 5 4 3 2 1

LSC-C

Printed in the United States of America

Once again to Grevel Lindop and Robert Morrison,
for guiding my journey into all things Thomas De Quincey;
and to historian Judith Flanders, for leading me along dark Victorian streets

TABLE OF CONTENTS

Ruler of the Night

INTRODUCTION

A NEW KIND OF DEATH

I**T'S DIFFICULT TO** imagine the extent of the British Empire during the nineteenth century. British maps of the era depicted its territories in red, vividly illustrating that they stretched around the globe: Canada, the Bahamas, Bermuda, Gibraltar, Cyprus, a large swath of Africa, India, Burma, Malaya, Singapore, Hong Kong, Australia, New Zealand, on and on. As the saying went, the sun never set on the British Empire. It dominated a quarter of the planet's landmass and a third of everyone living on it, far more than Alexander had conquered or the Romans had dreamed of possessing.

Britain—the nation that controlled this immensity—was, by comparison, small. At first, this might be surprising, but Britain's compact size gave it a major advantage over larger areas such as Europe and the United States. Ideas and innovations could spread rapidly throughout its limited space, creating a strong core for the empire's globe-spanning might—a power that increased dramatically after the invention of a new wonder of the world.

The distance between the port of Liverpool and the factories of Manchester is thirty-five miles. Today, that distance can be traveled in as little as half an hour. But in the early 1800s, wagons and barges were the only ways to transport raw materials and finished products. Both methods were difficult and time-consuming, limited by potholed gravel roads or narrow congested canals, requiring at least a day's travel under the best of conditions and weeks of delays during the worst of winter.

But in 1830, something astonishing was created—a railway between Liverpool and Manchester, the first of its kind. That railway was so expensive and experimental that many financiers considered it a folly, yet it proved so successful that only a month after it opened, a railway from Manchester to London was proposed. Ten years later, almost two thousand miles of tracks crisscrossed England. By 1855, a mere twenty-five years later, *six thousand* miles of tracks united every corner of the nation, with more being planned.

Materials, products, and coal could now be transported with such speed and profit that more and more factories were built until, within a few amazingly rapid decades, England became the first nation to take full advantage of the Industrial Revolution, achieving unprecedented world dominance.

Thomas De Quincey, one of the most notorious and brilliant literary figures of the nineteenth century, mourned the change. "Out of pure blind sympathy with trains, men will begin to trot through the streets," the Opium-Eater wrote, "and in the next generation, they will take to cantering." In his nostalgic essay "The English Mail-Coach," he eulogized the horse-driven vehicles upon which he'd traveled in his youth. Their dependable ten miles an hour had been fast enough for him. He'd felt a unity with the landscape through which he'd passed and a sympathy with the mighty animals that charged him forward. Now, as trains reached an unimaginable velocity of fifty miles an hour, it seemed to him that "iron tubes and boilers have disconnected man's heart." He recalled the excitement with which a trumpet had once heralded the arrival of a mail coach into a relay station and the awe of the spectators at the thunder of the horses. "The gatherings of gazers about a mail-coach had one center and acknowledged only one interest. But the crowds at a railway station have as little unity as running water and own as many centers as there are separate carriages in a train."

Always interested in violent death, De Quincey was quick to note that on the first day of the Liverpool to Manchester railway, a politician named Huskisson had climbed down from the ceremonial train when it stopped to put water in its boiler at the midpoint of the inaugural journey. Huskisson wanted to apologize for his recent argument with England's then prime minister, the Duke of Wellington, whose victory over Napoléon at the Battle of Waterloo had made him one of the most revered men in the nation. Huskisson proceeded along the tracks, reached the prime minister's compartment, and shook hands with him, becoming so distracted that only at the last moment did he notice a locomotive speeding toward him on a parallel set of tracks.

The prime minister's train began to move forward. Huskisson hurried next to it. He grabbed a door to climb inside, but the door swung open into the route of the approaching train. He dangled, lost his grip, fell onto the tracks, and was run over.

The news of Huskisson's gruesome death spread across the country, making him famous, causing people throughout England and the world to become aware of this stunning invention and a new kind of transportation that they couldn't previously have imagined.

But the railway also brought a new kind of death, and as De Quincey—an expert in the fine art of murder—discovered, there were many more deaths to come.

I seemed every night to descend into chasms and sunless abysses, depths below depths, from which it seemed hopeless that I could ever re-ascend.

—Thomas De Quincey,
Confessions of an English Opium-Eater

The Opium-Eater is [the] ruler of the night.

—Ralph Waldo Emerson to Thomas De Quincey

ONE

THE LOCKED COMPARTMENT

London

ON THURSDAY EVENING, 22 March 1855, a frowning gentleman studied a two-page document that lay on his substantial desk. His name was Daniel Harcourt. Fifty years old, the solicitor was stout, a consequence of his sedentary profession. His gray frock coat and waistcoat were of the finest tailoring. His gold watch chain indicated his respectability. The glowing coals in his fireplace worked to remove the damp chill from a recent rain, but at the moment, a fire wasn't necessary. As Harcourt looked up from the pages, he felt the internal heat of triumph.

"Are you quite certain about these details? The house in Bloomsbury? Everything?"

The man who stood on the opposite side of the desk wore a faded greatcoat of inferior quality. His raw face had the creases of someone who worked outside for long periods in all kinds of weather.

"I did the job myself, Mr. Harcourt. If you patrol the streets the way I did for ten years, you get to know who to talk to. Newsboys, crossing sweeps, water boys at cabstands—that sort don't miss a thing, and for as little as sixpence, they'll prove it. The best street artist in Bloomsbury drew the man's face. What I gave you is gospel."

Harcourt removed a piece of paper from a desk drawer and slid it toward the man. He dipped a pen into an inkwell and handed it to him. "Write your name."

"But you already know my name. It's John Saltram."

"Write it anyhow."

"You think I don't know how to write?" Saltram asked with muted indignation. "You think the Metropolitan Police Force hires constables who can't write?"

Harcourt set a gold sovereign next to the piece of paper. "Humor me. Write your name."

After a long look at the gold coin, Saltram obeyed, scratching with the metal nib. "There, you see," he announced, returning the pen and the piece of paper.

"This isn't the same handwriting that's on the pages you gave me," Harcourt observed.

"I said I could write. I didn't say I could write neatly. My missus wrote those pages. She put down what I told her. I wasn't about to trust it to anybody else."

"How do I know she didn't make a copy? How do I know you won't try to sell these pages to the man you followed?"

"That wouldn't be too smart of me, would it, Mr. Harcourt? I want steady work, not trouble, from a man the likes of you."

Harcourt thought a moment and put five more gold sovereigns on the desk. They were the equivalent of five weeks' pay for a constable.

"Here's what we agreed upon," he said. "Keep the other sovereign as a bonus."

"Thank you, Mr. Harcourt. Thank you kindly." Saltram stuffed the coins in a pocket of his trousers. "Any more work you need me to do…"

"I can always use a man who controls his tongue. In fact, your services might be required very soon. But right now, it's late, and I'm certain you want to return to your wife."

"Yes, Mr. Harcourt. Very good, Mr. Harcourt."

As Saltram backed away, he wiped a hand across his lips in a manner that suggested he intended to go to a tavern rather than to his wife.

Harcourt watched him step into the lamp-lit corridor outside the office and shut the door. He listened until he could no longer hear Saltram's footsteps descending the stairs.

Only then did he allow the heat of triumph to thrust him into motion. He quickly removed his gold watch from his waistcoat. The time was twenty-seven minutes after eight. He seldom worked this late, but there hadn't been a choice—his meeting with Saltram had needed to occur when the building was deserted and no one would see the man arrive.

In a rush, he tossed the piece of paper with John Saltram's name into a wastebasket under his desk. Then he hurriedly put on his overcoat, gloves, and top hat. He shoved the two-page document into a leather case, grabbed his umbrella, extinguished the lamps in his office, and stepped into the hall. After locking the door, he swiftly descended the stairs, extinguishing more lamps as he went.

Harcourt's office was in Lombard Street, which tonight was cold and thick with mist. It was one of the shortest streets in this exclusive business district of London, a square mile known reverently as the City, always with a capital C. But despite the modest length of Lombard Street, its location near the palatial Bank of England and the Royal Exchange made it one of the most influential places in the world.

Harcourt took long steps over the dark, wet pavement and reached a cabstand at the corner. During the day, there were as many as twenty cabs here, the most that the law permitted at one time, but now, after business hours, he felt lucky to find two.

Climbing rapidly into the first, he called up to the top-hatted driver on his roost at the back, "Euston Station! I need to be on a nine o'clock train!"

"That doesn't give us much time, guv'nor."

"Triple your usual fare."

The driver enthusiastically cracked his whip, and the sprightly two-seated cab surged forward. The clatter of the horse's shoes echoed off the deserted stone buildings. At once, the driver dodged this way and that through a sudden chaos of vehicles coming north from Blackfriars Bridge. Cracking his whip harder, he urged his horse along Holborn Hill and turned right into Grays Inn Road.

Harcourt patted his leather case with the pages inside it. As the cab passed a mist-shrouded streetlamp, he studied his watch and saw that he now had only ten minutes to reach the station.

Harcourt tried to breathe slowly and calmly. He never failed to be nervous whenever he needed to make a railway journey. He remembered the mail-coach era, when speed was exhilarating rather than threatening.

"Nearly there, guv'nor," the driver called, swerving left into the New Road.

"It's almost nine o'clock!"

"No fears, guv'nor. Just have your coins ready when you jump out."

As Euston Square appeared before him, Harcourt clutched his document case and umbrella, waiting anxiously for the cab to pass through the immense Roman arch that led to the station. At the curb, he threw the coins to the driver and raced into the Great Hall. Ignoring the pillars, statues, and grand staircase, he reached the only ticket window that remained open.

"The nine o'clock to Sedwick Hill," he told a clerk, shoving a crown toward him.

The clerk didn't need to ask if he wanted first class; Harcourt's gold watch chain told him everything. "Better hurry, sir."

Harcourt grabbed the ticket and rushed away.

"You forgot your change, sir!"

Ignoring the shout behind him, Harcourt pushed through a gate and reached the platform. After the classical architecture of the Great Hall, the ugliness of an iron-and-glass ceiling stretched before him. Smoke from countless departing engines had coated the glass with soot.

Harcourt showed his ticket to a guard and hurried along the waiting train, its hissing engine seeming to indicate impatience. He passed the third-class carriages in which passengers could only stand. Then came the second-class carriages with their hard benches. The social importance of wealthy passengers required them to take precedent and be at the front, even though that put them behind the noise and sparks from the belching engine.

Out of breath, Harcourt finally reached two first-class carriages. Each had several compartments, and each compartment had its separate entrance.

He peered through the first open door, but that compartment had passengers. He loathed sharing a confined space with strangers. Propriety obligated him to exchange a few pleasantries with them, but after that, the situation became awkward. During daylight, he could ignore the other occupants by reading a newspaper that he'd purchased from the W. H. Smith bookshop in the station, but at night, the single lamp in each compartment wasn't sufficient to allow him to read, forcing him to avoid conversing with strangers by staring out the window into the darkness.

The passengers Harcourt saw through the open door didn't look like they belonged in a first-class compartment anyhow. One was a short elderly man who wore what appeared to be a suit appropriate for attending a cheap funeral. Even the single lamp in the compartment was enough to show that the little man was agitated. Although he was seated, he moved his boots up and down as though walking in place. He clenched and unclenched his hands. His face was beaded with perspiration.

Seated opposite him, the elderly man's young female companion looked peculiar also. She was attractive, Harcourt admitted, with lustrous blue eyes that turned to focus on him through the open door, but her clothing had the same look of belonging to a mourner at a cheap funeral, and she wore, in place of the fashionable hoops of ladies in society, trousers, which were evident to the observer because they extended below her skirt. No, Harcourt was definitely not inclined to spend even twenty minutes locked in a compartment with two such people.

He hurried nearer to the front of the train and peered through the next open door. Mercifully, the lamp on the wall revealed that there weren't any occupants.

The small compartment had four seats on the right and four on the left, facing each other. A farther door allowed access if the train arrived at a station that had a platform on the opposite side. There wasn't a corridor linking all the compartments; instead, each set of passengers occupied an isolated chamber.

Harcourt climbed inside and settled onto a thick cushion of blue satin. As he placed his document case and umbrella next to him, he realized how agitated he'd become during his rush to reach the train. He removed one of his gloves and touched his face, discovering that his cheeks were slippery with perspiration. Reminded of the little man in the compartment behind him, he wondered if he'd been too quick to pass judgment.

"Just in time, sir," a guard said at the open door.

"Indeed," Harcourt replied, concealing his relief.

But he wasn't the person whom the guard had addressed.

An out-of-breath man climbed into the compartment, politely looking down so that he and Harcourt wouldn't be forced to converse. In fact, the newcomer was courteous enough to move all the way over and sit near the other door. He even sat on the same side as Harcourt, relieving them of the awkwardness of facing each other.

Harcourt leaned back but couldn't relax. There hadn't been time to send a telegram to the man he was hurrying to see, but he assumed that when he reached Sedwick Hill, someone in a local tavern would be eager to earn a half crown and take a message to the nearby estate. A carriage would soon arrive for him. The household would be in a state of confusion, having been roused by his urgent summons, but when Harcourt delivered the two precious pages, he had no doubt that his client would be immensely grateful.

The guard shut the door, inserted a key, and locked it. Despite the hiss of the locomotive, Harcourt heard the scrape of metal as the guard locked the next compartment also—and the next and the next.

When Harcourt was a child, his two older brothers had locked him in a trunk in a storage room. Squeezed by the dark, narrow confines, he'd pounded at the lid, begging to be let out. The trunk's interior had become warm and damp from the accumulation of his frantic breathing. His shouts had weakened, his breath slowing, his mind blurring. Abruptly, light had blinded him as his brothers threw the lid loudly open and ran away, laughing.

Harcourt couldn't help remembering.

The man who shared his compartment seemed anxious also, sitting rigidly straight.

As the locomotive made chugging sounds, the iron pillars on the platform outside appeared to move. Through the window, Harcourt watched the soot-blackened glass ceiling recede as the train departed the station, heading north. He had difficulty concentrating on the view, if it could be called that, because of the distraction of the brass bars at the window. The bars prevented passengers from leaning out and being killed by a blow to the head from an object that the train passed. For a similar reason, each compartment was locked from the outside, lest someone accidentally open a door or even do so deliberately, foolishly peering out for a better view and then perhaps being struck by something or losing his or her balance and falling.

Harcourt knew the practical reasons for this arrangement, but his face was nonetheless covered with perspiration, since he didn't think of this as a train compartment. With its barred windows and locked doors, it felt like a prison cell.

The man who shared the narrow enclosure stood. He shifted past the armrests and sat opposite Harcourt, their knees almost touching.

What unmitigated rudeness, Harcourt thought. *Is he a speculator? Does he hope to sell me something?*

Peering resolutely toward the darkness beyond the window, Harcourt ignored the man.

"Good evening, Mr. Harcourt."

How the deuce does he know my name? Unable to resist, Harcourt turned his gaze in the stranger's direction.

The stranger had kept his head down when he'd entered the compartment. But now he raised it and looked into Harcourt's eyes.

"You!" Harcourt exclaimed.

As the man lunged, Harcourt grabbed his umbrella, hoping to defend himself. But the man yanked it from his grasp and threw it onto the floor. Squeezing Harcourt's throat with one hand, he drove a knife toward Harcourt's chest with the other.

The knife struck something solid and slid off.

The attacker cursed. Harcourt gasped, struggling to push away the hand that choked him.

Hell began.

From the Journal of Emily De Quincey

After our three-month stay in London, I did not expect that the respite Father and I enjoyed from our infinite bill collectors would end so abruptly. In the weeks since the threat against Queen Victoria had been eliminated, I took advantage of my twenty-second birthday to appeal to Father's sentiments and compel him to admit that his decades-long reliance on opium could not continue without lethal consequences. Two days of remaining awake were followed by twenty-four hours of twitching sleep in which all of history's armies marched through his nightmares and the ghosts of his sisters and my mother spoke to him. He could eat almost nothing except bread soaked in warm milk. He confessed to consuming as much as sixteen ounces of laudanum—a concoction of powdered opium dissolved in brandy—each day. That amount of spirits would have been destructive enough even without the addition of an opiate.

Under Dr. Snow's guidance, Father reduced his intake by half an ounce for three days and then another half an ounce for three days and so on. At the slightest sign that his body was rebelling, Father was instructed to add a quarter ounce to the level he had reached and remain there until the headaches and tremors abated. Then Father was to continue attempting to reduce his intake in half-ounce stages.

This method not only made sense but also appeared to be effective. Father managed to reach a level of eight ounces per day. It remained an enormous amount, considering that people who weren't accustomed to opium might die if they swallowed a full tablespoon, but Father had accumulated more than four decades of tolerance for it.

His blue eyes became clearer. He ate broth and eventually dumplings. He began writing again, adding new material to the volumes of his collected works that his Scottish publisher was preparing. Having received new pages, Father's publisher actually sent us ten pounds, an unexpected kindness given that Father had long since spent the money that his publisher was obligated to pay him.

Our dear new friends Sean and Joseph (I refer, of course, to Detective Inspector Ryan and Detective Sergeant Becker) were delighted by Father's progress and gave him every encouragement, as did I. But they did not know Father the way I did, and all the while he reduced his intake, I couldn't help remembering the several times in which I had made this journey with him. In particular, it troubled me that one of Father's writing projects was a new version of his Confessions of an English Opium-Eater—not merely a revision but an enlargement. Just when I'd hoped that he could free himself from the drug, he was revisiting the tormented text he'd written a lifetime ago, once more describing the harrowing events that had contributed to his need for opium. Again he wrote about having nearly starved to death as a seventeen-year-old beggar in the wintry streets of London. Again he wrote about tragic Ann, his first love, a fifteen-year-old girl of the streets who'd saved his life when he collapsed from hunger but who had then disappeared forever.

I did my best to distract him. On that Thursday evening, to celebrate the halfway point in Father's opium reduction, Sean and Joseph accompanied us to a much-talked-about newly opened chophouse in Soho. Sean's abdominal wound had healed properly this time, and Joseph no longer suffered the double vision that the blow to his head had caused. All in all, our improved conditions were reasons for celebration. Father even offered to use part of our recently acquired ten pounds to pay for our feast.

"No need, sir. We forgot to tell you that Joseph and I are now rich," Sean reported.

"Rich?" Father asked, looking puzzled.

"Indeed. Because of our injuries, we each received a bonus of five pounds from Scotland Yard's special fund. We can't think of a better way to spend some of our vast wealth than by treating you and your daughter to a meal."

The chophouse's floral-patterned ceiling was a wonder to behold, as were the brightly colored segments of glass in the overhead lamps and the elaborately framed mirror above the fireplace. Everything was so pleasant that in the hubbub of conversations, no one paid attention to my bloomer skirt or the scar on Joseph's chin or Sean's Irish red hair when he took off his cap. Customers didn't even seem to notice how short Father was.

But no sooner did we all sit at our table than my smile died, as I saw a change—much too familiar—come over him. It always began with his eyes. Their blue acquired the brittle look of ancient porcelain. Then his face became pale and glistened with sudden sweat. His cheeks seemed to shrink and develop more lines. He clutched his stomach.

"Rats," he said, trembling.

A man at the next table dropped his fork. "Rats? Where?"

"They gnaw at my stomach." Father moaned.

"The chophouse served you rats?"

"My father is ill," I told the man. "I'm sorry we disturbed you."

"Rats in his stomach? Then he needs a cat *in his stomach."*

As Father groaned, Sean and Joseph helped him outside. A rain earlier in the evening had given London a rare sweet scent. I hoped that it and the cold mist enveloping us would brace him and moderate his torment.

"Emily, should we take him to Dr. Snow?" Sean asked.

"I don't believe it would help. I've seen this happen before. There's always a level of opium below which Father can't descend."

Obeying the doctor's instructions, I removed a laudanum bottle and a teaspoon from my pocket.

"Here, Father."

From painful experience, I knew there was no other way. The teaspoon of the ruby liquid did its work. Father's breathing became less agitated. Gradually he stopped trembling.

"Mr. De Quincey, you had only a slight relapse," Joseph said. "Tomorrow, you'll be on track again."

"Yes, only a slight relapse," Father murmured.

In the faint light from the streetlamp, I saw tears in his eyes.

Father normally walks briskly, reacting to opium as if it were a stimulant, not a sedative. But that night, his steps were slow with discouragement as we returned along Piccadilly to Lord Palmerston's house across from Green Park.

The immense house is among the few in Piccadilly that are set back from the street. It has two gates, one for arriving and another for departing traffic. Beyond them, a curved driveway leads up to the majestic entrance through which Queen Victoria had often passed when her cousin the Duke of Cambridge owned the structure, which is still known as Cambridge House.

A porter—looking none too happy to be outside in the cold mist—opened a gate for us.

"Lord Palmerston's been waiting for you," he said. "There's been a telegram."

"For me?" Sean's tone suggested that he feared another terrible crime had been committed.

"For Mr. De Quincey."

Father raised his head in confusion. "What? Who on earth would…"

"Your publisher, perhaps," Joseph offered.

Father regained some of his energy as a footman opened the large door. We entered the vast hallway, which was brightly illuminated by a chandelier and gleaming crystal lamps along the walls. The Greek statues, the Oriental vases, and the huge portraits of Lord Palmerston's noble family never failed to impress me. Given the various cramped, leaking accommodations where Father and I had lived, I had never in my dreams expected to reside in what I considered a palace, although Lord Palmerston always referred to it as a house.

His Lordship instantly appeared at the top of the immense staircase, making me suspect that he'd been listening for our return.

"I have something for you!" he announced.

Holding an opened telegram, he hastily descended. It was the swiftest that I had seen His Lordship move since he'd become prime minister in early February, so heavily did his new responsibilities weigh on him. His chest and shoulders still exuded power, but the burden of the war against the Russians had created extra lines in his once-handsome features, and the brown dye in his thick long sideburns no longer disguised his seventy years.

Quickly reaching the bottom of the staircase, Lord Palmerston handed Father the telegram. "It appears that the nation's prime minister has become your social secretary. I opened this before I realized it was for you."

Although Father and I were grateful for His Lordship's three months of hospitality, I continued to feel that he gave us shelter not to indicate his appreciation for the help we'd provided during the recent emergencies but rather to keep us near him so that he could sense if we learned anything about him that might be compromising. "Keep your enemies closer than your friends," I had once heard him say to a cabinet minister about a member of the opposition, and I was certain that he felt the adage could also be applied to us. But after so much time, he was clearly sick of us, especially of Father's noisy pacing along corridors in the middle of the night. If not for the fondness that Queen Victoria and Prince Albert had for us, he would no doubt have long since asked us to leave.

"It appears that you've been summoned," Lord Palmerston said.

What little color there was in Father's complexion drained as he read the telegram and moaned in despair.

"Father, is everything all right?" I asked.

"It's a catastrophe! As bad as the burning of the Alexandrian library!"

"The burning of what?" Sean asked.

"The Pope! The Dryden! It has to be stopped! A Bradshaw! Get me a Bradshaw!"

No matter how baffling Father's outburst was, at least one reference was clear. Father was demanding to see a copy of Bradshaw's Railway Timetables.

"You heard the man," Lord Palmerston told his footman. "Bring him my Bradshaw."

The footman scurried away, although he seemed eager to remain in the hopes that the mystery of Father's behavior would be revealed.

"The Shakespeare. The Spenser. No!" Father moaned.

I took the telegram from Father and read it to the group. "'Patience ended. Books to be auctioned noon Friday.'"

"I told him he'd receive his blasted money!" Father insisted.

"But that was six months ago, and you didn't send it," I reminded him gently.

"I explained to him that I just needed a little more time! Why won't he listen?"

"Explained to who, Emily?" Joseph asked.

"A landlord," I replied.

"*In Edinburgh? I thought your landlord knew that for now you're living in London and he should rent out your lodgings.*"

"*In Grasmere. The Lake District,*" I told the group. "*Where Father lived for many years. One reason we're in debt is that he collects books.*"

They seemed perplexed.

"*Many, many books,*" I continued reluctantly. "*Wherever Father lives, he fills room after room with books until there is barely space in which to move. He finally locks the door and rents another dwelling.*"

"*How many places filled with books are you talking about?*" Sean asked.

"*Three. There used to be others.*"

"*Three? But how in creation does your father pay the rent?*"

"*He can't. He keeps promising, and occasionally he sends payment for a month or two, leading the landlords to expect that additional money will arrive. Eventually some of them lose patience.*"

"*Perhaps if he sold a portion of the books, he could pay the landlord and retain the others,*" Joseph offered.

"*Sell my books?*" Father sounded horrified.

As Lord Palmerston stepped forward, I had the impression that he concealed his delight. "*You asked for a* Bradshaw. *Does that mean you contemplate a journey? Perhaps to the Lake District? Perhaps to Grasmere?*"

"*The books will be auctioned at noon tomorrow! I must leave at once!*" Father said.

"*Yes, absolutely at once,*" Lord Palmerston agreed.

When the footman rushed back with a copy of Bradshaw's Railway Timetables, *Lord Palmerston searched eagerly through the thick volume.*

"*Aha. A train leaves at nine o'clock tonight from Euston Station. It stops at Manchester. Tomorrow morning at six, a train leaves Manchester for Windermere, arriving at ten. A swift carriage ought to get you to Grasmere by noon. You can save your books. Quickly. There's not a moment to spare.*"

"*But it's already after eight.*" I pointed toward the great clock in a corner of the entrance area. "*There's no time to pack.*"

"Easily taken care of," Lord Palmerston assured me. "I'll instruct the servants to gather your things and send them to Grasmere. You'll have them by tomorrow evening." He turned to the footman. "Summon a cab," he ordered. He told another servant, "Bring my overcoat, hat, and gloves."

"You're coming with us, my lord?" Father asked. "Aren't you needed at Parliament tonight?"

"I wish to give you a proper good-bye."

Thus it happened that the five of us were crammed into a hackney cab that was meant to hold only four. A woman with a hooped dress could not have fit into the crowded vehicle, but my bloomer skirt allowed me to share the close space between Sean and Joseph, feeling them on either side of me.

I'd gone to the chophouse in high spirits. Now those spirits plummeted as we rushed through the misty streets, arriving at Euston Station with only five minutes to spare. In the cab, in the presence of Lord Palmerston, I wasn't able to tell Sean and Joseph how much I didn't want to leave them. "I shall miss you" was all I could manage as we crossed the station's Great Hall.

"But you'll come back soon, I hope," Joseph said quickly.

Before I could tell them I would try with all my heart, Lord Palmerston thrust two tickets into my hand. "First class. Nothing's too good for you and your father. Here are five sovereigns to help you along the way. Now hurry or you'll miss your train."

His Lordship looked shocked when I kissed first Sean and then Joseph on the cheek.

But he didn't allow my show of affection to distract him. He urged us through a passageway onto the gloomy glass-and-iron-roofed platform, where a guard examined our tickets.

Hurrying toward the hiss of the train, I looked back and waved to Sean and Joseph at the gate. Their faces were bleak. In contrast, Lord Palmerston smiled brightly and returned my wave, happy to be rid of us in a way that wouldn't antagonize Queen Victoria. I imagined him telling the queen, What else could I do, Your Majesty? It was their idea.

We found an empty first-class compartment, where I told Father, "We ought to sit against the far window." He looked so distracted, clenching and unclenching his hands, moving his feet up and down even after he sat, that I wanted us to keep a distance from anyone else who entered. As it was, a hurried man peered through the open door, saw us, obviously didn't approve, and rushed on.

The guard locked our door. Although I disliked being trapped in the prisonlike compartment, at least we wouldn't have the awkwardness of sharing the limited area with strangers who would judge us.

The train jolted into motion. Outside the terminal, the mist cleared. We passed the gaslights of factories, then the lesser lights of decayed buildings in slums. Finally there were only trees and pastures revealed by starlight and a half-moon.

The compartment was cold. The single lamp on the wall against which I sat did little to dispel shadows. The train swayed as it accelerated, and the clatter of its wheels intensified.

"Emily, will you allow me to open the window?" Father asked. "I think a sharp breeze might help to calm me."

He slid the window up.

"Perhaps another teaspoon of laudanum would help also," he suggested.

"Not yet, Father."

"No, alas, not yet."

With a sigh, he leaned back against a cushion. My position across from him, with my back toward the engine, was such that the wind created by the train rushed in toward Father but not me. A cinder flew through the open window and stopped glowing a moment before it landed on him.

"Watch for sparks, Father."

He brushed at his coat.

The train moved faster.

"In the days of the horse-driven mail coach," Father said, "especially when I rode on top, I could readily see what lay along the road and what stretched ahead. But in here, we might as well be blind."

I felt a thump behind me.

"What was that?" I wondered.

"What was what?" Father asked.

Again something thumped behind me, this time with greater force.

"The wall," I said. "Something banged against it."

Father leaned forward. Even in the meager lamplight, I could see that for a change, his eyes showed interest rather than despair.

The next thump was so strong that the partition trembled.

Now there were several loud thumps in a row, followed by a muffled shout. All at once, the vibrations seemed to come from the side of the compartment instead of the wall, many of them, loud and rapid.

Abruptly the stars and the half-moon disappeared as we entered a tunnel. The enclosure amplified the roar of the engine and the fierce clatter of the wheels while the thumps and the shouts in the next compartment became silent.

As the train rocketed from the tunnel, its noise diminished. A dark liquid covered the area of the window that wasn't open, rippling in the wind created by the train's rush.

"It must have started to rain," Father said. "Drops of it flew in. I feel them on my face."

"But before we entered the tunnel, I could see the sky, and it was clear," I told him. "I don't understand how clouds could so suddenly have overtaken us."

"Then why did I feel rain strike my face?"

Father wiped the cheek that was near the open window. He peered down at his hand.

"Emily," he said. His tone chilled me as he showed me the dark liquid on his fingers. He seemed to fear that he was suffering an opium delusion.

"It's real, Father. Turn your face toward the light."

When he exposed that section of his face, I shivered. His cheek was covered with the same dark liquid that smeared the window, and there wasn't any question that it was blood.

* * *

LESTER ALDRIDGE HAD a cough. By itself, that wasn't remarkable. After an unusually cold, snowy winter, many people had coughs, but Aldridge was a train guard, and his employment put a different perspective on the condition of his health. He'd noticed that many train guards developed coughs, and his wife had a theory that being constantly exposed to the smoke and cinders from locomotives affected his lungs the way soot in a chimney affected a sweep's lungs—and no one had ever met a chimney sweep who didn't have a cough.

As the nine o'clock from Euston pulled into its first stop, Aldridge raised his fist to his mouth, coughed yet again, and turned the wheel on the brake van at the rear of the train. Because none of the carriages had a braking system, one of Aldridge's jobs was to bring the train to a halt.

He jumped down to the platform and ran along it, using his key to unlock all the compartments. In the event of a collision or a derailment, that task was essential. Otherwise, the passengers would be trapped amid the chaos of the wreckage.

He heard shouts ahead but decided not to attend to them until he came closer. Right now he needed to keep the train on its strict schedule. Quickly, he unlocked the freight carriage. That was easy. There was only one door, in the middle.

He hurried to the third-class carriages, but ahead, the shouts grew louder, a woman demanding, "Guard! Guard!" So he kept rushing forward.

People on the platform gathered to learn the cause of the commotion. Aldridge made his way through them and found a blue-eyed young woman at an open window, her attractive features distorted with alarm. He remembered when she and a small elderly man had boarded the compartment at Euston Station. Considering the trousers that extended below the hem of the young lady's hoopless skirt, Aldridge was surprised that they could afford first-class tickets; they most likely belonged in a third-class carriage.

"Let us out!" she insisted.

After another cough, Aldridge inserted his key into the door. "Is there a problem, miss?"

"My father has blood on his face!"

"Blood?" someone in the crowd exclaimed. "Where?"

"Did your father have an accident, miss?" Aldridge inquired in distress, hurrying to open the door. "Did he somehow cut himself?" Even as Aldridge asked the question, he couldn't think of anything in the compartment that was sharp enough to cause an injury.

"The window!" the young woman told him, helping the small elderly man hurry from the compartment. The lamps on the platform revealed the blood covering one side of his face.

"My God!" a man said, lurching back.

"Did something crash against the window, miss?" Aldridge asked, trying not to appear as agitated as he suddenly felt. He knew that ruffians sometimes threw rocks at passing trains, and on rare occasions, birds flew against the windows, breaking the glass.

"No. No. The window was open."

"Let us out!" the passengers in the second-class carriages were yelling.

A platform guard rushed to Aldridge. "What's wrong?"

"I don't know yet," Aldridge said. He suppressed another cough and acted as if he were in control of the situation. "Unlock the other doors. Let the other passengers out."

Returning his attention to the young woman, Aldridge said, "A station guard will bring medical help. What happened?"

"Blood came through the window."

"Blood through the window?" someone in the crowd repeated in horror.

"Open the next compartment," the elderly man said. The crimson that dripped from his face made him look so grotesque that the crowd stepped even farther back.

"But what does the next compartment have to do with—" Aldridge started to ask.

"Listen to my father," the young woman instructed. "Unlock the next compartment."

Suddenly in motion, Aldridge unlocked and opened the next door. He frowned when the faint light from the single lamp showed that the compartment was empty.

"But passengers were definitely here," Aldridge insisted. "I remember one of them spoke to me before I locked the door. Then a second passenger boarded at the last minute. Where did they go?"

The woman's father squeezed next to him and peered inside. "The floor mat is in disarray," he noted. "So are the cushions."

Aldridge started to climb inside.

"No, not that way," the little man objected. "Quickly. Come with me."

Confused, Aldridge felt the woman in the bloomer skirt tug his arm. Her authority was such that he couldn't resist following her father into the compartment they had occupied.

"The door on the opposite side," the man said. "See the part of the window that isn't open? See the blood on it? Unlock that door."

"But it's dark on that side of the tracks. We won't see anything out there."

Trying not to brush against the young woman, Aldridge made his way outside and grabbed a lantern that hung on an iron post.

Again, he maneuvered around the woman. As the little man sat sideways on cushions, Aldridge reentered the compartment and gave him the lantern. Then Aldridge removed his key from his uniform, shoved his arm between the brass bars at the open window, twisted his hand down, and managed to unlock the far door.

He felt relieved to step down onto the gravel and have sufficient space not to bump into the woman. She and her father descended behind him and stood between two sets of tracks, one on which their train had arrived and another set for trains heading in the opposite direction.

"Good Lord," Aldridge said when he raised the lantern toward the exterior of the next compartment.

The iron step below the door was covered with blood. So was a wheel between that compartment and the one from which he'd just descended. The side of the latter compartment was spattered with blood, as was the closed portion of the window.

"What in heaven's name…"

"Unlock this door," the woman's father said.

By now, Aldridge was so accustomed to receiving commands from this strange pair that he automatically obeyed. But when he put the key into the lock, he didn't need to do anything. At his touch, the door swung open.

"It isn't secured," he said. "But I know all the doors on this side were locked. I did it myself."

"The latch has been broken," the woman said, pointing.

Aldridge brought the lamp closer. Not only was the latch broken but the interior of the door showed severe damage to its polished mahogany— or, rather, what had once been polished mahogany; much of the battered wood was now covered with blood, as were the upended cushions and the twisted mat. Even the ceiling was spattered with crimson.

Aldridge coughed and raised a boot toward the metal step, intending to look inside.

"No!" the little man warned. "You'll disturb the blood on the step. You mustn't touch anything until the police arrive. Give the lantern to my daughter, and lift me under my chest and legs. Put me inside so I can look around without standing on anything."

Again the authority of this strange couple was such that Aldridge obeyed, pleased that the little man weighed almost nothing.

"All I see is a hat and a blood-covered umbrella," the man said, his voice sounding muffled beyond the compartment's open door. "Maybe the umbrella was used as a weapon."

"There isn't a leather case?" Aldridge asked, continuing to hold him above the floor in there. "I remember the first passenger carried both a document case and an umbrella."

"Only the hat and the umbrella. No, wait—I see something under this seat. Tilt me down closer." The little man hovered over the floor and peered under the seat. "I'm wrong," he said. "It's nothing."

"Your cough sounds persistent," the young woman told Aldridge.

"From the train smoke, miss."

"Boil water in a pot. Add a chunk of pine resin. Inhale the steam," she advised. "The vapor from the pine resin will open your airways."

"You know about medicine?" Aldridge asked. His chest began to feel the effort of holding up the woman's father.

"A doctor is teaching me. Your lungs will feel better for a time, but they won't improve if you continue to be exposed to the smoke."

"What can I do, miss? With four children and a wife, I need the work."

"Perhaps a mask would help when you're alone at the back of the train."

"You're kind to think of me, miss."

Suspended within the compartment's interior, her father said, "There doesn't appear to be anything else inside. You may set me down now, thank you."

Aldridge's chest continued to ache even after he returned the little man's boots to the gravel. "Nothing like this has ever happened on a train before. I don't know what to do."

The locomotive hissed. A fierce whistle sounded.

Aldridge quickly closed the compartment's door but couldn't lock it, so damaged was the latch. At least it stayed shut. "I'll summon the constable at the station. He'll try to make sense of what happened."

"Just be certain the constable doesn't enter that compartment and disturb anything," the young woman insisted. "Send a telegram to Detective Inspector Ryan at Scotland Yard. Tell him that Miss De Quincey and her father are here. He'll come at once."

The train's whistle blew again.

"It doesn't matter how swiftly the inspector arrives," Aldridge told her. "The train will be gone."

"What?"

"We're behind schedule."

"I don't understand."

"The train has to depart immediately and try to gain the time it lost."

"But someone was attacked here!" the woman said.

"There's no choice. Railway time is relentless. Nothing can interfere with the schedule. If one train falters, the rest of the system falters also. Everything comes to a halt."

"Uncouple the carriage and leave it here for Inspector Ryan to examine," she told him firmly.

"Impossible! This station doesn't have a siding on which to shunt the carriage. We need to reach Manchester for that. This carriage can't be brought back here until noon tomorrow."

The train's whistle shrieked again, this time longer.

Aldridge hurried to climb into the compartment that the little man and his daughter had occupied. "You'd better get aboard."

"How far behind us is the tunnel?" the woman asked.

"The tunnel? A quarter of a mile. Why do you wish to know?"

"The attack happened when the train passed through it." She turned to her companion. "You know what we need to do, Father."

"Yes."

"I'm sorry about your books."

"As am I," her father said.

"Give me your lantern, please," the woman told Aldridge.

"But—"

She took it from him and started along the tracks.

"Wait!" Aldridge demanded. "What are you doing?"

"The victim might still be alive!" she called back. "I might be able to help him! Perhaps I can stop the bleeding!"

"But it isn't safe out here!"

"Send guards as quickly as you can!" she urged.

Aldridge watched her run along the tracks, her elderly father managing to stay with her. The light from the lantern swayed in the darkness, becoming smaller. Then the train's whistle was even more insistent, and Aldridge rushed to obey it.

THE COLD AIR stung De Quincey's cheeks.

"Father, I truly meant what I said about the loss of your books," Emily told him as they hurried along the shadowy tracks. "I understand the sacrifice you're making."

"The sacrifice was made a long time ago, Emily. Finally I realize how much I deceived myself."

Behind them, the train made rapid chugging sounds. The connections between carriages clanged. Wheels scraped. Peering over his shoulder as he hurried, De Quincey saw the red lanterns at the end of the brake van recede into the night. Then all that remained were the distant lamps on the platform and the shadows of the countryside.

"Even if I reached Grasmere in time, how could I possibly stop the landlord from auctioning my books? I'm forced to admit that they were doomed the moment I locked the door on them."

Gravel crunched under their rapid footsteps.

"I see the tunnel," Emily said, raising the lantern.

The looming, dark entrance made her stop.

"Can you hear me?" De Quincey yelled into the tunnel. His words reverberated in the blackness.

"We've come to help you!" Emily shouted.

But the only sound was a rumbling echo.

"Maybe he's too weak to answer us," Emily said. "God grant that we're not too late."

She gripped De Quincey's hand. They stepped into the void.

Instantly, the air became colder and heavier. They heard the echo of their footsteps and the sound of water dripping from the ceiling.

Emily aimed the lantern between the two sets of tracks, but the light wasn't powerful enough to chase the darkness from the widely spaced, curved walls.

"The abyss of an opium nightmare," De Quincey said.

"Perhaps you should have remained at the station. Father, do you feel strong enough to continue?"

"What this makes me feel is..."

"Yes?" Emily asked.

"...alive."

The adrenaline of having a purpose suppressed the weariness of De Quincey's sixty-nine years, stifling decades of regret for the snare in which he'd allowed opium to entrap him. His habit of walking as much as fifteen miles each day to subdue his craving, his compulsive midnight pacing that Lord Palmerston complained about, gave his legs the strength to keep up with his daughter.

"Ahead." De Quincey pointed. "There's something on the gravel."

The lantern revealed a dark shape lying between the two sets of tracks. Emily rushed forward but then stopped abruptly.

Even if the victim hadn't been motionless in the way that only corpses can be, clearly the man was beyond help. His neck had been slashed. His forehead was pulped. One of his legs was almost severed.

"Oh," Emily murmured.

She set the lantern down and dropped to her knees at the edge of the considerable blood that surrounded the body. After a moment's hesitation, she reached over and touched one of the man's wrists, searching for a pulse.

She shook her head despondently.

"In December, I believed I'd seen the worst that I would ever encounter," she said. "After what happened in February, I became even more certain. But now…" She sighed. "God help this man—because there's no way I can."

De Quincey tried not to inhale the coppery odor from the blood.

"I hope you don't think this is murder as a fine art," Emily said.

"Aristotle would be the judge of that, not me. Pity and terror—those are the great philosopher's requirements."

De Quincey helped his daughter to stand. "Without question, what was done to this man produces terror." He turned Emily away from the corpse. "But what about pity?"

"Father, I know what you're doing."

"Merely trying to create a reality in your mind that's greater than what lies behind us."

"Thank you."

"The helplessness that this man felt, trapped in a locked cell on a speed-ing projectile, is something we all feel every time we step into a train, and now the vileness of the human imagination prompted someone to commit murder in one of those locked compartments. Will there come a time when the world moves so fast that there'll be no place in which we're not afraid? Yes, I pity this man." De Quincey's voice dropped. "I pity us all."

They faced the far-away curved entrance to the tunnel. The moon-light beyond it provided a pale contrast to the dense blackness around them.

"You shivered. Are you cold, Father?"

"You shivered also," he told her.

"But we can't leave," Emily said, the tunnel echoing. "Not until station guards arrive to make certain that everything remains the way we found it. Sean will want to have all the details preserved."

"Do you see the lights of the station?"

"No, Father. It's too far away."

"Do you see the outlines of guards hurrying toward us?"

"No, I don't see them either," Emily replied. "What do you suppose is taking them so long?"

"But I do see something. Perhaps because of laudanum, it's only in my mind."

"What are you talking about, Father?"

De Quincey extended the arm that held the lantern. At the level of his knees, several eyes gleamed from the light's reflection.

Emily stumbled back. Something growled.

"Dogs!" Emily said.

The eyes moved closer—three pairs, four, five.

"The odor of the blood must have attracted them! They want the corpse!" De Quincey said.

Another dog growled.

"Maybe they also want us!" Emily said. She waved her arms and shouted, "Go!"

The eyes vanished as the dogs turned and darted away.

"That's right!" Emily yelled. "Leave us alone!"

But now the eyes reappeared, floating back to where they'd been.

"I couldn't help this wretched soul, but by God, I'll protect what's left of him!" Emily shouted.

Teeth suddenly flashed, snapping at her.

Emily lurched back so quickly that she almost fell.

"Gravel!" De Quincey said.

He picked up a handful and hurled it. They heard numerous yelps, and the eyes again vanished as the dogs scurried away.

"Yes!" Emily said. She grabbed one handful of gravel and then another, throwing it with all her strength.

De Quincey heard more yelps.

But then he heard more growls. Turning, he saw yellow eyes drifting toward him from the opposite direction.

"Emily, I'll take this side while you take the other! Keep throwing gravel!"

As he held the lantern with his left hand, he found the strength to grab stones with his right, throwing them, hearing them clatter on rails while many of them thumped against flesh. He wore gloves, but the rough edges of the gravel tore the tips off the gloves.

"Blast you!" Emily yelled as she threw the gravel. "I won't let you have this man!"

"Make as much noise as possible!" De Quincey told her with effort. His arm cramping, he began to sing a hymn that he remembered from the terrible events in February. " 'The son of God goes forth to war / A kingly crown to gain!' Sing it, Emily! As loudly as you can! 'The son of God goes forth to war!' "

Their bellowing voices rebounded off the curved walls.

De Quincey abruptly switched to a hodgepodge of Shakespeare. " 'Hell is empty and all the devils are here!' But I shall send you all back to hell! I shall be a dog of war!"

"Father!" Emily called out in warning.

The echoing roar of their shouts was nothing compared to the fierce din that rushed toward them. Suddenly the entrance to the tunnel was blocked by darkness except for two red lights that grew larger and larger.

Emily grabbed her father and tugged him down onto the gravel a moment before an express locomotive raced from the north toward London. The fury of the wind it created gusted at De Quincey's coat. He felt the ground beneath him shudder and clamped his hands over his ears. Carriage after carriage rushed past, the clatter and clang of myriad wheels adding to the chaos. Thick smoke filled the tunnel, sparks burning De Quincey's forehead. The air became so dense with swirling soot that he couldn't breathe. He coughed and choked, scrunching his eyes shut against the grit that threatened to clog them.

All at once the clatter and clang were gone. As the smoke and the cinders settled around him, De Quincey opened his raw eyes and saw the red lamps at the end of the train hurtling away into the night toward London. The tunnel's thundering echo subsided until the only sound he heard was the ringing in his ears.

"Are you all right, Emily?"

As the two of them struggled to their feet, De Quincey raised the lantern. The eyes were no longer in evidence.

"The train must have frightened the dogs away," he said.

Then Emily said, "No."

The eyes reappeared, dark shapes stalking near them. The growls came closer.

Teeth snapped at Emily.

"Damn you!" She kicked, her boot striking a dog's nose. With a bark of pain, the dog bolted away.

"Until tonight, Emily, I never heard you say 'blast' or 'damn.'"

"You might hear worse, Father."

A dog bit into his trouser cuff and tugged, nearly pulling him off his feet.

His chest tight, De Quincey hopped on one foot, swung the lantern, and slammed it against the dog's head. Stunned, the dog released its grip and staggered away.

De Quincey drew a painful breath as he reached for more stones, but what his fingers grasped instead was a piece of metal. Raising it to the lantern, he saw that it was the end of a broken rod that must have fallen from a passing train.

He mustered the energy to bang it repeatedly against a rail on the tracks. The angry ringing noise he created was so unfamiliar that the eyes darted back.

"It's working, Father!"

But as he kept striking the rod against the iron rail, his heart raced with such force that he feared he might collapse.

"I don't have the strength to keep doing it, Emily!"

Slumping to the gravel, he handed her the rod. Sweat dripped from his face and soaked his clothes.

Emily pounded the rod again and again on the rail, but the earsplitting, high-pitched sound of the impact only made the dogs hesitate and assess the danger.

De Quincey fought to calm the frenzy of his heart.

"They're coming back!" Emily said.

Certain that he was in an opium nightmare, that none of this was happening, that he was asleep in Edinburgh and had never come to London, De Quincey forced himself to stand.

He took off his overcoat.

"Father, what are you doing?"

"I love you," he told her.

He raised the glass on the lantern and stuck the hem of his coat into the flame.

"Father!"

Gripping the coat's collar, he swung the burning hem toward the dogs. The fire illuminated the matted fur and ulcerating sores on the grotesque animals, some without an ear, others with maggots dripping from them, all looking like creatures from hell.

Certain that his heart couldn't beat any faster without killing him, he shouted, "Go back to hell!" and flailed the coat at the animals, sparks flying. Smoke carried the stench of scorched fur. His speeding pulse made him dizzy.

Emily followed his example, removing her coat, igniting its hem. As he sank to his knees, she was suddenly next to him, lunging toward the dogs, swinging the fiery garment.

Lights rushed into the tunnel. For an instant, De Quincey feared that another train was coming, but these lights swayed as though they were being carried by people who ran. Voices accompanied them, men shouting, "Go, you bastards! Get away!"

The lanterns showed truncheons rising and falling. Dogs cried out and fled, their shadows becoming silhouettes that disappeared at the tunnel's mouth.

"Are the two of you all right?" a man asked, rushing closer. His lantern revealed his railway guard's uniform. "Oh my, look at you! Sir, you have blood on your face. Your gloves are covered with blood too. So are yours, miss! You're both layered with soot. What happened to your coats? They're almost ashes."

"We didn't think you'd ever arrive," Emily said.

"We had trouble finding a doctor, miss."

"But I won't be needed," a man standing over the body said. "No one could recover from injuries as severe as these."

"I felt for a pulse," Emily told him. "He is indeed beyond help."

The doctor gave her a puzzled look, apparently unable to imagine that a woman would know how to detect a pulse.

"It's important to stay away from the body," Emily told them. "The police will need everything to be undisturbed so they can investigate."

"I'm the local constable," another man said, stepping forward.

"Then you understand everything needs to remain the way it is so that Inspector Ryan can do his work," Emily told him.

"Yes, the train's guard said you were emphatic that Detective Inspector Ryan needed to be summoned from Scotland Yard and that the telegram should also say Miss De Quincey and her father are here. De Quincey? That name sounds familiar."

Feeling the rats reinvading his stomach, De Quincey said, "Emily, please, my medicine."

When she removed the laudanum bottle and the teaspoon from her skirt, he ignored the spoon, took the bottle, and drank from it.

Recognizing the kind of bottle it was, the three men gaped.

"Now the name comes to me," the constable said. "You're the Opium-Eater."

TWO

"IT'S SOMETHING THAT PEOPLE DIE FOR"

UNMARRIED SCOTLAND YARD detectives had the option of sleeping in a police dormitory in the Whitehall area, not far from the headquarters for the Metropolitan Police Force. The former private residence consisted of several rooms filled with narrow beds.

Ryan later determined that it was ten minutes after eleven when a constable woke him, speaking softly so as not to disturb everyone else. "Sorry to do this, Inspector, but you have a telegram."

"Telegram?" Ryan needed just a moment to gather his thoughts. He'd felt so distressed by the sudden departure of Emily and her father that sleep had not come easily. "Who sent it?"

"The Great Northern Railway."

"The *railway?* Why would…"

Ryan got out of bed and stepped into his trousers with a minimum of sound. He followed the constable to a hallway and shut the door to prevent its lamp from waking the others.

He read the telegram once. Then he read it again.

"Thank you," he said, concealing his agitation.

He reentered the room and walked through the shadows to the corner where Becker slept.

When he put a hand on Becker's shoulder, Becker's eyes opened.

"Emily's in trouble," Ryan said.

THEY HURRIED DOWNSTAIRS to an office.

"There aren't any trains at this hour," Ryan told the constable on duty. "We need a police wagon."

"I wish I had one for you, but all of them are being used."

Ryan turned to Becker. "Looks like we're going to spend our reward money."

They rushed outside, barely taking time to button their coats against the night's chill. With Parliament sitting until after midnight, traffic in Whitehall was scant at this hour. But a short run brought them to the Strand with its brightly lit theaters, taverns, chophouses, and, most important, numerous cabs.

"We're with Scotland Yard," Ryan told a driver as two well-dressed men stepped out of his vehicle. He showed his badge.

"Always 'appy to 'elp a detective inspector," the driver said. "Where to?"

"It's a distance."

"As long as you pay, I'll get you there."

Becker named their destination.

"But that's ten miles!" the driver objected.

"Here's two sovereigns," Ryan said. He and Becker each handed the man a coin. "You won't earn that much driving around London tonight."

"And ten miles back. My 'orse'll be worthless for tomorrow."

"Another two sovereigns," Ryan said. He and Becker dug into their pockets. Four pounds was probably more than the driver had ever seen at one time.

"Scotland Yard must have an awfully important reason to get there," the driver said.

"The most important reason in the world," Becker told him.

"Well, nothin' is more important than a pretty woman."

"Exactly," Ryan said.

"In that case, you'd better 'ang on, gents!"

From his perch at the back of the cab, the driver cracked his whip, urging his horse forward.

Ryan and Becker sat tensely, neither of them saying a word. Forty years old and twenty-five years old, respectively, both of them knew all too well that they were attracted to the same twenty-two-year-old woman.

Late at night, trying to sleep, Ryan often reminded himself that he was almost twice Emily's age and that his feelings toward her ought to resemble those of a brother. Becker—so close in years to Emily—was the obviously appropriate suitor. But try as he might, Ryan couldn't subdue his attraction toward her. During the rare times when he believed he'd succeeded in thinking of Emily only as a sister, his resolve would crumble the moment he again encountered her blue eyes and the ringlets in her light brown hair—and her spirit, her wonderfully exasperating independent spirit.

The cab reached the factories and slums of London's northern outskirts. After stopping to pay the toll at the turnpike gate, they hurried along a dark, deserted road, its pulverized stone surface allowing the horse to maintain its footing in the dim illumination from the cab's exterior lamps.

No matter how swiftly the vehicle moved, Becker tapped his fingers impatiently on his knees while Ryan stared outside. The haze dispersed, revealing shadowy trees, fields, and streams.

But all Ryan saw was Emily's face.

"I pray she's all right," Becker said.

"If she isn't, someone will pay dearly," Ryan vowed.

"Indeed," Becker said firmly.

"You 'ired the right man, gents," the driver yelled down. "Hear that church bell marking the hour? I got you 'ere in ninety minutes."

Ryan frowned as the cab's two lamps revealed stacks of bricks and piles of sand along the road. Weathered boards dangled from the exposed frames of cottages. Heaps of debris seemed everywhere.

"What happened to this place?" Ryan shouted.

"The railway!" the driver called down. "Land speculators started buildin' cottages for people who want to live in places that are now closer to London. The speculators got beyond themselves and built so many cottages there's no one to buy 'em. My brother was a carpenter here, but he got put out of work and had to join the army to eat, God 'elp 'im. Now they sent 'im to the war."

Ahead, Ryan saw a cluster of shops and houses next to railway tracks. The streets were unpaved and lit by a few old-fashioned lamps that had coal-oil reservoirs.

The moment the cab stopped, he and Becker jumped out and hurried across a rumbling wooden platform. The station had only a ticket office, a telegraph office—both of them dark—and a waiting room, the lamps of which were illuminated. Ryan glanced through its windows, but the room looked deserted.

A station guard stood outside.

"I'm Detective Inspector Ryan from Scotland Yard. This is Detective Sergeant Becker. Where are Emily De Quincey and her father?"

"In there," the guard told them, gesturing toward the waiting room.

But when Ryan entered, he didn't see them.

"Where—"

Becker pointed, and Ryan saw that Emily and her father were stretched out on benches.

They weren't moving. Afraid that they'd been killed, Ryan hurried to them, only to stop in relief as Emily raised her head. His relief changed to shock when he saw that her face was dark with soot. Her bonnet was askew. She didn't have a coat. Her bloomer dress was torn and grimy. Her hands were covered with blood.

Then her father sat up, and he looked even worse, with blood as well as soot on his face, the whites of his eyes a stark contrast.

"My God," Becker exclaimed.

"A man was murdered on the train," Emily said. "His body's in a railway tunnel. We tried to protect it from dogs."

This information came so quickly, Ryan could say only "What?"

As Emily described what she and her father had done in the tunnel, the two detectives looked at each other in astonishment.

"You did all that to keep the dogs from destroying evidence?" Becker asked.

"We didn't want to disappoint you," Emily answered.

"You can't possibly disappoint us."

"Perhaps *I* have," De Quincey said.

"Under the circumstances, I can't imagine how." Ryan stirred the coals in the fireplace, trying to chase the dampness from the room. "We need blankets for you."

"I removed an object from the murder scene," De Quincey said.

Caught by surprise, Ryan turned. "You did what?"

"A guard told us that the train had to keep moving, that the carriage in which the attack occurred couldn't be left at this station."

De Quincey raised a laudanum bottle to his lips and tilted it all the way up to drain a final precious drop of opium.

Ryan looked at Emily and silently expressed his regret.

"The guard said that the carriage couldn't be brought back here until noon," De Quincey continued. "One door on the murder compartment was so damaged that it couldn't be locked. I had no confidence that during fifteen hours, the murder scene would remain intact as it journeyed from town to town, then to Manchester, and then back here. Surely the news would spread. The first murder on an English train—surely the place where it happened would attract crowds. When people discovered that one of the doors couldn't be locked, would their curiosity prompt them to open it and go inside and touch things? Would they want souvenirs? I told the guard to lift me under my chest and legs and insert me into the compartment so that I could see without disturbing any evidence. I found a blood-covered umbrella. According to the guard, there should have been a leather document case also, but it wasn't there. Then I noticed something under a seat. At first, I thought it might be a trick of the lamp-light, so I instructed the guard to lower me near the floor. But it wasn't a trick of the lamplight."

De Quincey reached into a pocket. The object he withdrew was yellow and flat and round, almost filling the palm of his hand.

"Certainly someone would have taken *this* souvenir," De Quincey said.

For a moment, the only sound was the crackling of coals in the fireplace.

"Good heavens, a gold watch," Becker marveled.

"*More* than a gold watch," Ryan said, reaching for it.

It looked to be almost four inches wide. That amount of gold felt heavy in Ryan's hand. Although the gold was polished, some of it had streaks of dried blood.

A portion of a gold chain dangled from it.

"Must have snapped in the struggle," Ryan said.

On the watch's back were three large, elaborately engraved letters.

"With all the curlicues, it's hard to be sure, but it looks like *JWB*," Becker said. "Do you suppose those are the initials of the victim?"

When Ryan opened the case, he exposed two dials, one for hours and minutes, another for seconds.

He glanced at the large clock on the waiting room's wall. Every morning, each railway station in England received a telegram indicating the current minute and hour as determined by the Royal Observatory in Greenwich.

"They both agree," Ryan said. "Fourteen minutes after one."

On the watch's face, a name was displayed in simple, elegant letters.

J. W. BENSON
LONDON

"So the engraved letters on the back refer to *him*," Becker said.

Ryan nodded. "This is more than a gold watch. It's officially known as a Benson chronometer."

He opened the back of the case and revealed two small holes where a key could be inserted to wind the springs. "The many pieces of the intricate mechanism are hand-tooled at Benson's shop on Ludgate Hill." Ryan referred to a prestigious street near St. Paul's Cathedral. "Can any of you guess how expensive this is?"

"Fifty pounds," Becker said.

"Anyone else?" Ryan asked.

"Perhaps eighty," Emily replied, her tone suggesting that she really didn't believe it.

"One hundred," Ryan told them.

"I suspect that Inspector Ryan means guineas, not pounds," De Quincey said.

The group stared at the watch with greater amazement. Guineas were coins valued at one pound and one shilling. Although the coins were no longer minted, the term *guinea* was still used when referring to prices for costly items such as jewelry, racehorses, and country estates. The magnificent watch in Ryan's hand was worth one hundred and five pounds.

"Something so small," Emily said, "and so valuable."

"Touch it," Ryan said, giving it to her.

Emily looked surprised by the weight.

"Eighteen-karat gold," Ryan said. "You too, Becker. Hold this. It's not every day you get to experience what two years of salary feels like in your hand."

"Sometimes I think there isn't anything you don't know about," Becker said.

"It's only a matter of experience. Fifteen years from now, someone younger will say that to *you*."

Ryan instantly regretted drawing attention to his age compared to Becker's. But Emily didn't seem to notice.

"I once investigated a robbery in Belgravia," he explained. "The earl whose house was violated displayed more concern about the loss of his Benson chronometer than about the theft of his wife's jewels. I decided that something so treasured was something I ought to learn about."

"Did you find who stole the chronometer?" Emily asked. "Were you able to return it?"

"The thief tried to sell it to shops that specialize in secondhand jewelry," Ryan answered, "but no one would dare accept it, realizing that the police would look everywhere for an object so valuable and unusual. Several shopkeepers remembered the man who offered it to them. We easily located him and found the chronometer in the false bottom of a drawer in his room. I asked the thief why he didn't just throw the chronometer in the Thames when he couldn't sell it. He told me that it was too beautiful to be destroyed and that he often took it out to admire it. I wonder if he still felt that way when he was…"

Ryan didn't need to say "transported to a penal colony." Everyone in the room knew the extreme penalty, a potential death sentence, for stealing something so valuable.

He changed the subject. "Emily, you and your father look frozen." He opened the door and asked the guard outside, "Is there a lodging house in town?"

"Across from the station, Inspector. But I already inquired—its rooms are taken."

"Perhaps, for a fee, its proprietor would allow Miss De Quincey and her father to wash the soot and blood from their hands and faces," Ryan said. "And perhaps he or she would also rent pillows and blankets to allow them to sleep here with some comfort."

"That hadn't occurred to me, Inspector. I'll look into it."

Ryan turned to Becker. He disliked saying this, but there were too many things that needed to be done, and as the senior detective, he was the one who had to do them: "Take care of Emily and her father. I'll go to the tunnel and examine the body."

Becker gave him a look of respect, understanding that Ryan would much sooner have traded places with him.

HOLDING A LANTERN, Ryan entered the tunnel's smothering darkness. Ahead, the lights of two other lanterns guided his way. In the penetrating cold, he reached a constable and another railway guard. The metallic odor of blood was strong.

"Constable, I'm Detective Inspector Ryan from Scotland Yard. With your permission, I'd like to examine the victim."

"You know more about this kind of thing than *I* do," the constable said, sounding grateful to surrender the responsibility.

"In that case..." Ryan prepared himself. "Please, raise your lanterns over the body."

He crouched, breathing shallowly. What he saw was as bad a killing as he'd encountered, even when the events of December and February were considered. Based on harsh experience, he knew that the only way he could tolerate doing this was to focus on objective details. The victim was a man of average height, around five feet seven inches, stout. Despite the injuries to the body's neck and forehead, Ryan could tell that he was bald and that he had what was called a rim beard—whiskers along the line of his jaw only and no mustache.

The victim seemed expensively dressed, although the quantity of blood on his clothing made it difficult to judge exactly *how* expensively dressed. A boot remained on one of his feet, the other having been hurled off by the force of the impact. Despite scuff marks from the gravel, the leather of the boot showed evidence of having been meticulously polished. The heel had little sign of wear. Yes, the victim had been someone of means.

His right leg was held to the body only by a length of muscle, most of the limb having been severed by what Ryan guessed was a train wheel. The blood on the victim's clothes appeared to have come from wounds to the chest in addition to those in the throat and the forehead.

The guard made a gagging sound and turned away.

So did the constable.

"No breakfast or lunch for me," the guard said.

"How can you bear to look at that?" the constable asked Ryan.

"I remind myself that the victim felt much worse than I do," Ryan answered. Thinking of Commissioner Mayne, he added, "Thirteen years ago, the man who trained me to be a police detective told me that I should ignore what I feel and concentrate on the details that'll help me find the monster who did this."

"And can you do that?" the constable asked. "Ignore what you feel?"

"No."

Ryan brought his lantern closer to the body. He guessed that the wounds to the chest and the throat were caused by a knife. But what about the pulverizing damage to the forehead?

Emily and her father had mentioned blood on the compartment's outside step, on one of the train's wheels, and on the side of the next compartment, the one in which Emily and her father had sat.

Ryan imagined that the victim's weight would have prevented the killer from lifting the body to its feet and hurling it from the compartment after kicking the locked door open. More likely, the murderer had dragged the heavy victim to the doorway and dropped him straight down. The victim's head might have struck the metal step. The body could have flipped toward the train and hit a wheel, the spinning motion of which had caused blood to spray upward toward the De Quinceys' compartment.

Possibly, Ryan thought. He would know more when he examined the compartment in which the attack had occurred. He was curious about whether he'd find streaks of blood on the floor, indicating that the victim had indeed been dragged.

The victim lay on his side. Ryan reached over and, with effort, pushed him onto his back.

He noticed a broken watch chain attached to a buttonhole on the victim's waistcoat. Before leaving the station's waiting room, he'd taken the Benson chronometer from Becker's hand. Now he removed it from his trousers.

"What's that?" the constable asked, braving another look toward the body.

"It's something that people die for," Ryan said.

The chronometer had a section of broken chain attached to it. Ryan compared the chain to the fragment attached to the victim's waistcoat. The style of the links was identical, and their broken parts matched.

After putting the chronometer back into his trousers, he searched through the victim's pockets.

"You're tougher than *I* am," the constable said.

"If you needed to, you'd do what was necessary," Ryan assured him. "Do you have a photographer in this town?"

"We did until we didn't grow as fast as the speculators promised. He moved back to London."

"How about a portrait artist? Is there someone here who draws true-to-life sketches?"

"I know a retired army officer who draws birds. They look like they'll fly off the page."

"Retired army officer?"

"He was wounded in the Crimea."

"Then maybe he saw enough in the war that he won't be shocked. When I finish, one of you needs to waken him while the other stays here."

"Waken him?"

"We can't move this body until detailed sketches are made, and it must be done soon. We don't want to be in this tunnel when the trains come through in the morning."

He continued to search. Most of the victim's pockets had been slashed open. If he'd carried a purse and money, they'd been taken. All Ryan found was a small key—presumably for the chronometer—and a train ticket in a waistcoat pocket, both of which he removed.

"This ticket's to Sedwick Hill," he said, holding it close to a lantern.

"That's the next stop," the train guard said. "What a shame. To be struck down so cruelly so close to his destination."

"Why, though?" Ryan murmured.

"Begging your pardon, Inspector, but the slashed pockets tell the story. He was killed for his money."

Ryan thought about it.

"Perhaps," he said.

* * *

"This won't be as comfortable as Lord Palmerston's house, Emily, but you'll be warm, and perhaps you'll be able to sleep. You also, Mr. De Quincey."

Becker spread blankets on two benches in the station's waiting room, then set down pillows.

"Thank you," Emily said, her eyes expressing her appreciation.

"I'm happy to help. You know I'd like to do more."

"Yes," Emily said. "I know."

The looks they exchanged indicated that they were both mindful of a conversation they'd had a month earlier in which Becker had asked her opinion about marriage and Emily had explained that her responsibilities to her father made it impossible for her to think about the future. Perhaps one day, Becker hoped, she would change her mind.

"What about you, Mr. De Quincey? Can I help you in any way?" Becker asked.

"You can bring me some laudanum."

"I'm afraid the shops are closed, sir."

De Quincey sighed. "Unfortunately, the shops are indeed closed." He sank onto a bench.

"Sleep well," Becker told them, directing his gaze toward Emily.

She touched his arm. "We're grateful, Joseph."

The feel of her hand lingered as Becker dimmed the lamps. After watching Emily stretch a blanket over her father and then pull a blanket over herself, he stepped from the waiting room and closed the door.

"Watch over them carefully," he told the man outside. "The people in there are very important to me."

"I'll keep them safe," the guard promised.

The glow of a lantern came through the darkness, following the railway tracks toward the station. In a moment, Ryan climbed onto the platform.

"Emily and her father are inside trying to sleep," Becker reported.

"How much did the lodging house charge to rent the pillows and blankets?"

"Two shillings."

Ryan searched in his pockets and gave Becker his share.

"I've been trying to imagine what happened after the murderer dropped the body into the tunnel," Becker said.

"Good," Ryan told him. "Act it out in your mind. Put yourself in the killer's place."

"He wouldn't have risked jumping from the train while it was moving, not in the dark, not knowing what he might land on."

"Agreed," Ryan said.

"He'd have waited until the train stopped at the station," Becker suggested. "Emily and her father were shouting to the train guard, demanding to have their compartment unlocked. In the commotion, the killer could have stepped from the broken door into the darkness on the opposite side of the train without anybody noticing. Then he could have walked around the back of the train, climbed onto the platform, and mingled with people there, pretending to be as shocked as everyone else."

"You think the killer reboarded the train?" Ryan asked.

"Emily told me that the driver was in a hurry to depart and maintain the company's strict schedule. It's possible the killer's in Manchester by now."

"But he isn't."

"Oh?" Becker looked surprised by Ryan's confidence.

"Keep putting yourself in the killer's place. Remember how Emily's father looked."

Becker realized his mistake. "I didn't imagine strongly enough. Mr. De Quincey had blood on his face."

"And the killer would have been splattered with it also," Ryan said. "If he climbed onto the platform and tried to mingle with the other passengers, they'd surely have noticed."

"Then where did the killer go?"

Becker followed Ryan's gaze toward dark trees beyond the two sets of tracks.

* * *

"Who's there?" a frightened voice asked. "Leave us alone. We ain't done nothin'."

No matter how cautiously Becker moved through the leafless bushes, branches scraped. Wary, he emerged into a clearing, where his lantern revealed the wooden frame of a half-completed building. Considerable debris suggested that work had been halted abruptly, perhaps another failed speculation.

"Scotland Yard! I'm Detective Sergeant Becker!"

"Scotland Yard's in London!" another voice objected. "Tell the railway to quit botherin' us. We done no harm. The opposite. We're watchin' this place so nobody steals its bricks and boards."

Now Ryan's lantern came through the bushes, joining Becker's.

"Gentlemen," Ryan said, "we'd be pleased to let you go back to your dreams, but we need a favor."

"'Gentlemen,' he calls us. Ha."

"Truly, we need a favor," Ryan told them. "In exchange, we'll speak to the railway about letting you protect this building for a few nights longer."

"Without anybody botherin' us?" a voice asked.

"We can make it happen."

"What kind of favor?" The voice belonged to a ragged man who now limped into view.

A scrawny figure joined him, crawling from a hole in a hollowed-out stack of bricks. A third man squirmed from the building's foundation. His tattered clothes hung on him.

"You look like you set yourselves up very smartly," Ryan said. "Do you manage to avoid getting wet?"

"We keep dry enough. But there's not much we can do about the cold."

One of them wheezed from deep in his lungs. "Except tonight. Harry over there had good luck tonight."

"Oh? What sort of good luck?"

"Someone else came through here."

"Indeed?" Becker asked. Following Ryan's example, he acted as if this were nothing more than a casual conversation. "And how was that good luck?"

"Because he threw *this* away as he ran past," a frail voice answered. "It landed right in front of where I live under that pile of boards. All I had to do was reach out and pull it inside."

A man tottered forward. He had long dirty hair and whiskers to match, although the whiskers didn't conceal how scabbed his features were. In contrast, he wore an overcoat of exceptionally fine quality.

"May I look?" Ryan asked.

"Promise you won't take it from me," the spindly man implored.

"What I'd like to do is make a trade."

"A trade?"

"Yes." Ryan aimed his lantern toward the overcoat. "Your coat has blood on it. A lot of blood."

"*Blood?*" The beggar flinched. "Where? My eyes ain't too good lately."

"Harry, he's right," one of his companions said. "In the light from the lantern, I see blood all over your new coat."

Harry made a sound that might have been a sob. "And I was thinkin' my luck had finally changed."

"Take *my* coat," Ryan offered. "It's warm, and I guarantee there isn't any blood on it."

"You're sure? If my coat has blood on it, animals will attack me while I sleep. There's wild dogs around here, you know. Every night, I'm frightened."

"Maybe we can do something about that—help you not to be frightened," Becker said. "But first we need that favor. Did anybody see the man who ran through here?"

"*I* did," answered a beggar who leaned on a board, using it as a crutch. "At least, I saw his outline. There's a half-moon, and unlike Harry, I have pretty good eyes, but he was movin' awful fast. I can't tell you much about him."

"You might be surprised how much you can tell us," Becker said. "Was he tall or short?"

"Sort of on the tall side."

"Young or old?"

"The speed with which he ran, he had to be young."

"Thin or heavy?" Becker continued.

"Nobody heavy could run that fast."

"Did he have a beard?"

"Couldn't tell."

"Did he have hair or was he bald?"

"Couldn't tell that either. He was wearin' a hat."

"I noticed he dipped his boots in a stream farther along this path, then brushed them with a handkerchief," another beggar said. "And now that I think of it, he was carryin' somethin'."

"Carrying what?" Becker asked.

"A leather document case. I used to be a clerk in the City. That was before..." The beggar peered down sadly, remembering better times. "Anyway, he had the kind of case that I used to see businessmen carry."

"Where did he go after that?"

"Farther along the path."

"There, you see? You noticed quite a lot. Do you gentlemen trust each other?" Ryan asked.

"We'd better. We've been on the tramp together for three months."

"Then if I give you a shilling, I can rely on you to share it with these other gentlemen. It ought to be enough for all of you to cross the tracks tomorrow morning and treat yourselves to tea, bread, butter, and marmalade at the lodging house."

"They'll think we're beggin' and chase us away like they always do."

"Not tomorrow. We promise," Ryan said. "Gentlemen, we hope you see better times."

"Bein' called 'gentlemen' is already better times."

"Buying food for beggars. You sounded like Emily," Becker said, proceeding along the dark path.

"Three months ago, I wouldn't have dreamed of it," Ryan agreed. He shivered as he held the bloodstained overcoat.

"Here's my half of the tea and marmalade money. We'll soon be poor again," Becker concluded.

They reached the stream where the killer had been seen washing blood from his boots. Their lanterns showed a log that stretched across the trickling water. Beyond it, they came to a narrow dirt road with darkness to the left and the streetlamps of town on the right.

"Which way?" Ryan asked.

"Well, it's been ten minutes since you gave up your overcoat," Becker replied. "You're shaking. So is the killer. I doubt he'd brave the open road and risk freezing to death."

"He might find a farmhouse and take shelter in a barn," Ryan said, testing him.

"He might also find a farmer with a yappy watchdog and two strong sons who'd make him wish he hadn't," Becker countered.

"Point granted," Ryan said.

Becker felt encouraged, adding, "It's simpler for him to go back to town. He'll hide until the trains start coming in the morning."

"Where would he hide in town?" Ryan asked.

"A shed or a stable. One of them might even have an old rug or a horse blanket to keep him warm."

"And then?" Ryan persisted.

"Well, just as I said, he could buy a ticket and board a train with no one being the wiser."

"Without an overcoat? Wouldn't he be conspicuous in the cold?"

Becker suddenly understood what Ryan wanted him to conclude. "Of course. The killer needs to—"

A bell clanged fiercely. The commotion came from the direction of town. In the distance, men shouted.

Becker started running even before Ryan did. They crossed the two sets of train tracks and hurried toward buildings, following the urgent din of the bell.

"There!" Ryan said.

A fire illuminated a shadowy side street. Rushing closer, they saw flames rising from a stable, where some men hurled water from pails while others worked the squeaking handles of a pump linked to a huge barrel on a wagon. Two other men held a hose and sprayed water at the flames crackling through the stable's roof.

Smoke filled the street. As Ryan and Becker made their way through it, men, woman, and children talked nervously, hugging rumpled clothes that seemed to have been put on in a rush.

Ryan showed his badge to the man who seemed to be in charge.

"What's Scotland Yard doing all the way out here?" the man wondered.

Evidently he hadn't heard about the attack aboard the train, but that would soon change, Ryan knew. "What caused the fire?"

"Not sure yet, but I always assume it's because of an accident with a lantern."

Another man stepped forward. "I told you I wasn't in the stable after dark. I didn't go anywhere near it with a lantern. Thank God I saw the flames in time and was able to lead my horse out."

"Was anybody injured?" Becker asked.

"Thank the Lord, nobody," the man in charge answered.

"What I meant was," Becker said, "could someone have been in the stable, planning to spend the night there?"

The owner and the first man looked at each other.

"Someone hiding inside?" the owner asked. "I was distracted bringing my horse out, but I didn't see anyone."

The other man stepped closer to the flames. "With so much smoke, I can't see if there's a body."

"A body?" a woman in the crowd exclaimed.

"We don't know that, madam," the owner assured her.

"Is there a shop around here that sells gentlemen's overcoats?" Ryan asked.

"What does *that* have to do with anything?" the man in charge wanted to know.

"*I* have a clothing shop," a man in the crowd said. He wore spectacles and had a narrow, worried face. A frightened woman and two young children stood next to him.

"Take us there," Ryan said.

"You wish to buy a coat at *this* hour?" the man asked. "But you already have one draped over your arm."

"It's evidence, so in fact I do need a coat. Where's your shop?"

"Around the corner." Baffled, the man led the way, his wife and children following. "We live upstairs. We were asleep when the fire bell clanged. At first, we feared that it was *our* house on fire, but when we hurried outside, we discovered that it was the stable around the corner."

In the light from the lantern, the man pointed toward a modest two-story house with stairs at the back. All the windows were dark.

"Does the shop have a back door?" Ryan asked.

"Yes, but it's bolted from the inside. The only way to enter is by unlocking the front door with this key."

"All the same, I prefer to see the *back* door," Ryan said. "Becker..."

"I'll take special care of this lady and her children," Becker assured him.

The woman looked pleased by the attention.

Ryan and the owner approached the rear of the house.

As Ryan's lantern revealed the back door, the owner suddenly pointed. "The window's broken!"

The door was ajar. Ryan pushed it all the way open and studied the darkness within.

"Stay behind me," he told the owner.

He extended the lantern into the shop, dissolving its shadows. Numerous overcoats and frock coats hung from pegs. Some looked like the outline of a man, but Ryan couldn't imagine that whoever had broken into the shop would have lingered. Nonetheless, he proceeded carefully between counters.

"We didn't hear the glass being smashed," the owner said behind him.

"Not with the bell clanging and the neighbors shouting," Ryan explained. "After he started the fire, he waited for you and your family to rush down the stairs and see what was happening. Then he broke in."

"This is the fault of the blasted railway's making it easy for thieves to come here from London."

"Has anything been stolen?"

"Business is so poor, God help me if it has." As the owner stepped into the shop, another thought occurred to him. "Maybe he also broke into where we live!"

The man hurried back through the door.

Hearing him rush desperately up the outside stairs, Ryan felt the cold seeping into him and walked toward a rack of shapeless coats of a type that laborers wore. He found a dark blue one that wouldn't attract attention among ordinary people. After putting the blood-spattered coat on the floor, he pulled on the woolen garment and finally started to feel warm again.

The owner returned, breathing rapidly. "The upstairs door is intact. At least he didn't—"

Then he saw that Ryan had put on a coat. "Oh." His tone indicated that he believed Ryan planned to take advantage of him.

"What's the price?" Ryan asked.

"Uh...for Scotland Yard?" the man said, looking uncomfortable. "No charge."

Ryan noticed a card indicating prices next to the rack of coats. He pulled his remaining sovereign and a few other coins from his pocket. "Will these do?"

"Thank you." The man looked relieved.

"Now show me your *best* coats—the kind that you'd expect someone to wear in a first-class train compartment."

"Over here." The owner led him toward a wall. "Wait! This peg wasn't empty when I closed the shop tonight! My most expensive coat is gone!"

WHEN THE HORSE lurched, the cabdriver jerked his head up. He'd done his best not to fall asleep, but at this late hour, with a long, lonely stretch of road back to London in front of him and nothing to keep him alert, his eyelids had relentlessly closed.

The horse righted itself and continued along the pulverized-rock surface. Starlight and a half-moon added to the illumination from the cab's exterior lantern, providing a view of the ditch on either side of the road.

Perched on his high seat at the back of the two-wheeled vehicle, the driver sat straighter, trying to rouse himself. It had been a profitable night's work—four pounds. On a typical evening, if he could earn a couple of shillings after feeding and stabling his horse, he was happy. Compared to dodging the chaos of theater traffic near the Strand, this was easy duty, but it wouldn't do to fall asleep and lose control of the horse, spoiling his good fortune by getting killed in a tumble into a ditch.

The weary animal proceeded steadily onward, its hooves plodding in a measured, hypnotic beat that caused the driver's eyelids to droop again. He forced them open and worked to stay awake by thinking about his brother, who—as he'd told the detectives—had joined the army in order to eat and who, poor soul, had been shipped to the war in the Crimea. Two months and several battles later, there wasn't any word if he was alive or—

The driver suddenly leaned forward, staring at the window in the tiny trapdoor that allowed him to see into the compartment below him.

From this angle, the light from the lantern didn't reveal much of the interior, but without question, the driver was looking at a hat.

A gentleman's hat.

On someone's head.

"What the devil?" The driver yanked open the small window. "Where did *you* come from?"

The man shifted to the side, the angle preventing the driver from seeing his face.

"I noticed you taking the road back to London," a voice answered. "As it happens, I too need transportation back to London. You were sleeping so peacefully that I didn't want to wake you, so I simply climbed aboard."

The driver saw enough to determine that the man was well dressed, with an expensive overcoat. "Out 'ere? At night?"

"I admit the circumstances are unusual."

"*I'll* say. Why couldn't you wait to board a train in the mornin'?"

"Well…" The gentleman coughed in embarrassment. "You see, to be perfectly candid, there was a lady involved—and a husband who wasn't supposed to be on the last train from London. My exit was hasty. The husband stormed through the town, searching for me. With nowhere to hide, I decided that I needed the exercise of walking the ten miles to London."

"In the cold and the dark?"

"The alternative would have been worse. Then, like a miracle, *you* came along. I'm willing to pay two sovereigns if you'll continue to take me back to London."

The driver decided to be bold. "Make it *three* sovereigns."

The gentleman sighed and handed three sovereigns up through the opening.

The driver silently rejoiced. A total of seven pounds! This was indeed his lucky night.

A TURNPIKE GATE BLOCKED the road. Next to it stood a booth in which a toll-taker slumbered on a chair. In former times, he'd slept in the cottage next to the road, relying on night travelers to be honest and drop a six-pence into a box. Back then, because few vehicles traveled at this hour, it hadn't been much of a loss if anyone sneaked through without paying. But the coming of the railway meant that fewer vehicles passed through even in the daytime, and the officials in charge of maintaining the road could no longer afford to allow even occasional drivers to cheat them out of revenue, so the gatekeeper had been ordered to sleep in the booth.

He woke to the sound of approaching hooves and the rattle of wheels. Yawning, he stepped from the booth, removed the lantern from the gate, and held it high to stop the driver of what he saw was a hansom cab.

"You came through here earlier," the gatekeeper said.

"And now I'm 'eading 'ome to sleep. It's been a good night. I even found a passenger to take back."

"At *this* hour?" The gatekeeper leaned into the cab. In the glare from the lantern, he saw a well-dressed man protecting his eyes by turning away. "Must be a fine story that brings a gentleman in the road at *this* time of night."

"An embarrassing one," the man said, still averting his eyes.

"Embarrassing? I'd enjoy hearing…Say, are you hurt?"

"What makes you ask?"

"You have blood on one of your trouser cuffs."

"Blood?"

When the man didn't look down, the gatekeeper wondered why.

"No, that's wine," the man explained. "I spilled some earlier. I was certain that I'd cleaned it off."

"Looks like blood to me."

From his perch in back, the cabdriver sounded amused. "Maybe you hurt the lady's husband when he discovered you."

"The lady's husband?" the gatekeeper asked. Leaning farther into the cab, he finally got a view of the man's features.

HAVING BLOODIED ONE expensive overcoat and gone to considerable effort to obtain a replacement, this time the well-dressed man chose to employ the blunt end of his knife. He grabbed the gatekeeper's throat with one hand while he used the other to drive the hilt against the man's temple, striking repeatedly with such force that he cracked the fragile bone and drove fragments of it into the victim's brain.

The tight fingers around the gatekeeper's throat prevented him from gasping. As he slumped into the cab, the well-dressed man grabbed the lantern and kept it from crashing to the floor.

"What 'appened to 'im?" the driver asked.

"I don't know. He seems to have fainted. I'll get out and try to help him."

But when the passenger stepped from the cab, he set down the lantern and climbed swiftly to the driver's perch.

"What are you doin'?" the driver demanded, his hands on the cab's reins.

The passenger used the blunt end of his knife to shatter the driver's temple the same as he'd done to the toll-taker. He dropped the body to the ground. After removing the driver's hat and cloak, he dragged the body into the booth, then went back and pulled the gatekeeper's body into the booth as well.

He put on the driver's hat and cloak, wrapping the latter around himself so that it concealed his expensive clothes. After raising the gate, he returned the lantern to its position there. He grabbed the horse's bridle and led the animal and the cab through the opening. He lowered the gate, climbed to the driver's perch, and proceeded into London, fog enveloping him.

At that late hour, few people saw him drive past the dark factories and slums on the city's outskirts. Those who did chance to notice the cab's lantern concluded he was only a driver taking his vehicle home after a long night's work.

In a deserted street near his destination, he stepped down. Hearing the clink of coins in one of the cloak's pockets, he found the three sovereigns he'd given to the driver, plus four others.

The coins meant nothing to him. What he needed was far beyond anything that money could purchase. Nonetheless, he took the coins so as to confuse the police. He angrily realized that he should have stolen the coins from the toll box also to make this seem like a robbery. In the train compartment, he'd made an even greater mistake by failing to take the gold watch.

Furious at himself, he threw the driver's cap and cloak into the vehicle. Then he put on his top hat, elbowed the horse so that the empty cab continued onward, and walked away into the darkness. But his night was far from finished. There was much that remained to be done.

THREE

THE CENTER OF THE WORLD

From the Journal of Emily De Quincey

I awoke to the chugging sounds of a train coming into the station. On the bench next to me, a pot of tea sat next to bread, butter, and marmalade. Presumably gifts from Sean and Joseph, they made me smile. But then I looked toward where Father had been sleeping and saw only a pillow.

Movement beyond a window attracted my attention. In the morning's pale light, Father paced on the station's platform, his breath coming out as frost, his blanket clutched around him.

Sean and Joseph were on the platform also, exhaustion straining their features as they studied the people who waited to board the early train. A thin, nervous-looking bespectacled man was with them but seemed interested only in the overcoats that the male travelers wore. Not that there were many people on the platform. Their uneasy looks gave me the sense that they'd heard about the murder on last night's train and doubted the wisdom of exposing themselves to a possible repetition of what had happened.

The large clock on the waiting room's wall showed twenty minutes after six when the train squealed slowly to a stop, its voluminous smoke dispersing.

As I peered through the window, several surprises greeted me. This early, I expected hardly anyone to be coming from London. But when a guard unlocked the third- and second-class carriages, dozens of men burst from them, all in a state of excitement.

They accosted everyone they saw: Sean, Joseph, the town's constable, the people waiting to board the train, and even a boy who carried bags.

"What do you know about the murder?"

"Who was killed?"

"Was he stabbed? Did anybody see the killer?"

"That little man holding the blanket. He's the Opium-Eater! He knows more about murders than Scotland Yard does!"

As the newspaper writers surged toward Father, Sean and Joseph intervened, shielding him while they guided him to the waiting room.

But Sean and Joseph didn't follow him inside. Their attention became fixed on another surprise: a solitary man stepping from a first-class compartment.

The man's shoulders were stooped, giving the impression that he carried a burden. His long gray sideburns emphasized his gaunt features. I knew that he was fifty-eight years of age, but he looked older, and from my experiences with him during the emergency in December and again in February, I understood the nature of the weight upon him. He was Sir Richard Mayne, joint commissioner of London's Metropolitan Police Force since its inception twenty-six years earlier. Without him, Scotland Yard's detective division, which he'd created thirteen years ago, wouldn't exist. No one deserved more credit for establishing law enforcement in England. But it came at a cost. He still hadn't recovered from the attack on him and his family six weeks earlier.

Two constables joined him from a second-class carriage. When the newspaper writers recognized him, he became the next target of their hurried questions.

"Who's the killer?"

"Who did he murder?"

"How many times was the victim stabbed?"

Sean and Joseph shielded the commissioner as they'd shielded Father, guiding him into the waiting room. The London constables remained outside and kept the reporters from entering.

"Sir, I didn't expect my telegram to reach you so quickly," Sean told him, closing the door on the commotion. "And I didn't expect reporters to learn about the murder so quickly either."

The station's public telegraph office was closed during the night, but I'd learned that the railway company's own telegraph system never closed, making it available to relay information in case of an emergency.

"I assumed you'd want to be informed," Sean continued. "Although this happened a distance from London, it involves London all the same."

Commissioner Mayne nodded solemnly. "The first murder on a train. I alerted the home secretary and the prime minister at once. A crime of this sort affects the entire nation. When reports of the killing appear in the newspapers, there'll be a panic. We need to assure everyone that railway travel remains safe, and there's no better way to assure them than to apprehend the murderer as quickly as possible."

"We have a general description of the attacker: young, tall, and thin," Joseph told the commissioner. "Not much, but it's better than nothing. We have this bloodstained overcoat that he dropped. A local shopkeeper can identify an expensive coat that the killer seems to have stolen to replace it. We're watching everyone waiting to board trains."

"But won't he assume you'll do that?" Commissioner Mayne asked.

"There aren't many ways to leave the area," Sean replied, taking over for Joseph. "We warned carriage men to tell us about anyone who wishes to rent their services. There was a hansom cab that brought us here from London, but a station guard made certain it was empty before the driver returned to London."

"Immanuel Kant," Father said.

Everyone turned toward where he trembled beneath the blanket. They *perhaps thought he was still reacting to the cold, but I knew that he trembled for a different reason.*

Proving the point, Father removed a small laudanum bottle from beneath the blanket, its clear glass showing a telltale ruby liquid.

"Father, where did you get that?"

"I bought it at the lodging house across the street." The anguish on his face was heartbreaking.

"Please give me the rest of the money that your publisher sent to you."

Father absently obeyed. "Immanuel Kant," he repeated. "The great philosopher asks whether reality exists outside us—"

"Or only in our minds." Sean quickly completed the proposition with which the group had become all too familiar.

"A moment ago, Inspector, you mentioned that we're a distance from London, but in my youth, those ten miles were much longer," Father said.

"No," Commissioner Mayne objected. "Ten miles can't be stretched."

"The astonishing speed of a train has accustomed us to conclude that the only way to travel is swiftly," Father told him. "Ten miles in twelve minutes—we say that's a short journey. But in the mail-coach era, ten miles in an hour was a short journey, and before mail coaches, ten miles in two hours was a short journey. Now, two hours to cover that distance seem immense. But only if your reality is that of the railway era."

"Are you saying…"—Joseph hesitated, absorbing Father's logic— "…that the killer walked?"

"On foot? All the way back to London?" Commissioner Mayne asked in disbelief. "A gentleman would never dream of doing such a thing."

"Or probably even be capable of it," Sean added.

"Which suggests that the killer is not what his clothing makes him seem," Father said. Within the voluminous blanket, he looked even smaller than usual. "It might be useful to inquire at the turnpike on the London road. Ask if a well-dressed man walked through there around one o'clock in the morning."

Somebody knocked on the door. It was the local constable, who man-

aged to squeeze past the reporters and enter the room. He shut out a barrage of questions.

"Inspector, we found this in the burned stable."

The constable held an object that I didn't recognize at first. Then I realized that it was the charred and twisted remnant of a leather document case.

The flap nearly broke away when Sean opened it.

"Is anything inside?" Joseph asked.

"No."

"Nothing?" Father stepped closer. "Not even the ashes of burned documents?"

"It's totally empty."

"But the victim wouldn't have bothered to carry the document case if it were empty," Father said emphatically.

"Inspector, there's something else," the constable told him. "This telegram came to me from Scotland Yard. I don't know if it relates to what happened here, but I thought you should see it."

Troubled, Sean unfolded the message.

For the first time in this busy conversation, Commissioner Mayne had the chance to turn in my direction. "Forgive my manners, Emily. I should have greeted you sooner." Assessing my soot-covered garments, he asked, "Are you hurt?"

"No, but I'm grateful for your concern, Commissioner."

"We'll return you to London as soon as possible."

"Unfortunately, that might not be as soon as you'd wish, Emily," Joseph said. "If you're willing, we'd like you and your father to stay until the noon train brings back the carriage in which the murder occurred. It would help us if you could determine whether anything in the compartment has been disturbed since you saw it. Otherwise we might come to false conclusions."

"If we're willing?" Father asked. "I can't think of anything else I'd rather do."

"Sean?" I noticed that he looked more troubled as he lowered the telegram. "Has something further happened?"

"The bodies of a cabdriver and a toll-taker were found at the turnpike booth outside London," he answered starkly. "The police here have been asked to watch for anyone suspicious who comes in this direction."

"But the killer was actually going into London, not away from it," Father said, fingering the laudanum bottle. "He must have set out on foot before the cab left the station. Eventually the vehicle reached him, and he commandeered it."

"Presumably he killed the driver and the toll-taker to prevent them from identifying him. There's no mystery about that," Commissioner Mayne said. "But why did he attack the man on the train in the first place?"

"At first impression, the motive was to steal money," Sean replied. "The victim's pockets were cut open. His wallet and any coins or bank notes he carried were taken. The only objects I found on him were a watch key and a railway ticket to Sedwick Hill, the next stop up the line."

"I'll send a constable there to ask the villagers if anyone was expected to arrive last night but didn't," Commissioner Mayne said. "That might give us a name for the victim."

Father drank from his laudanum bottle. "But stealing money and other valuables wasn't the motive."

"Indeed." Sean removed the Benson chronometer from a trouser pocket and showed it to Commissioner Mayne. "Mr. De Quincey found this in the murder compartment."

The commissioner regarded it with wonder. "I've had the opportunity to see only a half dozen of these."

"During the struggle, it was broken from its chain," Sean told him. "Why didn't the killer make certain he had this in his possession before he escaped? True, it's so rare that sellers of secondhand jewelry would assume it was stolen and refuse to buy it for fear of trouble with the police. No matter—could a thief have resisted taking this, if only to admire it for a brief time?"

Sean turned the precious object in his hand, admiring its golden luster.

"No. The killer wants us to believe that his motive was to steal items of value. But that is not why he killed the man on the train."

Commissioner Mayne boarded the next train to London, taking the blood-spattered overcoat with him so that one of his other detectives could show it to proprietors of expensive clothing shops in London and possibly learn who'd purchased it. Despite their fatigue, Sean and Joseph waited on the platform for the noon train from Manchester. In case the murders at the turnpike turned out to have nothing to do with the man they were hunting, they and the nervous-looking shopkeeper persisted in studying the even fewer passengers who boarded the later trains.

When the shopkeeper wasn't occupied, I gave him some of the money from Father's publisher, asking him to bring us the most practical, inexpensive overcoats that he had. He seemed grateful for the purchase.

Finally the noon train arrived from Manchester. Sean, Joseph, the London constables, and the station guards formed a passage for Father and me so we could move through the horde of reporters.

"What was the victim's name?" one of them blurted out.

"Where's the body?" another shouted.

As wheels screeched to a halt and the smoke dispersed, I had a view of the first-class carriages. The one in which the murder had taken place was immediately obvious.

"No! This is wrong," I said in alarm.

During its long journey, the carriage had been turned around, so the dried blood was now on the side that faced the station.

The reporters pressed forward to get a better look at the gore.

Amid the jostling, a train guard hurried from the brake van at the back. It was the same guard who'd spoken to us the previous evening. Running strained his lungs and made him cough.

He ignored the badges that Sean and Joseph showed him, directing his attention to me. "I'm so sorry, miss. I tried to do what you told me. I sent a telegram to Scotland Yard. I did my best to keep everyone away from the compartment, but it was impossible to stop them."

"*Stop* whom?"

"Miss, you know that the lock was broken. I couldn't keep people from opening the door and…"

I looked down at the metal step, where the previous night the blood had been undisturbed. Now there was an obvious boot print, and when the guard swung the door open, I saw boot prints in the dried blood there as well. The cushions were missing.

"What on earth happened?" I asked.

"The first murder on an English train, miss. The hat, the umbrella, the cushions, the floor mat. I did everything I could, but I couldn't stop them from taking souvenirs."

I was the only member of our group who had the means to buy four railway tickets back to London. Because of the soot that Father and I deposited on everything we touched, we traveled in a second-class compartment, where there weren't any cushions that would need to be cleaned. In truth, given our debts, a second-class compartment was more expensive than I would have chosen, but Sean and Joseph had been awake for most of the night, and I wished to save them from standing in a third-class compartment, which is what the police force would have paid for. They insisted that they'd reimburse me, but I declined their offer, mindful of how swiftly and generously their reward money had been expended. I salvaged their pride by assuring them that I'd used some of the five sovereigns that Lord Palmerston had given me.

On a hard bench, I sat next to Joseph while Sean sat next to Father. At the sound of the guard's key locking us in, my heart beat faster. With a jolt, the train departed from the station.

"I hate to think of the panic when people read tomorrow's newspapers," Sean said. "Every train will be empty."

"One of the reporters asked a question that made me curious," I told him.

"Oh? What question is that, Emily?"

"*He wanted to know what happened to the victim's corpse.*" Three months earlier, I would never have imagined being in a circumstance that required me to discuss this topic.

And Sean no doubt would never have imagined so frank a conversation with a member of the opposite sex. He no longer seemed embarrassed. "I asked the local undertaker to put the corpse in a coffin and hide it at his place of business. This morning, the coffin was loaded into the baggage compartment of the train that took Commissioner Mayne back to London. The undertaker's neighbor accompanied the coffin. He wore a black armband and pretended to be a grieving son in case the reporters asked who was in the coffin. By now, the body should be at Westminster Hospital, where Commissioner Mayne is instructing surgeons to examine the wounds to see if they can tell us something about the killer, whether the stab wounds came from the right or the left, for example, suggesting which hand he favored."

When the rattling train sped around a curve, I gripped one of the support straps that dangled from the ceiling. The carriage seemed poised to fly from the rails at any moment.

Father removed his laudanum bottle from a pocket. "Twenty-five years ago, on the first day of the Liverpool-to-Manchester railway, at the start of the new era"—he concentrated on the bottle's skull-and-crossbones label, seeming to read his words from it—"a historian noted that a plover raced against this new smoke-belching creature. The bird flapped its wings mightily in a desperate attempt to match the locomotive's increasing speed, but the effort was futile. Realizing that an immense change had come over the world, the bird broke away from the race and took solace in the nearby woods. As everything moves faster, perhaps we'll all wish for the solace of the woods."

"GOOD GOD, LOOK at you!" Lord Palmerston said, hurrying down his staircase. "When I heard about the murder on the train, I immediately reported to Buckingham Palace. Her Majesty and His Royal Highness are shocked. No one will feel safe anywhere. The queen and the prince are also worried about the two of *you*. What happened to your fingers? You have"—he shuddered—"scabs on them."

"My lord, we were forced to throw gravel at wild dogs," De Quincey said.

"What?"

"To protect a corpse in a railway tunnel, but the dogs persisted, and we set fire to our overcoats."

"Wild dogs? Corpse? You set fire to your…" Lord Palmerston groaned. "I promised Her Majesty and His Royal Highness that I'd take care of you. If they see you like this, they'll blame me."

He turned to a servant. "Take Mr. De Quincey and his daughter upstairs. Fetch them hot water. They'll need clean clothes. Get one of the maids to remove the soot from their hair. Quickly. The queen said she might visit at the earliest opportunity."

"Lord Palmerston, what my father needs is a chance to rest," Emily said. "Inspector Ryan and Sergeant Becker could use some rest also."

"Thank you, but we'll rest when we have time," Ryan told her. "Right now, we need to hurry to Ludgate Hill."

LUDGATE WAS ORIGINALLY an actual gate, the western entrance to the ancient Roman settlement of Londinium. Most of the walls of that settlement had disappeared long ago, but the word *Ludgate* survived as part of a street name situated in the exclusive district known as the City.

Although the City was only a portion of greater London, Ryan was very aware that it had its own police force and government and that the Metropolitan Police had no authority within it.

He and Becker passed the offices for the *Times,* the *Morning Chronicle,* and other newspapers in Fleet Street. The two men had no doubt that tomorrow's editions would increase the alarm.

A constable stood on a corner, surveying his busy domain.

"I expect no one would object if we asked a few questions here without permission," Ryan told Becker. "But it's better to make it official."

He approached the constable and showed his badge. "We need to speak with someone in your district. Would you mind accompanying us to a shop?"

The constable looked uncertain.

"My commissioner will make it right with your guv'nor, I promise," Ryan said. "And it's a very interesting shop."

They entered a short, narrow street, where a drover navigated cattle through a din of carts, cabs, and omnibuses.

This was clamorous Ludgate Hill, at the end of which loomed the immense dome of St. Paul's Cathedral. But all Ryan and Becker paid attention to were the signs above the shops.

"Lloyd's Pharmacy, Grayson's Cigars and Fine Tobaccos, Bryant's Millinery," Becker murmured. *"Here."*

J. W. BENSON
WATCH, CLOCK & CHRONOMETER MANUFACTORY
GOLD AND SILVER TIMEPIECES
OF EVERY DESCRIPTION, CONSTRUCTION, AND PATTERN

Bars protected windows on both sides of the entrance. Far out of arm's reach, an array of polished gold and silver watches lay on a blue felt counter.

"What? You're going in *there?*" the constable asked.

"I told you it would be interesting," Ryan answered.

When they opened the shop door, an overhead bell rang, and a well-dressed clerk glanced up from wiping a speck of dust from a counter. The moment he saw the common clothes that Ryan and Becker wore, his look of expectation changed to one of dismissal.

Then he saw the constable entering behind them, and his rigid face tried to form a smile. "Good afternoon."

"Good afternoon," Ryan said as he, Becker, and the constable peered around in admiration. Despite the noises from outside, Ryan was conscious of multiple ticking sounds throughout the shop.

"I wonder if you could tell me something about this." Ryan set the gold chronometer on the counter.

The clerk straightened at the sight of it, then frowned at the Irish red hair visible beneath Ryan's cap. "Where did you get this?"

"It's a police matter. That's why I asked this constable to accompany us."

The clerk reverently turned the chronometer one way and then another. "Surely this isn't dried blood. Who would do such a thing to so fine a timepiece?"

"That's what we're trying to learn," Ryan said.

The clerk peered at it through a magnifying glass. "There's a scratch under the blood," he said, appalled.

"Yes, from the point of a knife."

Now the clerk directed his attention toward Becker and the scar on his chin, seeming to believe that *he* was responsible.

Behind the counter, a door opened, and a smooth-cheeked, pleasant-featured man in his late twenties entered the shop. In back, clinking and scraping sounds came from a brightly lit work area that had rows of benches with magnifying lenses attached to armatures. Apron-clad laborers peered through the lenses, measuring, shaping, and polishing small pieces of metal.

Like the workers, the young man wore an apron. He held a pair of unusually thick spectacles.

"Ah, Mr. Benson, there's something here you'll wish to see," the clerk said.

"*You're* J. W. Benson?" Ryan asked.

The man noticed the constable and frowned. "Is there a problem?"

"Forgive me, but somehow I expected someone older," Ryan said.

"My grandfather and father were watchmakers. If you purchase a timepiece from this firm, regardless of my age, you're acquiring a hundred years of skill."

"They brought us this chronometer," the clerk explained.

"With dried blood on it?" Benson asked with concern. He needed only a moment to evaluate the watch. "This is our Ludgate model. Top of our line. Thirteen jewels."

"Jewels?" Becker asked.

"Rubies." Benson removed a small tool from his apron, inserted it into the case, and opened the inmost portion of the timepiece, revealing the magic of its many moving parts.

Ryan, Becker, and the constable peered down in reverence. The mechanism's numerous revolving wheels seemed alive, its levers like arms. Its ticking resembled the beat of a heart.

"A creature unto itself," Benson said. "But where one piece of metal pivots against another, friction will wear it down. We attach a ruby to every spot where the moving parts touch."

Benson noted the position of the hands on the watch and compared them to those on a tall, oak-encased clock that stood in a corner.

"Every morning, we obtain the exact time from the Royal Observatory. This chronometer is one minute slow, which tells me that it hasn't been wound recently."

"Here's the key," Ryan said.

Like the watch, the key was made of gold. Benson opened the back of the case and inserted the key into one small receptacle, then another, each time carefully turning. "It's important to stop as soon as there's a slight resistance."

He pulled out the watch's stem and adjusted the minute hand.

"Treated with respect, my chronometers are designed to outlast their owners," Benson said. "But given the dried blood on it and your presence here, I suspect that this particular chronometer outlasted its owner much sooner than he anticipated." His expression suggested that he would welcome gory details.

"I regret that we can't discuss it," Ryan said.

"Of course," Benson told him, disappointed. "This timepiece was purchased within the past three months. I don't need to look at its serial number to tell you that. The engraving of my initials alone on the back indicates my sole ownership of the company, which is a recent development. Prior to January, my brother was in partnership with me."

"Can you tell us who purchased it?"

"Certainly."

Benson opened a door marked PRIVATE, revealing an office. From a shelf, he took down a long, narrow wooden box in which cards were arranged.

"The serial numbers are matched with the owners." Benson searched through the cards and held one up. "The gentleman who purchased this chronometer is Daniel Harcourt."

"Does the card indicate where he lives?"

"No. But he did provide his office address." Benson's tone emphasized the significance of the location. "In Lombard Street."

OUTSIDE, THE JANGLE and jolt of traffic was again overwhelming.

As Becker hurried eastward toward St. Paul's Cathedral, he wasn't surprised when Ryan again tested him.

"We had only a quick glimpse of the workers at the back of Benson's shop. What did you notice about them?" Ryan asked.

"They all wore aprons that went up to their chins," Becker replied.

"What kind of aprons?"

"Leather."

"What kind of leather?" Ryan persisted.

"Polished."

"Why was the leather polished?" Ryan asked. "And did you notice anything about the workers' faces?"

Becker concentrated. "They were all clean-shaven. So was Benson. So was the clerk."

"Five years ago, that wouldn't have seemed unusual," Ryan said. "But fashions changed. Wouldn't you have expected a few of the laborers to have beards or at least mustaches?"

Walking northward past the looming cathedral, Becker struggled to work out what Ryan wanted him to deduce. He concentrated on an image in his memory: the numerous workers leaning over benches, peering through magnifying lenses on armatures, adjusting tiny pieces of metal.

"Hair," he replied.

"It's hardly a revelation that mustaches and beards are composed of facial hair," Ryan said.

Becker recalled the clerk wiping a speck of dust from a counter. "But a tiny facial hair might fall into a watch that's being assembled." He grinned at Ryan, knowing that he had the answer. "It might not be noticed even through a magnifying lens, but it would interfere with the intricate mechanism. And Benson chose aprons that were made from polished leather because dust can easily be seen on them and wiped off before specks fall into a watch."

"I'm starting to believe you have the makings of an excellent detective," Ryan told him, then smiled.

Becker's grin broadened, his exhaustion lifting from him, as he followed Ryan eastward along Cheapside. They passed a poultry market from which the squawking protests of imprisoned fowl could be heard despite the grinding noise of traffic.

Then they arrived at a deafening intersection of six bustling streets. The huge nexus resembled the spokes on a gigantic wheel. At the north end, two massive buildings dominated the scene. One of them seemed as enormous as the newly built Houses of Parliament.

"Ever been here?" Ryan asked.

Becker shook his head in awe. "Never. When I came to London, I worked in a brick factory in Spitalfields and hardly had the chance for sightseeing. Then I joined the police force and spent nearly all my time on patrol in Wapping." Becker gaped at the imposing hub of six streets, feeling the power that radiated from them. "I've never seen so many richly dressed men in one place—and look at all the carriages with crests on the doors!"

"You're standing at the center of the British Empire," Ryan told him.

"The center? But what about Buckingham Palace, Parliament, and Whitehall?"

"Governments come and go. Monarchs come and go as well. I mean no disrespect or ill wishes to the queen," Ryan quickly added. "But wealth controls everything, and when it comes to money, there's no more influential site on the planet than here. That monumental structure with all the pillars is the Bank of England. The one that looks like a Roman temple is the Royal Exchange, where almost every ship in the world and all of their contents are insured. The columned colossus beyond it belongs to the East India Company. These enterprises are the true controllers of the empire, far more than Parliament or anyone on the throne. This is where wars begin and colonies are created. And directly across from us"—Ryan pointed—"is Lombard Street."

THEY REACHED A varnished maple door between the stone offices of a real estate agent and a stockbroker. A gleaming copper plaque displayed the number 42.

A constable approached them, obviously wondering about these men in their shapeless clothes when everyone else was dressed in luxury.

"Scotland Yard detectives," Ryan said, showing his badge. "We're investigating a murder. Since we don't have authority here, would you mind accompanying us upstairs?"

"Perhaps I should consult with my sergeant."

"If you help us find the murderer, I'm sure that your sergeant will take note of your self-reliance."

Ryan opened the door, revealing lamps that illuminated a handsomely carpeted stairway. They climbed to a hallway of doors with shiny letters—A, B, and C on one side, D and E on the other.

A deserted secretary's desk occupied the space where F would have been expected.

"No directory downstairs. No names on any of the doors," Ryan told Becker. "The people who use these offices are so successful they don't need to identify themselves."

Ryan knocked on the door that had a brass letter A, part of the address he'd been given.

He knocked again.

"May I help you?" a voice behind them asked.

They turned toward a fastidiously dressed man approaching along the corridor. He was unusually lean with thin lips and spectacles perched on the tip of his slender nose.

"We've been told that this is Mr. Daniel Harcourt's office," Ryan said.

"Indeed," the man replied. Obviously disapproving of how Ryan and Becker looked, he spoke to the constable. "I'm Mr. Harcourt's secretary. May I ask the purpose of your visit?"

"We're from Scotland Yard," Ryan said. He and Becker showed their badges.

"That means nothing here."

"It's something about a murder," the constable explained in confusion.

"Murder?"

"Is Mr. Harcourt approximately fifty years old, of average height but heavy?" Ryan asked. "Bald? With a beard but not a mustache?"

The secretary's stunned features indicated that the description matched his employer. "Good heavens, has something happened to him?"

"We need to speak to his wife."

"He never married. Why is that important?"

"Perhaps his parents are still alive."

"No."

"Brothers and sisters?"

"Brothers. But both of them are dead."

"Then unfortunately it comes down to you. Are you willing to go to Westminster Hospital and determine if a corpse there is that of Mr. Harcourt?" Ryan asked.

"Determine if…" Now that the secretary understood, his face turned gray. He took a breath. "God save him, yes. Whatever I can do to help…All day, I had a terrible feeling. Several important clients arrived for appointments, but Mr. Harcourt failed to come to the office. These aren't the type of people whom it's wise to keep waiting."

Ryan reached for the doorknob.

"That won't do any good. When Mr. Harcourt isn't here, he keeps his office locked," the secretary advised.

"Then open it, please."

"I can't. Mr. Harcourt has the only key."

"Which wasn't on his person," Ryan said.

On impulse, he tried the knob. As the door swung open, the secretary gasped.

"You didn't test it?" Ryan asked.

"I wouldn't have dreamed of doing so!" the secretary answered.

Cold air drifted from a shadowy office dominated by a substantial desk and a splendid Oriental carpet. When Becker entered the room and opened the curtains, he revealed two red Moroccan leather chairs, a pedestal with a globe of the world on it, and a painting of a stream flowing past the ruins of an abbey. Ryan took for granted that the painting was by a noted artist.

"What was Mr. Harcourt's profession?" Becker asked the secretary.

"He...uh...a lawyer." The secretary removed his spectacles. His eyes looked smaller. "He was a lawyer."

"A barrister?" Ryan referred to the type of lawyer who could make a presentation in a criminal court.

"No. A solicitor."

"At so important an address?" Ryan asked, puzzled. Solicitors were considered inferior to barristers. They dealt with the administrative aspects of the law, mostly drawing up documents such as wills, contracts, and loan agreements.

"Mr. Harcourt wasn't an average solicitor," the secretary replied.

"Please explain."

"I can't without violating the confidentiality of my position. I need to speak to one of his associates in these other offices and find out what my legal responsibilities are."

"By all means, do so."

But the secretary remained, suspiciously observing Ryan as he walked around the office and noted details.

"That isn't right," the secretary said.

"Pardon me?"

The secretary pointed to an oak cabinet in a corner. "Mr. Harcourt kept his most important documents there."

"And what troubles you?" Becker asked.

"The framed daguerreotype on the cabinet."

"Yes, it's an excellent image of Her Majesty," Becker noted.

"A gift from one of Mr. Harcourt's clients," the secretary explained with an undertone of significance. "But it's too close to the front of the cabinet." He stepped forward and moved it. "Morning sunlight comes through that window and strikes here. Mr. Harcourt was warned that sunlight could destroy the daguerreotype. 'We mustn't ever let Her Majesty fade,' he told me. To protect her picture, he kept it farther back."

Ryan tugged at one of the drawers.

When it opened, the secretary exclaimed, "But that cabinet's supposed to be locked also!"

Ryan opened another drawer and another, revealing folders with names on tabs in alphabetical order. Stunned, he forced himself not to show a reaction when he realized how many of Harcourt's clients were members of the peerage and of Parliament. He was staring at the names of some of the most powerful men in the land.

One in particular struck him: *Temple, Henry John.*

That was the family and given name of Lord Palmerston.

The secretary intervened, putting a hand on one of the drawers. "I really must insist on consulting with Mr. Harcourt's associates."

"Do you have a way to determine whether any folders have been removed?" Ryan asked.

"No. Mr. Harcourt kept the master list to himself."

As the secretary closed the drawers, Ryan redirected his attention toward the rest of the office. He passed the chair at the rear of the desk and approached the pedestal upon which the globe of the world sat. Abruptly he returned to the desk, pulled out the swivel chair, and took a wastepaper basket from an alcove.

"Mr. Harcourt hid the basket under his desk so clients couldn't see what he referred to as 'disorder,'" the secretary explained.

"When was the last time you saw him?"

"Around seven o'clock last night. He told me that he had a few documents to review and wouldn't need me."

Ryan lifted a single piece of paper from the basket.

The secretary frowned. "Mr. Harcourt must have put it there after I spoke to him. All our wastepaper is collected and incinerated at six."

"Do you know who John Saltram is?" Ryan asked.

"Who?"

"John Saltram. The name on this piece of paper." Ryan showed it to him. "Is this Mr. Harcourt's handwriting?"

"No, and I never heard the name before. Without violating confidentiality, I can tell you that he definitely wasn't a client."

"John Saltram?" Becker asked with interest.

Ryan turned to him. "Does that name mean something to you?"

"Perhaps." Becker stepped close and lowered his voice so that no one else could hear. "He might not be the same man, but a John Saltram was a constable when I walked a beat in the East End."

"Find him," Ryan said.

THE TERM EAST End had only recently become synonymous with the worst part of London. Four years earlier, in 1851, journalist Henry Mayhew had published his exposé *London Labour and the London Poor,* about the horrid conditions in the East End, and the appellation had entered the language. For people of means in wealthy districts such as Mayfair and Belgravia, the East End seemed not just half a city away but half a *world,* its disease and filth as remote as the worst parts of India and the empire's other eastern regions.

But Becker had spent five years patrolling the East End's Wapping district and was so familiar with its horrors that, as he walked past the Tower of London, one of its boundaries, he felt he was almost coming home, although his memory of the murders there in December made it a reluctant homecoming.

Some of Wapping's structures were as old as any in London, a few having even survived the Great Fire of London almost two hundred years earlier. Each building's listing walls and buckling roofs provided meager shelter for dozens of wretched families. The odors were as revolting as the filth on the cobblestones. Ragged creatures huddled in doorways and alleys, sobbing. The smoke-laden fog always seemed darkest and thickest here, an effect that was now emphasized by the lowering sun.

As a figure came around a hazy corner, Becker braced himself in case of trouble. Anywhere else, Becker's apparel looked ordinary, but here, his common clothes made him appear temptingly wealthy.

The figure turned out to be a constable. He studied Becker in the fading light, apparently trying to understand what someone who was not in rags was doing there.

"Come back to commit more crimes, have you?" The constable grinned. "I never thought I'd see *your* ugly face again."

"Evans? Is it you?"

Laughing, they shook hands.

"I didn't think I'd ever see *your* ugly features again either," Becker said.

"Almost didn't recognize you out of uniform. Come to lord it over me, have you? How does it feel to be a detective?"

"I wish I knew. It'll be a while before I learn enough to feel that I'm truly a detective."

"At a guess, it could only be business that brings you back to this miserable place," Evans said.

"I'm on my way to the station house." Becker stomped his boots on the squalid stones to keep his feet from turning numb as he'd done so many times when he'd patrolled this area. "I need to talk to a constable here. John Saltram. Maybe you remember him from roll call."

"Indeed. I don't suppose you can tell me why you wish to talk to him." Evans looked eager for gossip.

Becker shrugged.

"Become a cagey devil, have you? Well, never mind. I'll save you the walk to the station house. Saltram left the force."

"Left the...when did *this* happen?"

"Not long after you were promoted. Headquarters gave Saltram permission to marry. His bride's a laundress with ambition. She persuaded him that, with his experience as a constable, he ought to hire himself out as a private-inquiry agent."

Evans put significance into the final words. Until three years earlier, private-inquiry agents had been almost nonexistent in England. But that had changed in 1852, when London's most famous police officer, Inspector Charlie Field, resigned and opened a private-inquiry bureau. Claiming that he'd been the model for the mysterious Inspector Bucket in Dickens's novel *Bleak House,* Fields attracted numerous clients by offering confidential investigative services that the police weren't willing to provide.

"Saltram's wife turned out to be as smart as she was ambitious," Evans continued. "She told him to go where the money is and advertise himself to lawyers in the City."

"Advertise himself to lawyers?" Becker managed to keep his voice neutral.

"Apparently it worked," Evans said. "I heard that Saltram's situation improved enough that he moved to better lodgings. Maybe *I* should become a private-inquiry agent and get out of this godforsaken place."

"Any idea where Saltram lives?" Becker asked.

"He bragged about going to Southwark."

As ITS NAME implied, Southwark was south of the Thames. A working-class neighborhood with a weekly market and a well-known cathedral, it managed to avoid the despair of the East End.

Surrounded by bitter-cold fog, Becker walked across London Bridge. As he chewed the last of three stale biscuits he'd purchased from a bakeshop that was about to close, his fatigue tempted him to return to the police dormitory and postpone his quest until the morning.

But what would Ryan do? he asked himself.

He found a constable in Wellington Street, near the London Bridge railway terminus. "Where's your station house?"

"Two streets that way."

It was literally a house—or, rather, two adjoining houses that had been combined to accommodate offices and cells.

Welcoming the heat from a corner fireplace, Becker showed his badge to a sergeant behind a desk. "Ever heard of John Saltram?"

"I heard of him, all right," the sergeant answered. "He came in here two weeks ago, making certain we all knew he'd been a constable. He said he was a private-inquiry agent now, as if he was royalty. He told us we could count on him in an emergency, and he hoped he could count on *us* to help him in return if he ever needed information. He was so full of himself, we had quite a chuckle after he left."

"Do you know where he lives?"

"Oh, he told us several times where we could reach him if we needed his help. He even gave me a note with his address and suggested that maybe his street could have a little extra attention. What do you want with him?"

"Just something he might remember from when he patrolled in Wapping."

"And you came here after dark, shivering in the cold, simply because you're curious that he might remember something from when he patrolled in Wapping?"

"Well, maybe I want a little more than that. Maybe I could use a constable to come with me."

"I'll go with you myself. Could be I'll find a chance to needle him." The sergeant called to a constable in a hallway, "Williams, take charge. I'm stepping out for a while."

Mercifully, Becker didn't need to walk much farther. Guiding the way with a bull's-eye lantern, the sergeant led him to a tavern at the next corner.

"This is where Saltram spends most of his time," the sergeant said, opening the door.

The narrow interior was filled with pipe smoke, loud conversations, and the odor of stale beer. The sergeant squeezed his way between two burly men at the counter and told the barkeep, "We're looking for John Saltram."

"Haven't seen him since last night," the barkeep said, wiping a wet rag across the counter. "He bragged about coming into some extra money and bought drinks for everyone."

Becker and the sergeant returned to the street. Halfway along it, the sergeant pointed to an open stairway between a butcher's shop and a grocer. "He lives there, above the butcher shop."

Becker peered up at the window but didn't see any lamplight.

"This early, he wouldn't be asleep," the sergeant said. "He and the missus must be spending the money he bragged about. If it's important, you can go back to the station, drink some hot tea, and try again later."

The offer was tempting. Becker's legs ached. He hadn't sat down in hours.

But what would Ryan do? he thought again.

A lamp glowed in the butcher's shop. A window revealed a man in a stained apron putting away chunks of meat. When Becker opened the door, the butcher looked hopeful that this was a customer, but then he saw the sergeant behind Becker.

The shop was cold. March's low temperature helped to prevent the meat from spoiling. Even so, the pungent odor of blood was strong.

"Have you seen John Saltram today?" Becker asked.

"No, and it's a good thing for him I didn't."

"Why is that?"

"I've got some choice things to say to him about waking me up," the butcher said.

"What do you mean?"

"I live behind the shop." The butcher pointed toward the ceiling. "Early this morning, Saltram and his wife had a row. I never got back to sleep."

"Early this morning?" Becker repeated.

"Shouts and pounding and such."

Becker closed the shop door and peered up the dark stairway. An uneasy feeling grew inside him, making him feel colder.

"Stay behind me," he told the sergeant.

"Why? What's the matter?"

Becker climbed the narrow steps. The sergeant followed with his lantern. The creaking of the boards sounded unnervingly loud.

At the top, Becker reached a door. In the gathering silence, he listened but didn't hear anything behind it.

He drew a knife from a scabbard under his right trouser leg. Ryan had taught him to carry it. *But use the blunt end before you use the sharp one,* Ryan had warned. *And make sure you have an explanation ready for Commissioner Mayne.*

"Hey, what are you doing with *that?*" the sergeant asked.

"Quiet."

Becker knocked on the door. It moved.

He pushed it open. Maybe he smelled blood because of the butcher shop below, but he didn't think so.

With the lantern behind him, he saw a small room that had a chair and a table. The chair lay sideways on the floor.

A man lay next to it.

"Sergeant, stay where you are," Becker said.

The lantern revealed dried blood on the floor. Careful not to step in it, Becker approached the body.

The man was sprawled on his back. Standing, he would have been tall. He looked solidly built and had the weathered face typical of constables. His nightshirt was crusted with dried blood.

Recognizing Saltram from when they'd worked together, Becker tried to control his breathing. *Remember what Ryan told you,* he thought. *Distract yourself with details. Focus on finding evidence so whoever did this won't be able to do it again.*

His mouth dry, Becker glanced behind him toward the open doorway, trying to reconstruct what had happened. The nightshirt suggested that Saltram had been in bed. Had a knock on the door wakened him? When he groggily opened the door, had a knife to his chest caused him to stumble back and collapse, gripping the chair and pulling it over as he toppled?

Becker stared at a farther doorway. Forcing himself, he proceeded toward a small bedroom. He prepared for an attack, although he couldn't imagine that the killer would still be here after all this time.

At the bedroom's entrance, he saw more dried blood on the floor. The lantern cast a shadow that prevented him from seeing farther. Only when he stepped to the side did he discover a woman lying crossways and face-up on the bed.

Her eyes peered toward the ceiling, dull and unblinking. The front of her nightdress was covered with dried blood.

Becker's heart beat faster as he led the sergeant outside and closed the door. "Stay here," he said quickly. "Don't go back in, and don't let anyone past you unless it's someone I sent."

No longer caring about the noise he made, Becker raced down the stairs, his frantic footsteps thundering.

FOUR

THE WOMAN WHO THOUGHT THAT RATS WERE GHOSTS

Parliament usually didn't adjourn until at least one in the morning. Standing in the yellow light from gas lamps along the walls, Lord Palmerston silently bemoaned the fact that it was only a few minutes past midnight. England's most powerful politician, a former war secretary, foreign secretary, and home secretary, he'd hoped that after five decades of service, he'd have learned to tolerate the tedium of government, but the truth was, as he sank into his seat after having delivered a defense of his war policy, he felt tired.

Despite the cold March weather outside, the chamber—no matter how large it was—felt hot and smothering. The faces scowling at him from the tiered benches across the aisle made him wish that he'd never acceded to the queen's request to become prime minister after the previous government had collapsed because of its gross misconduct of the war. Now he himself was being accused of the same ineptness, and it took all his resolve not to blurt to these fools that if they left the matter in his hands, if decisions didn't need to be passed through countless committees, suffering compromise after compromise at each stage, if he could act on his own authority, using his own resources, he would defeat the Russians within the year.

An opposition member made a jeering remark to someone speaking on Lord Palmerston's behalf. Palmerston almost stood to rebut the rebuttal of the rebuttal when a messenger bent beside him.

"This came for you, Prime Minister, from Commissioner Mayne." The messenger gave him an envelope sealed with wax. "He said it was urgent."

Lord Palmerston attempted to look unconcerned. Glancing around the chamber, he noted that his home secretary, Sir George Grey, was being handed a similar envelope. Hoping that he appeared merely irritated by a minor disturbance, Lord Palmerston broke the envelope's seal, pulled out a sheet of paper, and shielded the stark words that informed him

THE VICTIM ON THE TRAIN WAS DANIEL HARCOURT.

Despite the note's brevity, he felt stunned. It had been shocking enough that, for the first time, someone had been murdered on a train—slaughtered, in fact—and not merely a common laborer in a third-class carriage but a gentleman in the very best accommodation that the railway could provide. Now the shock was magnified as Lord Palmerston learned the victim's identity. He didn't dare allow his enemies to detect the note's impact. Trying to look annoyed by an unimportant interruption, he slid the piece of paper back into the envelope.

"The commissioner is waiting in the corridor," the messenger said, then retreated.

Lord Palmerston put a hand to his mouth, seeming to stifle a yawn. He glanced toward Sir George, nodded slightly, and stood as another opposition member began a complaint. Lord Palmerston hoped that his exit would communicate indifference and not urgency. After passing through swinging doors, he reached a long stone corridor that was mercifully cooler than the chamber he had left.

Commissioner Mayne, looking his usual gaunt self, stood near an alcove, the gas lamp of which had been dimmed. When Sir George came through the swinging doors, Lord Palmerston led the way to the alcove.

The three of them stepped into its shadows.

"Are you certain that the victim was Daniel Harcourt?" Lord Palmerston asked the commissioner, keeping his voice low.

"Inspector Ryan was able to determine his identity only this evening. He assures me there's no doubt."

Lord Palmerston's mind continued to reel from having learned that his personal solicitor—a friend and one of the most influential lawyers in all of England—was the victim on the train. "Heaven help him."

"What would possess anyone to do this?" the home secretary asked tensely. His cabinet position made him Commissioner Mayne's superior, putting him in charge of all police matters in Great Britain.

"Ryan doesn't believe the motive was money," Mayne answered. "He thinks—and De Quincey thinks this also—that it had something to do with documents Harcourt was carrying."

"De Quincey," Lord Palmerston murmured, his annoyance intruding on his grief.

"He and Inspector Ryan believe that's why Harcourt was going to Sedwick Hill—to deliver documents to someone. But the constables I sent can't find anyone there who knows him."

Sedwick Hill, Lord Palmerston thought. As when he'd first heard about the murder, he felt his stomach tense at the mention of the victim's destination. This was the worst possible time to draw attention to Sedwick Hill. Of all places, why the deuce had Daniel been going there?

"If Inspector Ryan and De Quincey are correct, we need to wonder what sort of documents would have caused Mr. Harcourt's murder as well as that of a private-inquiry agent who was employed by him," Commissioner Mayne continued.

"What? A private-inquiry agent was killed also?" the home secretary asked.

"We only recently learned about him. Does the name John Saltram sound familiar to you?" the commissioner asked.

"No."

"Nor to me," Lord Palmerston said. "A private-inquiry agent? Are you suggesting that Mr. Harcourt was killed because of something the agent learned during an investigation?"

"That's a possibility, given that numerous members of the government were Harcourt's clients."

"How do you know this?" the home secretary asked abruptly.

"Inspector Ryan saw various names on folders in Mr. Harcourt's office, including yours, Sir George, and yours, Prime Minister," Commissioner Mayne replied.

"Surely you don't suspect that we or anyone else in the government killed Mr. Harcourt," Lord Palmerston said.

"Of course not," the commissioner answered. "But he had secrets that were evidently important enough for someone to kill him in order to learn those secrets or perhaps to prevent those secrets from being exposed."

"Who else knows the names of Mr. Harcourt's clients?" Lord Palmerston demanded.

Down the corridor, the swinging doors were brushed open. A member of the opposition stepped out, noticed them in the alcove, nodded, and proceeded past them, obviously curious about their intense discussion.

They waited until the reverberation of the man's footsteps diminished into silence. The only sound became the droning of a speech beyond the swinging doors.

"Who else is aware of the names?" Lord Palmerston repeated.

"Inspector Ryan told no one except me," Commissioner Mayne responded. "Prime Minister, forgive me for seeming forward, but I'm obligated to explore every possibility. Did either of you enlist Mr. Harcourt to investigate anyone as part of an unofficial government inquiry?"

"I made no such request of him," Lord Palmerston said.

"Nor did I," the home secretary added. "What sort of government inquiry are you imagining?"

"Again, I apologize if I seem to be overstepping, but given Mr. Harcourt's close relationship with members of the government, and given that there's a war in progress—"

"The war? You think this has something to do with the Russians?" Lord Palmerston asked in surprise.

"The newspaper reports have yet to appear, but already rumors about Mr. Harcourt's murder are swirling. In the streets, my constables heard people wonder if the Russians are attempting to make them fear the trains. Prime Minister, could your foreign secretary or possibly someone in the War Office have requested Mr. Harcourt to conduct a secret investigation, perhaps about a Russian spy?"

LORD PALMERSTON RESUMED his seat and tried to look as if his absence had been merely an unavoidable nuisance. Known for his oratory, he provided a spirited response to another complaint from the opposition, doing his best not to appear disturbed by the troubling report that Commissioner Mayne had just given him.

He and the other members didn't leave the Parliament buildings until half past one in the morning, emerging into a cold, brown fog that was thick with the bitter smoke from London's half a million chimneys. Lord Palmerston was accompanied by two members of Parliament and his private secretary, a broad-shouldered man whose clerical skills were less important than his combat experience in the Crimea. The emergencies in December and again in February had taught the prime minister to take precautions, and his tense meeting with Commissioner Mayne had reinforced his belief that those precautions, once unthinkable, were necessary for politicians in the modern world.

At the end of a parliamentary debate, there was invariably a demand for cabs, and Lord Palmerston always arranged for the same driver to be waiting at the same spot. But tonight, even with his escort, he had difficulty finding his way from streetlamp to fog-shrouded streetlamp. As he turned the corner into Abingdon Street, he tried to carry on a conversation with the two members who walked with him. He was grateful that the discussion required him merely to agree with whatever they said.

"Good night, Prime Minister," they told him.

"Good night."

He reached the lamppost where his driver waited.

"To Cambridge House as usual, my lord?"

"Yes."

Shivering, he climbed inside the cab, sank onto the seat, and covered himself with a rug. His escort joined him, peering from the vehicle toward whatever might lurk in the fog.

The impact of the iron horseshoes on the granite pavers sounded louder than usual. As the cab swayed, Lord Palmerston stared ahead, feeling that he'd disappeared into a void. Because he knew the driver's habitual route, he sensed when the cab passed the hulking darkness of Buckingham Palace on the left and proceeded up the slight incline of Constitution Hill. Eventually the cab turned to the right at the unseen Hyde Park Corner and continued along Piccadilly.

"You can stop here," Lord Palmerston told the driver.

"But we're not at your house, my lord."

"The short walk will do me good."

"But it might not be safe," his escort warned.

"After sitting for so many hours, I wish to stretch my legs. You needn't accompany me."

"Prime Minister, I really must insist on going with you."

Lord Palmerston stared at him. "You *insist*?"

The escort lowered his eyes. "As you prefer, my lord."

Lord Palmerston removed the rug from his lap and stepped down from the cab. Even in the fog, a corner streetlamp allowed him to see where Park Lane extended north from Piccadilly.

That was the direction he took. As the cab clattered away, he kept a tight grip on his walking stick and listened for footsteps, but the only ones he heard were his own. Mayfair's church bells tolled twice, sounding the hour. Dogs barked. A cat screeched, then another.

The fog thinned somewhat, partially because this district of London—with several parks—had fewer structures (and thus fewer chimneys) than the rest of the city. To his right, Park Lane had houses only. To his left stretched the expanse of Hyde Park, the openness of which he sensed, even if he couldn't see it. While his Cambridge House was one of the most valuable properties in London, the houses in Park Lane were even more so. The trees and meadows of Hyde Park provided a rare rustic setting in the world's largest city. With their pillars and towers, the buildings resembled castles, all the more remarkable because they were separated from one another, unlike the adjoining structures found in most of London. Vast balconies provided dramatic views that in some cases included Hyde Park's Serpentine River. Unusually large, upper-level bay windows allowed observers to admire the magnificent vista on each side as well as straight ahead. Having a residence in Park Lane said volumes about one's background and resources.

A quarter of the way along it, Lord Palmerston reached a streetlamp that allowed him to determine that he'd found his destination. He opened a gate and walked along a white gravel path that led to impressive stone steps. He climbed to a portico illuminated by a hazy lamp above large double doors, the majestic blue of which had been varnished until, even in the fog, the doors shone.

A fan-shaped window over the doors showed that a single lamp in the interior hall was lit. Other than that, the immense structure was dark.

He hesitated only briefly before raising his hand to the lion's-head knocker, preparing to disturb the house's residents.

"Henry?" a woman's voice asked behind him, sounding puzzled.

He turned. A portion of the fog appeared to waver. A cloaked, hooded woman emerged from it, her footsteps sounding on the gravel path.

Henry. Not many people had the freedom to address Lord Palmerston by his given name, only his wife, his blood relatives, a few members of the peerage with whom he'd attended Harrow and the University of Edinburgh, one or two politicians whom he'd known forever—and the woman who climbed the steps, extending her gloved hand to greet him.

"Is something wrong, Henry? What are you doing here at this hour?" she asked.

In the light from the lamp above the door, the woman's oval face—

framed by her cinnamon-colored hood—showed that she was perhaps in her early sixties. She was beautiful, lines of maturity adding substance to her elegant features. Her back was regally straight, her shoulders poised with confidence. Strands of hair framed her face as much as the hood did, and although those strands had streaks of gray, their color mostly resembled the cinnamon of her cloak.

"Carolyn…" He didn't feel ready to answer her question. "Where did you come from? I didn't hear your carriage."

"I was walking in the park." Carolyn's voice had a resonance as attractive as her features.

"In the park? Surely not."

"I go there when I can't sleep."

"In the *fog?*"

"The smooth paths are easy to follow. The place is calming."

"But it isn't safe." All at once, Lord Palmerston recalled his protective escort warning him that it wasn't safe for *him* to walk alone.

"No one of means would be expected to walk there at night, so criminals don't have a reason to go there. But just in case…" Carolyn showed him a walking stick that was stouter than his.

Lord Palmerston couldn't help smiling at her confidence. There was a time when his amorous nature would have compelled him to try to make their relationship even more than it was. But he was no longer Lord Cupid, as the newspapers had nicknamed him in his prime.

"Despite your smile, your eyes are gloomy." Carolyn removed a key from her cloak. "My husband is in Manchester on business. Nonetheless, you'd better step inside."

EXCEPT FOR THEIR footsteps on the marble floor and the echo of the door as she locked it, the enormous house was silent. In the vast entrance hall, the only light came from one of the gas lamps on the walls, illuminating a few of the paintings, pedestals, and ancient Roman sculptures that Lord Palmerston's visits here had made familiar.

What wasn't familiar was a curious green glow on a saucer at the bottom of the curved staircase. A similar saucer gave off a green glow at the staircase's top.

Noticing his confusion, Carolyn explained, "At night, I tell the servants to bring them out so people won't trip on the stairs in the dark."

"Is the glow caused by phosphorus?" he asked.

"A paste that contains it. My husband advises a company that's testing it as a product to prevent such accidents."

They spoke softly to avoid waking the servants. Lord Palmerston's stealth filled him with bittersweet memories of his youthful midnight visits to mistresses.

Carolyn turned to an elaborately carved side table. Next to an Oriental vase of red roses, she took a match from a box, struck it, and lit the wick in a silver lamp.

Parting the shadows, she led the way to a door beneath the curved staircase. From his many visits, Lord Palmerston knew their destination. They entered a high-ceilinged library that was handsomely appointed with a stately mahogany desk, thickly cushioned armchairs, and abundant shelves filled with countless books, many of which had spines with gold-embossed titles.

To avoid scandal, Carolyn left the door open, although if a servant discovered them alone together, especially at this hour, rumors would still spread. It was a further mark of her confidence that she felt free to meet him like this.

She set the lamp and her walking stick on the desk. Then she pulled the hood from her head, exposing her lustrous auburn hair streaked with gray.

"Henry, you didn't answer my question. What's wrong?"

"Your informants sometimes know things before *I* do. But just in case you aren't aware..."

"Of what?"

"You heard about the murder on the train Thursday night?" Lord Palmerston said.

"Everyone who owns railway stock heard about it. The price has declined by twenty percent since the incident."

"Indeed, the price declined," Lord Palmerston repeated somberly. "The man who was murdered…"

"You know who he was?"

"I just found out. Daniel Harcourt."

For a long while, Carolyn didn't move.

"Daniel Harcourt?" she murmured. She looked down at an intricate Persian carpet. Finally, she drew a breath and peered up from the swirling pattern.

"Yesterday, in my husband's absence, I needed to meet Daniel about a matter that couldn't wait, but when I arrived at his office, he wasn't there for my appointment," Carolyn said. "At first, I thought that he was showing his usual distaste for doing business with a woman, but then his secretary assured me that he'd missed appointments all day and no one could explain why. I never dreamed that he was the man who'd been…" Her voice dropped. "Do the police have any idea who killed him?"

"No."

"Daniel lived in London. What on earth was he doing on a train, especially at that hour?"

"The police don't have an answer for that either," Lord Palmerston replied. "The newspapers haven't had a chance to print any of this yet, but I assume your informants told you that the victim had a ticket to Sedwick Hill."

"It startled me," Carolyn answered. "I finally decided that it was only a coincidence, that the murdered man was a bank clerk or some such on his way home to Sedwick Hill after a late night at the office. But now that I know who the victim was…"

"Do you have any idea whom Daniel might have been going there to see?"

She shook her head. "My daughter's husband has a country house in the area, but if Daniel had acted for him, I'm sure I'd have known. Other members of the peerage own property there. And of course, there's the hydropathy clinic."

"The last thing we want is for the police to get interested in the clinic," Lord Palmerston said. "The inspector in charge of the investigation thinks Daniel was bringing documents to someone near there."

"Documents?" Carolyn frowned. "Of what sort?"

"Important enough that someone would kill for them. A Scotland Yard—what should I call him?—adviser whose opinion is reliable despite his opium raving believes the same thing."

"Opium raving?" Carolyn asked.

"Yes. The man is infamous for having written *Confessions of an English Opium-Eater.*"

"*Confessions of…*" Carolyn sounded amazed. "Surely you don't mean Thomas De Quincey!"

"You've heard of him?"

"More than heard of him! Good heavens, he and I were childhood friends."

"What?"

"When Thomas was a beggar in Oxford Street, my father—a solicitor—took pity on him! I haven't seen him since—"

"You call him Thomas?"

"This is astonishing! I thought he lived in Edinburgh. Did you say he's an adviser to Scotland Yard?"

"For the past three months. Lord help me, because the queen and the prince find him amusing, he and his daughter stay with me."

"Thomas has a daughter?" Carolyn asked in surprise. "And they're just around the corner?"

"The newspapers mentioned him in connection with some murders he helped to solve in December and February. He's been a common topic of conversation. You didn't notice?" Lord Palmerston suddenly remembered. "But no, you couldn't have. You were in Italy during that period."

"After all these years…and Thomas believes that the killer's motive was to obtain documents in Daniel's possession?"

"Well, as we know, Daniel's files do indeed contain secrets," Lord Palmerston said.

"Yes. But not after tomorrow," Carolyn told him.

Lord Palmerston nodded. "I'll make certain that it happens."

STANDING ON THE portico, Carolyn watched Lord Palmerston descend the stone steps and disappear into the fog.

Thomas, she thought.

As Mayfair's church bells tolled the half hour, she closed the door and locked it.

Thomas, she repeated to herself with greater amazement.

She returned to the library, set down the lamp, and opened a cabinet door to reveal numerous shelves crammed with books that had the same author's name on their spines: Thomas De Quincey. Here were the collected works that an American publisher had released, as well as the first volumes of a set that a Scottish publisher was in the midst of releasing. Here were all the individual books that Thomas had written throughout the years. Here were stacks of magazines in which his essays and stories and reviews had appeared—shelves and shelves of them.

Thomas has been living in London, just around the corner in Lord Palmerston's house, and I didn't know it? Carolyn thought.

She drew a hand reverently along the books, but there was never any doubt which title she would choose. She pulled down *Confessions of an English Opium-Eater* and took it to the lamp she'd set on the desk.

The aged volume opened automatically to a worn page that she had turned to countless times.

Reading Thomas's account of his ordeal as a beggar in London's wintry streets when he was seventeen, she remembered his tormented voice from a lifetime ago. She could almost hear him describe the day when they'd met in the vile house in Greek Street.

I suffered the anguish of hunger as bitter as ever any human being can have suffered who survived it. A few fragments of bread from one individual constituted my whole support, and these at uncertain intervals. I seldom slept under a roof. When colder weather lengthened my sufferings,

*the same person allowed me to sleep in a large unoccupied house. Unoc-
cupied, I call it, for there wasn't any furniture. But I found that the house
already contained one single inmate, a poor friendless child, apparently
ten years old. I learned that she had lived there alone for some time, and
great joy the poor creature expressed when she found that I was to be her
companion through the hours of darkness. From the want of furniture,
the noise of the rats made a prodigious echoing on the spacious staircase,
and amidst the fleshly ills of cold and hunger, the forsaken child suffered
still more from the self-created one of ghosts. We lay upon the floor, with
no other covering than a horseman's cloak. The poor child crept close to
me for warmth and security against her ghostly enemies. I took her into
my arms.*

Carolyn stared at the page, reliving the heartbreaking way that distant
winter had ended. She returned the book to its appointed place and closed
the cabinet door. As memories rushed at her, she picked up the silver lamp
and her walking stick and left the library.

The saucer of green-glowing paste illuminated the bottom of the
curved staircase.

She'd told Lord Palmerston that a company her husband advised was
testing it as a product to prevent accidents in the dark. That was the truth,
as far as it went. But the manufacturer hadn't invented the product, and it
had originally served quite a different purpose. The recipe—flour, sugar,
lard, brandy, and a dirty white chunk of something covered with water in
a jar—had been a gift from Thomas to her the last time she'd seen him so
long ago.

"I can make biscuits with these!" she'd rejoiced, her stomach growling.

"No. You mustn't eat them," Thomas had warned.

"But I'm hungry!"

"Carolyn, which would you prefer? To quiet your stomach or be free
of rats?"

"I can't bear the rats."

"Then I'll show you what to do."

In the cobwebbed kitchen of the abandoned Greek Street house, Thomas had removed pieces of coal from his ragged pockets and set them in the empty fireplace.

"Where did you get the coal?" she asked in astonishment.

"I had some good fortune."

"Tell me, tell me!"

"In a while." He sounded strange.

He built a fire and poured some of the brandy into an old pot. As the liquid heated, he added portions of the lard, sugar, and flour.

"Now pay attention, Carolyn. This is the really important part."

Using a twig, he broke off some of the dirty white chunk that was in the jar of water and added it to the simmering mixture.

"What's *that*?" she asked in confusion.

"Phosphorus."

Only ten years old, she asked in greater confusion, "What's phosphorus?"

"A substance you must always keep covered with water except when you put it in the mixture," Thomas answered with the wisdom of his seventeen years. "Without water, phosphorus bursts into flame. Like *this*."

He blew on the twig, drying the water and exposing a remnant of the dirty white material. The twig suddenly started burning.

Carolyn gasped.

"Keep shaking the mixture until everything blends together. See how it's thickening into a paste? The phosphorus is safe when it's combined with the paste. Good. Now come with me. We'll put some of this paste outside every rat hole we can find. In the night, the bits will give off a green glow without starting a fire. Spellbound, the rats will come to the glow and smell the sugar and the brandy. After they eat this, the phosphorus will burn away their stomachs. In the night, with the numerous glows, you won't feel alone."

"Alone? Of course I won't. You'll be with me."

The sorrowful look that Thomas had given her filled her with fright.

"What? What's happened? What's wrong?" she'd begged him to tell her.

A half a century later, Carolyn still recalled the acid feel of her tears after he'd told her that he had to leave.

Clutching her walking stick, which she needed only as a club, she aimed the lamp and climbed the curved staircase toward another green-glowing saucer. On the next level, where the staircase continued upward, a third saucer dispelled shadows. Her grip tightening on her stick, she climbed toward a fourth glowing saucer.

Scrittle-scrattle.

Tension made Carolyn pause. Unlike in that hateful Greek Street house from long ago, here the staircase and the corridors had plush carpeting. The only exposed surface where rats' claws could *scrittle-scrattle* was the black-and-white marble floor of the entrance hall, but the sound had not come from that direction.

No, it came from inside my head, Carolyn decided.

She resumed her ascent. At the next level, she aimed the lamp along a shadowy corridor and proceeded toward the first door on the left.

Her bedroom faced Hyde Park. Earlier, a maid had drawn the curtains, turned down the bed coverings, and stoked the coals in the fireplace. After shutting the door, Carolyn set the lamp and the walking stick on a bureau. When she removed her top garments, one fashionable item was missing: a corset. Her waist was so trim that she didn't need it. Moreover, she disliked being constrained. Similarly, she preferred the freedom of a stiff, flared crinoline rather than the weight of the metal underdress hoop that had been in fashion since the Crystal Palace Exhibition four years earlier. Stripped to her final layer of underclothes, she reached for a nightdress on the bed.

And froze as she again heard *scrittle-scrattle.*

It was only the rustle of my nightdress when I touched it, she tried to assure herself.

Thomas had written that there was no such thing as forgetting, that the mind was like a page upon which words were constantly inscribed and then erased and then inscribed again. But the earlier words could never be erased totally. They always remained underneath.

Yes, the bottom layer always remains, Carolyn thought.

She removed a green-glowing saucer from her closet and set it beside the bureau. Only then did she blow out the lamp and climb into her bed, where she drew its curtains tightly around her. As much as she wanted to see the glow, that would require leaving a gap in the curtains, a space through which something might creep while she slept.

As a child, she had believed that the *scrittle-scrattle* of the rats was actually the sound of ghosts, and even now, when her situation had improved so much that she slept on the finest of feather pillows beneath silk sheets and a satin bedspread, she still sometimes jerked awake with a stifled scream wedged in her throat, certain that ghosts were coming to eat her, and in her long life, she had certainly accumulated ghosts, *one* ghost in particular.

FIVE

THE HOUSE IN GREEK STREET

From the Journal of Emily De Quincey

I awoke to the sound of someone knocking on a door—not mine but Father's. Sunlight seeped past the curtain in my room.

"Mr. De Quincey, you have a visitor." The voice belonged to one of Lord Palmerston's footmen.

"A visitor?" Father's immediate response told me that he'd been awake in his room for a while. I hoped that he was writing, but I feared that he was pacing to take his mind away from his need for laudanum.

"A woman, Mr. De Quincey."

"A woman? Who on earth…"

"Her card says Mrs. Edward Richmond."

"I don't know anyone by that name," Father's muffled voice responded.

"She claims that you and she were friends a long time ago."

"I still don't—"

"Does the name Carolyn Brunell mean anything to you, Mr. De Quincey? She wrote that name on the back of the card."

"Carolyn...oh my God." Father's door banged open.

Throughout this exchange, I hurriedly dressed, grateful that I didn't need to bother with a corset or a hoop. I managed to reach Father and the footman as they descended the final section of the grand staircase.

"Father, who is Carolyn Brunell?" I asked.

He didn't seem to hear me. He rushed outside into the cold when the footman opened the front door. It had been weeks since I'd seen him move so eagerly.

In the driveway, I ignored the clatter of traffic in Piccadilly and focused on a woman who stood behind the bars of the gate in front of Lord Palmerston's house.

She wore a cape and a hood, but the hood only partially concealed her hair, the most lustrous auburn I had ever seen. It hung loose, framing her features, emphasizing her elegant cheekbones and the unusual brightness of her eyes. If not for a slight amount of gray in her hair, I would not have believed what I soon learned: that she was in her early sixties. She sensibly didn't wear a hooped skirt but instead one that had a flared petticoat, making her dress the narrowest that I'd seen apart from mine.

"Thomas?" she asked.

I have rarely seen Father as dumbfounded as he was at that moment.

"Is it you, Thomas?" the woman continued. "After so many years, I wouldn't know unless you told me. Nor would you know me."

"Carolyn?" Father seemed to doubt his senses.

"Do you remember teaching me how to read?" she asked. "Do you remember the Chatterton poems you made me recite to distract me from the rats?"

Father did something that was unusual for him of late. He laughed. Then he reached between the bars and clasped her gloved hands.

"'When a strong tempest rising from the main / Dash'd the full clouds, unbroken on the plain,'" she quoted. "'Nicou, immortal in the sacred song, / Held the red sword of war, and led the strong.'"

Father laughed again and continued the recitation. "'From his own tribe the sable warriors came, / Well tried in battle and well known in fame.'"

"Chatterton. Wondrous Chatterton," Carolyn said. "Night after night, you recited him until I knew his verses as well as you did. And in my mind, Chatterton's red sword of war chased the rats. 'Well known in fame,'" Carolyn quoted again. "I read every essay and book you published, Thomas. You achieved your goal. You became famous."

Father lowered his head. "Many would use the word infamous.*"*

Carolyn turned her attention to where I stood behind Father. She never once looked askance at my bloomer dress, as so many people do when they first see me. Instead, she focused solely on my face. "Thomas, your manners have failed you."

"Oh." Father suddenly realized that I was with him. "Emily, this is a friend from long ago, Miss Carolyn Brunell, although I gather that you're now Mrs. Edward Richmond. Is that true, Carolyn?"

She smiled and nodded.

Father continued, "And this is my daughter Emily."

"Your daughter?" Carolyn asked with wonder. "I have a daughter also." She studied my face more intently. "Thomas, she has your blue eyes!" She reached between the bars to shake my hand. "I'm truly delighted, Emily."

"And I as well. It's seldom that I meet one of Father's friends without already knowing about them."

"But Emily, you do *know about Carolyn," Father said. "You've read about her."*

"I have?"

"I didn't mention her by name, but in my Confessions, *Carolyn was the ten-year-old girl with whom I shared the abandoned house in Greek Street when I was a beggar in London."*

"Of course!" I exclaimed. "There was something about the reference to rats that tugged at my memory. You and Father slept beneath a horseman's cloak."

"If I hadn't been so young, I might blush," Carolyn told me, "but as Thomas says, I was only ten, and it seemed perfectly modest to sleep with him." Carolyn pointed toward the bars. "Thomas, is it possible to speak without this barrier between us?"

"Barrier?" Father was so entranced that only now did he seem to become aware of the bars. We stood at the gate through which carriages departed from Lord Palmerston's driveway. He turned to the porter. "My good man…"

After the porter opened the gate and we stepped through it, Father clasped her hands again, peering happily up at her. "It seems that you have grown while I remained the same size. What else have you been doing all these years, Carolyn? How in creation did you know where to find me?"

"It came as quite a surprise to discover that you lived just around the corner from me," Carolyn said.

"Around the corner from you? I don't understand."

She pointed to the left, toward Hyde Park. "Park Lane."

Father and I must have looked stunned by the significant address.

"Yes, Thomas, I've come up in the world. No more sleeping beneath a horseman's cloak, listening to rats in a deserted house."

"You married well?" Father asked.

"Very. And as to how I learned that you were here, one of my acquaintances—your host, in fact—told me."

"Lord Palmerston?"

"As I said, I had the good fortune to come up in the world."

Shouting from nearby attracted our attention. A newsboy held up a paper, yelling, "First murder on a train!" People crowded around him, buying copies as quickly as he could sell them. "Respected solicitor brutally killed! Murderer escapes!"

Carolyn listened somberly to the newsboy's cries.

Seeming to imagine the fearful scene, she turned to us and said, "I read that you were in the compartment next to the struggle. Thank God neither of you was hurt. Thomas, could you use a distraction?" She clutched *her windblown cape.* "*Let's go somewhere that's warm. After a half a century without seeing each other, let's celebrate.*"

To my delight, Carolyn took us to the newly opened chophouse in Soho where Father and I and Sean and Joseph had hoped to enjoy ourselves two nights earlier.

"*Everyone tells me that the food here is excellent. Look at the colored glass in those lamps!*" *Carolyn marveled, pointing with childlike wonder.*

No one seemed to notice my unfashionable clothes or how short Father was. The diners were too busy discussing the murder on the train.

"*Bad enough that we need to worry about collisions and derailments,*" *a man complained.* "*Now we have to dread passengers too.*"

"*Someone told me that the trains had a lot fewer passengers this morning,*" *his companion lamented.* "*It's a good thing the stock market isn't open on weekends or the price of my railway shares would have plunged even lower.*"

As with the newsboy's cries, this conversation made Carolyn look troubled. When she returned her attention to us, she needed a moment before she was cheerful again.

"*Tea for everyone,*" *she informed our waiter.* "*Would you like something substantial, Thomas?*"

"*Something sweet.*"

"*Bring us a variety of confections,*" *Carolyn told the waiter.* "*And you, Emily?*"

"*Well, since this is a chophouse*"—*I did my best to sound casual*—"*I can hardly go away without having a chop, can I?*"

Lord Palmerston's grudging hospitality was uncertain from day to day. I'd learned to eat when the opportunity presented itself, especially if the nourishment was free.

"*Yes, a chop, and greens, and boiled potatoes, and cabbage,*" *I said offhandedly.* "*Oh, and why not bring some cheese and bread and butter?*"

"*Indeed,*" *the waiter said, his expression leaving no doubt that he heard my stomach rumbling.*

Father's brow glistened with sweat. He clutched his hands to steady them.

"Thomas, if you feel the need for laudanum, please don't hesitate on my account," Carolyn said. "You look as if you're coming down with typhus. But I suspect the malady is of another type."

"You won't mind?" Father asked.

"It won't be the first time I've seen someone drink laudanum," Carolyn replied.

The waiter brought tea and bread and biscuits. After I poured for Father, he discreetly removed the bottle from his frock coat and added some of the ruby liquid to the steaming cup.

His right hand trembled when he raised the cup to his lips. He blew on the steam, then took a deep swallow. He waited and drank again. The film on his brow seemed to be absorbed back into his skin.

"Thomas, if you'll forgive this question from an old friend, how much laudanum do you drink?" Carolyn asked.

"Too much."

"Are you imitating Chatterton?"

Father didn't answer.

Carolyn looked at me. "As you know from your father's Confessions, in his youth he attended a school where the headmaster mistreated him. Thomas begged his mother to send him somewhere else, but she refused to believe his accusations. Finally he ran away to London."

I nodded.

"What your father didn't write in the book is that one reason he chose London was his fascination with the poet Thomas Chatterton, who came to London when he too was seventeen. That Thomas shared a first name with Chatterton wasn't lost on him. In fact, Thomas wanted to be as famous as Chatterton."

Uneasy, I recalled the sad legend of the boy poet. Raised in poverty by his mother and sister, Chatterton had admired stories about knights in the Middle Ages. Exploring a neighborhood church, he discovered old parchments from the 1400s and fantasized about those earlier times until he *wrote poetry that sounded as if it had been written back then. Attributing the poems to Thomas Rowley, a name he'd seen on one of the parchments, Chatterton convinced wealthy patrons that the Rowley poems were hundreds of years old. At the age of seventeen, he set out for London to earn fame and fortune. A mere four months later, the city had so crushed him that he poisoned himself. Almost all the great poets of a later generation— Wordsworth, Coleridge, Keats, and Shelley—idealized him as an undiscovered genius who'd suffered and died for his art.*

"Thomas, do you remember the type of poison that Chatterton used?" Carolyn asked.

"Arsenic."

The reference to the poison made me hesitate before biting into a piece of buttered bread.

"Do you also remember the liquid that he swallowed before he used the arsenic?" Carolyn asked.

Father didn't reply.

"It was laudanum," she said. "A half a century ago, following Chatterton's path, you nearly succumbed to London's cruelty. But you escaped. And you can escape again."

"Would that it were so," Father replied.

"Eat a biscuit, Thomas."

Father did, and in fact another biscuit after that. He was so delighted to be with Carolyn that his gloom about the laudanum lasted only a moment. I began to see that, in Carolyn, I had an ally.

"Thomas, would you be interested in going to Greek Street?"

"Greek Street?" Father asked in surprise.

"I haven't seen that wretched house since I was a child, but memories of it never stopped haunting me," Carolyn said. "Perhaps if I went back there with you, I could banish them. You appear doubtful. Do you truly believe, as I read in one of your books, that there's no such thing as forgetting?"

"Like the stars, our memories disappear during the day but come back in the darkness." Father looked down at the laudanum bottle he clutched in his lap. "The house won't help you anyhow."

"What do you mean?"

"There's nothing left of the place. An explosion destroyed it."

"Take me there," Carolyn said.

Greek Street was in Soho, sufficiently near the chophouse that, in spite of the cold wind, we walked. Learning from Carolyn that she'd been in Italy in December, Father explained about the murders at that time and the killer's obsession with the house that Father had described in his Confessions.

Even from a distance, the location was obvious. What had once been number 38 was nothing more than a huge gap in the row of buildings. In the three months since the explosion, the bricks and other debris had been removed, revealing open sky and a courtyard at the back, but the scorch marks on the adjacent buildings indicated the violence of the blast and the resulting fire. A wooden barrier prevented passersby from falling to the bottom level.

"If the owners of the other properties hadn't paid their monthly fees to the fire brigade, the entire street might have been consumed," Father said. "Emily, when I first came here as a youth, I had to knock several times before a nervous-looking man finally looked out at me from behind a curtain, and he wouldn't allow me to enter until he'd peered up and down the street. I'd been told that he might take pity on me and allow me to sleep there. That turned out to be the case. His name was Brunell. Carolyn, you wrote that name on the card you sent to me. I always assumed he was your father."

"If he was, he never admitted it. Once when I did call him Father, he became very angry." Carolyn raised a gloved hand to her right cheek, seeming to feel the effect of a slap.

"Brunell was a lawyer who worked for moneylenders," Father explained to me. "He sometimes used the alias Brown. He came to the house only every few days, to sort through legal documents in a room in the back. He was afraid of someone and gave the impression that he never slept in the same place two nights in a row."

Carolyn pointed up the street toward the bare trees of Soho Square. "Thomas and I often begged up there at the park."

"And along Oxford Street with Ann. Do you remember Ann?" Father asked Carolyn.

"How could I forget her? We were like a family. The three of us couldn't have survived without one another."

"So long ago." Father's voice broke. "Ann."

The most vivid passage in Father's Confessions describes Ann, the fifteen-year-old girl of the streets who was Father's first love. The two of them had walked hand in hand among the heartless crowd, sometimes pausing to watch a man play a barrel organ while they imagined a better life. On one occasion, when Father collapsed from hunger on the steps of a house in Soho Square, Ann had saved his life by racing to Oxford Street and using some of her meager coins to buy spiced wine, the only substance that his stomach could tolerate. If not for fate, Father would have married Ann before he ever met my mother.

"Carolyn, what happened to you back then?" Father asked with sudden intensity. "I told you that a friend of my mother recognized me begging in the street. He knew that she and I had argued and that I'd run away rather than let a schoolmaster mistreat me. He gave me money to travel to Eton, where another family friend lived, one with more influence on my mother. There was a chance that he could persuade her to let me go to another school."

"I could never forget," Carolyn said, clutching her cape in the bitter wind.

"I brought you the ingredients for the phosphorus rat poison, hoping that its glow would make you feel less lonely in the dark, and I promised that I'd see you again in five days," Father continued with great emotion. "But when I returned to this house, there wasn't any sign of you. The place had a terrible odor. It was emptier than before. Even Brunell's legal documents were gone from the back room."

"The stench was from all the dead rats," Carolyn explained. "But that wasn't why we left. Something happened that made Brunell more afraid, *something about the man he was always trying to elude. He forced me to go with him to Bristol. I begged him to let me stay and wait for you, but he was too frightened to agree. All I could do was make him promise to write a note saying where we'd gone so that you could follow me. But you never came."*

"A note?" Father shook his head, devastated. "Where did he say he left it?"

"On the floor where we used to sleep."

"I never saw it."

"Maybe Brunell didn't leave the note," Carolyn said, sounding betrayed. "Damn him."

The wind made a whistling sound through the chasm. Low gray clouds swept over us. Because of the worsening weather, few people were in the street.

"Father, you'll catch your death. Please, let's go back to Lord Palmerston's house," I said.

But he persisted with the conversation, asking Carolyn, "Do you know what happened to Ann?"

"What happened to Ann? After you left, she kept me company here for a couple of nights. Then Brunell took me away. As I grew up, I assumed that you and Ann went on as before. How I wished I could have been with the two of you. But then, years later, I read in your Confessions *that she'd disappeared."*

Father drank from his laudanum bottle. He stared at the emptiness where the house had stood. He shivered, but I doubted that it was because of the wind.

"The night I boarded the mail coach for Eton, I told Ann the same thing that I told you—that I'd return in five days. I promised to meet her in Great Titchfield Street at six o'clock in the evening, but when I arrived, she wasn't there. I came the next night, and the night after that. But she still wasn't there. She'd been sick with a cough. I worried that perhaps her illness had become worse. But when I went to the street where she lived, no one knew what had become of her. Again and again

I returned to Great Titchfield Street—and to this house, looking for you, in case you knew what had happened to her. As the years lengthened, whenever I chanced to be in London, I continued my search, but I often feared that in the city's labyrinth, Ann and I might pass within a few feet of each other and not know it in the teeming crowd. Carolyn, do you ever think that there was one particular moment in your life that changed everything—that if something hadn't happened or if something else had happened, your life might have taken a different course, and it might have turned out better? Is there a moment you wish you could change?"

"Not at all," she answered. "If my life hadn't followed the course it did, I wouldn't be enjoying the good fortune I've achieved. Instead, I might be in the gutter—or in the grave."

Father stared at his laudanum bottle. "If I hadn't gone to Eton to try to regain my mother's graces, if I'd accepted a destiny as a beggar and stayed in London with Ann and you, perhaps my life would have been happier."

"Thomas, how do you imagine your daughter feels when you talk like this?"

Father looked confused.

"If you hadn't gone to Eton, if you'd stayed with Ann and me, you wouldn't eventually have met the woman who became your wife," Carolyn told him. "I read about her in your various writings. You seem to have loved her."

"Wordsworth belittled me for marrying what he called 'a milkmaid.' But Margaret had more value and dignity than he ever did. Margaret and I were husband and wife for twenty years—far too short a time before she died. I miss her every day." Father's voice dropped. "Yes, I loved her."

"But if you'd stayed with Ann and me, you would never have met her, and Emily would never have been born."

Father's eyes glistened as he turned toward me. "Emily, you're the one thing in my life I would never wish to change. I'm sorry if I said anything just now that might have hurt you. I love you as much as it's possible for a father to love his daughter. With all my heart, I promise to try to do better."

"Thomas, perhaps I can help you to do better," Carolyn said.

"Oh?" He sounded puzzled. "In what way?"

"Tomorrow, I plan to travel to see my daughter. Her husband is so infirm that they can't come to London. I visit their country house each Sunday. Would you and Emily care to accompany me? Your presence would be a diversion for my daughter. We could spend the night, and the next morning, I'd like you to meet a doctor who manages a nearby clinic."

"A doctor?" Father asked.

"His name is Dr. Wainwright. The clinic is a hydropathy retreat. He tells me that a water cure is very effective for a number of ailments—gout and rheumatism, of course, but also melancholy and a dependence on alcohol."

"Perhaps also a dependence on opium?" Father asked.

"Indeed."

Father considered Carolyn's statement and shook his head. "As much as I welcome the invitation to meet your daughter, it's important for me to remain in London. I need to assist with the murder investigation, which gives me all the distraction from laudanum that I require."

"Then why did you appear to need laudanum so intensely during our visit to the chophouse?" Carolyn asked.

Father evaded the question. "I'm confident that my need for the drug will lessen as the investigation intensifies. Really, I would feel uneasy being separated from Scotland Yard's detectives at this critical time in the hunt for the killer."

"Father, a day might not matter," I said.

"Or it might make all the difference in finding the murderer," he responded.

"Thomas, would it help if I told you that my daughter lives near Sedwick Hill?" Carolyn asked.

"Sedwick Hill?" Father repeated.

I felt something in him come to attention at the reference to the village to which the murdered man had been traveling.

"Carolyn, is the clinic near Sedwick Hill also?" I asked.

"It is."

"In that case, Father would get what he wants, and so would you and I." Without giving him a chance to object any further, I said, "He accepts your invitation."

RYAN HURRIED UP the rumbling stairs to Daniel Harcourt's office, pleased to find two business-district constables guarding the door.

His good feeling didn't last long, changing abruptly to suspicion when a well-dressed man stepped out of the office. The man carried a leather document case that appeared to be heavy. In the brief time that the door was open, Ryan heard voices, some of which he recognized. Then the man closed the door and descended the stairs.

Ryan showed his badge to the constables.

"You're out of your jurisdiction," one of them noted.

"I have an appointment with your captain."

"They said not to disturb them."

"They?"

Footsteps made Ryan turn toward another well-dressed man, this one climbing the stairs. He too carried a document case. When he showed his card to the constables, one of them said, "Yes, sir. Please go in."

The man entered and shut the door behind him.

"I thought you said the people in there didn't want to be disturbed," Ryan told the constables.

"He was expected."

"But I'm expected also."

"You're not on this list." The constable showed him names on a sheet of paper, none of which was Ryan's. "Why don't you step away and we'll sort this out when they finish inside?"

The door opened again. This time, the man who emerged was

Harcourt's thin-lipped secretary; he looked over the spectacles on his slender nose, surprised to see Ryan.

Before the secretary could say anything, Ryan slipped past him and entered the room.

"Hey!" a constable objected.

The men in the office looked startled. Ryan had expected to see the captain of this district's police force, but not Commissioner Mayne, who didn't have jurisdiction here any more than Ryan did. And he certainly hadn't expected to see a rigid-looking man he recognized as the home secretary, Sir George Grey, the official who controlled *both* of London's police districts as well as law enforcement everywhere in Britain.

The man who'd entered the office was removing a thick folder from the cabinet. Ryan's sudden entrance made him look sharply over his shoulder.

"What's the meaning of this?" the home secretary demanded.

"Sir George, this is one of my detective inspectors," the commissioner explained.

"But what's he doing here? He can't just barge in and—"

Ryan pointed toward the cabinet. "Why is this man removing evidence?"

"Evidence?" the home secretary asked.

"Daniel Harcourt's killer wanted something in those folders," Ryan said.

"And no doubt removed it when he came to this office last night," the home secretary told him.

"But we don't know that, sir. The killer might have missed something. These folders might contain information that will help us find—"

The home secretary cut him off. "What they contain are private documents that Mr. Harcourt's clients wish to retrieve before they too are stolen and their confidential details become public knowledge. Do you have what you need?" he asked the man at the cabinet.

"Yes, sir. Thank you."

Another man entered, carrying a document case.

"Half of that drawer is empty," Ryan objected. "How many other people are going to take—"

"What's your name?" the home secretary demanded.

"Ryan, sir. Detective Inspector Sean Ryan."

"Perhaps not a detective inspector for much longer. The name comes to me. Ryan. Are you the man who has Mr. Harcourt's gold chronometer?"

"It was found at the location of the murder," Ryan said.

"And needs to be returned to his estate," the home secretary insisted.

"Returned? But it's valuable evidence, sir."

"It's definitely valuable. Where is it?"

"At Scotland Yard headquarters," Ryan lied, conscious of the weight of it in his coat pocket.

"Wait outside, Ryan," Commissioner Mayne ordered.

"But sir, the information in this cabinet is—"

"*Outside,*" the commissioner repeated in a stronger tone.

Feeling heat in his face, Ryan took a moment to control his emotions. He breathed deeply. With his hands at his side, he dug his fingernails into his palms. "Yes, sir."

"Such insubordination," he heard the home secretary complain as he turned toward the open door. "Commissioner, I'm surprised you haven't dismissed him."

"That would be difficult, sir. Her Majesty and His Royal Highness are fond of him. In fact, Inspector Ryan saved the queen's life when John Francis shot at her thirteen years ago."

The home secretary muttered something. Then the door was closed behind Ryan, and the voices became muffled.

As Ryan waited, Harcourt's secretary sat stiffly at his desk, making notes and trying strenuously not to look at him. The two men carried their crammed document cases from the office. Another man arrived, and then another. Finally Commissioner Mayne stepped from the room, gave Ryan an unhappy look, and descended the stairs, gesturing for him to follow.

* * *

"IN THE CHAOTIC street, the commissioner glared angrily at him.

"Sir, I apologize for being disruptive," Ryan said, "but how can we investigate if possible evidence is being removed from—"

"Not here," the commissioner said sharply.

Impatient, Mayne led the way through a tangle of cabs, carts, and complaining drivers to a tavern on the opposite side of the street. A sign, THE LUCKY CROWN, had a painting not of the kind of crown that royalty might wear but of a shiny coin.

Inside the smoke-filled establishment, the noise of conversations was almost as loud as the din in the street. Passing crowded tables, Ryan saw four men stepping from a booth. He quickly commandeered it. Mayne sat across from him, and some of the wealthy-looking patrons seemed puzzled that an obvious gentleman would sit with a commonly dressed man who had Irish red hair peeking from beneath his newsboy's cap. Perhaps concluding that Ryan was the foreman of a work crew to whom Mayne needed to give instructions, the patrons returned to the important financial matters they were discussing.

"Sir, really, my intentions were only for the good of the investigation. I—"

Mayne surprised Ryan by leaning toward him and lowering his voice. "First thing this morning, I received a summons from the home secretary. When I arrived at Harcourt's office and saw what was happening, I realized that my purpose in being there was to ensure that members of the Metropolitan Police Force—particularly *you*—understood that those files were out of their jurisdiction and didn't concern them."

"Even if the files might help to solve these killings?" Ryan asked, speaking more quietly and tensely than the commissioner did. "If people believe that murderous thieves, madmen, and Russians are lurking aboard trains, there'll be chaos. Surely the home secretary doesn't want us to stop investigating Harcourt's murder."

"To the contrary, I get the impression that numerous powerful people would like Harcourt's murder solved as quickly as possible. But they wish to make clear that certain areas don't concern us. You told me about the names you saw on the folders in Harcourt's cabinet."

"Peers and politicians," Ryan said. Uneasy, he scanned the tavern's patrons, trying to determine if anyone watched them.

"When I reported to the prime minister and the home secretary last night, they were upset that anyone knew who Harcourt's clients were," Mayne told him. "Harcourt was no doubt privy to the kind of secrets— lawsuits against his clients, gambling debts, money paid to scorned women, indiscretions committed by sons, and similar private matters— that would be devastating if they became public."

"You think this is about blackmail?" Ryan asked.

"Clearly that's what *they're* afraid of," the commissioner replied. "But who would get the most benefit from using blackmail as a weapon? Suppose the objective was to make these powerful people afraid rather than to extort money from them?"

"Then once again, in the worst case, we come back to the Russians," Ryan said.

"Whatever the motive," Mayne told him, "I'm certain that when we apprehend the killer, Harcourt's former clients will use their power to make certain that very few people are permitted to talk with the murderer and that he's hanged as soon as possible."

As church bells rang twelve times, a stooped man entered Waterloo Station. One of the nine railway stations that encircled London, it was located south of the Thames, a short walk from the bridge that provided its name.

The man wore a thick greatcoat and a cap pulled low over his forehead. The bottom part of his face was wrapped with a scarf against the cold. But despite all this, he shivered as he bought a second-class ticket to Portsmouth. Now that London's newspapers had confirmed the rumors about the first murder ever to occur on a train, fewer travelers (all of them nervous) passed through the station on what should have been a busy Saturday, and the guard who examined tickets before allowing passengers onto the platform had time to notice that the man was trembling.

"Are you feeling all right, sir?" the guard asked.

Instead of replying, the man trudged toward a waiting train. But then he faltered, set down his canvas travel bag, and leaned unsteadily against an iron pole.

When he coughed, other travelers looked at him with concern, keeping their distance as they passed.

The man coughed more deeply. Abruptly he leaned over the platform's edge and vomited onto the tracks.

"Guard!" someone yelled.

The man vomited again. What he ejected had the crimson of blood.

"Guard, hurry! This man needs help!" someone else shouted. None of the well-dressed people were so bold as to help the man themselves.

When he reversed direction and staggered toward the gate through which he'd come, people saw the crimson liquid on his coat and lurched away.

"A doctor," he murmured to the guard who'd examined his ticket. "I need a…"

"I'll find a cab for you!" the guard said quickly.

"India," the man found the strength to say.

"What?"

"Came back from India three days ago. Fever."

"Fever?"

Streaks of red dripped from the man's chin.

"He has a tropical disease!" someone yelled.

The man stumbled through the gate.

"Follow me, sir! The cabs are this way!" the guard called, leading him past the ticket stalls, carefully not touching him.

"Stop!" someone yelled. "He forgot his bag!"

The guard turned. "What?"

"He left his bag on the platform!"

"Sir, wait at this door while I run and fetch it."

But the man seemed not to hear and disappeared through the exit.

"Somebody go out and stop him while I get his—"

A sudden roar lifted the guard off his feet. Powerful hands seemed to slam his chest, thrusting him backward, taking his breath away. Amid smoke and screams, the guard landed so hard that his ears rang and his vision dimmed. Debris crashed onto him.

"YOUR MAJESTY. YOUR Royal Highness," Lord Palmerston said, concealing his trepidation.

He stood in the throne room in front of a dais upon which the two solemn figures sat glowering down at him. With his head at the level of their knees, he was very aware that the setting was meant to make him feel small and inferior.

He had no idea why Queen Victoria had summoned him. Only yesterday he'd met with her and Prince Albert. Their dislike for him—in particular because of a scandal several years earlier in which he'd tried to seduce one of the queen's ladies-in-waiting—was such that a single meeting each week seemed the most they could tolerate. Whatever the reason he'd been told to come here, it couldn't be good.

Queen Victoria remained silent for a long while.

"Prime Minister," she finally said.

The silence resumed, varied only by the whistle of a cold wind across the tall windows.

The dark blue of the queen's elaborate satin gown made her look more regal than the less ostentatious dress she'd had on when he'd spoken to her the day before. She now wore additional jewelry: several rings, a bracelet on each wrist, a necklace, and prominent earrings, the pearls, rubies, and diamonds exuding power more than wealth.

Prince Albert wore an authoritative military uniform in place of yesterday's frock coat. Its gold epaulets and polished brass buttons reflected light from a strategically placed lamp, as did the numerous honorary medals on his chest.

They were a study in contrasts. She was short and stout, while he was tall and thin. She sat rigidly straight, while he tended to slouch. She had a round face, while his features were narrow. What they had in common was that they both regarded him severely.

As their silence persisted, Lord Palmerston felt an impulse to clear his throat but resisted it.

"*Civis Britannicus sum,*" the queen told him sternly.

"I beg your pardon, Your Majesty?"

"The Latin expression means 'I am a British subject.'"

"Indeed, Your Majesty."

Queen Victoria continued in the same harsh tone. "I intended it to echo an expression that *you* used in a speech to the House of Commons five years ago. *Civis Romanus sum.* You argued that the British Empire could never be as great as the Roman Empire until we defended the rights of our subjects as the Romans had—anywhere and to any extreme."

"It was an attempt at a rhetorical flourish, Your Majesty."

"Exactly *how* extreme do you feel it is necessary to defend British subjects?" Prince Albert asked. Although he had lived in England for a decade and a half, his German accent remained strong. "Five years ago, without anyone's approval and certainly not that of Her Majesty, you dispatched the Royal Navy to Greece to defend the rights of a single British subject whose property had been destroyed by an Athenian mob."

"Your Royal Highness, if I may be so bold as to qualify what happened, it was a *squadron* of the Royal Navy, not the entire fleet, and—"

"If you went that far to defend one British subject, how far would you go to defend a great many?" Queen Victoria interrupted. "And indeed the empire?"

"I'm afraid I don't understand, Your Majesty."

"What do you know about Dr. Martin Wilhelm von Mandt?"

"Dr. Mandt, Your Majesty? The name isn't familiar to me." Despite his uneasiness, Lord Palmerston managed to keep his voice steady.

"He is German," Prince Albert said, his accent emphasizing a kinship. "He is…I should say he *was* the personal physician to the czar."

"Was, Your Royal Highness?"

"A message reached us early this morning that the czar died two weeks ago."

"The czar is dead?" Lord Palmerston asked in a tone of astonishment.

"Ten years ago, he visited us at Windsor Castle," Queen Victoria said. "We had pleasant conversations about our cousins in various royal houses throughout Europe. Between social events, he tried to persuade us that it would be in Britain's interest if we sided with Russia in its plan to dissolve the Ottoman Empire. He returned to Russia under the misimpression that we agreed to his plan when in fact it had merely been discussed as a possibility."

"You were wise not to commit to it, Your Majesty," Lord Palmerston said. "Our goal should be to let the countries on the Continent fight among themselves. That way, we remain strong while they become weaker."

"But some of those countries are ruled by our relatives," Prince Albert reminded him with annoyance.

"I didn't mean *those* countries, Your Royal Highness," Lord Palmerston said quickly.

"And as our war against Russia drags on, we no longer exhibit strength," Queen Victoria pointed out. "Perhaps it would have been better to listen more carefully to the czar's suggestion about siding with him against the Turks."

"Your Majesty, if I'd been in office when Russia first threatened the Crimean Peninsula, I'd have dispatched our navy to the Black Sea immediately rather than wait for diplomatic channels to prove fruitless. If the czar had realized how committed we were to opposing his aggression against our trading partner, he would not have persisted in his intentions."

"Well, as we know, you're all too happy to dispatch our navy," Queen Victoria said, then abruptly changed the subject. "It was from one of our royal relatives on the Continent that we learned about Dr. Mandt. He so distinguished himself as a physician throughout the German States that the czar chose him as his personal doctor. The czar's advisers protested that he should rely on Russian doctors, but he dismissed their objections, saying that he wanted only the best medical treatment, no matter its source. When the czar died two weeks ago, Dr. Mandt recorded the cause of death as pneumonia."

"But rumors swirled," Prince Albert added.

"Rumors, Your Royal Highness?" Lord Palmerston asked.

"Yes. That the czar didn't die from pneumonia and that Dr. Mandt in fact poisoned him."

"But that's unthinkable."

The queen leaned forward on her throne, staring down at him from the dais. "How else can one explain the doctor's sudden disappearance from the czar's palace, and indeed from St. Petersburg? While the czar struggled through his last breaths, Dr. Mandt was seen carrying a travel bag and hurrying into a carriage. Members of the czar's security force pursued him, but he vanished."

"Your Majesty, perhaps he was afraid that jealous Russian doctors would accuse him of negligence."

"Do you truly believe that?" Queen Victoria asked. "Mindful of the attempt against us only a month ago, we would be distressed to discover that someone had indeed persuaded Dr. Mandt to assassinate the czar in an effort to influence the war's outcome. If that was true, it would encourage elements in Russia to seek reprisals against us. Soon nothing would be sacred. There'd be no rules whatsoever."

"You have my word that I'll look into this."

"Look into it carefully, Prime Minister." Queen Victoria emphasized his title. "If anyone in your government was responsible for the czar's death, we would be most displeased. It would be well for you to do everything possible to prove that these suspicions are false. Already, people in the street fear that the Russians were behind the murder on the train, and there's a possibility those people are right. Is Scotland Yard any closer to finding the killer?"

"They're working as hard and fast as they can."

"Perhaps not hard and fast enough. Has Mr. De Quincey's help been enlisted?"

"Mr. De Quincey, Your Majesty?"

"His unique perspective helped to protect us six weeks ago. We believe that he can be helpful again. Make certain that he's consulted."

As Lord Palmerston inwardly groaned, someone knocked on a door. An attendant stepped into the room, saying, "Your Majesty, my apologies, but the home secretary sent a message for Lord Palmerston and asked for it to be delivered immediately."

Queen Victoria gestured for the attendant to step forward. He gave Lord Palmerston an envelope.

Troubled, Lord Palmerston broke the seal and removed a sheet of paper.

"What is the urgent matter?" Queen Victoria asked after the attendant left the room.

"A bomb exploded at Waterloo Station, Your Majesty."

SIX

WYLD'S MONSTER GLOBE

An AGITATED CROWD blocked the street in front of the station. Alarm bells clanged. Smoke swirled.

"Police. Make way," Ryan said.

"Sod off," someone told him. "You're no more the police than I'm Prince Albert."

The man suddenly groaned and lurched to the side.

"Sorry. Didn't mean to elbow you," Ryan said. "That bloke over there pushed me."

After struggling forward for a few moments, he and Becker reached a line of constables.

"Stay where you are," a policeman ordered. "Nobody moves past this line. Oh, sorry, Inspector Ryan, I didn't recognize you in the commotion. Go ahead. The commissioner's inside."

"Thanks, Harry."

The constable looked pleased that Ryan remembered his name from when they'd worked together the previous year.

The odor of burned gunpowder hovered as Ryan and Becker entered the chaotic waiting area. Debris covered the floor. Normally the pastry room and bookshop would have been crowded with travelers preparing for their journey. But this afternoon, the fewer-than-usual occupants lay groaning among the rubble. While surgeons bandaged wounds, constables carried severely injured people on stretchers, taking them outside to wagons.

Seeing Commissioner Mayne talking to another detective, Ryan approached him.

"Right away, sir," the detective told the commissioner and departed.

Commissioner Mayne turned to Ryan and Becker. "The bomb went off a few minutes after noon. Two people are dead, thirteen seriously hurt. The only bright side is that if people hadn't been avoiding train stations, there'd have been a lot more casualties."

"Now even *more* people will avoid train stations," Ryan said. "Where did the bomb go off?"

"On one of the platforms. It was in a travel bag that the perpetrator abandoned. This train guard spoke to him before the explosion."

The commissioner led the way to a pile of rubble where a guard sat, leaning wearily forward, his elbows on his knees. His blue uniform had bloodstains, as did the bandage around his head.

"Do you have the strength to describe him one more time?" Mayne asked.

The guard winced. "Anything to catch the bugger—excuse my language, Commissioner."

"Under the circumstances, you don't need to be excused."

The guard drew an agonized breath. "He was dressed like he expected today's cold wind to become a blizzard. A cap was pulled down over his forehead. He had a scarf wrapped around the bottom of his face, and a thick greatcoat. But for all that..." The guard closed his eyes, mustering his strength. "But for all that, he kept shivering. I asked him if he was ill, but he just walked toward the train."

"Through that archway." Commissioner Mayne pointed to a gate that led to the platforms.

"Perhaps he trembled more than shivered," a voice interrupted.

Ryan turned, surprised to find De Quincey standing next to him.

"Good afternoon, everyone," the little man said brightly.

"Why are you—" Before Ryan could finish the question, he realized that if De Quincey was here, Emily would be here also. But where *was* she?

Immediately he heard her voice.

"Doctor, there's no trick to applying bandages and astringent," she was saying. "Please let me tend to this man while you take care of that seriously injured woman over there."

Ryan turned farther, seeing Emily take a bottle from a physician's bag, tilt its liquid onto a cotton pad, and apply it to a man's bleeding forehead.

Ryan suppressed a smile.

"I didn't expect you," he told De Quincey.

"Not that we aren't pleased to see you," Becker quickly added, looking toward Emily.

"Emily and I spent the morning with an old friend," De Quincey said. "When we returned to Cambridge House, we found a message from Lord Palmerston telling us that Queen Victoria and Prince Albert wished for us to come here and join the investigation."

Ryan, Becker, and Commissioner Mayne appeared stunned.

"The queen and the prince sent you here to help?" Ryan asked.

The little man nodded. "But I'd have come anyway." He turned toward the guard. "My good sir, have you heard of Immanuel Kant?"

"Is he the sod who set off the bomb?"

"No, but Kant might help us find who did this," De Quincey replied. "The man was dressed as though the cold wind would bring a blizzard, is that correct?"

"Yes."

"He made agitated motions?" De Quincey continued.

"Yes. His hands shook. So did his shoulders."

"Because you thought he was cold, you concluded that he was shivering."

The guard winced, raised a hand to his bandaged head. "There is no doubt that he was ill."

"How can you be certain?"

"He vomited blood. He told me he needed a doctor."

Ryan saw where this was going. "Now it's my turn to show how much I learned from Immanuel Kant. Where was the man sick?"

"He leaned over the edge of the platform and vomited onto the tracks," the guard replied with difficulty. "At the first post. That's where he left his bag."

Ryan walked toward the archway, hearing the others follow him. The odor of smoke became stronger as he emerged from the stone columns of the waiting area and reached the iron poles of the platform.

The blast had shattered the glass roof; shards of it crunched under Ryan's boots.

"Becker, do you see those three places where the blood spreads away, looking like wings, becoming fainter? That's where the nearest victims stood. If you stretch a cord from the middle of each blood pattern, the point where the cords come together indicates the center of the blast—this shattered pole, where I assume the man left his bag."

Ryan reached over and picked up a piece of glass covered with blood. Then he stepped to the edge of the platform and jumped down to the tracks.

"Mr. De Quincey, would you care to join me?"

De Quincey looked puzzled but nodded.

Ryan gripped his waist and lowered the small man as if he were a youth.

The air was colder near the tracks, the smell of oil and grease replacing that of the explosion.

"If you hadn't mentioned Kant, I might not be down here," Ryan said. "Does reality exist outside us, or do our minds create it? The train guard said that the man vomited blood. But how would the guard know it was blood? The only possible way is that its color was crimson. He made an assumption."

"And saw his own version of reality," De Quincey agreed.

Ryan pointed toward a splatter of crimson on the gravel next to the tracks. "One day, perhaps a chemist will invent a test to determine what is blood and what is not. But for now…"

He crouched, placing the blood-covered shard of glass next to the splatter of red liquid. "Blood becomes reddish brown as it dries. The substance on this piece of glass has begun to turn that color, but this other liquid remains bright red. The substance on this glass has thickened as it dries, but the substance down here has not."

De Quincey nodded. "Before coming to the station, the man ingested a quantity of water that was dyed crimson. He bent over the edge of the platform so that no one would notice him stick a finger down his throat and force himself to vomit. Because he'd swallowed an excessive amount of crimson-dyed water, it wouldn't have been difficult to encourage his body to eject it. The volume of what appeared to be blood would have horrified anyone around him."

" 'Appeared to be.' That's how you see things," Ryan said.

"There are many realities. Because of opium, I sometimes have difficulty distinguishing them."

"What version of reality do you think happened here?"

"This was theater. An actor on a stage. His thick coat prevented anyone from seeing how bloated his stomach was from the considerable water in it. His low hat and scarf wrapped around the bottom of his face concealed his features. At the same time, the conspicuous costume drew attention to him so that when he vomited what appeared to be blood, people would already have noticed him and couldn't help seeing the crimson liquid."

"But why the charade in the first place?" Ryan asked.

"So that the guard at the gate wouldn't question why he wanted to leave the station just after he'd arrived," De Quincey answered. "The man said he needed a doctor, and the guard was no doubt eager to help him leave the station before he vomited more of what appeared to be blood. In all the commotion, no one noticed that he didn't have his travel bag—until it was too late."

Below the platform, next to the tracks, the air suddenly felt even colder.

"So, if he wasn't sick, then he only pretended to shiver," Ryan said.

"He wasn't pretending, but his movements had nothing to do with illness."

"I don't understand."

"How do you suppose the bomb was detonated?" De Quincey asked.

"The only practical way is to light a fuse. I've heard of attempts to use a clock that causes a hammer to strike a percussion cap and set off gunpowder. But it's not reliable. A slow-burning fuse is the safest and most dependable method."

"Then you believe he paused outside the station and found a place where no one could see him light the fuse inside his bag. After it was ignited, he closed the bag and carried it into the station," De Quincey said.

"I can't imagine a better way."

"As he carried the bag past the guard and onto the platform, knowing that the fuse was burning and that the bomb might go off at any moment, he didn't need to pretend to make movements that looked like shivering. What he actually did was tremble—because of fear."

Ryan studied him. "The opium should addle your brain, but instead...Listen to me. I never believed I'd ever say this, but you, Becker, Commissioner Mayne, and Emily might be the only people I can trust. Today Lord Palmerston tried to impede the investigation."

"Impede the...But why would he do that?" De Quincey asked.

"That's what I intend to find out."

CAROLYN STEPPED THROUGH her Park Lane gate, walked along the white gravel path, and climbed the wide stone steps, noting that the servants had dutifully scrubbed them.

A footman opened one of the splendid green doors. "Good afternoon, Mrs. Richmond."

"Is everything prepared?" she asked.

"As you instructed, madam."

Carolyn glanced at a tall clock in a corner and saw that the time was almost twenty minutes to three. She wouldn't have an opportunity to change clothes for the three o'clock event, but it took only a moment for her to decide that her well-tailored costume would be more than suitable.

After handing her gloves and cape to the footman, she climbed the curved staircase to the next level, turned to the left, and entered a large room that was normally used for dinner parties but that now contained five tables with four chairs at each. A finely woven floral-patterned linen cloth covered each table. A long mahogany sideboard supported a generous selection of special confections—especially lemon cakes—next to cups, saucers, and plates from the most approved china manufacturer.

The spoons and forks were silver, polished to a luster that was visible from the room's entrance. If examined closely, which they were by every visitor, the utensils revealed tiny hallmarks that indicated where, when, and by which superior silversmith they'd been crafted. When owners of such high-grade tableware went traveling, they commonly arranged for it to be taken to a bank and stored there.

Carolyn crossed the deep reds and greens of a much-admired Oriental rug and made certain that the wine-colored satin draperies were open to their full extent. As a rule, residents of the West End did not open their draperies lest unworthy outsiders peer in. But Carolyn didn't at all mind if passersby saw the luxury in which she lived. More important, she wanted her guests to see the immense balcony and the rustic magnitude of Hyde Park across the way.

She returned her attention to each table, examining the fresh pads of notepaper and the silver-encased pencils (all from the best stationer in Regent Street and with his mark on them to prove it). The decks of cards (printed for her and labeled, amusingly, CASINO DE RICHMOND) lay on the tables in their sealed packets.

She went to the sideboard and inspected the four silver caddies, each with an elegant card that identified the tea it contained: green, red, white, or yellow.

"Marybeth?" she called to a servant, taking for granted that the girl was waiting near a side entrance to the room.

"Yes, ma'am?" Nineteen-year-old Marybeth, wearing an immaculate white apron, stepped into view and curtsied.

"The water for the tea?"

"Is hot, ma'am, and I'm making sure it *stays* hot. When your guests are ready, we'll carry it in. Should I bring in the surprise before or after the tea?"

"Before. Is your mother feeling better?"

"She *is*, ma'am, thanks to the doctor you sent."

"Well, you can't do your work properly if you're worried about your dear mother."

"You're very kind, ma'am."

The sound of the door knocker alerted Carolyn that her guests were arriving. She gripped the staircase's gleaming bronze handrail and descended to the entrance hall, where she greeted each lady as she stepped through the door. Each indeed had the right to the title Lady; every guest was the wife of a duke, marquis, earl, viscount, or baron. Only members of the peerage attended Carolyn's twice-monthly whist parties.

Each guest had a female servant who helped her mistress take off her cape and gloves. Outdoor bonnets were replaced by indoor caps adorned with blue ribbons and ornate lace.

"Perfectly frightful day," one lady said.

"And it seems to be turning colder," another replied. "With the clouds gathering, I feel as though it will rain."

"Well, it's March," a third lady added. "What do we expect other than clouds? No matter—it would take a much worse afternoon than this to discourage me from attending one of Mrs. Richmond's gatherings."

"You're too generous, Lady Warwick," Carolyn said.

Looking through the open door, past more arriving ladies, Carolyn saw hooded carriages departing, their pairs of horses magnificent.

Colorful crests on the doors indicated the importance of the owners, as did the equally colorful livery of the drivers.

"Mrs. Richmond, how wonderful to see you!" a guest declared.

"Thank you, Lady Beresford, and as always, it's a pleasure to see *you* again. You're looking well."

"I owe it to a week at Dr. Wainwright's clinic at Sedwick Hill. I'm so delighted that you recommended him. At first, I thought that the wet sheeting, the plunge bath, and the shoulder douche were much too aggressive, but after the attendant shampooed my back, I never felt so relaxed. Sometimes I felt I was in a waking dream."

"I'm going there next week," a countess said.

"How fortunate. I hear the doctor's schedule is filled until June," Lady Beresford said. "I'm trying to persuade my husband to consult him. Dr. Wainwright says that the relaxation would improve His Lordship's dyspepsia."

"If anyone can feel relaxed after what's been happening on the trains," Lady Montagu said.

"Trains? Plural? Don't tell me there's been another—"

"Haven't you heard? A bomb exploded in Waterloo Station."

"Good gracious!"

"What's this country coming to? The man who was murdered Thursday night—Daniel Harcourt—he was our solicitor!"

"And ours! I don't know if I'll ever feel safe on a train again."

"I've *never* felt safe on one," Lady Garvis said. "I always expect the contraption to fly off the rails."

Carolyn gestured toward the staircase. "Ladies, if you please…"

Amid the whisper of velvet, they mounted the staircase one at a time, their wide hooped dresses preventing them from going in pairs.

"And the war keeps raging. I asked my husband why he voted to allow the country to get into such a mess. He still hasn't given me an answer I can understand."

"When can you ever understand them when they talk about money and politics? I'm not sure they themselves understand what they're saying."

When the group entered the parlor, they found name cards at each table. Carolyn always varied the seating arrangement so that cliques couldn't form and sets of players couldn't dominate.

"My husband's in a state about what happened to the price of railway stocks," a lady said as a servant adjusted her chair.

"It's a temporary setback," Carolyn told the women.

"Temporary?" Lady Beresford asked, opening a pack of cards.

"Yes, the stock market is like a person," Carolyn explained. "It needs to adjust to the shock of the first time a particular calamity occurs."

"As I adjusted to the calamity of my wedding night," a lady at another table said.

Several women laughed.

"But just as people adjust to shock, so will the market," Carolyn continued. "I'm sure my husband can explain this better than I can."

"Mrs. Richmond, when men explain finances, they make it sound like Greek. But I always understand *you*."

"Thank you, Lady Garvis. Listening to my husband, I've concluded two things about the stock market."

"Do tell." Lady Warwick finished dealing. "Thirteen. Does everyone have thirteen cards?"

"The first secret of success is to be an investor, not a speculator," Carolyn said. "People who have an urge to gamble should confine themselves to playing cards."

"Ha," a lady said, beginning the play at her table with a nine of clubs. "And the second secret?"

"Patience," Carolyn replied.

"Well, anyone who's been married to a politician as long as I have knows about patience," Lady Garvis said.

"Hearts are trumps," a woman reminded the players at her table.

"I'm sure that my husband would advise people to buy *more* railway stock because the price will eventually return to its previous level—and higher. That's what always happens."

"Spades," someone at another table said.

"Enough of this depressing topic," Lady Beresford said. "Mrs. Richmond, you always have something clever for us. What is it *this* time?"

"Tonic water."

"Tonic water?"

"It's a beverage that Dr. Wainwright will soon offer to his guests. If they find it refreshing, he'll make it available to the better shops in London."

"But what is it?"

"Carbonated water with quinine added to it. As you ladies perhaps know, quinine is a substance that our soldiers in India use to ward off malaria. It's a powder that dissolves in water. It's very bitter. But Dr. Wainwright discovered a way to make it refreshing by adding sugar and carbonation. Perhaps the best part is that, unlike London water, there isn't a risk of anyone becoming ill from drinking it."

"Dr. Wainwright boils the water to rid it of impurities?" someone asked.

"There's no need," Carolyn replied. "Those of you who've been to his retreat know that the springs at Sedwick Hill have a rare purity. Even the queen is said to favor its water."

"But why are you proposing this as something clever?" Lady Beresford asked. "Surely we're not all in danger of coming down with malaria."

"Quinine also happens to be useful for controlling leg tremors, which some of you admit you have. But Dr. Wainwright's primary motive is to combat intemperance, since, unfortunately, our soldiers in India have decided that the only way to make quinine palatable is to mix it with gin."

"Gin?" someone exclaimed in horror.

"Dr. Wainwright's tonic water tastes so pleasant on its own that he intends to ship bottles of it to India in the hope that our soldiers there will get their necessary quinine from that rather than by mixing it with gin. But he believes that Britain will be his principal market. His goal is to promote health through pure water and a taste so refreshing that it discourages people everywhere from drinking not only gin but even brandy and soda."

"How commendable!" Lady Garvis gushed.

Carolyn turned toward a side door and called, "Marybeth."

The young servant appeared, carrying a tray of bottles that resembled small bowling pins.

After corks were popped and the fizzing water was poured, each lady sipped from the crystal stemware she was offered. Some of them wrinkled their noses as bubbles tickled them.

"It is indeed bitter, but with a pleasant sweetness also," Lady Montagu noted. She took a second sip and debated. "And it does have a bracing tonic quality."

"I have bottles for all of you to give to your husbands. Perhaps *this* time, they'll be interested in what happened at our card party."

"As long as it keeps my husband's mind off the railway stocks," Lady Garvis said.

In the echoing cavern of Paddington Station, railway guard Matthew Harrigan hurried along the carriages of the train to Bristol, locking each compartment. Only a third of them were occupied. Word about the explosion at Waterloo Station had traveled quickly, and the relatively few passengers on what would usually have been a crowded Saturday-night train looked at him apprehensively as his key made a scraping sound at each door. The expressions on their faces suggested that they felt like prisoners being consigned to their doom. Unless they were traveling with people they knew, the passengers took pains to find compartments in which they would be alone. Given the circumstances, that solitary arrangement wasn't difficult for them to manage.

Harrigan finished locking the final compartment and climbed aboard the brake van at the rear of the train. Despite the smoke and cinders, not to mention the cold wind that would soon overpower him back here, he considered himself lucky. Four months earlier, he'd been a soldier in the Crimea. When he wasn't eluding enemy bullets and cannonballs, he was nearly starving from the meager food allotted to him while the officers dined in high style. During sleet storms, he'd shivered in a summer uniform in a leaking tent while the officers wore thick greatcoats and warmed their hands over stoves on their commander's yacht. After an explosion during a Russian attack knocked Harrigan unconscious, the universe had shown him mercy, for his almost frozen body had been gathered with other casualties and shipped to the military hospital near Constantinople. There, his good fortune had persisted when none other than Miss Nightingale, the blessed Lady with the Lamp, had taken pity on him, nursed him back to health, and arranged for him to be sent home.

Fate had continued to smile on him in England. A boyhood friend, now a senior clerk for the Great Northern Railway, felt sorry for him and gave him a job as the brakeman on this train. Because of the health hazards of the job, few people wanted it, but to Harrigan, this was easy duty compared to the horrors of the Crimea.

He turned the wheel that released the brakes. He leaned out and waved his lantern, signaling to the driver that everything was ready.

Far ahead, the engine made a loud chugging sound that reverberated throughout the station. Similar sounds followed in quick succession. After a jolt, the brake van moved forward with the rest of the train.

Normally, Harrigan raised his hand in a friendly farewell to the people who remained on the platform, but tonight, most of the people he saw were guards, porters, and beggars wearing tattered war uniforms.

"Wait until Monday," a porter had told him, obviously hoping for a return of his customers. "People 'ave a short memory. They'll be back as soon as they can't put off goin' on a business trip or visitin' a sick grandmama."

But that had been before the explosion at Waterloo Station.

The train increased speed, clattering past the shadows of factories and slums. As smoke and cinders drifted back toward Harrigan, he made certain that the white lamps at the front of the van—and the warning red lamps at the rear—were lit. Then he stepped inside the van's shed, put a hand against its trembling wall to brace himself, and peered earnestly through the grimy window.

After three weeks on this route, Harrigan was starting to know every straightaway and curve on the tracks. As the train rattled over a familiar bridge, the air became clear. The van's lanterns reflected off a stream that he recognized, and he estimated that the first stop was ten minutes away. To the right, he saw the silhouette of a farmhouse.

Ahead—again on his right—he saw a glow that he would usually have assumed was from the lanterns at the next station, but that station was too far away to be seen. If clouds hadn't obscured the moon, he might have concluded that what he saw was its light reflecting off a window as the train rounded a curve.

The glow grew brighter.

Harrigan opened the shed's door and stepped into the wind. The irritating odor of the engine's smoke was unusually strong. He gripped a pole and leaned out as far as he dared, though not so far that he risked being struck by something. Focusing along the side of the swaying train, he saw that the glow was even larger, and in fact it wasn't a glow any longer. Its crimson light rippled and pulsed. Black smoke billowed, rushing toward the back of the train.

My God, it's a fire in one of the compartments, Harrigan realized.

He grabbed red filters from the shed and put them over the lamps at the front of the van. He grabbed another red filter and put it over his lantern. Then he leaned out and swung the red lantern to warn the driver to stop.

Lord in heaven, make him look back! Harrigan mentally pleaded.

The carriages didn't have a corridor that linked the compartments within each carriage or that linked one carriage to another. There wasn't a way for passengers in the burning compartment to escape. Harrigan could only pray that it wasn't occupied.

He swung the red lantern in a greater frenzy. On the left side, flames now erupted from a window. The rhythm of the train faltered, suggesting that the driver had finally looked back and seen the fire. As the train's speed lessened, Harrigan grabbed the wheel that projected from the floor of the van. He turned it, desperately applying the brakes.

They squealed, sparks shooting from them.

The train lurched, making Harrigan fight for balance. All at once the train slowed enough for him to jump to the gravel. He ran beside the tracks, the light from his lantern barely sufficient to keep him from stumbling in the smoke.

He paused only long enough to remove the key from his uniform and unlock the door to the baggage compartment.

"There's a fire!" he yelled to the guard. "Hurry out here and help!"

Harrigan raced onward, feeling the urgency and fear that he'd known in the war. He passed people shouting from a third-class carriage, where the passengers were herded together in one large area. He hoped that the baggage-compartment guard would unlock them, but he himself couldn't stop to do so—his attention was directed solely toward the burning carriage.

Coughing from the smoke, he ran past a second-class carriage. Ahead, he saw the flames in the first-class area. He heard their roar.

He also heard screams.

He shoved the key into a lock, twisted, and pulled at a door. Two men dove out with such force that Harrigan couldn't get away from the door quickly enough. Its painful impact knocked him onto the gravel.

Dazed, he struggled to his feet and forced himself to move closer to the blaze. When he unlocked the next door, a man in flames hurtled out, colliding with him. Before Harrigan could try to help him, the screaming man tumbled down a slope, setting fire to the dry grass.

Harrigan tugged off his overcoat and charged down the slope. He threw the coat over the shrieking, writhing figure and worked to suffocate the flames. He stamped on the burning grass.

"Help!" people screamed from the other compartments.

Where's my key? Harrigan thought in a panic. *What's happened to my key?*

Flames revealed where he'd dropped it in the grass. He grabbed it and ran up the slope. This time, he knew enough to stay clear when he unlocked the door and two men surged out.

He hurried to the next carriage. In the roar of the fire, the door bent. Heat lifted the roof.

Stumbling away, he suddenly heard a different roar, terrifyingly familiar, intensifying, rushing toward him.

He swung toward the back of the train and saw the lamps of a locomotive speed around a dark curve. The approaching train was going too fast to stop.

Its whistle shrieked.

"Run!" Harrigan yelled. He shoved passengers down the slope.

The whistle kept shrieking, growing louder.

"Hurry! Go!"

Looking back as he raced away, Harrigan saw the speeding train strike the brake van, upend it, and propel it from the tracks. Sounding like the thunder of cannons in the Crimea, the other carriages rammed into one another, some of them rising, others overturning. They flipped down the slope and across the field.

The engine from the oncoming train surged off the rails and plowed down the slope. Next to him, a woman tripped and fell. Harrigan grabbed her and dragged her along the grass. The engine's boiler exploded. Steam burst across the field, chunks of metal flying. As Harrigan threw himself over the woman to protect her, heat scorched his back.

"WYLD'S MONSTER GLOBE," Lord Palmerston told the driver as he and his guard climbed into a cab.

"Beggin' your pardon, guv'nor, but it ain't open at this time of night."

"Tonight it will be."

Lord Palmerston didn't take the precaution of instructing the driver to use an indirect route so that he and his escort could see if the lanterns of a vehicle followed them. On this occasion, it would in fact be better if someone did follow them.

The Monster Globe had been constructed four years earlier to coincide with the arrival of the millions of visitors coming to London for the Crystal Palace Exhibition. Sixty feet in diameter, one of the tallest buildings in the West End, the globe occupied much of Soho's Leicester Square, a once-pastoral area with lawns and trees that had degenerated into weeds, trash, and dead cats. An entrepreneur named James Wyld had persuaded the square's owners to lease it to him, promising to improve the grounds immensely. Wyld's idea of improvement was to fill Leicester Square with his Monster Globe. For the price of a shilling, visitors could step inside and admire plaster models of the world's continents, oceans, rivers, and mountains. As many as three million people did so, and none seemed to think it bizarre that they viewed a world turned outside in, where mountains that normally rose toward the sky now pointed inward toward the Earth's core.

"Again, beggin' your pardon, guv'nor, but you can see the place is dark," the cabdriver said when they arrived.

"Thank you anyway," Lord Palmerston told him as he and his guard stepped down. He paid twice the normal rate so that the driver would be sure to remember bringing him here.

As the cab clattered away, a member of Lord Palmerston's security team stepped from the shadows.

"Did she arrive?" Lord Palmerston asked.

"Five minutes ago, Prime Minister. At this streetlamp. As lovely as she is and with her pink costume, anyone watching couldn't have failed to notice her."

"You searched the globe everywhere?"

"It's deserted, sir, except for your guest."

Despite the cold wind, Lord Palmerston unbuttoned his overcoat. The streetlamp revealed a bright blue waistcoat beneath his gray suit. The festive garment was noteworthy, given that, according to current fashion, vibrant colors for men were considered undignified. In Lord Palmerston's youth, his present costume would have been considered dull, but by contemporary standards, he looked daring.

Straightening his back and expanding his chest to make himself appear younger than his seventy years, he walked toward the silhouette of the huge globe. Although the place wasn't illuminated, the door was unlocked. Inside, he waited for his eyes to adjust to the shadow of the revolving gate next to the ticket booth. Then he pushed through and reached a vestibule in which there were cases he couldn't see well but that he knew displayed various rocks and diagrams of the Earth's geological levels.

A light seeped past the edge of an Oriental curtain. His footsteps echoing, he swept the curtain aside and entered the globe.

He encountered four platforms, one atop another, accessible by wooden stairs. Lamps hung from the platforms. During the day, light came through a glass cap in the ceiling in the position of the Arctic Circle. He noted the outlines of continents and oceans projecting from the inside of the globe everywhere around him. Feeling as if he were encircled by stalactites in a cavern, he wondered if this was the sort of crazed perspective that the Opium-Eater dreamed about.

The first landmass Lord Palmerston recognized was Australia. A Crown colony, he noted with approval. As he proceeded up the first staircase, he identified other regions that belonged to the British Empire— India, Burma, Singapore, Hong Kong, New Zealand…

Of course, those were the British colonies in only one area, and as he climbed, he looked in other directions and saw even more British colonies. The empire's extent made him proud. He had power over more territory and people than anyone else had ever possessed in the history of the world.

But despite that power, when he reached the third level, he felt short of breath. His determination gave him the strength to hide it, just as he felt compelled to hide his advancing age by dyeing his sideburns brown.

A young woman waited for him on the top level. Astonishingly beautiful, she wore a beguiling pink bonnet and matching dress. The pink provided extra luster to her lips. Her name at the moment was Charlotte, but she had used many different names in her acting career. Currently performing roles on an international political stage, she found diplomats, generals, and men of wealth to be more amusing than the gentlemen who'd applauded her in blood-drenched melodramas in London theaters.

"I hope you feel as radiant as your appearance indicates," Lord Palmerston said.

"It's no wonder you survived in politics for half a century," Charlotte responded, kissing his cheek. "Your compliments always sound as if you mean them."

"But I *do* mean them," he said, kissing her in return.

They stood beneath ventilation tubes that whistled from the wind outside and distorted what they said. If, despite the thoroughness of his security team, someone happened to witness this meeting, it would be from a distance, and the spy could report only that they kept their heads together, evidently exchanging endearments. What else would one expect from a man whose dalliances over the years had made him notorious?

"Dr. Mandt reached England this morning," Charlotte whispered in his ear. "At this moment, he should be arriving at Sedwick Hill."

Sedwick Hill. The reference made Lord Palmerston exhale. To an observer, it would have seemed that he reacted to stroking her neck.

"Finally. The last report was from Antwerp, and that was three days ago. I feared the Russians had captured him." In contrast to his tender gestures, Lord Palmerston's voice was quietly angry. "But now the police are interested in Sedwick Hill because of Daniel Harcourt's murder. None of this effort would have been necessary if Dr. Mandt hadn't run. If he'd kept his wits, he could have waited for a month and then told the new czar he had family business that required his return to the German States. The czar did have pneumonia, after all. No one would have questioned that he died from lung failure."

"Dr. Mandt claims he didn't have a choice," Charlotte said, pressing her cheek against his. "The moment the czar died, jealous Russian doctors accused him of negligence. He believed that it wouldn't be long before they accused him of much worse. He escaped while he could."

"But if Russian agents keep chasing him, if they capture him and force him to tell the truth, if the Russians accuse me..." Lord Palmerston felt a moment's dizziness as he glanced from the top platform toward the inward-projecting continents and oceans of the world.

"A great risk—a great result," Charlotte murmured close to him. "It turns out the new czar's appetite for war isn't as strong as his father's."

"I knew I was right."

"Russia's commoners are rioting because of food shortages the war inflicted upon them," Charlotte continued. "At your instructions, my operatives spread reports that Russian soldiers are starving by the thousands while the rich stuff themselves with caviar and vodka. We told peasants the locations of food warehouses reserved for the aristocracy. We organized attacks on those warehouses. We set fire to mansions and made it seem that angry peasants were doing it. The new czar doesn't know which is worse, the cost of continuing the war or the possibility of a revolution at home. His resolve is weakening."

"Maybe *our* resolve is weakening also," Lord Palmerston said. "Tonight there was yet another incident involving a train. No one will feel safe anywhere. I worry that the Russians are turning my tactics against me."

THE WAGON LURCHED to an unexpected stop. In back, a nervous man peered from under a canvas cover. Beneath stars and a partial moon, all he saw was a shadowy field.

"Dr. Mandt, it's time to get out," the driver said in English-accented German.

"But there's nothing here," Mandt objected.

"Those are the instructions we were given," the driver's partner said. His German was English-accented also.

"But...but it's dark."

"I'll go with you."

"You plan to kill me here, is that it?"

"Kill you?"

"Slash my throat and bury me in this field."

"Doctor, I guarantee that if we meant to kill you, it wouldn't be after all the effort it took to arrange your escape from the Russians. Please step down. This young man is going to lead us to where you'll spend the night."

"I was foolish to agree to—"

"Look at it this way. If the plan was to kill you, there's nothing you could do about it, so save yourself a lot of worry. Be optimistic. Step down and let this young man lead us to where you'll be staying for a while."

Trembling, Mandt crawled from beneath the canvas cover. His legs almost didn't support him when his boots touched the dirt road.

The only light was a lantern so shielded that it barely allowed the wagon's horse to see where to put its hooves.

"A young man? Where?" Mandt asked.

Saying something in English, a tall man stepped around the side of the wagon.

The driver translated. "He says that where you'll be staying is down that lane."

"What lane?"

"Over there. He says we can't just drive up to the entrance because the sound of the wagon would wake up some of the patients. In the morning, there'd be questions about who'd arrived in the middle of the night, and we don't want any questions."

"Patients?"

"It's hard to describe. You'll understand when you get there."

"You're going to imprison me in a madhouse?"

"Doctor, please calm yourself. It isn't a madhouse, although the prices the patients happily pay—they're referred to as guests—might make it seem that they're crazy. Now let's go, and from here on, no talking."

Without a lantern, the young man led the doctor and his escort down the lane. A cold wind forced Mandt to clutch his overcoat and tremble more severely. After his long, fearsome journey, he expected dark shapes to jump from the murky trees that he passed and attack him.

Ahead, a hill loomed against the starlit sky. Three tall buildings stood next to it, none of their windows illuminated at this late hour. The wind whistled as the doctor and his escort were led toward a side door of the middle building.

The door opened, revealing only darkness. The young man guided Mandt inside.

"It's safe here." The escort from the wagon whispered so softly that Mandt could barely hear the words. "Don't be afraid."

It's easy for him *to say,* Mandt thought. *He isn't the one who's been terrified for the past two weeks.*

The escort started to return to the wagon.

"Wait," Mandt pleaded. "Don't leave me."

"Quiet," an educated voice said in German as a hand shut the door.

In total darkness, a match flared, hurting Mandt's eyes.

"What he told you is true," the voice continued. "You're safe here."

SEVEN

THE HOUSE OF ICE

"Good morning!" a distinguished-looking man said to De Quincey and Emily. After they'd knocked on the door, he'd opened it himself rather than relying on a servant. "I'm Edward Richmond. Carolyn's husband."

In his midsixties with a fashionable goatee and mustache, he wore a tailored frock coat, a ruffled white shirt, and a dark blue cravat that suggested financial success without being vulgar.

"Come in, come in. That's a nasty cold wind out there. Please set down your travel bags."

He didn't react to De Quincey's short stature or to Emily's bloomer dress. Nor did he react when Emily shook hands with him rather than curtsying.

For her part, Emily tried not to react to an entrance hall that was more opulent than that at Lord Palmerston's house. Its staircase was more impressive, its brass handrail flaring outward to accommodate the widest of dresses. Ancient figurines and exquisite landscape paintings surrounded her, but they didn't seem to have been chosen to impress visitors and proclaim wealth. Instead of being garish, they exhibited remarkable taste.

"My wife will be with you in a moment. After I returned from Manchester last evening, she couldn't stop gushing about her discovery that you were staying just around the corner from us, Mr. De Quincey."

"Please, call us Thomas and Emily," De Quincey said.

"I'd be honored, provided that you call me Edward. I think we can allow each other the liberty, given your relationship with Carolyn. How long has it been since she last saw you? Around fifty years? She almost made me jealous when she described the horseman's cloak that the two of you slept beneath when she was a child and how you protected her from rats that she feared were ghosts."

"With a poison I invented," De Quincey said. He reached into a pocket of his overcoat, apparently about to produce a bottle of the substance.

"No, Father," Emily said, knowing the type of bottle that he actually reached for.

Reluctantly, De Quincey lowered his hand. "I mixed phosphorus with sugar, lard, flour, and brandy. Attracted by the glow, the rats would eat what amounted to an uncooked biscuit and die. That was my parting gift to her and—"

"And it worked," Carolyn's voice interrupted.

They turned to see her coming down the steps gracefully, carrying a small overnight bag. She wore a flattering travel costume of blue wool, finely textured and soft-looking, its color enhancing her auburn hair. As on the previous day, her cape matched her dress, and the billow of the dress was created by several petticoats instead of a hoop. The ease with which she spoke as she descended the staircase indicated that, like Emily, she didn't wear a corset.

"Carolyn still uses the paste," Edward said. "But now it's mostly to provide illumination at night so no one will trip in the dark. I have a business relationship with a company that's considering manufacturing it. Thomas, because the idea came from you, perhaps I could arrange for you to get a small royalty if the product ever goes on the market."

Carolyn leaned down to kiss De Quincey on the cheek. "What an excellent idea."

"It is indeed a good thing that I'm not a jealous man," Edward said in a tone of amusement.

"Good morning, Emily," Carolyn said, hugging her.

"Good morning!"

"I hope you don't think less of me because I'm not going to church on Sunday. Our daughter's personal difficulties—her husband's health problems—are more important to me than sitting in a pew."

"I told a servant to bring a cab," Edward said. "But Carolyn, I still recommend that you postpone your journey."

"Absolutely not. I won't let them make me a hermit."

"Them? Is something wrong?" Emily asked.

"Last night, there was an accident after a train left Paddington Station," Edward explained. "The train caught fire. After it stopped, another train crashed into it. Several people were killed."

"Good Lord!"

"Only a third of the usual number of passengers were aboard," Edward continued. "Otherwise, the casualties would have been greater. Last night, my train arrived at Euston Station an hour after the crash. But in that limited time, reports had already sped from Paddington to Euston, causing a panic. Passengers who had tickets for the next train didn't board it. My business associates include officers of several railway companies. This morning, they summoned me to an emergency meeting at the Royal Exchange."

"A fire?" De Quincey asked, his blue eyes sparkling with interest. "Was it deliberate or an accident?"

"The police don't know yet, but the rumors are that the blasted Russians did it. Excuse my language, but tomorrow, the effect on the stock market will be disastrous. The financial damage will cascade onto shopkeepers, innkeepers, grocers, tailors, and even potboys in taverns. Carolyn, because of the emergency meeting, I can't accompany you. I ask you to reconsider and stay here until the situation is resolved."

"And surrender to fear? Hardly. I promised our daughter that I'd visit her today, and with all the trouble she has, I don't intend to disappoint her. Thomas and Emily, I promise I won't be offended if you remain in London, but—"

"Remain in London?" Emily said. "Perish the thought. We agreed to accompany you, and that's what we'll do. We're looking forward to meeting your daughter. And the doctor at the clinic. Isn't that right, Father?"

THE AREA AROUND Euston Station normally teemed with cabs, but today, theirs was one of the few to be found. The wind blew dust and debris through the massive Roman arch. Two dogs ran past, so pathetically thin that their ribs showed. Otherwise, except for a couple of desperate beggars in ragged Crimean War uniforms, the expansive courtyard was deserted. De Quincey, Emily, and Carolyn hurried from the cab, a few drops of rain pelting them as they ran inside the station.

The silence of the Great Hall felt ominous. The rumble of the copper-covered door reverberated from pillars and granite staircases that normally were barely visible because of bustling passengers.

At a booth, a spectacled ticket seller looked shocked to see them.

"Three first-class tickets to Sedwick Hill, please." Carolyn put coins on the counter.

"Are you certain, madam?" the astonished man asked.

"To Sedwick Hill. Yes," Carolyn responded. "That's where we wish to go."

"That's not what I meant. Are you certain you wish to go *anywhere*?"

"Why would you ask so strange a question?"

"Haven't you heard about all the trouble yesterday?"

"And on Thursday night also," Carolyn said. "But that's no guarantee that something untoward will happen *today*. Please give us our tickets."

"You mean you know about everything, and you still intend to board a train?"

"My dear man, you don't sound as though you're employed here."

"By tomorrow, I probably won't be. You're the first people I've seen all morning. At this rate, I'll be out of work."

"Passengers will return when they realize they're being foolish," Carolyn told him. "Our tickets, please."

"Happily, madam. I look forward to seeing more people with your attitude."

The three of them went through a short, dusky tunnel and reached a turnstile, where a guard—looking equally shocked—examined their tickets.

Except for a waiting train and idle porters, the iron-and-glass-roofed platform was empty. The rumble of myriad conversations was normally deafening, but this morning, the hiss and an occasional chug from the train's engine were the only sounds.

They reached a first-class compartment, the door of which was ajar.

Carolyn paused, peering into the small, shadowy chamber, seemingly undecided about whether to board.

Then she drew a breath and climbed inside. Emily and De Quincey followed and sat opposite her.

As they settled onto the thick, blue cushions, Carolyn pointed toward the empty seats next to them. "Well, at least there's one thing we don't need to worry about—someone joining us."

The moment De Quincey removed his laudanum bottle from his overcoat, a guard appeared at the open door. After a suspicious gaze at the bottle, the guard told them, "We're ready to depart." His tone implied that what he actually meant was *Are* you *ready to depart, or are you having second thoughts?*

"The sooner we leave, the sooner we'll arrive at our destination," Carolyn told him.

The guard nodded, closed the door, and locked it, the scrape of his key seeming louder than usual. Through the barred windows, they watched him proceed to the next compartment and lock it also.

Carolyn reached into her purse, surprising De Quincey and Emily when she pulled out a large key that looked to be the same as the one that the guard had used to lock them in.

"Where did you find *that*?" Emily asked in amazement.

"Last summer, Edward requested it from a railway executive who's one of his clients. Can you guess how the executive reacted? 'Good idea,' he told Edward. 'I never board a train without a key either.' If there's an emergency, we can raise a window and reach out to unlock the door."

The compartment lurched as the train moved forward. Carolyn pressed her hands solidly on her knees. Emily stared at the cocoa-fiber mat on the floor. De Quincey sipped from his laudanum bottle.

"I'm sure that nothing will happen so soon after yesterday's incidents," he said.

"Oh?" Carolyn asked. "What makes you think so?"

"Because murder as a fine art depends on suspense along with pity and terror. What grips an audience more, a shocking surprise or the tension of waiting for something terrible to happen?"

The train increased its speed. The clouds hung lower. Rain speckled the dusty windows, forming streaks.

"No—whoever is responsible for this," De Quincey said, "will wait for people to feel the full impact of the previous horrors."

The compartment tilted as the train rounded a curve. Now both Carolyn and Emily stared at the mat on the floor.

"What's more, the next incident won't be on the Euston line, or the Waterloo line, or the Paddington line," De Quincey said. "Rather, it'll occur on one of the other six lines that radiate from London. For the nation to be truly paralyzed, other railways will need to be attacked. Carolyn, how long does it take to reach Sedwick Hill?"

"Twenty minutes," she answered. Looking up, she seemed to welcome the distraction of the question.

"Then we have time for you to tell us."

"Tell you…"

"What happened to you and your father after I left that accursed house in Greek Street."

"My God," Ryan murmured as a police wagon carried him and Becker along a dirt road that paralleled the railway tracks.

The devastation seemed to stretch forever: A jumble of carriages scorched by flames had been thrown from the rails, upended, overturned, twisted, and ruptured. A locomotive appeared to have struck the motion-less train and now lay on its side in the middle of a charred field, a deep furrow behind it, its boiler split open. Rescue workers searched the field for more victims while hospital wagons rumbled away with the injured. Telegraph poles had been snapped, their wires tangled among the wreck-age. A far section of the field—near the first locomotive—had a row of what seemed to be bodies covered with sheets.

"Stop here," Ryan told the driver.

He and Becker jumped down and walked forward, gaping at the chaos.

"I was never in a war, but this is what I imagine it looks like," Becker said, appalled.

"No, this is worse," a dirt-and-blood-covered train guard told them, approaching. "Are you the detectives from Scotland Yard?"

Ryan and Becker showed their badges.

"In the Crimea, I saw craters in the mud, and arms and legs of bodies sticking up from it. A *lot* of craters. A lot of…" The guard gestured with his bandaged hands as if trying to force his memories away. "After a while, I got to the point that I thought it was normal. But *this*…five miles outside London, with an English hedgerow over there and a field where cattle will start grazing in a month and where women and children don't expect to be slaughtered…no, this is worse."

"Do you know what might have caused the fire?" Becker asked.

"There's no 'might have' about it. Come over here to this carriage. Look out for that sharp chunk of metal sticking up from the grass. Be careful of that wheel."

As Ryan and Becker made their way through the wreckage, they saw bandaged people being lifted into another hospital wagon.

"That's where it started." The guard pointed to the middle compart-ment of a carriage that had shattered windows, twisted doors, a scorched side, and an upwardly buckled roof.

Ryan and Becker stepped closer.

"The heat made the door pop open even though it was locked," the guard said. "See that pile of ash on what's left of the seat to the right? That was a travel bag."

"The door was locked?" Ryan asked. "Whoever was inside couldn't have escaped, but I don't see a body."

"Because there wasn't anyone in that compartment," the guard replied. "When I locked it, I'm certain it was empty—and I'm certain the windows were closed, so the fire couldn't have been started by engine sparks flying inside."

"No one was in the compartment? Then how the devil did a travel bag get in there?" Becker asked.

"Exactly what *I'd* like to know," the guard answered. "As far as I can determine, someone went in there and put a bag on the luggage rack at the top. Then whoever it was left the compartment and either stepped into a farther compartment or else somehow got past the guard at the exit from Paddington Station. The guard inspects the tickets before he lets anyone out of the station to make certain no one sneaked aboard the incoming train and tried to get a free ride. He'd definitely have asked questions if someone had tried to leave with a ticket for a train that hadn't even departed from the station."

"Whoever it was might have claimed he suddenly felt sick," Becker suggested. "That's what happened at Waterloo Station yesterday. Or he could have told the guard he needed to return to his lodging because he'd suddenly realized he hadn't turned off the gas."

Ryan gave Becker a nod of respect. "If so, it's possible the guard remembers someone making those kinds of excuses and can tell us what the person looked like."

"But what was in the bag that might have started the fire?" Becker wondered. "Another bomb with a slow-burning fuse?"

"I didn't hear an explosion," the guard told them. "But even if the noise of the engine kept me from hearing a bomb, do you see any sign of an explosion in this compartment?"

"None," Ryan said.

"Maybe a slow-burning fuse was linked to a container of loose gunpowder," the guard offered. "It wouldn't have exploded. It would only have burst into flames."

"Five miles outside London." Ryan shook his head. "It would need to have been an awfully slow-burning fuse."

THE TRAIN ENTERED a tunnel, darkness suddenly enveloping Thomas, Emily, and Carolyn, the noise of the engine intensifying. Both De Quincey and his daughter stared toward the far side of their compartment.

"What's wrong?" Carolyn asked.

"That's where Daniel Harcourt's body was dumped from the train," De Quincey answered.

"When the train stopped, we ran back to try to help him," Emily said, continuing to stare at the dark windows, "but there wasn't anything we could do."

Daylight returned as the train exited the tunnel. Instead of the blood that had appeared on the windows Thursday night, raindrops now streaked across them. De Quincey and Emily took a moment before they looked at Carolyn again.

"Thomas, you wanted to know what happened to me after you departed for Eton," she said. "Brunell was absent for three days. On the fourth, he returned in a state of fright. He ordered me to help him carry all the legal papers from the back room and stack them next to the nearest fireplace. He told me to look carefully through a gap in a front curtain and warn him if anyone approached the house. As soon as every document was burned, he dragged me out the back door."

"Do you have any idea why he was so afraid?" Emily asked.

Carolyn shook her head.

"He worked for moneylenders. Perhaps one of them was furious because Brunell vouched for someone who disappeared after borrowing considerable funds," De Quincey suggested.

"Whatever the reason, we hurried to a mail coach and went to

Brighton," Carolyn said. "But as soon as we arrived, we walked to an inn several miles away. The next morning, we walked to another town and boarded another mail coach. That became the pattern—walk, mail coach, walk, mail coach. Our route seemed aimless. After a week, we arrived in Bristol, and that's where he sold me."

"What?" Emily asked.

"I eventually learned that some of the work Brunell did for moneylenders involved investigating people who hoped to borrow money against inheritances they claimed were due to them. It turned out that he'd crossed paths with a man who should have inherited a large estate from his father, the owner of a shipping company in Bristol."

"What do you mean, should have?" De Quincey asked.

"The man was the only son," Carolyn explained. "There'd been three daughters, but the father had no fondness for females, and he showed only mild distress when they died from various illnesses over the years. It was a grim household. To make it grimmer, the son fell in love with a shopgirl. The father ordered his son to turn his back on her because of her inferior station. Instead, the son ran away and married her, hoping that the fact of the marriage would soften his father. To the contrary, the father became even more furious and disinherited him, naming his business partner as the new heir. Spiteful, he didn't bequeath his estate to his wife, fearing that his wife would be lenient to his son after his death."

The train swayed as it rounded a curve. Carolyn reached for the overhead strap.

"Events foiled his plan, however," she continued. "His business partner died when a sling broke and a container of goods fell on him as it was being loaded onto a ship. During the subsequent confusion—planning for the funeral, restructuring the company, and so on—the father neglected to name a new heir and died a week later when his carriage overturned.

"This was ten years after the father had disinherited the son. By then, the shopgirl was dead from cholera. The son had tried to reestablish himself in his father's affections, but with no success. Seeking a loan from a moneylender in London, he met Brunell, who read a copy of the will and interpreted it to mean that because no other inheritor was mentioned, the widow was the next in line."

De Quincey sounded puzzled. "But given the law of succession, didn't the father have a male relative, no matter how distant, who could be considered the next heir, even if he wasn't named?"

"Yes, but Brunell didn't expect to win," Carolyn replied. "His purpose was to threaten to introduce the will into the confusion of the courts. He hoped that the distant male heir—a third cousin, it turned out—would be willing to negotiate with the widow rather than have the estate destroyed by court costs and prolonged delays, as often happens."

"But how was this going to help the son?" Emily asked. "He'd been disinherited and still wouldn't receive anything."

"That was Brunell's stroke of brilliance. The son's wife had died without producing children. Brunell suggested that he pretend *I* was his daughter. Do you see? The widow had lost three daughters. Her husband had been an uncaring tyrant. By running away, her son had brought further misery into her life. She'd never imagined that in her late years she would know happiness, but now she discovered that she had a granddaughter."

"Was Brunell's scheme successful?" De Quincey asked.

Carolyn nodded. "For the sake of *me,* her supposed granddaughter, the widow welcomed her son. Brunell pointed out to the cousin that the court might favor a widow and a granddaughter—a granddaughter who'd been living in squalor because of the heartlessness of her grandfather—rather than reward a distant relative. In exchange for not contesting the will, the widow received a handsome yearly income, far more than she could have expected from her husband's niggardly business partner. It was more than enough for the three of us—the son, the mother, and me—to live on. The woman, whom I learned to call Grandmama, was deceived, yes, but the deception did no harm. Indeed, it gave her pleasure, and she gave *me* a life I could never have dreamed of. She educated me. She encouraged me to seek the independence that she herself had never been allowed to pursue. I made friends with the cousin who inherited the business and persuaded him to teach me how the financial world conducted itself. As I grew older, various financiers and lawyers courted me, and I learned a great deal from them as well. Finally I met Edward, the brilliant man who became my husband and who was wise enough to understand that independence meant more to me than anything. Together, we built quite an enterprise."

"What happened to Brunell?" Emily asked.

"He never stopped looking over his shoulder. The moment the son paid him his fee, Brunell boarded a ship and fled to the United States." Carolyn frowned. "Do you feel the train losing speed?"

A cottage appeared outside the window.

"Aha. No cause for concern," Carolyn told them. "We're here."

THE DRIZZLE PERSISTED as they hurried from the station toward a covered carriage waiting for them. The driver loaded their bags and urged the horses into motion. As Emily put a comforting rug over De Quincey, he peered outside.

Sedwick Hill was another village that had once been an inconvenient distance from London but, thanks to the railway, was now within easy reach of the metropolis. Men who wore business suits bought cottages here and in the evening arrived from their offices to appreciate the flower gardens that their wives hired local laborers to plant and tend. Even more appreciated was the pure air, so different from the gritty miasma of London.

But unlike the village where De Quincey and Emily had stopped on the night of Daniel Harcourt's murder, Sedwick Hill looked prosperous. Its streets had paving stones. Its shops were freshly painted, as were the numerous, obviously new dwellings on the outskirts.

"Carolyn, on Thursday night, we saw a village where speculators had built more cottages than they could find buyers for. Abandoned, half-completed buildings were everywhere. The villagers were discouraged," De Quincey said. "Why is Sedwick Hill, farther from London, in a better condition?"

"The hydropathy clinic we're going to visit tomorrow," Carolyn responded. "See, up ahead, there's the hill from which the village gets its name, and next to it…"

The carriage approached a huge estate on the right, with a white gravel lane that led to a grassy promenade that had benches and shrubbery. Beyond these, silhouetted against the hill, were three wide, tall buildings. Separated by trees and pristine walkways, they resembled luxury hotels. Their numerous gables made their five stories seem even higher.

A sign next to the gravel lane announced

DR. ERNEST WAINWRIGHT'S
WATER-CURE ESTABLISHMENT

"Combined, there must be three hundred rooms in those buildings," Emily said in astonishment.

"And as a rule, each of them is occupied," Carolyn told her. "Sometimes for a weekend. Often for a full week. But usually for a month at a time."

"A month?" Emily sounded surprised.

"The people who require Dr. Wainwright's help tend to have chronic diseases such as rheumatism and kidney stones. Considerable care is needed to reverse the symptoms. But many also have a vague debilitated condition that requires reenergizing a patient's core. I should say, a *guest's* core. Dr. Wainwright never refers to his clients as patients. As you can imagine, an establishment of this size can't function without numerous attendants, especially for the laundry, kitchen, and dining room. The water technicians are, of course, trained medical personnel, but otherwise, all the workers come from the village. That's the reason for the difference between Sedwick Hill and the other place you mentioned: a major source of employment. The residents feel very fortunate that heaven blessed them with the local springs—some of the purest water in England. As Dr. Wainwright likes to say, 'You can't have a pure soul without a pure body, and you can't have either without pure water.'"

"He sounds like a philosopher," De Quincey said.

"I know he'll enjoy talking with you tomorrow," Carolyn told him.

THE JANGLE OF a passing vehicle compelled Dr. Mandt to risk approaching an attic window. Nervously parting the curtains as little as possible, he saw raindrops on the glass. He stared beyond the pathways, shrubbery, and lawn toward a carriage that moved along a country road, coming toward the lane to the clinic.

The vehicle was covered, preventing him from seeing the occupants. He imagined grim-faced Russians, angry and impatient after a two-week pursuit. He imagined that they had weapons hidden in their pockets; knives, certainly, and probably firearms. He imagined that the carriage would turn when it reached the lane and then stop in front of the buildings and...

To Mandt's relief, it proceeded past the lane and continued along the road toward whatever beckoned its passengers on so dismal a morning.

Voices now prompted him to make his way around boxes and old furniture and peer through the curtains of the attic's back window. *This* window provided a view of the hill behind the luxurious buildings. The voices he heard came from people who ran up the hill or walked up steadily or plodded up. Young and old, men and women, they each held a cup, and despite the cold, wet wind, they seemed to be in a contest over who would be the first to reach a grotto halfway up the hill or perhaps over who would reach the grotto at all. Some of those who struggled up the slope needed an attendant. Others, having achieved their goal and quaffed water from a fountain up there, ran down the hill, laughing, while those who took labored steps appeared to wheeze.

Insanity.

Knuckles rapped three times on a door. Mandt waited. Again, the knuckles rapped three times. Only when they rapped another three times did he approach the door, having been told that he could trust anyone who used that pattern. With a trembling hand, he pushed a small hatch aside.

Through it, he saw the top of a narrow, shadowy stairway. But even in shadows, the man's now-familiar silvery mustache was identifiable.

"The water of life," the man said in German but with an English accent.

Like the pattern of raps on the door, the expression was another indication that nothing was amiss.

Mandt freed the bolt on the door, but despite having been reassured, he stepped back apprehensively.

The man whom he knew as Dr. Wainwright entered the attic, carrying a wicker basket. *"Guten Morgen,"* he said, and he continued in German. "Were you able to sleep?"

"Very little."

"Understandable. Your arrival must have been nervous-making. I apologize for the accommodations." Wainwright indicated the dusty clutter that filled the attic. The cot on which Mandt had tried to sleep was hidden in a corner, behind boxes.

"What *is* this place?" Mandt asked.

"A water-cure clinic."

"Hydropathy? Surely you don't mean the sort of thing that's at Gräfenberg?" Mandt referred to a controversial institution in the Austrian mountains.

"Indeed. I studied there for two years."

"But the man who established it was a farmer's son without an ounce of medical training."

"Unlike him, I *do* have medical training—from the University of Edinburgh," Dr. Wainwright said, standing straighter.

"Forgive me. I apologize if I gave offense."

"None taken. Your nerves are on edge. Perhaps some refreshment will help." Wainwright set the basket on a table and removed items. "I don't know what you were accustomed to eating in St. Petersburg, but I thought that some simple bread, cheese, and boiled ham wouldn't upset your stomach. And here is something to drink."

He placed two bowling-pin-shaped bottles on the table.

"What's *that*?"

"I call it tonic water."

"Water? What I need is schnapps."

"You won't find any alcohol here, I'm afraid," Dr. Wainwright said. "I can tell from the tone of your skin that you need a cleansing."

"Cleansing be damned. How long must I stay here? When do I leave for the United States?"

"The plan was for you to be taken by train to Bristol and put on a ship tomorrow, but you might need to wait a day or two longer."

"Wait? I was promised there wouldn't be a delay," Mandt said.

"Unfortunately, there have been some incidents involving trains."

"Incidents?"

Wainwright made a calming gesture. "A fire. A collision. Nothing to concern you. But travelers are staying away from railway stations. We need to assume that Russians are watching the stations. Without a crowd around you, there's a risk you might be noticed. In fact, when the railways return to normal, as an extra precaution your escorts might take you to Liverpool instead of Bristol. It's farther from London and might seem less likely for you to choose it."

Mandt groaned. "I should never have agreed to this."

THE AIR BECAME grayer. Sporadic raindrops pelted the top of the carriage as it turned into a lane and proceeded between rows of tall, leafless trees.

"Normally the trees have started to bud by now, but this strangely cold weather..." Carolyn let the sentence fall away. "This estate belongs to my daughter's husband, Lord Cavendale."

They approached a huge manor house that could have been mistaken for a castle.

"Your daughter married well also?" De Quincey asked. "You must feel proud."

"The union isn't as fortunate as it might seem." Carolyn peered down at her hands. "My daughter's name is Stella. She met Lord Cavendale on various occasions—at dinners, balls, and champagne receptions at the Henley regatta and the Epsom Downs races, that sort of thing—that I organized for my husband's clients."

The casual mention of those major social events made De Quincey and Emily glance at each other. It was a world they couldn't imagine.

"Lord Cavendale lost his first wife in a boating accident five years ago," Carolyn said. "When he met Stella, he'd been a widower for two years. He was understandably lonely, and Stella, as you'll discover, is beautiful. There's a difference of ages that perhaps argued against a union between them."

"Difference of ages?" Emily asked.

"Lord Cavendale is sixty years old. Stella is half that. At the time they married, he had two grown sons, approximately Stella's age. I heard from a source that the sons felt they could hardly accept her as a stepmother when she was only old enough to be their sister. But evidently Lord Cavendale had a stern conversation with his sons. His intentions prevailed."

"You said that *at the time* he had two grown sons," De Quincey noted.

"Yes. The elder son died from typhoid fever soon after Lord Cavendale and Stella were married. Stella did her best to console her husband even though the son had resented her. Naturally, the death put a sense of gloom over the start of the union."

"Unlucky indeed," De Quincey said.

"The bad luck continued. In due course, Stella found herself in a family way, but the child, a daughter, died from a fever only a week after she was born. Stella and her husband have had a second child, but my daughter can't stop fearing that something terrible will happen to *this* infant also. In fact, she worries about everything. She..." Carolyn shook her head. "I'm beginning to think that I shouldn't have brought you here, Thomas. Stella's troubles are too much to inflict on you. But I hoped that you might be a distraction for her. In a magazine to which you contribute, I read that your friends consider your conversation to be so entertaining that they're tempted to hold you captive, put you in a box, and bring you out, like a child's toy, to enliven dull parties."

"Of late, I regret that my conversation hasn't been lively," De Quincey said, holding his laudanum bottle, "but for your sake, I'll try."

"It would be appreciated. The bad luck persisted when Lord Cavendale suffered—"

Before Carolyn could finish her sentence, the carriage halted in front of the granite steps that led to columns flanking the huge door of the stone manor house. Holding an umbrella, a liveried servant ran outside and down the steps. Another liveried servant held the carriage door open.

From the Journal of Emily De Quincey

Despite its commanding exterior, it was the gloomiest house I have ever entered. Granted that the day was damp and cold, and granted that the dark clouds made the interior shadowy, but every fireplace I saw was blazing and every oil lamp was lit, and still the place felt like a tomb. Its stone walls were covered with tapestries that depicted bucolic scenes of shepherds and frolicking nymphs, but the partially clad state of the nymphs only made me sympathize with how cold they must feel.

"Mother!" a voice said with relief.

It belonged to a young woman who hurried toward us from a huge sitting room on the right.

"When this morning's Times *finally arrived and I read about all the trouble on the trains"—she hugged Carolyn tightly—"I worried that you wouldn't be able to visit me today."*

"Nothing could stop me," Carolyn said, returning the hug. "Thomas and Emily, this is my daughter, Stella—and Stella, I've brought you a famous visitor..."

Father looked uncomfortable.

"Thomas De Quincey."

"De Quincey," Stella repeated as though she felt she ought to know the name.

"Confessions of an English Opium-Eater," Carolyn explained. "A friend from long ago."

Stella gave Father a delighted smile, seeming not to notice how short he was. "A famous author. What an honor. I hope you won't think ill of me if I admit that I haven't read your Confessions. I know of it, of course, everyone does, but Mother thought it wouldn't be suitable for me to read when I was young."

"Your mother was correct," Father said. "My Confessions shocked adults, so I hesitate to imagine the effect the book might have had on a child."

"But I'll read it now," Stella promised, "and I look forward to speaking with you about it; about all your work, in fact. Conversation hasn't been the brightest here. The distraction will be welcome."

"See, Thomas?" Carolyn asked. "I was right."

Carolyn was right about something else. She hadn't exaggerated. Her daughter was indeed beautiful, but in a way that I had not expected. Unlike Carolyn, with her cinnamon hair, Stella had the fair hair and light skin of her father, but somehow her delicate—I imagine that some might say exquisite—features made her appear radiant in her own unique way. She had green eyes that reminded me of emeralds. She glistened.

"Quickly, come in where it's warm," she said, beckoning us toward the sitting room, where a crackling fire worked to dissipate the chill.

Carolyn, Father, and I stood in front of its fender, extending our hands, rubbing them together over the warmth.

"The servants will take your outdoor clothes."

My chill was such that I hesitated before I surrendered my coat.

"Please, sit," Stella told us. "Over here, next to Robert."

I glanced toward where she pointed and for the first time noticed a man in a wheelchair.

* * *

No part of him moved, not even his eyes, even though Stella leaned down and spoke directly to him. He just kept staring straight ahead, through *her instead of at her.*

"Look, Robert. Mother arrived with guests. Isn't that wonderful? A famous author, Thomas De Quincey. Do you know his work, Robert? Did you ever read his* Confessions of an English Opium-Eater? *We're going to have an afternoon of fascinating conversation."

Perhaps so, *I thought.* But not with the man in the wheelchair.

Stella might as well have been speaking to a lamp. He just kept staring through her. Carolyn had told us that Lord Cavendale, whom I assumed was the man in the wheelchair, was sixty years old, but he could have been a hundred, so sunken were his cheeks and eyes. His face was creased with wrinkles, far more than Father's, and Father is sixty-nine. The man's hair had the drabness and lifelessness of cobwebs.

A blanket covered him. Stella tucked it closer around him and then turned to us, saying, "Please, please, sit down. Robert doesn't respond to what we say, but perhaps he can hear us. Perhaps his mind is starved for stimulation. Perhaps something we say will finally prompt a reaction."

Stella's tone was bright, but I couldn't help noticing the sadness beneath the surface, a sadness—and indeed a desperation—that seemed barely under control.

"I can only imagine how nervous you felt coming here, given all the calamities on the trains, and it's such a dreary day, with the wind and the rain." She turned to a servant. "Send in tea and biscuits." She quickly looked at us and asked, "But perhaps biscuits aren't to your liking? Perhaps you'd enjoy—"

"Stella." Carolyn put a comforting arm around her. "Why don't you sit down also? You might not know it, but you're speaking as quickly as the trains you referred to."

Stella looked surprised. "Am I speaking quickly?" She directed the question to Father and me.

"Perhaps just a little," I said, smiling. "But I'm used to it. Sometimes

Father and I don't speak to anyone for long stretches as we flee from debt collectors. Afterward I sometimes speak quickly also."

"Debt collectors?" Stella asked, confused.

Inwardly I rejoiced that my attempt to divert Stella had been success-ful. "Yes; the life of an author is uncertain."

"Scribble, scribble," Father said. Following my lead, he gestured with his right hand, seeming to write with a quill pen on paper. "I'm at the mercy of fickle editors. One day, they can't get enough of what I write. The next day, they say that I'm out of fashion. But I press on, tossing page after page behind me, littering the floor until it appears covered with snow."

Stella studied the way we smiled. She appeared uncertain. "Surely you exaggerate."

"A landlord once kept me a prisoner for a year, forcing me to write constantly until I'd paid off the enormous amount of money I owed him," Father continued.

"You were kept a prisoner for a year? That can't be true."

"Unfortunately it is," I told her.

"Escaping debt collectors, I once fled all the way across Scotland— from Edinburgh to Glasgow," Father continued. "An acquaintance al-lowed me to hide in Glasgow's observatory. What a joy to gaze up at the infinite heavens each night and know that my troubles were nothing com-pared to the immensity of the universe."

Stella considered what he'd said, then nodded. "Indeed. Perhaps I should stare at the stars more often."

She turned to her husband, adjusted his blanket, and used a handker-chief to wipe spittle from a corner of his mouth.

"I suspect that you're wondering but you're too polite to ask," she said. "Two months ago, my husband suffered an accident. He and his son went riding on one of those clear, cold, bracing winter afternoons that my hus-band could never resist. Too soon, his son came galloping back in a panic, calling for servants to help him. Something had startled my husband's horse. Harold thinks it was an animal in a thicket next to the trail."

"Harold?" I asked.

"My husband's son. That is, his grown son, of course. Not Jeremy, the infant that Robert and I have. Yes, Harold thinks it was an animal in a thicket, or perhaps it was a piece of a dangling, dead branch that finally fell from a tree. Whatever the cause, the noise startled my husband's horse." She hesitated. "The horse reared. The ground was frozen. Robert fell, struck his head, and..."

Stella looked down.

"There's no need to continue," I said.

Carolyn stroked Stella's shoulder, taking up the burden of the explanation. "Lord Cavendale has been in this condition ever since." She was careful not to speak of a peer with the familiarity that her daughter, the nobleman's wife, had a right to do. "The only physician in Sedwick Hill is Dr. Wainwright at the clinic. He was sent for at once. He noted that Lord Cavendale's pupils were dilated and concluded that he'd sustained a brain concussion, that blood was gathering inside his skull, building pressure.

"Dr. Wainwright considers the practice of applying leeches to be a discredited treatment from the Middle Ages. Nonetheless, he recommended that in this case, leeches could save Lord Cavendale's life if they were applied to his temples. There, they could absorb the excess blood that created pressure in his brain. The alternative, he said, was to drill into the skull and relieve the pressure that way. Lord Cavendale's son wouldn't hear of it, arguing that the operation was too dangerous and that the stress of moving his father to an operating theater in London might kill him. Of course, without the operation, His Lordship might have died also. But it turned out that after three days of having leeches applied to his temples, His Lordship's eyes returned to normal. The pressure was apparently relieved. But as you can see, he was never the same."

"I'm very sorry," I told Stella.

She studied her husband. "Can you hear us, Robert?"

He showed no reaction.

"I must believe that he can hear us," Stella said. "I must believe that somewhere inside him, he's aware of what's happening but isn't able to tell me. I haven't given up. Three times a week, I go with him to Dr. Wainwright's clinic. The water treatments there keep Robert's muscles from withering."

Two servants entered, one carrying a tray for everything necessary to make tea, the other carrying an ornate platter of biscuits. Normally I greet food eagerly lest another opportunity not come along for a while, but given the circumstances, I could only pretend to welcome the arrival of refreshments.

"I'll do the honors," Carolyn said. But as she opened a silver caddy and prepared to spoon tea leaves into the porcelain pot's steaming water, something in the doorway caught her attention.

A tall, thin man whom I judged to be about thirty stood there. He was starkly handsome, with thick, dark hair and intense eyes. His boots shone. Trouser straps were anchored under them to keep the trousers perfectly straight. His frock coat and cravat were the height of fashion. Only one thing about him wasn't in fashion—he didn't have facial hair. I suspected that was for reasons of vanity, because his jaw was unusually strong, contributing to his handsomeness. An aggressive handsomeness, I might add, and the intensity of his dark eyes was the consequence of anger, I soon discovered.

"Harold, I didn't realize you were there. Please join us for tea," Stella said.

Harold opened an ivory snuffbox and inserted a pinch of the pulverized tobacco up each nostril. He absently brushed specks of it from his cravat. "I've been listening. So you and your mother believe that my judgment was wrong and that my father would have recovered fully if he'd been taken to London and undergone the operation?"

"I was merely explaining to our guests about the seriousness of Robert's accident," Stella replied.

"Indeed, your guests." Harold considered us dubiously. "I missed their introduction."

"My name is Thomas De Quincey." Father nodded to him with respect. "And this is my daughter Emily."

"De Quincey?" Harold frowned. "Surely to God you're not the Opium-Eater. Stella, can't you find better people to bring to the house?"

Carolyn provided the response. "They came at my invitation, Harold. I thought they would amuse her."

Possibly intending to annoy the man in the doorway, Father withdrew his laudanum bottle from his coat and drank from it, the only time I was ever happy to see him do so.

"Oh, for the love of God." Gesturing in disgust, Harold walked from the doorway and disappeared along a corridor.

"Please forgive his rudeness," Stella told us. "What really troubles him is that he blames himself for his father's accident. The day it happened, he kept berating himself, saying that if he could only have grabbed Robert when he'd started to fall from the horse—"

"Enough gloom," Carolyn said, spooning the tea leaves into the pot. "Tell us an amusing story, Thomas. Tell us about"—she thought for a moment—"the fraudulent Sir Walter Scott novel that you wrote."

"You know about that?" Father asked in surprise.

"I saw a reference to it in a magazine. But the reference only tantalized me; it didn't explain anything."

"Walladmor," Father said. "That was the title of the fraudulent Sir Walter Scott novel. The feel of the preposterous syllables on my lips makes me want to chuckle. Thirty years ago, Sir Walter was so popular in Germany that an unscrupulous publisher there decided to pay a hack writer to create a new novel in Sir Walter's Waverley series. The German author's pen name was Willibald Alexis, as ridiculous to say as the novel's title. Willibald Alexis, the author of Walladmor."

I looked at Stella and was pleased to see her smiling.

"The German publisher advertised the novel as a translation of Sir Walter Scott's latest work," Father continued. "That's how Willibald managed to have his name on the covers—as the supposed translator. The work consisted of three bloated volumes filled with smugglers, ship-wrecks, long-lost heirs, and demons. Everything went along splendidly until Sir Walter heard about this mysterious book attributed to him. He *asked a London bookshop to obtain a copy. Meanwhile, a magazine heard about this dubious publication and asked me, because of my knowledge of German, to write a summary of the novel for its next issue.*

"The task was how to get my hands on a copy. The only one in England seemed to be in the London bookshop from which Sir Walter had ordered it. I bribed a clerk, who told me that Sir Walter was expected to pick up the novel in two days. That left little time for me to take all three volumes to my lodging, read them, write a plot summary, and return the novel before Sir Walter arrived to pay for it."

"This can't be true," Stella said, her green eyes brightening.

"I swear. The next problem I faced was that the three volumes had uncut pages. I couldn't very well take a knife to them and separate the pages without Sir Walter suspecting that something was amiss, so I was reduced to prying the pages apart as much as possible and peering up them in the attitude of a man looking up a chimney."

Father pretended to hold a circular object above his head and attempt to read it. Despite her troubles, Stella chuckled.

"As you might expect, being unable to read the material on the far left and right sides of the pages, I inevitably missed some of the niceties of the plot, but at least I accomplished the task in time, with Sir Walter acquiring the volumes and never suspecting the intrigue. When the magazine appeared, my plot summary of Walladmor"—*Father's tone mocked the title*—"aroused such interest that a dishonest English publisher offered to pay me to translate the full text. Always in need of money, I gladly accepted the offer, thinking,* How hard can the task be? That the novel is in German won't be a problem. I can translate as quickly as I can write. *By then, other volumes of the German text had arrived in England. I obtained a set, slit the pages open, and began to scribble a translation, only to discover to my horror that my previous peering-up-a-chimney tactic had caused me to miss even more than I thought. The text by the esteemed Willibald was beyond dreadful and included such preposterous scenes as a man swimming on his back from Bristol to the far side of Wales.*

"I told the publisher that if I eliminated all the deplorable spots, I might be able to deliver an acceptable single volume, but no, the publisher said, he had paid me for three volumes, and by heaven, three volumes were what he expected, and so, as I have experienced many times, what looked like an easy task and easy income turned out to be quite difficult. In the end, I was forced to write what amounted to an original novel in Sir Walter Scott's manner. On the title page of Walladmor, *I wrote,* Freely translated into German from the English of Sir Walter Scott and now freely translated from German into English."

Both Stella and Carolyn laughed, and indeed I couldn't help laughing also.

"It became more preposterous when Willibald so liked my improvement of his text that he translated it into German and arranged for his *version to be removed from German bookshops and replaced by mine. Wordsworth's sister-in-law happened upon the English version that I wrote and told me that she didn't think Sir Walter had ever written a better novel."*

Stella clapped her hands and turned to her husband, who remained immobile in the wheelchair. "Robert, did you ever hear anything so amusing?"

If he had, alas, he wasn't able to tell us about it.

Harold appeared again in the doorway, thrusting another pinch of snuff into each nostril. He glowered at our laughter and walked away.

EIGHT

THE WATER-CURE CLINIC

As THE TRAIN swayed around a curve, Ryan sat on the bare bench of a second-class compartment and stared at the rain-streaked window. His focus was such that he didn't see the gray countryside beyond the glass. His thoughts dwelled on the almost deserted Euston Station from which they'd departed after a police wagon had returned them to London. There couldn't be more than ten other passengers on this train, all of them making certain that they were in widely separated compartments.

"We'll soon arrive at Sedwick Hill," he told Becker and withdrew the Benson chronometer from a coat pocket. The train's jostle seemed no longer to exist as he studied the watch's golden luster and the glinting crystal that covered the blue porcelain in which the two mesmerizing dials were set. The time was eighteen minutes and twenty seconds after one o'clock. Ever since he'd come into possession of the watch, he'd felt a compulsion to open it and determine the precise time. Although he didn't know what benefit that knowledge provided, he was very aware of how much the constant ticking movement of the second hand captivated him, showing him how quickly the present was becoming the past.

"You'll feel lost when you're forced to surrender that watch," Becker said from the bench across from him.

"When all of this is settled. For now, it's evidence."

"Of course," Becker said.

"I need to protect it. The moment I hand it over, it'll go missing."

"Certainly," Becker said.

"All right, I admit that it'll be difficult to give up," Ryan conceded. "After my parents came here from Ireland, my mother used to take me for a walk every Sunday. It was the only day she didn't work in a factory, and at first, I wondered why she didn't rest when she had the chance. All five of us lived in a single room of a lodging house in King's Cross, and each Sunday after our family went to church, she always took me to the fancy shops in Regent Street. She wore her best clothes, but in Regent Street, they were almost rags, and constables used to regard us with suspicion. I soon realized that my mother had a fantasy about working hard enough and being lucky enough that one day she might be able to afford one of the beautiful dresses she saw in the windows or something from one of the jewelry shops. It was a foolish dream, of course."

Becker shrugged. "But without dreams..."

"Yes, we'd never move forward." For a moment, Ryan thought about Emily and his own foolish dream that they could have a future together. Becker had the same dream, he knew, but because Becker was closer in age to Emily, he was more likely to achieve it.

Ryan shut out the thought.

"Anyway, eventually I wondered if my mother perhaps wanted *me* to see what was in the windows of those fancy shops. Maybe she hoped that if *I* worked hard enough and was lucky enough, I could be one of the people who frequented those places. To give me a better chance, she insisted that I hide my Irish accent and keep a cap over my red hair. She paid a bookseller to teach me to read, and only the better books."

"I wondered why you were able to speak the commissioner's type of English," Becker said.

"'Never stop trying to better yourself,' she kept telling me. 'You can be anything you want as long as you work hard enough.'"

"I wish," Becker said.

"Until three weeks before she died from what amounted to overwork, my mother and I were still taking that Sunday walk to Regent Street. If only she were still alive so that I could show this chronometer to her. She wouldn't have been able to stop looking at it."

"Did she know that you became a constable and then a detective inspector?" Becker asked.

"She did."

"Was she proud, or did she think you hadn't reached the mark she wanted for you?"

"She told me, 'Just take care that you never look down on poor people the way the constables in Regent Street looked down on *us*.' I got the feeling she thought that maybe *my* children would have a chance to frequent the shops in Regent Street."

Again, Ryan thought about Emily.

Buildings appeared beyond the window on the right and then a sign announcing SEDWICK HILL.

"I still think we should have told Commissioner Mayne that we planned to come here," Becker said.

Ryan shook his head. "Lombard Street is already out of bounds for us. I don't want to risk being told that anything else is out of bounds. There's something going on that at least one of Harcourt's powerful clients doesn't want us to know. Everything started when Harcourt made a sudden decision to come here. If we can find out why, maybe everything else will make sense."

The train clanged and jolted, slowing to a stop. When a guard unlocked the door, they were the only two passengers who disembarked. Smoke enveloped them as the train chugged onward from the station.

A clerk opened a window, surprised to see travelers.

"Where will we find the hydropathy clinic?" Ryan asked.

"In town, there's a crossroads. Go east for a quarter mile. You can't fail to see it."

As they followed a gravel road, the worst of the weather held off, light raindrops striking their shoulders and caps, the air feeling colder.

The clerk hadn't exaggerated that they couldn't fail to see it.

"Look at the size of this place!" Becker marveled.

Three tall, gabled buildings were situated at the bottom of the hill for which the town was named. Parkland surrounded them. The stones of the lane that led to the grand structures were impressively white, as were the structures themselves, lustrous in the gloom.

"I wonder what happens in there," Becker said.

"That's exactly what *I'd* like to know," Ryan told him.

THE MIDDLE BUILDING had a veranda that extended across the entire front and along both sides.

A rumble of footsteps made Ryan and Becker turn. Six corpulent, expensively dressed gentlemen marched around the corner on the right. They spaced themselves so that they didn't strike each other as they swung their arms inward and outward as if rowing a boat, all the while breathing with effort.

Lest there be a collision, Ryan and Becker stepped back into the rain. The six men tromped past and turned the next corner.

A seventh man—corpulent and expensively dressed also—rounded the first corner, swinging his arms in and out as the others had. His face was alarmingly red.

Ryan and Becker stepped back onto the veranda.

"Good afternoon," Ryan said.

The man assessed their ordinary garments. Normally he might not have responded to someone of a lower station, but he seemed grateful to stop marching. "Good afternoon." He continued to swing his arms toward his chest and then outward.

"A *cold* afternoon," Becker said.

"Dr. Wainwright says it's good for the constitution."

"Do you know where we can find him?"

"His office is in this building." The man took a labored breath. "Near the entrance hall. But he could be anywhere. Even on Sunday, he supervises treatments."

"What's that object hanging around your neck?" Ryan asked.

It was round, made of ivory, and had numbers painted on it.

"That's my water dial. Each time I drink a glass of water, I turn it a notch to remind myself how close I am to my goal."

"Your goal? How high do the numbers go?"

"Sixteen."

"You drink sixteen glasses of water a day?" Becker asked in surprise.

"It purges the toxins," the man replied. "I had an abundance of them until I came here two weeks ago. Dr. Wainwright made a new man of me."

A rumble of footsteps on the veranda's wooden floor preceded a different group of portly, expensively dressed gentlemen who marched around the first corner, swinging their arms in and out. They too had dials around their necks.

"If Dr. Wainwright sees me standing here, he'll be angry," the man said. He marched forward but turned his head and told them, "If you're looking for work, the tradesmen's entrance is at the rear."

"Unfortunately we don't lack for work," Ryan murmured.

He stepped back into the rain to avoid the next group of marchers. When they disappeared around the next corner, he returned to the veranda and pulled a cord next to an enameled blue door.

Inside, a bell rang.

When no one answered, Ryan tried the door and found that it wasn't locked. He and Becker entered a spacious hall where, despite the dismal day, a hardwood floor gleamed. Opposite the entrance, a staircase—gleaming also—led upward and downward.

Corridors stretched to the right and left. Secretarial desks stood in front of doors that had nameplates on them, one of which said DR. WAIN-

WRIGHT. Paintings depicted landscapes that included various water features: a well, a stream, a fountain, a pond, and a moonlit lake.

Footsteps approached. A white-coated man with a silvery mustache came along the corridor on the right. He moved toward one of the offices but then noticed Ryan and Becker.

"Yes?"

"We're looking for Dr. Wainwright."

"I am he." The doctor seemed annoyed that two men wearing common clothes had used the front entrance. He focused on Ryan's red hair and the scar on Becker's chin. "And *you* are?"

"Detective Inspector Ryan from Scotland Yard. This is Detective Sergeant Becker."

They showed their badges.

The doctor subdued his surprise. "Is this more about the murder on Thursday night?"

"Among other things," Ryan answered. "A constable visited you on Friday. He asked if you'd expected someone on Thursday night who hadn't arrived."

"That's correct. I told him that, for the entire week, none of my guests had failed to get here on schedule."

"The next day, the constable returned and asked if you knew Daniel Harcourt," Ryan continued.

"And I told him that I wasn't familiar with the name. I don't wish to seem rude, but some of my guests are in the middle of treatments that need to be supervised. Would you kindly wait here in the lobby until they're finished? Then I can devote all the time necessary to answer your questions."

"How many guests do you have?" Becker asked, ignoring his request.

Dr. Wainwright didn't need to think about it. "Three hundred and five."

"That many?" Becker looked at Ryan and told him, "This is going to take a long time."

Dr. Wainwright frowned. "A long time for what?"

"To speak to all of your guests," Ryan answered.

"Speak to all of my…But that's impossible."

"It's our understanding that on Friday and Saturday, the constable didn't question any of them."

"Of course not. My guests come here to escape the pressures that destroyed their health. They're not allowed to read newspapers or receive visitors or letters or hear anything about the tension in the outside world. Many are at a stage in their treatment where answering questions from the police would cause a ruinous relapse."

Ryan didn't bother responding to his objection. "We'll need a list of all their names."

"But those names are confidential!"

"Dr. Wainwright, you can deal with us or you can deal with the home secretary, the prime minister, and possibly Her Majesty. I guarantee that you'll be much happier dealing with *us*."

Stella gently opened a door, peered inside, then motioned for Carolyn, Emily, and De Quincey to follow her. A servant pushed Stella's husband in his wheelchair.

The room was a nursery. A female servant sat next to a brightly decorated infant's cot, the sides of which were protected by metal bars. The curtains were partially drawn, creating a soft light.

"I worried that Jeremy was sleeping too long," Stella told the servant.

"Just the right amount of time, my lady. No reason to fret. He woke a little while ago."

"Before his nap, did he accept the wet nurse?" Stella asked.

"He suckled normally, my lady. Everything is as it should be."

"Stella, you need to stop worrying about him," Carolyn said. She stroked a finger along the baby's cheek. "Look at how much he's grown!"

She turned to De Quincey and Emily. "I tell my daughter that she's the reason I come here every Sunday, but in truth, it's little Jeremy I want to see. Each week, the change in him is amazing."

"What a darling," Emily said. "I don't believe I've ever seen a finer-looking baby."

"Truly?" Stella asked. "You don't think he looks ill? Three nights ago, he had a cough."

"I don't hear anything wrong with his breathing," Emily said. "May I pick him up? Dr. Snow gives me medical instruction. Perhaps I can set your mind at ease."

"Dr. Snow?" Carolyn asked. "The queen's physician?"

"Yes, we shared some adventures," Emily replied. "I'm considering becoming a nurse in a hospital, but I haven't decided yet."

"A nurse?" Stella asked. "But how is that possible? Only men are allowed to be nurses in hospitals."

"Miss Nightingale's work with our wounded soldiers in the Crimea is changing all that."

The baby squirmed as Emily picked him up. She took off his cap and touched his forehead. She listened to his chest. She pulled off his stockings and moved an index finger along the bottom of each foot, watching the toes flex. The baby squirmed again, as if reacting to being tickled.

"Well, the only thing I can find wrong with him is he's too fat," Emily decided.

"What?" Stella said in shock.

"A bad joke. I couldn't resist. Forgive me."

Carolyn laughed, appreciating the humor even if Stella didn't.

"He's perfectly healthy," Emily said. "I'm certain that Dr. Snow would agree with me."

"Perhaps I worry too much," Stella admitted. "It's just that ever since our baby girl…People told me that even though Jennifer had a cough, there was nothing to be alarmed about, but then the cough became worse and she died of fever and…dear, sweet Jennifer."

"I'm sorry." Emily touched Stella's arm. "After that and after your husband's accident, I imagine you feel that doom hangs over you."

Stella drew a breath, making an effort to brighten her mood. "Robert, did you hear what Emily said? She's never seen a baby who's more adorable and healthy." Stella pressed the baby's cheek next to her husband's. "Feel how smooth his skin is." She put the baby's hand in his. "Feel how tiny his fingers are. Please get better so that you and your son can know each other."

Harold appeared in the doorway again. "I'm his son also."

"Of course," Stella told him impatiently. "Why do you feel the need to emphasize it? Harold, I've tried to be as friendly toward you as possible. Why won't you try to do the same? Why won't you let us all be a family?"

"With you as my stepmother?"

"I never asked you to call me that."

"And with the half brother you've given me?" Harold added. He scowled at the infant and walked away.

"So far, I don't see any Russian names," Ryan said.

He and Becker sat in Dr. Wainwright's office studying the several pages of the clinic's guest list.

"To the best of my knowledge, no Russians are staying here," Dr. Wainwright told him. "With the war going on, who would be foolish enough to identify himself as a Russian? Are you implying that a Russian killed the man on the train?"

"It's one of many possibilities we're investigating. The name Daniel Harcourt still doesn't spark a memory?"

"I'm afraid not."

"So many guests." Becker looked up from a page. "Are you always this busy?"

"Always," the doctor replied sadly. "People are determined to destroy themselves with overwork or overindulgence in their appetites. When it's nearly too late, they beg me to repair them. The modern age has much to be blamed for."

"Indeed," Ryan said. "Forgive my ignorance, but I don't understand what you do here."

"Most of it involves common sense. If a man comes to me stout, he'll benefit from a diet that's low in fatty meat. If he comes to me wheezing from too much tobacco and addled from too much alcohol, he'll benefit if tobacco and alcohol are taken from him. He'll also benefit from physical exercise—climbing the hill behind us, for example, to reach a fountain near the top. Mostly he'll benefit from copious amounts of the purest water in England. It clears the mind while flushing poisons from the body. Those are the simple cases. But there are other guests with complex physical and emotional ailments who require sophisticated water treatments such as douches and wet sheeting."

"Douches?" Becker asked.

"That treatment is more easily demonstrated than explained."

"Then by all means, show us," Ryan said.

A WOMAN WAILED.

Ryan hurried down the rest of the stairs. "Someone's in trouble."

"Don't be alarmed," Dr. Wainwright told them as they reached a basement corridor. "It's normal."

The woman screamed again.

"Normal?" Becker asked in confusion.

The corridor was made from granite blocks and felt damp, suggesting that it had been built over one of the area's springs. A series of doors stretched in both directions. The persistent shrieks came from behind the first door on the left.

The door had a window. Ryan stepped in front of it and saw a chamber. Its ceiling, walls, and floor were covered with white tiles that reflected light from lamps recessed in the ceiling.

In the middle of the chamber, above a drain, a woman wore a full-length bathing costume and leaned forward, bracing herself against a metal railing. The reason she cried out was that an attendant wearing a rubber coat aimed a hose and sprayed water forcefully onto her back.

"Truly, I don't understand," Ryan said.

"This woman is receiving a shoulder and back douche."

"It's too cold! Too cold!" she wailed.

"Good," Dr. Wainwright said. He turned to Ryan and Becker. "When this woman's husband brought her to me for treatment, he was alarmed by her listless demeanor, a general torpor that had settled over her for the past year. She has children, but she'd lost interest in them and indeed in just about everything, especially her social obligations as the wife of a peer."

"But how does this help?" Becker asked.

"The force of the cold water stimulates her skin, her blood circulation, and her muscular system, creating the vitality that she lacked when she came here. It also distracts her from whatever morbid thoughts created her torpor."

Dr. Wainwright opened the door and raised his voice above the sound of the spray. "Rick, that will be sufficient."

The attendant moved a lever on the hose, turning off the water.

A humid, perfumed scent drifted from the chamber.

"Do you feel energized, my lady?" Dr. Wainwright asked.

The dripping woman appeared to be in her midthirties. Her wet hair stuck to her head and shoulders. Her neck-to-ankle bathing costume clung to her. She hugged herself against the cold. "My blood is circulating fiercely, Doctor."

"Excellent. We're almost finished for the day. After the back douche, all that remains is the ascending douche. Afterward, I'm certain that you'll feel even more invigorated. Rick, continue to the next phase."

The doctor closed the door. Through the window, Ryan and Becker watched the woman proceed toward a shiny metal box. It was wide enough for her to sit on. It had numerous small holes.

The attendant turned a faucet on the wall. Water welled up through the holes in the box. The water was barely noticeable at first, but gradually it increased in volume.

"The water for the ascending douche is warm," Dr. Wainwright explained, "providing a contrast that creates another stimulation."

At first, the woman continued to hug herself, but as the spray of water beneath her increased to a gentle force, it also seemed to become warmer, prompting the woman to gradually lower her arms. She gripped the sides of the metal box and lowered her head.

Watching, Becker said, "She appears to be falling back into…what did you call it?…a torpor."

Responding to the water swelling beneath her, she gripped the sides of the box tighter. At the same time, she looked so drowsy that she seemed about to fall asleep.

Abruptly she trembled. She raised her head, opening her mouth, shuddering. The shudders became stronger. Slowly they subsided.

She drew a breath and leaned back against a wall.

Dr. Wainwright opened the door, instructing the attendant, "You may turn off the spray. My lady, I believe that's enough circulatory treatment for today. Do you feel invigorated?"

"Very much."

"We have a consultation scheduled for tomorrow morning. We'll discuss your progress."

"I can't thank you enough, Doctor."

"Your improving health gives me great satisfaction. Rick, please escort our guest back to her room."

Dr. Wainwright closed the door. Through the window, Ryan watched the attendant offer his arm to the woman and then lead her to a metal stairway in the background.

"Each malady requires a different treatment," Dr. Wainwright explained. "Plunge baths. Steam baths. Oxygen baths. We even have a compressed-air chamber for asthmatic and bronchial maladies."

"How much do your patients—I mean your *guests*—pay for this?" Becker asked.

"Six pounds a week."

"Six pounds?" Ryan tried not to show his surprise. He and Becker earned slightly more than a pound per week. Six times three hundred and five guests was—Ryan made a quick calculation—about eighteen hundred pounds a week. If that sum was multiplied by fifty-two…The mathematics became too complex for him to calculate without a piece of paper and a pencil, but he estimated that the clinic's yearly income was over eighty thousand pounds, a phenomenal amount.

"That includes treatments, consultations, lodging, and meals, of course," Dr. Wainwright said.

"Yes, of course. Do your guests eat their meals together?" Ryan asked.

"In the dining room. We have two seatings, the first one at four o'clock."

"Then that would be the best place for us to interview everyone."

THE DINING AREA was lavish, with immaculate white tablecloths covering twenty tables, each designed for eight people. Four chandeliers—unlit for the moment—hung over the tables, and numerous oil lamps lined the walls. Large windows provided ample illumination. Even with the gloomy clouds, the daylight caused the parquet floors to shine. Huge geraniums occupied the room's corners, their scarlet-flowered stalks climbing trellises.

Women in white dresses put plates and silverware onto the tables.

"You might as well speak to the staff also," Dr. Wainwright told Ryan and Becker. He gestured for the servants to gather round, which they did. "These men are police detectives."

The women took a step backward.

"There's no reason to be nervous. Just answer their questions truthfully, and everything will be fine." He turned to Ryan and Becker. "I have other guests whose treatments I need to supervise. When you finish here, you may speak to the personnel in the kitchen. I want you to feel that you have total access to my facility."

HIS HEART POUNDING, Dr. Wainwright left the dining room, walked along a corridor, and stopped at a watercolor of a bubbling brook. He pulled a notepad and a pencil from his pocket, leaned over a side table, and hastily printed a message. Abruptly, he descended the carpeted stairs toward the sound of splashing.

A swinging door opened onto a vast area that contained a rectangular pool with steps on every side. Fifty men wearing what amounted to loincloths and nothing else sat partially submerged on the steps, sometimes jumping into the middle of the pool to immerse themselves fully. The heated water caused beads of moisture to accumulate on the tiled walls.

Fragments of conversations echoed.

"While I'm here, my nephew is probably running my business into the ground," an ample-waisted man said.

"Don't think about it. Worrying about business is what got us here," his companion reminded him.

Wainwright scanned the pool area and saw that Rick, the attendant he'd spoken to earlier, had returned from escorting the woman to her room. He'd replaced his rubber coat with a white jacket and trousers and was offering glasses of water to men sitting at the edge of the pool.

More conversations echoed.

"I came here with kidney stones. Now I've swallowed so much water that I think my kidneys are *floating*. I'd give anything for a brandy and soda."

"…a railway extension from Brighton next year…"

"…perfect for a parcel of cottage retreats."

Humidity weighed down Dr. Wainwright's clothing as he walked to Rick and drew him aside. The boom of voices reverberated off the tiles, preventing anyone from eavesdropping.

"Did you hear what they said about a railway extension from Brighton?" Rick asked.

"Never mind that. Two Scotland Yard detectives are here."

"What?"

"They intend to speak to everyone." Wainwright handed him the note. "The next train to London arrives in half an hour. Board it and deliver this message. They threatened me with the wrath of the prime minister. We'll see how they enjoy their threat coming back at them."

* * *

DE QUINCEY CLIMBED onto a dining-room chair. His legs were so short that his boots didn't reach the floor. Blazing logs in a fireplace did nothing to dispel the cold.

"Thomas, I hope the menu pleases you," Carolyn said as a servant placed bowls of steaming food onto the table. "In one of your books, I read that, despite your stomach problems, you enjoy a boiled potato along with boiled beef in thin slices."

"Cut diagonally rather than longitudinally, exactly so."

"Diagonally?" Harold asked.

"Against the grain," Emily told him.

"Why didn't he just say that?" Despite how much Harold disapproved of De Quincey's opium habit, he had no reservations about his own prodigious consumption of wine at dinner. He took a long swallow and looked around. "What else are we having? A plate of cheese? Is that all? What kind of dinner is this?"

"One that our guests, especially Thomas, will enjoy," Stella said.

"They're *your* guests, not mine."

"Harold, if you're not happy eating with us, perhaps you'd enjoy dining in your room."

"And miss hearing you talk about me?" Harold poked at the beef with his fork, then sipped more wine.

Stella mashed a portion of potato, spooned a little water on it to make a paste, and raised a portion of it to her husband's lips. After it sat on his tongue for a brief time, he swallowed.

"Extraordinary," De Quincey said.

"Dr. Wainwright says that certain movements are automatic, such as breathing. In my husband's case, swallowing appears to be automatic also. Otherwise, I don't know how I would ever have been able to keep him alive."

"It would have been better if he'd died," Harold said.

"What a terrible thing to say about your father," Stella told him.

"Well, look at him. He's as good as dead. He can't think. He can't speak. He can't hear."

"We don't know *any* of that," Stella objected. The candelabra on the table shimmered over her delicate features and fair hair. Her green eyes had the depth of an ocean. "What if he *can* hear?" She turned to De Quincey and Emily. "I read to him for an hour every morning."

"You could read to him in Sanskrit for all the difference it would make—"

"Harold, allow me to take this opportunity to tell you I'm sorry about your brother," De Quincey interrupted.

"My brother?"

"Your older one, I believe. Carolyn told me. I gather he died a few years ago, but I know from experience that grief is difficult to shed. My condolences."

"Thank you."

"If what I heard was correct, the cause of death was typhoid fever. Bad water, I presume."

"In one of the German States. Given the location, I suppose it was to be expected," Harold said. "It's a miracle I didn't become ill also."

"I've always wanted to travel to Germany," De Quincey told him. "There's a mountain I'd like to visit. It's called the Brocken. People have seen monstrous apparitions there, but it turns out these are only the shadows that observers cast on the mist, begging the question of whether our minds create reality or whether it exists outside us."

Harold looked confused. "The Brocken? Never heard of it. My brother and I were visiting Homburg."

"Yes, there's a casino and a spa there, I've heard."

Harold opened his snuffbox. "There is indeed a casino."

"Does the name Daniel Harcourt mean anything to you?" De Quincey asked.

"Only because a constable came here yesterday asking about him. The constable wouldn't tell me why the man was important."

"Daniel Harcourt was the victim who was murdered on the train Thursday night," De Quincey explained.

"No thanks to the constable, I needed to wait until I read this morning's newspaper to discover his identity. A horrid business. Soon we won't be safe anywhere."

"The police believe that Harcourt was coming to Sedwick Hill with important documents that he intended to deliver to someone," De Quincey persisted. "Were you expecting any visitors?"

"The constable asked me that also. No, I wasn't expecting anyone."

"Perhaps you're familiar with a man named John Saltram," De Quincey said.

"Why are you asking these questions? You sound like the constable who came here."

"Thomas is fascinated by murder," Carolyn explained. "In fact, he's an expert in it."

"Really?" Harold studied him. "Well, I suppose I'm not surprised."

"Oh?" De Quincey asked. "Why is that?"

"Given the amount of laudanum you drink, most of the time you probably don't know what you're doing. If it's not indelicate for me to ask, how many people have you killed?"

THE RAILWAY TRACKS receded into the darkness. As a cold rain pelted the guard, he continued his inspection. Two hours earlier, a train had left him here, a few miles outside London, and then moved onward to drop off other guards at other sections of the tracks. Back then, the guard had been primed with the excitement of a hunter and the thought of what he'd do with the two-sovereign reward promised to anyone who found something amiss, but now all he cared about was how much longer he'd be forced to suffer in this terrible weather before his replacement arrived. Staying between the rails, he tried not to trip on the crossties while shifting his lantern back and forth and scanning the darkness. He searched for a bomb or a rail that had been pulled away—anything that might cause another catastrophe.

A trestle appeared in the gloom. As he stepped onto it, something scraped against a wooden beam below him.

The guard's chill now had nothing to do with the rain trickling under his coat collar.

Again something scraped. In a rush, he knelt and lowered his lantern over the side.

A shadow moved below him.

"Hey!" he shouted. "Who's there?"

He heard someone climbing hurriedly downward.

"Stop!"

The shadow descended faster.

The guard rushed to the slope next to the trestle and began to scurry down it, but the mud was so slippery that he lost his balance and fell onto his back. Desperately holding the lantern above him, he dug his heels into the mud and tried to keep from sliding out of control. The cold mud surged up his trouser legs and under his coat.

He struck a rock. Groaning, he jolted to a stop at the bottom.

A match flashed under the trestle.

Then something else flashed—a fuse.

"No!"

His lantern wavering, the guard struggled to stand as a figure ran away, splashing through a stream.

The guard raced toward the bottom of the trestle. He reached the fuse, yanked it with all his strength, and felt it break free from something above him.

The fuse hissed when he tossed it into the stream.

The guard hurried in the direction that the figure had taken. The sound of boots on mud led him from the stream toward an embankment. He charged up through tall, dead grass. Aiming his lantern, he reached the top, and suddenly his lantern shattered, glass flying.

The light died. But he'd seen the blur of a man swinging a club at him. As the guard dropped, he heard the club coming at him a second time, then whistling past him.

Sprawled in the wet grass, he kicked with both boots and felt them collide with the legs of the figure looming over him. He heard a groan and kicked again. He rolled to the side, screaming, "Help! Help!" as the club struck the mud next to him.

"Mother of God, save me!" he wailed.

Another voice suddenly yelled, "Who's down there!" It came from the top of the trestle, from another guard. "Joe? Is that *you*?"

"He's trying to kill me!"

"Joe?"

The guard kicked again. "For God's sake, stop him!" He struggled to squirm away from the blow that would break his skull. "Hurry!"

"Keep fighting, Joe! I'm coming!"

Again the guard kicked and rolled, and suddenly the figure was gone, racing away into the darkness.

Lying on his back, the guard felt the cold rain on his face. He struggled to stop trembling. He kept seeing the figure rush at him, swinging the club that had smashed his lantern.

"Joe, where are you?"

"Here! Over here!"

He felt hands pulling him to his feet.

"Are you hurt? What in blazes happened?"

"There's a bomb on the trestle."

"What?"

Fear dried his mouth. "He lit the fuse. I grabbed it." His tongue didn't want to work. "I threw it into the stream."

"Where *is* he?"

"Gone. *That* way."

"Did you get a look at him?"

"Just a glimpse before he smashed my lantern. But I don't think I was seeing properly."

"What do you mean?"

"His clothes."

"I don't understand."

"He was dressed like a soldier."

"A soldier tried to blow up the trestle?"

"Not exactly a soldier. I saw him only for an instant. Maybe I imagined it. But I'm certain he was wearing rags."

"Rags?"

"His uniform was in rags, like the kind those beggars wear at the train stations, the ones that just came back from the war."

"A BEGGAR TRIED TO *blow up a railway trestle?*"

Lord Palmerston paced as Commissioner Mayne and the home secretary reported to him in the hastily arranged meeting at his Downing Street office.

"Prime Minister, he was a particular kind of beggar," the commissioner said. "He wore the tattered uniform of a Crimean War veteran."

"You're telling me that the Russians aren't the ones behind these railway incidents, that it's somebody who's bitter about having fought in the war? Then how do you explain that the man who entered Daniel Harcourt's train compartment was dressed like a gentleman, not a soldier?"

"The tattered uniform might be another disguise," Mayne suggested.

"In that case, what he wore tonight is useless in helping you find him! He'll just keep changing his appearance."

"Perhaps not, Prime Minister. This particular disguise might be too perfect to abandon."

"Too perfect?"

"London has thousands of war veterans begging in the streets. They come and go as they please. No one questions them. In fact, most people ignore them. And any of those invisible beggars could be a spy."

LEAVING HIS DOWNING Street office, Lord Palmerston saw a small red chalk mark on a streetlamp.

"You're dismissed for the evening," he told his escort.

"But—"

Before the man could finish objecting, Lord Palmerston climbed into the cab that waited for him.

"To your house, Prime Minister?" the driver asked.

"No. Take me to Rotten Row."

"This late, Your Lordship? In this weather?"

"Do it."

Located on the south side of Hyde Park, Rotten Row was a bridle path where London society came to see and be seen, showing off their magnificent mounts and their fashionable riding costumes.

"Stop at the entrance," Lord Palmerston called up to the driver.

In the rain, traffic was sparse. They waited in the dark. A minute later, a carriage approached and stopped next to Lord Palmerston's cab.

"Remain here," he told the driver.

The carriage was covered, its interior dark. When its door opened, Lord Palmerston stepped from the cab, took three steps through the rain, and climbed into the carriage. As he shut the door, the vehicle moved forward.

Sandalwood perfume hovered around him. "I saw the chalk mark. What the devil happened?" he demanded.

The voice that answered belonged to the woman he'd met at Wyld's Monster Globe only a night previously. The stark difference in her tone was disturbing. "Do you know a detective inspector named Ryan?"

"Yes."

"And a detective sergeant named Becker?"

"Tell me."

"They're at Sedwick Hill."

"What?"

"They intend to question everyone at the clinic."

"God damn them."

"ARE YOU CERTAIN this is the place?" the man with a Russian accent demanded.

He was in the back of a canvas-covered wagon. Rain pelted it as he held a flap open, staring toward three large buildings at the end of a white gravel lane. Most of the windows had lamplight.

Behind him, a voice murmured in pain, "On my mother's soul, this is where I brought him."

The Russian turned toward his trembling captive. "If you're lying, my associate will cut off your remaining fingers. To which building did you deliver Dr. Mandt?"

"The middle."

The Russian tapped a knife against the blood-soaked bandage on the captive's right hand. "Which entrance?"

The captive inhaled in agony, making a stark whistling sound through his clenched teeth. "A side door on the right."

"And you have no idea where Mandt might be hiding in there?"

"I've never been inside the place." The captive nearly wept from his pain.

The Russian studied the middle building.

A new light appeared, this one in a window beneath the pitched roof of the topmost floor. The light was dim, filtered by an attic curtain.

The Russian kept watching.

CROUCHED BEHIND BOXES, Mandt felt his chest cramp while he listened to knuckles rap on the door, completing the code.

Even then, he still didn't feel reassured. As he groped through the darkness, faint lantern light glowed through cracks in the door.

He pushed the hatch to the side and saw Dr. Wainwright's face. But his relief lasted only for a moment. Mandt had treated too many patients for too many years not to notice that the pupils of Wainwright's eyes were larger than usual, a sign of stress.

"Unbolt the door," Wainwright said in German.

"The phrase," Mandt replied nervously, speaking German also. "I need to hear you say it."

"Sorry. 'The water of life.'"

Trembling, Mandt pawed at the bolt and freed it.

Wainwright hurried inside. "I don't have much time. Two Scotland Yard detectives are here."

"What?"

"They have nothing to do with you," Wainwright said hastily. "There was a murder on a train Thursday night—a lawyer coming to Sedwick

Hill from London. The police think he intended to deliver documents to someone here at the clinic."

"A murder on a train? But all you told me about were a collision and a fire!"

"I promise, none of it involves you."

Mandt wanted desperately to believe that.

"The police intend to talk to everyone," Wainwright continued. "They'll wonder where I went if I'm away too long. Here's more food and water. Is there anything else you need?"

"My chamber pot is—"

"That's a job for a maid. I can't stay." Wainwright stepped back into the stairway. "If I don't visit you tomorrow morning, it will mean that the police are still here."

"But—"

"Don't worry. You'll soon be on your way to Liverpool."

"Liverpool? Not Bristol? The situation is so unsafe that I'll definitely be taking the unexpected long route?"

Instead of answering, Wainwright quickly closed the door, returning Mandt to darkness.

Don't worry? Mandt thought, hurriedly bolting the door. He might have been convinced if Wainwright's pupils hadn't remained so dilated.

OUTSIDE, IN THE canvas-covered wagon, the Russian kept studying the attic window. After less than a minute, the light disappeared.

He wondered why anyone would visit an attic for so short a time at so late an hour.

NINE

NIGHT TERRORS

From the Journal of Emily De Quincey

A scream woke me. At first, I thought it was part of a nightmare I was having in which the sound of the rain pelting at my window belonged to fingers tapping, tapping, tapping.

The scream became fiercer.

It belonged to a woman—Stella.

"He's dead!"

The house was so cold, its gloom so oppressive that I hadn't changed into the nightclothes I'd brought. Still dressed in what I'd worn when I'd arrived at the house, I yanked away the curtains on my bed and ran to the door.

"Robert's dead!" Stella shrieked.

When I charged into the corridor, I saw Father—he, too, still wearing his travel clothes—hurrying from his room. Carolyn, wearing a dressing gown, was already there.

"Dead!"

The screams came from the level below us. As we rushed toward the wavering lamplight, Stella must have heard us. The moment we veered from the staircase, she ran along the hallway to us. Her features were pale in the light from the lamp she held, her eyes gleaming with panic.

"I couldn't sleep. I went to check on Robert. I…something's wrong. He isn't…"

We quickly followed her. An open door gaped before what looked like an abyss.

Harold stepped from a room farther along the corridor. Fastening his robe, he took long strides toward us.

"What the deuce is wrong? What's all the screaming about?"

"It's Robert! He's…"

"He's what?" Harold demanded. "For God's sake, make sense!"

"I saw you," Stella told him.

"Saw me?"

"Coming from Robert's room."

"What in blazes are you talking about?"

"A minute ago, I saw you!" Stella insisted.

"This is insane."

While they argued, I took the lamp from Stella and hurried into the room—a man's bedroom, as I expected, with dark, masculine appointments.

The wind howled at the window, rain striking it with the sound of pebbles. The bed curtains were parted. Approaching, I saw Lord Cavendale lying beneath a blanket.

"Stella, did you say he was—"

"I could tell right away that something was wrong!"

The others followed me into the room. I brought the lamp closer, dispelling the shadows. I'd never seen Lord Cavendale move his body, so it wasn't surprising that the commotion of Stella's outburst and our sudden appearance in his room received no reaction.

"Dead? No, he can't be," Harold said. "He showed no distress at dinner. He swallowed food. He breathed without difficulty."

"I saw you coming out of here," Stella repeated.

Carolyn approached me. "Emily, you said you'd received medical training from Dr. Snow. Is it too much to ask for you to…"

"Please, hold this lamp for me."

"Of course. Whatever I can do to help," Carolyn said.

"Hold it higher, please."

Servants gathered at the entrance to the bedroom, their candles providing more illumination.

"Stay away!" Harold ordered. "Go back to your rooms!"

As I leaned over Lord Cavendale, I was reminded of Thursday night when I'd crouched to feel the wrist on Daniel Harcourt's mangled body, trying to find a pulse. It had taken all of my resolve to do what Dr. Snow had trained me to do, and now, while I still needed to muster resolve, I did my duty with less hesitation, not simply because Lord Cavendale's body was intact but because, heaven help me, I was becoming accustomed to feeling for a pulse.

Lord Cavendale's two months of being an invalid had taken their toll; his wrist was thin and frail.

"Can you feel anything?" Stella asked desperately.

In the stale air that had accumulated behind the bed's curtains, I bent lower. About to put my ear to Lord Cavendale's chest, I noticed something that made me stop.

"Carolyn, the lamp—please move it higher."

The changed angle allowed me to see the blue blanket that covered Lord Cavendale's chest. Brown specks of something attracted my attention.

"Father," I said.

When he leaned close to me, I pointed at the brown specks. He picked up some of them and brushed them between a thumb and forefinger.

"His heart. Can you hear it?" Stella pleaded behind me.

I put an ear against the left side of Lord Cavendale's chest, which neither rose nor fell. I couldn't hear even the faintest murmur of his heart.

"Is there a mirror on his dressing table?" I asked.

Stella ran to get it.

I placed it under Lord Cavendale's nostrils. Not even the slightest vapor accumulated on it.

Lord Cavendale's eyes were open, focused on nothing. But they hadn't been focused on anything when I'd first met him, so in itself that wasn't significant. However, when I moved Carolyn's arm, bringing the lamp close to his dull brown eyes, he didn't blink, and his pupils didn't react.

I pulled up the blanket and touched his feet, noting a phenomenon that Dr. Snow had taught me to look for. "His feet are already cold. In fact, the cold has crept up past his ankles." Nothing feels colder, I thought, but I managed not to say that. "Stella, I'm very sorry. Your husband is indeed dead."

She seemed paralyzed. Tears trickled down her pale cheeks. She stared through them toward the motionless form in the bed. She shuddered and turned toward Harold.

"You did this," she told him.

"What?" Harold asked.

"When you were here."

"You keep saying that. But I wasn't here."

Stella turned to the bed and saw a pillow next to Lord Cavendale. She picked it up.

"Did you smother him? That would have been the easiest way."

She studied the pillow and turned it, revealing an impression on its underside.

"Is this how you did it, pressing the pillow over his face? Robert's breathing was so shallow that it wouldn't have required much effort."

"You're delusional!" Harold said.

"Emily, what did you and your father notice on Lord Cavendale's blanket?" Carolyn asked.

When neither of us answered, Carolyn leaned between the parted curtains and noticed the same brown specks that I had. She rubbed some of the specks together in her fingers, as Father had. She smelled them.

"Snuff," she murmured.

"*That's impossible,*" Harold said, *reflexively raising his right hand toward his nostrils.*

"*You said it would have been better for him if he'd died,*" Stella told him.

"*It was a way of expressing sympathy about how woeful his life was.*"

"*No, Harold. It sounded to me as if you truly wanted him dead,*" Stella persisted.

"*Why would I have wanted my father to—*" Abruptly, he seemed to understand. "*You think I wanted him dead so I could inherit his estate?*"

"*You certainly went out of your way to point out that I wasn't really a part of the family and that the boy you dismissively called your half brother wasn't either.*"

"*I don't need to listen to this.*"

Furious, Harold walked toward the open door but suddenly turned. In the lamplight, his face was twisted with rage.

"*As you insolently remind me, I now do indeed own the estate. I'm no longer Harold to you. I'm Lord Cavendale, and I want the lot of you out of this house.*"

"*With delight; we'll leave in the morning,*" Carolyn said.

"*No, you don't understand. I'm not talking about the morning. I want all of you to leave* immediately.*"

"*You can't be serious,*" Carolyn told him.

"*Go downstairs, put on your coats and hats, and get the devil out of my house!*"

From a room farther along the corridor, the baby wailed.

"*And take your brat with you!*" Harold ordered. "*Do you think I believe for a moment that he's truly my father's child?*"

"*What a thing to say!*" Stella exclaimed in shock.

"*My father wasn't well even before his accident. My mother once hinted to me that there was a reason they produced only my brother and myself. I don't believe that my father was capable of siring more children!*"

I've never felt so dismayed about being in the midst of a family argument. Father and I looked at each other, as astonished as if we were witnessing people physically attacking one another.

From along the corridor, the baby kept crying.

"Didn't you hear me? Make your brat stop squalling!" Harold demanded. "I'm sick of hearing him night after night!" He swung toward Father and me. "Get your coats and hats and leave!" He stepped closer to Father. "Opium-Eater," he said with contempt. "Your presence in my house is an insult!"

The violence in Harold's voice was so startling that I couldn't move.

"No?" the man asked, his eyes raging in the light from the lamp Carolyn held. "No one wants to listen to me? Well, by God, I'll take care of that!"

He stormed from the room, thrusting aside servants who, despite having been ordered to their rooms, had nonetheless lingered in the corridor.

"Stella, I'm so terribly sorry," I repeated.

The rain kept striking the window, but its sound had changed, acquiring the force of hail.

"I'd better put some proper clothes on," Carolyn said, using her free hand to clutch her dressing gown.

"The baby," Stella murmured. She called to a servant at the door. "We need to take care of him."

"Surely Harold doesn't truly intend to thrust us from the house in the middle of the night," Father said. "In this storm."

Returning footsteps pounded along the corridor.

"Out of my way!" Harold shouted to the servants.

He charged into the room.

"All of you are still here? No one listened to what I said? Well, maybe you'll listen to this."

I gaped at the riding crop in his hand. He lashed it through the air. The short whip at its end made a sharp whistling sound.

"Out!" he ordered. "Downstairs! Leave! You!" he yelled to Father,

seeing him take a laudanum bottle from a coat pocket. "Your behavior disgusts me! Get out of my sight!"

He whipped with the riding crop, struck the bottle, and knocked it out of Father's grasp. The bottle fell to the floor, its ruby liquid spilling.

"No!" Father exclaimed, dropping to his knees and grabbing the bottle.

Harold struck the riding crop repeatedly across Father's back. "Go! Go! Go!"

I stepped forward to stop him from hitting Father, and the riding crop stung my intervening arm.

"Out! Out!"

He swung the short whip, and abruptly my cheek felt as if it were on fire. Startled, I jerked a hand to my face and gasped when I felt blood.

"You cut me!" I said in disbelief.

"Go! Go! Out! Out!"

Now Harold lashed the whip against Carolyn's shoulder. "Do you think I don't know your game? You try to assume the airs of the gentry, but you're nothing more than a moneylender. To raise yourselves in the world, you and your daughter conspired to trick my father into marriage."

The blood continued to ooze down my stinging cheek. Already the area was swelling. None of us had the size to confront Harold physically. I feared that he'd soon injure one of us in a far more serious way.

"Father, we need to leave."

"Yes! Finally, someone understands! Leave! All of you!" Harold struck Stella's left arm with the riding crop. "Go! Don't bother to pack your bags! Be thankful I'm letting you take hats and coats! Out! Out!"

Stella raced past him. Along with a servant, she rushed in the direction of the baby's wails.

Father, Carolyn, and I edged past Harold's fury. He crowded us, shaking his riding crop at us, urging us from the room.

The light from the lamp that Carolyn held cast grotesque shadows in the corridor. Father and I walked toward the staircase, but when we *reached it, Father didn't descend. Instead he turned to go up, presumably to his room.*

"No!" Harold whacked the riding crop against the railing. "Go down to the entrance hall!"

"But in my room...I have..."

The way Father clutched the almost-empty laudanum bottle told me that he wanted to get a much-needed full bottle from his travel bag before he was thrust from the house.

Harold struck his shoulder. "I know what you want up there! But I won't let you have it! Get out of my house!"

The flurry of blows that Harold delivered made Father stumble down the stairs.

"Leave him alone!" I shouted at Harold, stepping in front of him.

Harold pushed me. I fought for my balance, lost it, and reached for the staircase's railing, but I couldn't grab it in time, and I fell. With a groan, I landed on the stairs and rolled down, stopping only because my body veered to the side and collided with the stone supports of the railing.

"Emily!"

Father hurried to raise me to my feet. He noticed my cheek in the glow from the lamp. "You're bleeding."

"Go!" Harold yelled. His fury was now directed toward Stella, who'd reached the top of the stairs and was cradling her infant son in her arms. He almost pushed her the way he'd done to me, but a shred of decency made him hesitate. Instead, he whacked the riding crop against the brass railing, herding all of us—Father, me, Carolyn, and Stella holding her baby—down to the dimly lit entrance hall.

"You!" Harold ordered a servant. "Get their hats and coats! Pile them here!"

Hail rattled against windows.

"Stella and I are wearing only our dressing gowns and slippers!" Carolyn pleaded.

"The clinic is barely a half a mile away. None of you will freeze to death!"

"But the baby—"

"To hell with the baby, and to hell with all of you. Thank God I'll never have to set eyes on any of you again."

The servant dumped our hats and coats at our feet, giving us an apologetic look and shaking his head in sympathy when he saw the blood dripping from my face.

Harold unlocked the front door and yanked it open. A cold wind assaulted us. Even with the darkness outside, it was obvious that hail slanted across the driveway. I couldn't tell the difference between gravel and pellets of ice.

"Harold," Carolyn said.

"Lord Cavendale to you!"

"You'll regret this," Carolyn said, standing straighter. I was startled by how stark her face became; it was no longer beautiful but had contorted into a seething rage.

"Regret it? To the contrary." He came close to laughing.

"Your gambling debts have almost bankrupted the estate. With contempt, you called me a moneylender, but your father was able to continue managing his estate only because I kept loaning him money. A great many loans. A great deal of money. The scheduled repayments were never made. Tomorrow, the moment I return to London, I intend to call in those loans. Your gambler friends will suddenly be your enemies. When they demand the money for your debts that until now I've been honoring, they'll bring riding crops of their own and no doubt worse than that. Your tailor, your butcher, your wine merchant, everyone you depend on for your lazy, worthless life will demand payment for what you owe them. When you can't pay your servants, they'll desert you. You won't even be able to afford oil for your lamps and coal for your fireplaces. You'll sit here in rags, freezing and starving in darkness."

"That's what you think. In a few months, I'll have income from crops."

"Not if the crops can't be harvested. The tools, the wagons, the animals, everything was pledged to me as collateral. Even your furniture was pledged as collateral. Tomorrow I'll seize everything."

"I lied," Harold said, his wrath increasing.

"Lied? About what?"

"I did know Daniel Harcourt. I hired him to investigate you and your shameless daughter."

"Don't be absurd. Daniel and I were business associates."

"He hated you! He despised your common origins and the airs you put on. He was thrilled by the chance to expose you and your daughter and make everyone realize the charlatans that you are! He must have been rushing here on Thursday night to give me proof that your daughter's snot-nosed bawling brat isn't my father's son. Not that it matters any longer. I'm Lord Cavendale now. Neither your daughter nor her bastard belongs here! Go! Out!"

Slashing the air with his riding crop, he drove us through the front door and down the granite steps into the storm.

Hail gusted at me from the right, striking my shoulder, pelting my hat, stinging my injured cheek. The baby kept wailing under Stella's open coat.

"Let me help," I told her, grabbing her arm as her slippers slid on the ice pellets she walked upon.

"No, I'll do it," Carolyn said, urgently putting an arm around Stella. "Take care of Thomas."

Holding Father, I looked back at the house and the open door where Harold stared savagely at us. Abruptly, the lamplight vanished when he stepped inside and slammed the door, the noise as disturbing as a gunshot.

The hail pushed at us. The baby's cries intensified, prompting Stella to say, "Hush, Jeremy, we're going to be all right. Don't fear. You'll soon be where it's warm."

That couldn't happen soon enough. As the hail stung me, I felt its cold rising through the soles of my boots, and I couldn't imagine how the ice pellets must feel under the slippers that Stella and Carolyn wore.

"Harold hates me so much that he hired someone to investigate me?" Stella asked in outrage. "He doesn't believe Jeremy is his father's child?"

Her voice broke. "Does he also not believe that sweet little Jennifer wasn't his father's child?"

"Hate him in return, Stella," Carolyn urged. "I promise we'll punish him. Don't think about anything else. Make your need for revenge warm your body."

We struggled along the gravel driveway and turned right into the hard-to-see road that led to the clinic. The hail had gusted at us from the right, but now our change of direction resulted in the hail driving straight toward us. I lowered my head. Ice pellets struck the exposed back of my neck. I couldn't stop shivering as the hail melted, trickling beneath my coat and down my spine.

"Harold will wish that he'd died instead of his older brother," Carolyn vowed. "God in heaven, how I'll make him pay. Keeping thinking that, Stella. We'll make him suffer. When we finish with him, he'll be crawling in the gutter. Keep fueling your rage. The heat of your hate will warm your body. It'll keep the baby warm."

Father slipped on the ice pellets that covered the road. In the dark, I managed to grab him before he fell. Abruptly, the road seemed to tilt, and I realized that with the hail covering the gravel, we couldn't know which way the road went. Disoriented, we were veering off it.

"We're going into the ditch!" I warned, grabbing Stella and Carolyn before they would have fallen with the baby. "Move to the left! I'll stay on this side and try to judge where the ditch is."

They had to walk slower while I constantly tested with my right foot, feeling where the slope began. The hail felt like stones that street urchins hurled at me.

Father lost his balance again, and this time, he fell. Groaning, he managed to stand. "I'm not hurt. Keep going. Ahead. On the left. I think I see something. Or maybe it's only—"

"No, Father, it isn't opium. That's the silhouette of the hill."

"The clinic is at its base," Stella said, her voice trembling. She told the baby beneath her coat, "Jeremy, we're almost there. You'll soon be warm."

Wet and shivering, I walked as fast as I dared while using my right boot to continue testing where the ditch started. The hill became darker and taller. I began to see the outline of three large buildings at the bottom of the hill, all of them without illumination at this late hour.

"I see the lane!" Carolyn said.

As we turned to the left, hurrying, I noticed something farther along the road from which we'd veered. I couldn't be certain in the dark with the hail blurring my vision, but the object seemed to be a canvas-covered wagon that wasn't moving. I wondered what it was doing there.

SOMEONE POUNDED AT the front door.

"Help! Help!" a woman shouted.

Ryan slowly lifted his head from a sofa in Dr. Wainwright's office. After he and Becker had interviewed as many of the clinic's clients as possible before they retired to their rooms for the night, he'd gone back to the doctor's office to study the list of guests and the details about them. While some had come from London (or claimed that they had), many had arrived from as far away as Scotland and Ireland. He couldn't decide how many of them were truly sick and how many had come to the clinic because it was a socially expected thing for the wealthy to do. So far, neither he nor Becker had sensed that any of them were lying when they said that they'd never heard of Daniel Harcourt or that they were familiar with the name but had never had any business with him. He felt a growing sensation that he and Becker were wasting their time.

The pounding on the door became more frenzied.

"Help!" the woman kept shouting.

Ryan quickly rose from the sofa where he'd fallen asleep when his eyes could no longer focus on Dr. Wainwright's documents. He struck a match and applied it to a lamp on the desk.

Impossibly, the woman sounded like Emily.

Clutching the lamp, he hurried from Dr. Wainwright's office and crossed the entrance hall.

Becker ran next to him, having risen from a sofa in the waiting area.

Ryan aimed the lantern while Becker freed the bolt on the door and tugged at the handle.

Four people lurched through the doorway.

"Thank God," one of them exclaimed.

Ryan gaped. The woman was indeed Emily. Her father was hunched over next to her, and they were accompanied by two women whom he'd never seen before. Hail dropped from their shoulders and hats. They were drenched, shivering.

"Sean? Joseph?" Emily asked, seeming to fear that she was hallucinating.

"We're trying to find out if anyone here knew Daniel Harcourt," Ryan blurted. "Why are you and your father—"

His question ended abruptly when he saw that the other two women wore dressing gowns that showed beneath the bottom of their dripping outer garments. The only things on their feet were soaked slippers. More astonishing, the younger of the two women—a woman whose face, for all its beauty, was as pale as her fair hair—opened her wet coat, revealing that she held a baby.

"Help me to get him warm," she pleaded.

"Over here," Becker urged, leading them to a fireplace. "The coals are still burning. I'll get more."

"Blankets," Ryan said. "We need blankets. Hot tea. We need to wake—"

"What's all the commotion?" a voice demanded.

Ryan turned to see Dr. Wainwright holding a lamp and hurrying down the staircase.

"I don't know yet," Ryan answered. "Two of these people are my friends. I'm not certain how they got here or—"

Turning to Emily, Ryan felt a shock when he noticed her left cheek. It was dark. Initially he'd thought that he was seeing only a shadow, but now he realized what the darkness actually was.

"Emily, good God, you're bleeding."

The blood was all over her coat.

"Stella!" Dr. Wainwright said. "Carolyn! What on earth…"

Servants hurried down the stairs, adding more light from candles they held.

"Bring blankets and dry clothes!" Dr. Wainwright ordered. He spread his arms, urging the four refugees toward the fireplace.

Becker had already added fresh coal from a pail next to the hearth. He gripped a bellows that hung on the side and pumped it, exciting the flames.

"Help me get these wet coats off!" Dr. Wainwright told Ryan.

Still dismayed by the blood on Emily's face, Ryan roused himself into motion. As he took away Emily's coat and hat, he frowned at how heavy they were from moisture.

"Emily, what happened to you?"

"Harold did it," the woman hugging the baby managed to say. She trembled close to the fire.

Servants ran toward them with blankets.

"Harold?" Ryan asked. "Who's—"

"Lady Cavendale's stepson," Dr. Wainwright answered.

"My husband is dead," the woman with the baby said.

"What?" Dr. Wainwright looked stunned. "Lord Cavendale is…"

"Harold smothered him tonight."

"Smothered?" Ryan asked.

"Lord Cavendale's an invalid," Dr. Wainwright explained. "Two months ago, he fell from a horse and—"

"Tonight," the woman with the baby told them. "When Harold thought everyone was asleep, he sneaked into my husband's room. But I saw him coming out. When I went in after Harold left, I found my husband dead."

"These two men are Scotland Yard detectives," Dr. Wainwright said. "Lady Cavendale and Mrs. Richmond, if there's anything amiss, I'm certain that they'll determine the cause."

"Detectives?" Mrs. Richmond asked. She was older but with striking features. Gray streaks emphasized her fiery hair.

"Are you certain he's dead?" Ryan wanted to know.

The two women looked at Emily, who clutched a blanket around her.

"I used every test Dr. Snow taught me," Emily answered. "There's no doubt."

"But Dr. Wainwright said he was an invalid after a riding accident," Becker noted. "Maybe Lord Cavendale died of natural causes."

"His son uses snuff," the woman with the baby said. "Specks of it were on my husband's chest. A pillow was next to him. It had a contour as if it had been pressed against my husband's face."

"Specks of snuff?" Ryan asked.

"Emily and her father saw them."

"It's true," De Quincey said. The cold had made his face look like an aged plate with so many tiny cracks that it seemed any moment it would shatter.

"I saw the specks also," the older woman told them. "I even smelled them. They were snuff."

"Struggling to reach here, I kept thinking about my husband's riding accident," the younger woman said. "Harold was the only person with him when it happened. Could it be that my husband's fall wasn't an accident? At dinner this evening, Harold even said he thought it would be better if his father were dead. Harold has massive gambling debts. Could he have become impatient about waiting to inherit his father's estate?"

Dr. Wainwright examined Emily's cheek. "This is going to need stitches."

"Stitches?" Ryan asked, appalled. "For God's sake, someone tell me how this happened."

"Harold struck Emily's father with a riding crop," the woman with the baby replied.

"A riding crop?" Ryan barely controlled his fury.

"And when Emily tried to protect her father, Harold whipped her face."

* * *

THE NOISE OF the rain on the attic's roof prevented Dr. Mandt from sleeping. The din worsened when the rain became hail. He sat up on his cot and felt nauseated from the stench of his chamber pot.

He pawed at a wooden crate, finally locating matches and a lamp. He lit the wick and made his way through the maze of boxes that concealed him. When he reached the curtained window, he set the lamp onto a crate, parted the curtains, and pushed the window open.

Greedily he inhaled the fresh cold air, dispelling the terrible odor that clogged his nostrils. Hail slanted onto him through the window. He didn't care.

A cry for help made him straighten. It came from a woman below him. Straining to look down, he saw what seemed to be four people struggling through the storm to reach the entrance to the building.

"Help!" the woman kept screaming.

Even with the noise of the hail on the roof, he was certain that he heard someone pounding on the door. Then the pounding ended as someone evidently opened the door for them. Leaning out, ignoring the sting of the hail, Mandt saw a glow appear in many windows below him as the commotion roused people in the building.

IN THE WAGON, the Russian continued to study the middle building. A noise made him turn as his two companions climbed back under the canvas cover. Water dripped from them, but they didn't comment on it.

"Did you have any problem?" he asked.

"None," one of the men replied. "We found a deep furrow in the field behind us and covered him with mud. A farmer might find his body two weeks from now."

Nodding, the Russian returned his attention to the window in the attic of the middle building.

"What were the voices we heard?" one of his companions asked.

"Four people—I think three of them were women—went down the lane to the clinic and pounded on the door, shouting for help. They must have become stranded in the storm somehow. I worried that we'd have to deal with them if they tried to climb into the wagon for shelter."

He hadn't been worried about killing them but about the complication of dealing with so many bodies.

"Look at the attic window," he said. "There's a faint glow. It's difficult to tell in the storm, but I think someone opened the window and leaned out."

"Who'd be in the attic at this time of night?" one of the other men wondered. "Perhaps servants sleep up there?"

"No. I'd have seen a lot more activity. This is only one person."

Abruptly, the front door of the middle building opened. A man charged outside. Another man pursued him.

"Sean!" the second man yelled. "Stop! For God's sake, calm down!"

But instead of listening, the first man broke into a run, reached the road in front of the clinic, and charged away into the darkness.

As the hail changed to rain, Becker lengthened his stride, splashing through muddy puddles, desperate to catch Ryan.

A huge house loomed in the darkness.

"Sean, you need to calm down! Don't do anything you'll regret!"

Ryan raced up the front steps two at a time. Under a portico, he grabbed the brass knocker on the entrance. He pounded with such force that the door trembled. He kept on striking it, faster and louder.

"Harold! I want to talk to you! Open the damned door, Harold!"

Becker reached the top of the steps and grabbed Ryan's shoulders, but Ryan pushed him away and kept pounding the door.

With a scrape of metal against wood, someone freed a bolt on the inside. The door opened only enough to reveal lamplight and a male servant peering out in alarm. "Lord Cavendale is in his room. Go away before I send a messenger into town and summon the police."

"I *am* the police!" Ryan told him.

Ramming his shoulder into the door, Ryan forced it open and shoved past the servant. In a massive entrance hall, he yanked off his hat and threw it across the marble floor, spraying drops of water.

"Harold, where are you? I want to talk to you! You struck a friend of mine with a riding crop! You cut her face!"

A man wearing a velvet dressing gown appeared on the stairway. The lamp he held revealed that he was tall, with a strong-looking chest and arrogant features. He scowled at Ryan's red hair.

"I'm Lord Cavendale to you. As my servant warned, if you don't leave, I'll summon the constable from town."

Ryan stalked toward the staircase. When Becker ran ahead of him, Ryan pushed him away so hard that Becker fell.

"You cut her cheek, Harold!" Ryan shouted. "Now I'm going to—"

As he reached for something hidden under his right trouser cuff, Becker dove for his legs and toppled him.

They struggled.

"Get away!" Ryan yelled.

Becker's vision suddenly blurred. He lurched backward, realizing that he'd been struck in the face. He raised a hand to his bleeding mouth, ignored the pain, and used the other hand to push Ryan away from Harold.

"Sean, don't be a fool! If you hit him, the home secretary will make an example of you! It doesn't matter how much Commissioner Mayne supports you, you'll be dismissed for striking a peer!"

Ryan fought to get around him.

"But that's not the worst of it!" Becker pleaded. "We're only laborers! What happens to a carpenter who's insolent enough to strike a lord? *You're* the one who'll go to prison! Even if all the evidence is against this man, his judges will almost certainly be lords! They won't be able to forget that you assaulted one of their own! You're destroying the chance we have to punish him!"

Ryan's chest rose and fell. His gaze was the fiercest, angriest that Becker had ever seen.

"Emily," he said.

"Yes," Becker said. "Emily. Listen to me. I know she'd tell you the same thing. Be smart about this. Don't do anything that'll stop the law from punishing him."

Ryan glared at the man standing above them on the stairs.

"The law punish me?" Harold scoffed. "For what? Striking a common woman who refused to leave my house? I'd be equally justified in striking *you* for intruding in the middle of the night. Leave at once."

"What's that in your hand?" Ryan asked.

Becker realized that the man held a riding crop.

Ryan charged up the stairs.

"Sean!" Becker pleaded.

Ryan pulled out his badge, telling Harold, "I'm Detective Inspector Ryan. Where's your father?"

"You have no right to—"

"Harold, if you won't take us to your father's body, we'll go from room to room until we find it."

"I order you to leave." Harold swung with the riding crop.

In a blur, Ryan caught it, yanked it from Harold's hand, and raised it.

Harold cringed.

About to strike, Ryan's hand shook. Indeed, his entire body shook. All at once, he hurled the riding crop down the staircase.

As Harold opened his mouth in shock, Ryan and Becker ran up the staircase.

At the first level, a female servant looked astonished about what she had witnessed.

"Where do we find Harold's father?" Ryan demanded.

She glanced nervously toward the next landing.

Ryan took her lamp. He and Becker hurried farther upward.

"You don't have any right," Harold blustered, pursuing them.

On the next level, Ryan and Becker separated. The light from the lamp that Ryan held was sufficient for them to see past the doors they opened.

"This one," Becker said.

They entered a bedroom and approached a bed where parted curtains revealed a still figure.

As they stepped closer, the lamp illuminated the gaunt features of a man of many years. His eyes were open, dull and unfocused.

"Stop here," Ryan told Becker. "Don't go any closer. We'll do this the way we always do."

"Get out of this room," Harold ordered.

Ryan gave Becker the lamp and stepped carefully forward, scanning the bed for details. He leaned through the parted curtains and felt for a pulse, but the man's clouded eyes left no doubt that he was dead.

Ryan picked up a pillow that was next to the body. The man's wife had said that it had an indentation matching the shape of the corpse's face, as though it had been used to smother him.

But now the pillow had no such indentation.

"Did you touch this pillow?" Ryan asked Harold.

"Absolutely not."

Ryan studied the dead man's face, noting the yellow crust of dried spittle at the corners of his mouth. He looked at the pillow.

The stain of what looked like spittle was on it.

"Your father's eyes are open," Ryan said.

"I don't know why that merits a comment," Harold said. "I assume that many people die with their eyes open."

"Not when they're asleep," Ryan told him. "What would have wakened your father? A pillow pressed over his face, perhaps? I'm told he was infirm. It may be that the only sign of his struggle would have been his eyes opening in panic."

"Is my so-called stepmother still accusing me of smothering my father?"

Ryan leaned close to the blue blanket, searching for specks of the snuff that the man's wife and Emily's father had described.

The specks weren't there.

He thought a moment and told Becker, "Lower the lamp toward the floor."

"What are you doing?" Harold demanded.

Ryan crouched, studying the carpet next to the bed.

He moved his fingers across it.

"You have no right to do this!" Harold shouted.

Ryan's fingers touched specks of something. A few of the specks stuck to his index finger. He raised them and smelled them.

"Snuff."

"That's impossible!" Harold said.

Ryan stepped close to Harold, noting that specks of snuff clung to the underside of his nostrils and the top of his dressing gown.

"You reshaped the pillow so that it no longer had the contour of your father's face, but you failed to notice that your father left spittle on it when the pillow was pressed over his nose and mouth. After my friend and her father found snuff on your father's blanket, you came back here and brushed the specks away. But you should also have removed them from where they fell on the carpet. I'm arresting you for your father's murder."

TEN

HYDROPATHY

"I DON'T HAVE ANY spare bedrooms," Dr. Wainwright told the shivering arrivals. "But I'll arrange for cots to be placed in consultation rooms. Here are dry clothes for all of you. I apologize," he told Carolyn and Stella. "These maids' dresses are hardly what you're accustomed to." When he looked at Emily's bloomer dress, he seemed to decide that in her case she probably wouldn't mind. "But they'll keep you warm until we can dry the clothes that you're wearing. My assistant here is named Rick." Wainwright indicated a young man who wore the white uniform of the clinic. "He'll help this matron to get all of you settled."

"Tea," Emily said. "Is it possible for someone to bring us hot tea?"

"I don't allow tea or coffee here," Dr. Wainwright told her. "No stimulants of any kind. But the kitchen staff will bring you hot water with honey."

Emily held a handkerchief over her bleeding cheek.

"Miss De Quincey, I'm afraid I'm not a surgeon. I don't have the training to place the stitches you need."

She nodded, understanding that physicians had a revulsion about touching their patients and that only surgeons, at the low end of the medical hierarchy, dealt with blood and gore. "If you have the equipment, I'll do it myself."

Carolyn, Stella, and Dr. Wainwright regarded her with astonishment.

Dr. Wainwright seemed not to know what to say. "Well, I do have the equipment, but surely you don't really intend to—"

"I don't have a choice. Show me where it is."

He led her to a consultation room. Trembling, De Quincey followed.

Wainwright opened a drawer, revealing a curved needle and catgut sutures.

"I need white vitriol to clean and shrink the tissue," Emily told him. "And a small mirror. Father, you haven't stopped shaking." She touched his forehead with concern. "You have a fever."

"I need my medicine."

"I have no medicine here," Dr. Wainwright said, handing Emily the vitriol and the mirror. "Half the people I treat are sick because of the noxious pills their physicians prescribe, concoctions that are nothing more than powdered cabbage mixed with paste or chalk blended with licorice."

"This is the medicine I need." De Quincey showed the empty laudanum bottle. "Harold knocked it out of my hand, spilling its contents. I had another container in my room, but Harold wouldn't allow me to…" De Quincey trembled.

"That medicine in particular is something I don't allow. *This* is the medicine you need." Dr. Wainwright picked up a pitcher, poured water into a glass, and handed it to De Quincey.

"If only this were enough." De Quincey swallowed from the glass, his hands shaking.

Emily poured white vitriol into a bowl, then dropped the needle and catgut into the astringent. "Dr. Snow has been helping my father to reduce his laudanum consumption."

"You're familiar with the queen's physician?" Wainwright asked, impressed.

"We lowered Father's intake to eight ounces of laudanum per day."

Emily found a clean cloth in a drawer and poured white vitriol onto it. Wincing, she wiped the cloth over the cut.

"I thought your father's reputation was exaggerated, but obviously not!" Wainwright exclaimed. "Some people might die from swallowing even a tablespoon of laudanum."

"My habit was long acquired and hard-earned," De Quincey said, his face beading with sweat.

Emily picked up the mirror with one hand and the dripping needle with the other. "Lord, help me to avoid a scar." She threaded catgut through the needle.

As blood swelled from the cut, she drew a breath, pierced her cheek with the needle, winced, and pulled it through.

"Emily, I'd give anything to be the one who required stitches instead of you," De Quincey said.

"I'm thankful that it didn't come to that, Father."

"But you do indeed require treatment," Dr. Wainwright told De Quincey, watching him clench and unclench his hands.

"In the morning, as soon as the shops open," De Quincey said, "someone needs to go into town and buy—"

"I can't recommend it," the doctor warned. "Besides, that'll be several hours from now. You need immediate help. Since Dr. Snow's method hasn't been successful, perhaps you'll agree to try one of mine."

THE TREATMENT ROOM had white tiles and a drain. Two attendants held long, thick sheets drenched with water.

"It's called the wet-sheet method," Dr. Wainwright said.

"Anything that will help me to stop trembling," De Quincey told him.

"It will also reduce your fever. You can leave your wet clothes on. No matter what you wear, they'll soon be soaked."

"Dr. Wainwright," Emily asked, "did you ever consider that the term *hydropathy* is composed of the words for 'water' and 'suffering'?" Her left cheek was red and swollen, two dark stitches now at the center of the wound.

"That's very clever. But the word can also easily imply that water chases away suffering."

"Let's not talk about suffering," De Quincey said, shaking.

The doctor motioned for the attendants to wrap the wet sheets around De Quincey. Briefly, the little man continued trembling. But soon his arms and legs became immobile. Except that his face was exposed, he resembled one of the mummies in the British Museum.

The attendants picked him up and set him on his back on a table. After raising metal guards so that he couldn't roll off, they poured pails of water over the sheets that enfolded him.

"What do you feel?" Dr. Wainwright asked.

"Cold." De Quincey's voice continued to shake.

"Not for long. The heat of your body should create considerable warmth beneath the wet sheets."

The attendants brought thick wet blankets and placed them over the sheets wound around him.

"Yes," De Quincey said. "Now I'm starting to feel warm."

"Soon the toxins in your body will pour out of you," Dr. Wainwright said. "All the poisons that you've accumulated, especially from laudanum, will be expelled."

"I'm perspiring."

"Excellent! We'll make a new man of you in a couple of hours!"

"Dr. Wainwright," Emily asked, "how long have you practiced hydrotherapy?"

"After receiving my medical degree from the University of Edinburgh, I went to study water cures with Vincenz Priessnitz at his spa in Gräfenberg."

"And when did you open this clinic?"

"Two and a half years ago. Members of the peerage persuaded me, feeling a need for my services. Why do you ask?"

"I'm only trying to distract Father. How do you feel under there, Father?"

"Warm. Very warm."

"Excellent indeed," Dr. Wainwright affirmed. "Every toxin will be eliminated."

"I do definitely feel them being eliminated," De Quincey told him, encased within the tightly wound, dripping sheets.

"Doctor, the original plan was for Mrs. Richmond to bring us here to meet you tomorrow morning, which I suppose is now today," Emily said. "The gentleman at whose house we're staying in London has an extensive library. When I learned that we were going to have the honor of meeting you, I read some books about hydropathy."

"I applaud your curiosity, Miss De Quincey."

"It puzzles me that Mr. Priessnitz, who adhered to his water-cure principles, expired when he was only fifty-one, whereas Father, who frequently drinks sixteen ounces of laudanum per day, is sixty-nine and walks at least fifteen miles each day."

"But I didn't walk yesterday," De Quincey said in distress. "That may be why this relapse is so extreme."

"Some constitutions are stronger than others," Dr. Wainwright noted. "You're a medical miracle, Mr. De Quincey."

"Perhaps the laudanum preserved me. I wish I could move my arms and legs under these sheets."

"In three hours, my attendants will unwrap you."

"Rats," De Quincey said.

"What?" the doctor asked.

"They gnaw at my stomach."

"The wet-sheet method will smother the rats, I assure you."

De Quincey groaned, his features contorting, the fine cracks in his face seeming about to fracture. "What time is it? How soon will the shops open? Emily, when can you buy—"

Dr. Wainwright raised his hands in objection. "I don't believe we're ready to surrender yet. As long as we have a few more hours, what's the harm in continuing your treatment?"

"It's very hot under these sheets."

"Perfect!"

* * *

IGNORING THE RAIN, the Russian stopped at the side door of the middle building. Most locks could be opened with one of a half a dozen of the most commonly shaped keys. He was successful with the third attempt. He pushed the door open warily, satisfying himself that only darkness awaited him. To avoid being noticed, his two companions pressed themselves against the building. He stepped inside.

"HAROLD, PUT ON your overcoat," Ryan ordered. "You're coming with us to the clinic."

"I'm not going anywhere."

"Understand, now that you've been arrested, you and I have a different relationship," Ryan told him. "You're a peer and I'm a laborer, yes, but if you resist me, I'll say that you attempted to escape. My partner will agree with me. Is that true, Detective Sergeant Becker?"

"Absolutely, Detective Inspector Ryan. He tried to escape."

"Harold, not only will I be able to justify doing whatever's necessary to make you comply, but your attempted escape will make everyone believe that you had a reason to flee, that you are in fact guilty."

"But I didn't kill my father!"

"Certainly. Every man and woman who steps onto a gallows insists that they're innocent."

"Gallows? Wait! All right, I admit I reshaped the pillow and brushed the snuff from my father's chest, but that was just to prevent me from looking guilty."

"What you accomplished was making yourself look *more* guilty," Ryan said.

"I swear I wasn't in the room when my father died!" Harold told him. "*She* must have taken some of my snuff and…*She* did it."

"She."

"Stella. *She* killed my father."

"Why would she do that? Was your father's property entailed?" Ryan referred to the standard practice of establishing a trust that bequeathed land to the oldest male heir while preventing him by law from selling it. The new owner would then establish a similar trust that prevented his own male heir from selling the land.

"Yes, the property was entailed," Harold replied.

"In which case, you're the only person who could inherit the estate and benefit from your father's death," Ryan continued. "What could Lady Cavendale have gained? Nothing. Like most widows, she depended on the goodwill of the male heir, and we know how you handled that responsibility. You threw her out into a hailstorm."

A servant hurried down the staircase carrying two travel bags. "Mr. De Quincey and his daughter left these when they departed."

"Thank you," Becker said.

Ryan opened the bag that had De Quincey's name on it.

"What are you doing?" Becker asked, shocked by the invasion of privacy.

Ryan sorted through the bag's contents. "Making certain that something is safe."

He held up a laudanum bottle. "Three months ago, would you have guessed that I'd concern myself with delivering opium to Emily's father?"

"Things have indeed changed." Becker laughed, then winced, touching the blood on his mouth.

"I'm sorry for striking you, Joseph. You were right. I did something that I regret."

"I'd rather have you regret this than something worse." Becker glanced down at Ryan's right trouser cuff and the slight bulge where his knife was hidden.

"Thanks for being my friend," Ryan told him.

As the emotional moment lengthened, Ryan turned to Harold. "Put on your coat and hat."

"But…but it's raining outside," Harold objected.

"Imagine that."

"And carry one of these bags," Becker told him.

"What? That's a job for a servant."

"If you're carrying a bag, you'll be less able to run away. In fact, you'd better carry *both* bags," Ryan decided. He opened the door and studied the dark, gusting rain. "A fine night for a walk, don't you agree, Harold?"

THE RUSSIAN CLOSED the door and stood motionless in the dark. He listened intensely but heard only the storm. He withdrew a lantern and a box of matches from beneath his overcoat. The scrape of a match echoed as he ignited it and revealed narrow, dusty wooden stairs upon which footprints were evident. He lit the lantern, blew out the match, removed a revolver from a coat pocket, and began to climb.

DE QUINCEY LAY on the table, feeling the weight of the numerous layers of thick, wet sheets wrapped around him. His arms were pressed tightly to his sides, and his legs were squeezed together, leaving him unable to move. Even his fingers were immobile.

"I feel I've become cocooned," he said.

"A new man will emerge," Dr. Wainwright assured him. "It isn't necessary for me to remain while the wet-sheet method works its cure. Allow me to leave the two of you alone for a few minutes while I see if Lady Cavendale and Mrs. Richmond require attention."

The doctor stepped outside and closed the door.

Emily peered over the guardrail on the table. "Do you feel warmer under there, Father?"

"Considerably."

Initially he'd felt so cold that he shivered. But as more wet sheets had been wrapped around him, the movement of shivering wasn't possible. It was as though he'd been given a drug that paralyzed him. Soon, his body didn't need to shiver, as the heat from his body became trapped. The sensation was briefly comfortable, but then the heat increased until he was sweating.

Some of the sweat trickled from De Quincey's forehead into his eyes.

"Emily, please wipe my brow."

As she did, she frowned. "You feel very hot."

"Is that a pitcher of water on that table?"

She poured some into a glass, put a hand behind his neck, and managed to lift his head enough so that he could drink.

"When this is finished, you should acquire the habit of drinking more of this," she told him.

"At the moment, the rats in my stomach demand more than water."

"Dawn will soon be here," Emily said. "The shops will open. I never imagined that I'd be eager to purchase laudanum for you."

"It can't happen quickly enough. Does your cheek hurt? With those stitches, it looks very painful."

"It's numb."

"Well, sometimes that's the best we can hope for."

"Father, did you notice that Dr. Wainwright referred to Carolyn and Stella by their first names when he came down the staircase and saw the condition they were in? But a minute later and also just now, he referred to them as Lady Cavendale and Mrs. Richmond."

De Quincey felt more constricted as the sheets became heavier, absorbing the considerable perspiration from his body. "Yes, he's closer to Carolyn and Stella than he wants us to know." De Quincey drew a difficult breath. "Do you still have some of the money that my publisher sent to me?"

"I've been careful with it."

"Then you'll be able to send a telegram when you go into town to buy the laudanum."

"A telegram?"

Blinking sweat from his eyes, De Quincey explained where the telegram should be sent and what she should put in it.

"We ought to have a reply by this afternoon," he told her.

The feel of Emily's hand against the side of his neck distracted him, her fingers so refreshingly cool that at first he thought she was comforting him. But then he realized that she was feeling his pulse.

"Can you count quietly to sixty, Father? At the speed of *one thousand and one, one thousand and two,* and so forth?"

"Yes."

"Start now."

Concentrating, he managed to distract himself from feeling smothered.

"Sixty," De Quincey said.

Emily took her hand away from the side of his neck. "Your heart has a rate of one hundred and forty beats per minute."

"The look on your face suggests that isn't a good number."

THE PELTING OF the rain on the attic's roof diminished. Lying on his cot in the darkness, Dr. Mandt hoped that the silence would allow him to sleep.

Think about boarding the fastest train to Liverpool, he told himself. *Think about getting on the speediest ship to America, a steamship, not a sailing ship, only sixteen days from England to the United States. Think about the fortune waiting for you in a New York City bank. Think about—*

Stairs creaked outside his door.

THE RUSSIAN CAME to the topmost level of the narrow steps. He'd climbed slowly, passing a door at each level, listening, climbing higher, trying to make a minimum of sound. But despite all his caution, the bare wood creaked beneath his weight.

He put his ear to the final door and heard nothing. Gently, he worked the latch. The door didn't move when he pressed against it. He tried the various keys that he carried. One of them fit the lock, but when he twisted the key, he discovered that the lock had already been freed. The only explanation for the door not moving was that someone had bolted it from the inside.

WHEN THE CREAK of the footsteps paused, Dr. Mandt rose nervously from his cot and directed his attention toward the attic door. He shouldn't have been able to see it in the dark, but the light from what seemed to be a lantern glowed through the door's cracks.

He felt along a wooden crate and touched the basket in which Dr. Wainwright had brought food, its bread, cheese, and boiled ham long since eaten, its bottles of what Wainwright called tonic water long since consumed. He picked up one of the empty bottles in case he needed to defend himself. Then his trembling fingers touched something else that was in the basket, and in his fright, Mandt decided to rely on that instead.

His heart raced when he heard fingers scratching at the door.

"Dr. Mandt," a man's voice whispered in German. But he had a Russian accent, all too familiar after the considerable time that Mandt had spent in St. Petersburg, attending to the czar. "I know you're in there."

Mandt felt an invisible hand pressing against his chest.

"Doctor." The Russian kept his voice as low as he could and still be heard. "There's no need to make this situation difficult."

Again, he scratched his fingernails against the door, a sound that could be heard only by someone inside the attic.

"No reason for unpleasantness," he whispered. "You did your best to escape. Nonetheless, we found you. It's time to admit defeat."

He waited but didn't receive a response. He unbuttoned his overcoat so that he could lean even closer to the door.

"Doctor, I promise that no harm will come to you. It's in our best interest to keep you safe. My orders are to take you back to Russia, where you'll tell various foreign ambassadors and newspaper writers the details of the British plot against the czar, including the amount of money that Queen Victoria's government paid you to poison him. You won't be injured in any way. After all, how persuasive would your testimony be if there was even the slightest suspicion that we coerced you? You'll be given the best lodging, the best food and drink, anything you desire. After you convince the world that the British committed a crime against God and nature, we'll release you, not to the wealth that you were no doubt promised but at least to a reasonably comfortable existence."

He waited.

"Doctor, truly, there's no reason to make this unpleasant."

* * *

Mᴀɴᴅᴛ ꜰᴇʟᴛ ʟɪɢʜᴛ-ʜᴇᴀᴅᴇᴅ and suddenly realized that he'd stopped breathing. He gripped a crate and inhaled deeply, trying to steady his heart.

Does he mean it? he wondered.

"Doctor, I have a wagon waiting at the road," the voice whispered. "Regrettably, the three-hour drive into London will be uncomfortable, but we don't dare wait for the morning train. After we reach London, we'll board the first train to Dover and be on a boat to France before the British government realizes that you're gone. I emphasize that you'll be treated with comfort and respect. You're very important to us."

Mandt had no doubt that he was important to the Russians.

But after I testified, would I in fact be allowed to live in reasonable comfort? he asked himself.

And what about the British? How would they react to my betrayal? Would they allow me to live in reasonable comfort?

Trembling, Mandt walked to the door, where the lantern glowed through the cracks between the boards.

He slid the bolt free.

"You made a wise decision," the voice said.

When Mandt opened the door, he saw a mustached, burly man with broad shoulders. As the man smiled and took a step into the attic, Mandt noticed that while his left hand gripped the lantern, his right hand held a revolver.

The object that Mandt had taken from the food basket was a knife. The man's overcoat was unbuttoned. Propelled by panic and desperation, Mandt thrust the knife into the man's stomach.

The man bent forward as though he'd been punched. He gasped and tried to straighten. Mandt tugged upward on the knife, feeling the warmth of blood on his hand.

The revolver dropped, thumping loudly. With his now-free right hand, the Russian gripped his stomach, trying to stop the blood. As he fell backward onto the stairs, his other hand lost its grip on the lantern.

The lantern shattered on a step and rolled, its burning wick exposed to the wood.

"You feel on fire," Emily said in alarm as she removed her hand from De Quincey's forehead. "I need to unwrap you."

"*Unroll* me would be more accurate," he murmured.

She leaned over the metal railing on the side of the table. Before the attendants left, they'd placed drenched blankets on top of the bundle that enclosed him. She hurled these away and felt for the edge of the first of the many soaked sheets in which he'd been wrapped.

But she couldn't find the edge.

"I need to turn you, Father." Her voice echoed sharply against the room's bright tiles.

With effort, she rolled him onto his right side and then his stomach, where she finally found the edge of the first soaked sheet.

She pulled.

"I'm sorry I can't be gentle, Father."

"Quite all right," he said with his face on the table. "The bumps distract me from the rodents gnawing at my stomach."

"Perhaps I can distract you more," Emily said, tugging harder. "What are we to make of Harold's announcement that he hired Daniel Harcourt? Was he telling the truth or, in the heat of the argument, was he merely trying to spite Carolyn?"

"Emily, at the moment, please don't say *heat*."

Sweat dripped from his face as she yanked the wet sheet, turning him onto his other side and then his back.

"It was in Harold's hateful nature to want to ruin his stepmother," De Quincey said, exhaling from the impact of being rolled. "I suspect that he did hire the attorney. As Harold told us, he wanted to prove that Stella was unfaithful to his father. But would the fear of being exposed as an adulteress have been great enough for Stella, or even Carolyn, a fiercely protective mother, to arrange for Harcourt to be murdered?"

Emily kept pulling the soaked sheet, once more thumping her father onto his right side and then his stomach.

"I don't believe it," De Quincey said, dripping onto the table. "Harcourt's revelations would have caused Stella to be exiled from Lord Cavendale's estate, true." He winced as Emily tugged him onto his back. "But Carolyn's so wealthy that she could have supported her daughter and grandson in far greater luxury than they would ever have enjoyed in that terrible house." He groaned. "The only penalty would have been that Stella could no longer call herself Lady Cavendale, but is the fear of losing a title worth the risk of being hanged? No, I don't believe it."

"It must be difficult speaking this way about a long-lost friend who's so important to you, Father."

"The only person who truly matters to me is *you*," De Quincey told her, grimacing as she tugged the sheet and rolled him onto his left side.

"I feel the same way about you, Father."

"As you proved many times. Thank you for your sacrifice. No one could have a more loving daughter. I know your fondness for Sergeant Becker and Inspector Ryan. Under other circumstances, you might have felt free to choose one of them to be your—"

"There *aren't* any other circumstances, Father," Emily told him abruptly, avoiding the topic. "There is only here and now and you and I. That is what we must deal with."

"Yes, here and now."

"I reached the end!" Emily said in triumph. She threw the dripping sheet away and tried to find the edge of the next one. "Do you feel less hot, Father?"

He didn't reply.

"Father?"

"Is it close to dawn?" he asked. "I'm certain that I'd feel stronger if I had my medicine."

"Does your heart feel that it's beating slower?"

"Faster, I'm sorry to say."

Emily tugged furiously at the second of the many drenched sheets that encircled her father.

In a panic, Mandt stared at the shattered lantern on the steps below where the Russian lay. The lantern was on its side. Fuel leaked out of the slot from which the wick protruded. The flame spread farther across the wood.

Mandt remembered a sheet that covered a crate behind him. He grabbed it and prepared to charge down the stairs to swat out the flame.

But the Russian was sprawled on the narrow stairs, blocking the way, and the Russian was still alive, moaning and clutching his stomach, from which the knife's handle protruded. Mandt feared that if he tried to step over him, the Russian would grab his legs, topple him, and use the last of his strength to pull out the knife and stab him.

The flames rose from the step, touching a wall.

Mandt dropped the sheet, descended two steps, bent down, and gripped the Russian's ankles. Straining, he pulled, dragging the Russian up toward the attic.

The Russian's head bumped on one step and then another. With each jolt, he groaned.

Mandt pulled more fiercely when he saw the wall catch fire. He dragged the Russian all the way into the attic and left him bleeding on the floor.

As he picked up the sheet, Mandt remembered the revolver. Lest the Russian crawl to it, Mandt grabbed it, crammed it under the waistband of his trousers, and hooked the handle over one of his suspenders.

He hurried down toward the swelling brightness of the burning stairwell.

All at once, he noticed that the sound of his panicked movements seemed louder. The drumming of the rain had stopped.

He heard another sound, a hiss. It came from the overturned lantern where it lay amid the flames. The hiss became high-pitched, like the whistle on a kettle.

Mandt suddenly understood what was about to happen. Turning in a frenzy, he raced up the steps and threw himself onto the floor.

An instant later, the fuel reservoir in the lantern—its contents expanding because of the fire's heat—achieved a pressure that the metal couldn't contain.

The explosion disintegrated the lantern, spewing fuel and chunks of metal throughout the stairwell. The ceiling, the walls, the steps—everything burst into flames.

"LADY CAVENDALE AND Mrs. Richmond." Dr. Wainwright stood at the entrance to the consultation room. Before him, Stella and Carolyn sat on cots, holding blankets around their shoulders. Stella cradled her infant son in her arms. "Is there any way I can be of assistance?"

He said their formal names loudly enough that anyone in the corridor could hear, although now that the commotion had passed, most servants and guests had gone back to bed.

Satisfied that he wasn't observed, he took a step into the room.

"Why are police detectives here?" Carolyn asked.

"They don't believe that the inquiries about Daniel Harcourt were thorough. They want to assure themselves that no one here at the clinic had any dealings with him," Wainwright answered.

"Harcourt," Carolyn said, looking down at the floor. "I had no idea he hated me so much. I thought he was merely showing contempt for a woman in business, but in fact, it was I personally he felt contempt for." She finally looked up. "Bad luck that the police detectives decided to come here at this particular time. Did Dr. Mandt arrive?"

"He's in the attic. He was supposed to leave for the United States tomorrow night, but with all the trouble on the railways, he might be noticed among the few travelers. He can't be moved for a while."

"My plan was to bring my friend Thomas here today," Carolyn said. "The famous Opium-Eater would have been so great a distraction that no one would have suspected Mandt was here. Unfortunately, our entrance created a greater distraction than I anticipated."

"The police detectives are certainly distracted, one of them in particular," Wainwright noted. "Lord knows what that Irish inspector has done to Harold. They haven't returned yet. Stella, in all the chaos, I didn't have a chance to express my condolences. I'm extremely sorry about the loss of your husband."

"Thank you." Stella peered mournfully down at the baby in her arms. Her green eyes brimmed with tears. "I did my best to restore Robert's health after his riding accident, or perhaps I should say his *supposed* accident. The more I think about the way Harold acted after he galloped back to the house, shouting that something horrible had happened, the more I believe it wasn't an accident at all. I think Harold was terrified that his father would recover sufficiently to tell us what really happened."

"The law will deal with him," Dr. Wainwright assured her, "or perhaps that inspector will punish him even sooner than a judge. The Opium-Eater's daughter is obviously special to Ryan. I've seldom seen anyone more enraged."

"I envy her," Carolyn said.

"I don't understand."

"To be loved so intensely," Carolyn said. She looked older, creases showing around her eyes. The gray streaks in her hair seemed more pronounced.

THE HEAT FROM the fire pushed Mandt back into the attic. He managed to avoid stumbling over the Russian, who blinked in shock, his chest rising and falling with effort.

Desperate, Mandt pivoted toward the attic's front window and quickly dismissed it as a means of escape. He couldn't possibly squirm through the small opening, and even if he did, he would never survive the long fall.

He swung back toward the growing roar of the flames in the stairway. He drew a breath, raised his arms to protect his face, and rushed downward through the blaze. Heat singed his hair and burned the skin on the backs of his hands. His rapid footsteps thundering, he charged through the flames, lost his balance, and fell. With a groan, he landed painfully on the steps, sliding rather than rolling because the walls of the stairway were so close together.

He jolted to a stop on a landing and slapped the fire on his clothes, burning his palms, smothering the flames on his trousers and coat.

A noise startled him, coming not from the fire but from a door on the landing where he lay. It opened. A portly, bearded man in a dressing gown held a candle and peered from an otherwise dark corridor. In shock, the man gaped at the inferno on the stairs and then at Mandt lying sprawled on the landing.

The man shouted something, then turned and ran along the corridor, pounding on doors as he passed them. Mandt's English was so limited that he couldn't determine precisely what the man yelled, but in all likelihood, it was "Fire! Help! Run!"

Mandt ignored his pains and struggled to stand. His right leg almost buckled. The barrel of the revolver wedged under the waist of his pants had gouged his thigh, but he didn't have time to assess the damage. With the heat of the flames stretching toward him, he raced farther down the steps. He turned to charge down the next section, but away from the fire, darkness suddenly enveloped him. He placed a scorched palm against a wall so he could keep his balance as he descended cautiously.

Above and behind him, he heard more shouting. The fire's roar increased. The air in the murky stairwell became cooler. He reached yet another landing, turned, and kept descending.

Finally, he turned in the darkness and found there weren't any more steps. All he felt was a door. When he opened it, a few wall lamps revealed a granite corridor. He smelled water.

I'm in the basement! he realized.

He heard voices coming from a room—an elderly man and a young woman speaking urgently.

He hurriedly retreated and rushed up the dark steps to the next landing. There, he used his throbbing hands to paw along a wall. He found a door that he presumed would lead outside.

He opened it. The rain had stopped. A moon emerged from clouds. The night smelled sweet.

A man stepped away from a wall and asked in Russian, "Vladimir, did you find him?"

Mandt stumbled back.

A second man moved away from a wall.

"It's him! It's Mandt!"

Mandt pulled the revolver from his waistband as he continued to stumble away. He had no experience with firearms, but he'd seen others use them and knew enough to pull back the hammer.

As the Russian grabbed for him, Mandt pulled the trigger. The flash was blinding. The smoke added to the darkness of the night. The noise slapped his ears, making them ring. Not knowing if he'd hit the man, he lurched back all the way through the opening, slammed the door, and hoped there was a bolt to lock it.

He couldn't find one. Behind him was another door. He opened it to make it appear that he'd fled in that direction. Then, as fast as the darkness allowed, he raced up the stairs, opened the door on the next landing, and ran along a corridor. People wearing nightclothes rushed from rooms, holding candles that trembled.

"WHAT A PITY, Harold," Ryan said as they made their way along the muddy road, guided by a lantern that Becker held. "The rain stopped. I'd hoped that the hail would return. I wanted you to enjoy the same weather you forced my friends to experience."

"You can't treat a peer in this fashion," Harold objected, struggling to carry Emily's travel bag and her father's. "When I speak to your superiors, you'll learn the penalty for insolence."

"I look forward to your conversation with my superiors," Ryan told him. "Are those bags too heavy for you, Harold?"

"Stop calling me that."

"I don't remember if a peer has ever been hanged before. Detective Sergeant Becker, do you recall such a thing ever happening?"

"Wasn't there an earl a hundred years ago?" Becker replied.

"Yes, that's right! So peers can in fact be hanged. There ought to be a large crowd. At least twenty thousand people," Ryan said with great enthusiasm. "The street vendors will earn considerable money selling rotten vegetables for the crowd to throw at you, Harold."

"Stop talking like that! I didn't kill my father!"

"Of course not. You merely went out of your way to make it *seem* like you did. In which case, you ought to be hanged for stupidity."

"You can't talk to a lord in this fashion! I'll have you dismissed from the police force!"

Becker suddenly interrupted. "Sean, what time is it?"

"Time? It's the middle of the night."

"I mean precisely," Becker persisted.

Confused, Ryan removed the Benson chronometer from a trouser pocket, opened it, and held it close to the lantern that Becker held.

"Since when does a police detective carry a gold watch?" Harold demanded.

"It's evidence that I'm protecting." Ryan studied the two dials on the lustrous chronometer. "The time is exactly seventeen minutes and fifteen seconds after three o'clock," he told Becker.

"Too early for dawn. Anyway, we're walking toward the west, not the east."

"What are you talking about?" Ryan asked.

"Look ahead. Next to the silhouette of the hill. At a later hour, if we were walking east, it could be the glow from the sun coming up."

"A glow doesn't ripple," Ryan said in a rush.

Becker broke into a run. "The clinic's on fire!"

ELEVEN

INTO THE DEPTHS

SOMEONE FRANTICALLY RANG a fire bell. Remembering to conceal the revolver in his trousers, Mandt joined the chaos of people surging from their rooms. A few struggled to put on dressing gowns while most wore only nightclothes. Their voices were a babble, but he sensed that they were shouting something to the effect of "Help! Fire! Run!"

The swarm reached a large central staircase, where dozens and dozens of people charged down from the upper levels. They bumped against each other, merging into a larger mass, hurrying down toward where other panicked people gathered talking loudly in an entrance hall.

Mandt veered into the center of the frenzy, doubting that anyone who chased him would show himself to so many witnesses, hoping that no one would notice him among so many frantic people.

"BE CALM!" DR. Wainwright urged. He pulled a chair from a table, climbed onto it, and shouted to the growing crowd in the entrance hall, "Everything's under control! There's no reason to panic!"

"The building's on fire!" someone yelled back. "How can you say everything's under control?"

"There are two other buildings!" Wainwright answered. "If necessary, you can find shelter there! But the fire's limited to a stairwell. You're not in danger."

"Do you smell that smoke? What do you mean, we're not in danger?"

Wainwright's assistant hurried through the crowd. His once-white coat and trousers were smudged with soot. He motioned urgently for Wainwright to lean down from the chair.

"The entire attic's on fire," Rick reported, straining to keep his voice low.

The attic? Wainwright thought. *That's where Dr. Mandt is.*

"The flames dropped down into the rooms on the third level," Rick continued. "I heard small explosions, I think from the oil lamps on the walls. Then the flames spread even faster. The fire will soon be on the second level."

Wainwright realized that the explosions were caused by more than oil lamps. The maids used supply rooms on each level. They kept metal containers of coal oil there so that they could easily replenish the lamps in each room. When the fire reached those containers…

Wainwright nodded, trying not to show emotion. He straightened and faced the crowd.

"What did he tell you?" an imperious-looking gentleman demanded.

"Just that the staff has the fire under control. But as a precaution, to be prudent, please go to one of the other buildings."

"What about my clothes?" a woman protested.

"And my jewels?" another exclaimed.

"After the danger has passed, we'll search for your valuables," Wainwright assured them.

"Now he says we're in danger!" a man yelled.

Something exploded on a level above them.

The mass of people ran toward the front doors.

* * *

Mandt almost went with them. But he was one of the few people who wore day clothes, and with two men outside watching for him, he feared he'd be easy to notice as the crowd streamed past them.

Feeling something wet on his thigh, he looked down and saw that his right trouser leg was red with blood. When he'd fallen on the stairs, the barrel of the revolver had injured him more than he'd realized. His pain worsened. Even with all the commotion, it was a wonder that someone hadn't noticed the blood and drawn attention to it. If they discovered that he couldn't speak English, if they found out he wasn't a guest here...

He stepped backward. While everyone was focused on the frenzy to escape from the building, he reached the stairs that led to the basement. The Russians might be down there, but he thought it more likely that when they'd chased him into the building and encountered the panicked crowd, they'd retreated, positioning themselves for a less public opportunity to grab him.

Limping, he descended to the corridor in the basement. The smoke hadn't reached this far, but he had no doubt that it soon would. He didn't have much time to find another way out of the building.

The odor of water again filled his nostrils. He saw a door at each end of the basement corridor and started toward the one opposite where the Russians had been hiding. But then he thought that the Russians wouldn't expect him to return to the first exit that he'd used, so he changed direction.

He passed the door behind which he again heard the voices of the elderly man and the young woman, their English unintelligible to him.

Abruptly he stopped. The lamps in the corridor showed him that the door at the end of the corridor was opening. In a rush, he veered toward the door behind which the man and the woman spoke.

When he entered, surprise made the man stop in midsentence. He was in his late sixties, so short that from a distance he might have been mistaken for a youth. The woman—beautiful despite two stitches in her cheek—paused in the act of helping him from a table. Astonishingly, his clothes were soaked. Wet sheets lay around him.

Mandt shut the door. He raised his index finger to his lips, indicating that they should be quiet.

The woman asked him something in English.

Mandt gestured more forcefully for them to be quiet.

The woman said something else, pointing toward the blood on his right leg.

When Mandt pulled the revolver from beneath his coat, the woman became silent.

The room had several lamps that reflected brightly off the white tiles of the floor and walls. Mandt saw a partition on the left and stepped behind it, continuing to aim the revolver.

"Bitte, helfen Sie mir," he said, hoping that they'd understand.

The little man surprised him by replying in German. "Help you? How?"

Mandt gaped. "You speak German?"

The little man nodded, leaning against the table. His red face was beaded with perspiration.

"Two men are searching for me. If they enter and ask if you've seen anyone, I beg you to tell them that you haven't."

"Men?"

"Russians."

"Russians?"

"Don't talk to me. Pretend that you're alone."

Mandt stepped farther behind the partition, but the man and woman could still see him aiming the revolver.

Mandt heard the door being opened. He steadied both hands on the weapon.

A voice said something in English with a Russian accent.

The woman replied in English.

The voice said something else in English with a Russian accent.

This time, it was the elderly man who replied.

Mandt heard the door being closed, rapid footsteps, then a door farther along the corridor opening.

He peered from behind the partition and studied the door. Faintly, he heard other doors being hurriedly opened.

The Russians must have been watching the entrance hall through a window, Mandt thought. *They saw me go down the stairs toward the basement.*

"Thank you," he said in German as softly as he could.

"There was only one of them," the elderly man said, bracing himself against the table.

"Then the other must be watching from outside."

Or did I manage to shoot him? Mandt wondered. *No, I can't believe my aim was that lucky.*

"What do they want?" the elderly man asked.

"I cannot tell you."

"Surely you must have some idea why two Russians are searching for you."

Mandt didn't reply.

"What you mean is you can't risk telling me," the elderly man concluded. His trembling worsened.

"You're not well," Mandt said.

"I need my medicine."

"I'm a doctor. Perhaps I can help. What disease afflicts you?"

"Laudanum." The elderly man gripped the table. "My disease is laudanum."

"Then God is the only one who can help you."

The footsteps returned rapidly along the corridor.

The woman pointed at the tiles where Mandt stood. Puzzled, he looked down and was shocked to see that the blood had reached his right boot and was trickling onto the floor.

The woman grabbed a wet sheet and threw it in Mandt's direction. As he stepped back behind the partition, the sheet landed on the blood.

At once, the door opened again.

This time, the elderly man sounded impatient, evidently asking the intruder why he kept interrupting them.

The intruder made a surly remark and closed the door.

The footsteps hurried toward the end of the corridor and faded into silence.

"Look to be certain that he's gone," Mandt said. "We need to leave. The building's on fire."

"On fire?" the little man asked in alarm. "Why didn't you tell us?"

"You'd have run instead of helping me. Stop," Mandt ordered as the woman reached for the door. "Wait. Don't go out there yet."

He heard someone shouting in the corridor.

WITH HAROLD STRUGGLING behind them, Ryan and Becker veered into the lane and ran faster toward the clinic.

Flames burst from the roof. Windows exploded on the fourth and third levels. Amid shouts, people wearing nightclothes hurried from the entrance. On the veranda, they separated, racing toward one or the other of the two buildings that flanked the middle one. As soon as they were in the open, some of them slipped in the mud and fell, but the commotion was such that no one stopped to help them up.

Guided by Dr. Wainwright, two women emerged. They clutched blankets, their attention occupied by something that one of them held. Ryan recognized them as Lady Cavendale and Mrs. Richmond. The former's face was even paler, and yet her fierce attention to her baby made her radiant.

"How did the fire start?" Ryan asked when he reached Wainwright.

"I don't know," Wainwright answered, his voice breaking. "It's all ruined. Everything's ruined."

"With all the water here, didn't you plan for a fire? Don't you have pumps?"

"Pumps? No."

"What about buckets? Your staff members can form a line and—"

"No buckets either," Wainwright said in despair.

"Did your staff members check to make certain that all the rooms are empty?"

Wainwright gave him a blank look.

Ryan cursed and spun toward Becker. "We need to find out if anybody's still inside."

"Harold!" the woman with the baby exclaimed. She and Mrs. Richmond recoiled as Harold staggered toward them and dropped the bags. "Keep him away from us!" Lady Cavendale turned sideways, protecting the baby.

"I promise he won't hurt you," Becker said.

The roar of the flames forced Ryan to speak louder. "Why are you standing here?" he told Wainwright. "Take these women and the baby to another building! Go!"

The women were already running, doing their best to make their way through the mud to the building on the left.

"What about *me?*" Harold demanded.

"You're going to help us search for anybody who might still be inside."

"You want me to go in *there?*"

"Never mind, Harold. I have a better place for you." Ryan pointed toward the local constable who hurried along the lane, shielding his eyes from the blaze.

"How can I help?" the constable asked, out of breath.

Ryan showed his badge. "Do you have a jail?"

"Yes, but I almost never need to use it."

"Tonight, you do. This man's under arrest for murder."

"You arrested Lord Cavendale's son? That can't be true."

"He killed his father."

"God save us," the constable murmured.

"It's a lie!" Harold protested.

"Shut up, Harold." Ryan returned his attention to the constable. "Lock him up until I can arrange for his transport into London."

"Wait!" Becker yelled to Wainwright. "Where are Emily and her father? Which building did they run to?"

Wainwright looked back at him, seeming to wonder what in the world he was talking about. Then he suddenly realized. "The basement!"

"What?"

"They're in a treatment room in the basement!"

"In the…Oh my God," Ryan said.

THEY CHARGED THROUGH the open doors, coughing from smoke that swirled along the ceiling. Amid the fire's roar, something crashed on the floor above them.

They ran to the staircase, where flames blocked the upper level.

"If there's anybody up there, we can't help them," Becker said.

Ryan nodded. "Yes, the only people we can try to help now are Emily and her father."

They hurried down the stairs to a dimly lit basement corridor.

"Emily!" Becker shouted. "Mr. De Quincey! Are you down here?"

Smoke drifted down the stairs.

"Maybe they smelled the smoke and ran out of the building," Becker said, hoping.

"But maybe they didn't. Check the rooms on that side. I'll check the ones over here. Emily! Mr. De Quincey!"

Ryan opened a door and saw only shadows.

He opened another door. The smell of warm water was almost overpowering.

Movement to his right made him turn.

Becker was staring into a room, raising his arms as though someone threatened him. Seeming to obey an order, Becker stepped inside.

MANDT COULDN'T STOP the revolver from shaking, even though he grasped it with both hands.

The young man who raised his arms and entered the room had a scar on his chin. Tall enough to look menacing, he said something to the young woman and the elderly man. What saved his life was that he seemed to address them by their names and that he spoke English without a Russian accent.

"This man's a friend," the elderly man told Mandt in German. "He can help you against the Russians."

"How?"

"He's a police detective."

"No!"

"He'll protect you, I promise!"

The man with the scar turned his head and called to someone in the corridor.

To Mandt's increasing dismay, a second man appeared, in his forties, with red hair. The newcomer held up a police badge as smoke drifted into the room.

"We can't wait any longer," the little man told Mandt. He sagged against the woman. "You need to trust them. We need to leave."

THE RUMBLE OF the fire made Ryan think of a rapidly approaching train.

They reached the staircase, but the area at the top was completely obscured by smoke.

"Maybe it's *only* smoke." Ryan coughed. "Maybe the flames haven't reached there yet." He started to climb.

"Wait," Becker warned.

He raced back to the room and returned with an armful of the drenched sheets that had littered the floor. He gave one to Ryan and one to the German. He draped one over Emily's head and another over her father. He put one over himself.

Ryan led the way up the staircase. He raised a hand and waved it back and forth, trying to clear the smoke enough so that he could glimpse what was beyond it.

A section of fiery wood plummeted to the floor in front of him, landing with an impact so powerful that it shoved him back.

He forced himself to take another step, and a searing arc of flame whipped toward him.

"We'll never get through!" Becker yelled.

They retreated to the bottom. There was a door at each end. Ryan led the way to the exit on the right only to realize that Emily's father was too dazed to match his pace. He lifted De Quincey into his arms, amazed by how little he weighed, and half ran to the door at the far end of the corridor.

But even as he came near it, he saw smoke seeping under the bottom of the door.

Becker rushed ahead of him.

"The knob might be hot!" Ryan warned.

But Becker anticipated that, bundled the wet sheet over his right hand, and twisted the metal doorknob.

Steam rose from the wet cloth.

Becker tugged at the door, and the sudden explosion of flames propelled them backward. The German fell. Becker hauled him to his feet.

"Emily, are you all right?" Becker asked.

"Yes!"

They ran to the door at the opposite end of the corridor, but smoke seeped beneath it also, and the crackle on the other side made it obvious that there wasn't any hope in that direction.

Flames appeared through the smoke on the ceiling.

The German moaned.

"*This* way," Ryan told them, carrying De Quincey.

"Where? There's no other exit," Becker said.

"Hurry!"

Ryan remembered the door that he'd opened and the overpowering smell of water. There hadn't been a chance to step into the room when he'd glanced to the right and seen Becker raising his arms. But now he shouldered the door farther open. Although the area was in darkness, its echo indicated that it was immense, and the light from the lamps in the corridor reached far enough to reflect off a huge pool, perhaps forty feet square.

De Quincey coughed as more smoke descended from the ceiling. Embers dropped, hissing in the water.

Emily and the German made their way down steps at the edge of the pool. The water came to Emily's waist.

After setting De Quincey in her arms, Ryan noticed a long metal table next to the pool.

"Becker!"

They dragged it to the pool and tilted it down so that two legs sat on the rim while the other two legs were in the water, forming a shelter.

After doing the same with another long metal table, they hurried down the steps and crouched in the water. Ryan's soaked clothes weighed on him. The water was warm—evidently pumped through a boiler. But soon it would get much warmer, he knew.

More flames burst from the ceiling, allowing him to see how severely De Quincey trembled.

Emily held her father and stroked his forehead.

"Mr. De Quincey," Ryan said, "I have your medicine."

Both he and Emily looked stunned.

Ryan pulled the bottle from a coat pocket. "I took the liberty of removing it from your travel bag."

Ryan broke the bottle's seal as De Quincey grabbed for it.

"Not too much at once," Ryan cautioned. "Please give him to me, Emily."

He pulled the cork from the small bottle, then put an arm around the tiny, trembling man and held his head above the water while using his other hand to lift the bottle to De Quincey's lips.

A chunk of burning wood fell from the ceiling and splashed into the far end of the pool. With a hiss, steam rose.

"How far we have come from last December." Ryan withdrew the bottle after De Quincey swallowed from it. "Three months ago, I condemned you. Now I not only provide laudanum to you, I help you drink it."

With his arm around De Quincey, Ryan shifted him onto his back so that the little man floated in the water. He was reminded of the way Lady Cavendale had clung to her baby.

The smoke sank lower.

Emily coughed.

"Breathe through the wet sheet," Becker told her.

A bigger chunk of burning wood fell from the ceiling, thrusting a huge wave across the pool.

"Get under the tables," Ryan urged. "There's room enough to keep our heads above water."

Ryan crouched, pulled De Quincey under the table, and held him in a floating position.

"Here's another sip," he said, raising the bottle to the tiny man's lips.

A fiery beam almost struck the tables, hurling water over them.

"Hold tightly to the bottle," De Quincey said. "Don't spill it."

"I promise to guard it," Ryan said.

The smoke was almost upon them.

"Put the wet sheets over your heads," Becker urged.

Ryan used one sheet to cover both him and De Quincey. The rippling light coming through the sheet revealed that De Quincey's face had started to lose some of its anguish.

"Again," the little man said.

"Just a sip," Ryan told him. "Then you'll need to wait for a while."

"Yes. Yes. Just a sip."

Ryan gave it to him, then corked the bottle and put it in his coat pocket.

Despite the wet sheet over them, the smoke stung Ryan's throat. He coughed again. So did De Quincey.

So did Emily, Becker, and the German.

Objects clanged off the tables and splashed into the pool.

De Quincey told Ryan, "The German said that two Russians were hunting him. He said he was a doctor. That's the most I was able to learn."

"Why would two Russians be hunting a German doctor?" Ryan asked.

"Indeed." De Quincey coughed. "Another sip, please."

"Not for half an hour." Ryan felt like a father speaking sternly to his young boy.

More objects fell and hissed. More waves swept over them amid the thunder of collapsing debris.

"I'm having trouble breathing," De Quincey said.

"As am I," Ryan admitted.

"Father, are you all right?" Emily's voice came muffled from the wet sheet that covered her head.

"Much better now that I have my medicine. And *you*, Emily?"

"If we survive this, what is the one thing that you'd most like to do?"

De Quincey coughed. "Go to the chophouse in Soho again. To finish the dinner that the four of us so looked forward to on Thursday night."

Becker's muffled voice joined the conversation. "Then that's what we'll do."

A cluster of objects cascaded into the pool. The sound of their impact against the metal table was deafening. It threatened to collapse.

After stifling a cough, De Quincey said something in German.

The man they were trying to protect responded in kind.

"What did you ask him?" Ryan wanted to know.

"Where we should take him if we survive this."

"And what did he say?"

"That Dr. Wainwright would know. Another sip, please."

A half an hour hadn't passed, but Ryan felt heat around him and thought, *What difference will it make? We're all going to die anyhow.*

With the two of them sheltered beneath the wet sheet, Ryan uncorked the bottle and gave De Quincey another sip.

The reference to half an hour made Ryan think of the Benson chronometer in his trouser pocket beneath the water. Imagining how much his mother would have admired it, he sadly concluded that the glorious timepiece was now ruined.

De Quincey murmured something.

"I didn't hear you," Ryan said.

"Lord Palmerston."

"What about him?"

"The German doctor. The Russians."

"I still don't—"

"This has something to do with the war."

A massive object crashed into the pool. The wave that swept over Ryan nearly submerged him. He struggled to keep De Quincey's head above water.

The smoke and the heat were becoming unbearable.

"Emily," Becker said, his voice muffled. "Are you still all right?"

She didn't reply.

"Emily?"

"I feel...drowsy."

"Poke the stitches on your cheek," Becker said urgently.

She didn't reply.

"Poke them as hard as you can. The pain might keep you awake."

Again, she didn't reply.

"Emily?" Becker asked with greater concern.

Ryan heard splashing and raised the drenched sheet. Through smoke, he saw Emily sliding under the water.

Becker grabbed her and pulled her up. "Emily, breathe!"

THERE IS NO such thing as forgetting, the Opium-Eater had written. *A thousand events impose a veil between our consciousness and the secret inscriptions of the mind, but those inscriptions remain forever, just as the stars withdraw from the light of day but are waiting to be revealed when the night returns.*

Floating on his back, supported in Ryan's arms, feeling the laudanum course through his veins, De Quincey couldn't stop his legs from twitching as they had a lifetime earlier when he'd lain next to ten-year-old Carolyn beneath a horseman's cloak in the gloomy, empty house in Soho. Starving, freezing, he'd slept and wakened, slept and wakened, often not knowing the difference between the two conditions, just as he now believed everything happening to him was an opium nightmare that he currently suffered in Edinburgh, that he'd never come to London in December, that the events of the previous three months had never occurred.

Or perhaps that opium nightmare was part of *another* nightmare, one that he endured as he slept and twitched and moaned in starving, freezing anguish next to Carolyn beneath that horseman's cloak. Perhaps the rest of his life existed only in his imagination and he was still a seventeen-year-old beggar trying to sleep on that bare, cold floor next to ten-year-old Carolyn who was haunted by rats and ghosts.

Layer upon layer. Perhaps all of this was happening after he and his beloved Ann spent a numbingly cold day begging in Oxford Street without success. Unusually light-headed, unable to tolerate food, he stumbled around the corner to Soho Square, where he slumped on the steps of a house and rested his head on Ann's bosom. He sank from her arms and fell onto the steps, certain that he was dying. Uttering a cry of terror, Ann ran back to Oxford Street and returned with a glass of spiced wine that she'd bought with some of her few pennies even though she could scarcely afford the necessities of life herself and knew that he would never be able to repay her. The spiced wine restored him sufficiently that she managed to get him to his feet and take him to the wretched Greek Street house, where Carolyn cried out when she saw him stagger inside. She and Ann had nursed him back to as much health as he could hope for.

Perhaps his head was still slumping away from Ann's bosom. Perhaps he was still losing consciousness, toppling onto the steps in Soho Square.

Something jostled him. He heard faint voices: "Water's getting warmer," "Air's like a furnace," "Can't—"

"Breathe, Emily!" Becker yelled as she spit out water and managed to inhale.

Another massive burning object plunged into the pool. The wave that swept over Ryan and De Quincey filled Ryan's nostrils. He spit out hot, gritty water.

Next to him, Becker coughed painfully and held the drenched sheet to his and Emily's face.

The smoke wavered, revealing a door on the opposite wall.

Probably the boiler room, Ryan thought. *It needs to be close to the pool.*

The boiler.

What about it? The pump. Think. The pump.

Where does the water come from?

Continuing to hold De Quincey in his arms, Ryan squirmed from beneath the protection of the metal table and climbed the steps from the pool. Water dripped from him, the rush of hot air around him almost overwhelming.

"Becker, bring Emily and the German!"

"Where are you going?"

"It might be our only chance!" Ryan shouted amid the roar.

A chunk of burning wood walloped onto the tiles in front of him. He staggered around it, stepped over a fiery plank, winced from the burning sensation that came through his trouser legs, and kicked debris away from the door.

"Becker, where are you?" Ryan couldn't get a grip on the doorknob while holding De Quincey. "I need you to—"

Becker rushed in front of him, covered the doorknob with the wet sheet, and turned it, but the door wouldn't open.

"Something's blocking it!"

Becker raised a boot and kicked, then kicked again. The door jolted open far enough for Becker to urge Emily through. Ryan went next, squeezing sideways with De Quincey. Becker and the German followed.

The instant they entered the room, a post thundered down behind them, thrusting flames and sparks into the room.

"Sean, your trousers!" Becker yelled. He flung the wet sheet around Ryan's legs, smothering the steam that rose from them.

The light from the fire revealed the boiler and a pump, crushed by a fallen beam.

"There!" Ryan shouted, pointing.

Beyond the boiler was a low, narrow tunnel made of stone blocks. It provided access for several pipes to enter the building.

"We'll need to crawl! Mr. De Quincey, can you do that?"

"I crawl perfectly."

Ryan set De Quincey down, sank to his hands and knees, and squirmed forward into the darkness. The smell of moisture and mold was strong. Pipes scraped his right shoulder. The stone ceiling grazed his back. His hands touched water leaking from one of the pipes.

Behind him, he heard labored breathing as De Quincey, Emily, Becker, and the German struggled after him. The dark tunnel became lower and narrower, squeezing him on every side. He had difficulty drawing enough air into his lungs.

"Sean," Becker murmured with effort from behind him, "if the tunnel gets any smaller…"

Ryan didn't reply. He just kept squirming forward into the unseen.

"Father?" Emily asked. "Are you all right?"

"I've endured worse opium nightmares than this," De Quincey assured her.

The right knee on Ryan's trousers tore open from the rough surface of the stone blocks.

His head struck something.

A dead end, he thought in a panic. But then he groped forward and touched stone steps.

"Sean, why did you stop?" Emily asked, her voice reverberating off the close walls.

Ryan felt to the right and found that the pipes ascended from the ground, presumably from a spring. He dragged himself up the steps and reached a hatch, but when he tried to work its handle, it didn't move.

Fighting to breathe, he pressed his back against the hatch and strained upward, but he still couldn't budge it.

Something rattled on the other side.

A lock! he realized.

He pawed along the sides of the hatch and found two hinges on the right. He pulled his knife from beneath his right trouser leg, wedged it beneath the top hinge, and pried.

The hinge loosened, the tunnel's dampness having softened the wood.

"Sean, what's wrong?" Becker asked.

Too breathless to answer, Ryan pried with greater urgency. He felt a surge of emotion when the hinge fell away, clattering onto the stone steps.

He shifted his knife to the bottom hinge, digging and twisting with the blade. If he'd had air in his lungs, he'd have shouted in triumph when the hinge dropped free, also clattering down the steps.

He braced his back against the hatch, strained upward, and, with a sudden cracking sound, the hatch burst open.

Breathing greedily, he crawled from the opening, pulled De Quincey after him, and slumped onto the cold, wet ground. As Emily and Becker struggled from the tunnel, Ryan blinked from the harsh light of the inferno roaring near him.

Then the German's head appeared in the exit from the tunnel, and Ryan lunged to shove him back inside.

The German exclaimed in fright.

"Sean, what are you doing?" Becker asked.

"The Russians will be watching. To stop them from following him, we need to make them believe he's dead. Mr. De Quincey, tell this man to stay in the tunnel until I work out how to do this."

De Quincey did what Ryan requested, translating the instructions into German.

A wave of heat swept over Ryan as a section of the burning building crashed inward.

"Mr. De Quincey, tell the German to lie perfectly still. Becker, help me drag him out as if he's seriously hurt and probably dead."

After De Quincey translated, Ryan grabbed the German's right arm while Becker grabbed his left. They pulled him from the opening.

"Emily, pretend to look for a pulse. Do what you'd normally do to determine if someone is alive."

Without a pause, Emily followed his instructions. She felt the German's wrists and neck. She listened to his chest, put a hand below his nostrils, and examined his eyes. In an intimate act that puzzled Ryan, she even felt beneath the German's trouser cuffs, touching the lower part of his legs.

"Now stand up and shake your head. Raise your hands and lower them as if to say there's nothing to be done," Ryan said.

Again, she obeyed.

A figure ran toward them. Ryan prepared to defend himself but then realized that the man rushing toward him was Dr. Wainwright.

"Thank heaven you're safe," Wainwright said, then faltered at the sight of the man on the ground.

"What do you know about him?" Ryan asked. "He's a German doctor who was hiding in the clinic."

"A German doctor? I have no idea what he—"

"Before you tangle yourself in lies," Ryan said, "he told us that if he survived, you'd be able to inform us where to take him."

"I…My God, he looks dead."

"Do you in fact know where to take him?"

After a moment's hesitation, Wainwright said, "Yes. If he's dead, though, what's the point?"

"He *isn't* dead, but we want the Russians to think he is."

"You mean you also know about the *Russians?*"

"Pretend to examine him. Emily already did and acted as if she thought he couldn't be helped. Now it's your turn to examine him."

"Examine him?"

"That's what I said. If the Russians are watching, we don't want them to have any doubts."

Wainwright did what he was told, but he didn't act with the confidence that Emily had shown, and he didn't put a hand under the German's nostrils or examine his pupils.

"Aren't you going to feel his ankles?" Emily asked.

"Why in the world would I do that?"

"One of the first indications of death is the loss of heat in the lower legs," Emily answered.

Wainwright looked confused.

"Emily, perhaps you won't need to send the telegram we discussed," De Quincey said.

"Indeed, Father."

"Telegram?" Becker asked. "What telegram?"

"This man doesn't know what's he's doing," Emily told the group. "Today, Father and I planned to send a telegram to the University of Edinburgh inquiring if they had a record of Dr. Wainwright graduating from its medical school. We can save ourselves the expenditure from our meager finances. Even the most incompetent physician would know all the ways to determine if someone is dead."

"Who *are* you?" Ryan asked Wainwright.

Wainwright hesitated. "No one." His voice wavered. His silvery mustache no longer appeared lustrous. "As of tonight, I'm no one."

Another massive section of the building collapsed into the flames.

"Mr. De Quincey, please tell the German to allow us to carry him as if he's a corpse," Ryan said.

De Quincey did so. "Inspector, may I now have more medicine?" he added in English.

Ryan reached into his sodden coat and gave the bottle to him. Then he gripped the German's arms while Becker grabbed the feet. They lifted him and walked in a stooped position, suggesting the awkwardness of carrying a deadweight.

Blessedly, the air became colder as they lurched away from the blaze.

"Emily, we brought your travel bags from Lord Cavendale's house," Becker said.

"Did you hear that, Father?" she asked. "We'll soon have dry clothes."

But De Quincey lingered as Wainwright stared hopelessly at the burning clinic.

"*Mr.* Wainwright"—De Quincey pointedly didn't address him as Doctor—"you told Emily and me that members of the peerage felt the need for this clinic and encouraged you to open it."

Wainwright kept staring at the inferno, its flames illuminating his features, emphasizing their despair.

"Am I correct in concluding that it was actually Carolyn who encouraged you to open the clinic and that it is in fact she who owns it?" De Quincey asked.

"Carolyn," Wainwright said.

"Am I also correct that it was she who asked you to hide the German, at the request of Lord Palmerston?" De Quincey continued.

"Everything's ruined."

"We don't have much time. We must find a means to speed the German away," De Quincey said.

TWELVE

THE FIELD-WORKER AND THE ADDER

At six thirty in the morning, Commissioner Mayne arrived on the first train out of London. Late the previous night, a messenger had come to his house in Belgravia's Chester Square, knocking solidly on his door. Wakened, Mayne had dressed quickly and accompanied the messenger to the prime minister's residence, where he was ordered to go to Sedwick Hill and tell Ryan and Becker to report to him at once.

No explanation was provided. On reflection, however, Mayne wasn't surprised, given the way Lord Palmerston and his home secretary had arranged for Daniel Harcourt's documents to disappear before the police could use them to investigate Harcourt's murder. Now the prime minister seemed determined to restrict *another* area of the investigation.

Even fewer people were on the train than Commissioner Mayne had expected. After the guard unlocked the otherwise empty compartment, Mayne stepped onto the lonely platform and saw a dark cloud of smoke hovering outside town.

"Is that smoke coming from the water-cure clinic?" Mayne asked the ticket agent.

"Worst trouble we ever had. Most of the jobs in town are lost."

"I need a carriage to take me there."

"You won't find one. Every vehicle has been hired."

"It appears that they're returning."

Wagons and carriages rattled toward the station. Dozens of men and women—several without travel bags and wearing overcoats that appeared to cover nightclothes—hurried from the vehicles, surprising the ticket agent with demands to reach London or Manchester or wherever without delay.

Mayne hired a wagon driver to take him to the origin of the smoke, where he discovered that there were plenty of other angry, impatient people who wanted immediate transportation to the railway station.

The destruction was shocking. Flames had totally consumed the largest of three buildings. Smoldering timbers lay in a huge, wide tangle, the grass scorched around them. The bitter taste of the smoke hung everywhere.

He asked the people climbing into the wagon if they could direct him to Scotland Yard detectives Ryan and Becker, but no one knew anything about detectives being in the area, although they added that the man in charge of the clinic ought to be put in jail for operating a firetrap.

"Commissioner!" someone yelled.

Mayne turned and saw Ryan hurrying toward him from the building on the left. Ryan's face was pinched with fatigue, his cheeks streaked with soot. Puzzlingly, he wore a white coat and trousers, as if he were a medical attendant.

"The only dry clothes available," Ryan explained.

Mayne soon learned about the alarming events of the night before: Lord Cavendale's murder, the attack on Emily, and the fire.

"The world has gone insane," the commissioner said. "Where is Lady Cavendale?"

"She and her mother returned to Lord Cavendale's house," Ryan told him. "They're preparing to go to London to arrange the funeral. Lady Cavendale indicated that she intends to spend her year of mourning at her mother's Park Lane residence."

As they spoke, Ryan led Mayne toward the large structure on the left. Numerous agitated people hurried from it, carrying travel bags.

"Stop!" Ryan showed them his badge. "We need to speak with all of you in case you noticed anything that will help us investigate the—"

Ryan might as well have been speaking to a windstorm. They swept past him with relentless force.

In the lobby, Mayne saw De Quincey and Emily.

"I'm very sorry, Emily," the commissioner told her, shaking his head forlornly at the stitches on her cheek. "Indeed, the world has gone insane."

Becker joined them, he too wearing the white trousers and jacket of a medical attendant. "I asked all the guests if they knew how the fire started. Most of them merely said, 'Do you realize who I am?' and shoved past me."

"I think we probably know how the fire started," Ryan said.

"Yes, the man who was hiding here," De Quincey agreed.

"Someone was hiding here?" Mayne asked.

The conversation stopped as four men carried a coffin through the lobby.

"A beggar," Ryan answered. "It appears he sneaked inside to protect himself from last night's storm. The smoke killed him. The doctor in charge of the clinic doesn't recognize him, and everyone on the guest list has been accounted for. We suspect he lit a candle and knocked it over, starting the fire."

"There'll need to be an inquest," the commissioner said.

"Of course. But like so many beggars, he'll probably never be identified."

"You're not usually this quick to give up on something, Ryan."

"It was a tiring night, sir."

"Evidently."

Becker interrupted the conversation and changed the subject. "Commissioner, if you didn't know about the fire, why did you come here?"

"Lord Palmerston wants the two of you to return to London and report to him at once."

"At once? But we're not finished here," Becker said. "Did he tell you why he wants us to report to him?"

"He seemed very angry that you two are here."

"Another avenue of the investigation that he doesn't want explored?" De Quincey asked. "Perhaps I can resolve the problem if I speak with His Lordship alone."

"W<small>ITHOUT</small> <small>QUESTION</small>, <small>THE</small> funeral must occur at Westminster Abbey," Carolyn told Stella. "Lord Cavendale's family name and his government service merit it. Afterward, a train will transport him back here, where his coffin can be placed in the family mausoleum next to his parents and sweet little Jennifer."

They were alone in Stella's chambers in the dismal, cold house. Assisted by Carolyn rather than a servant, Stella put on a mourning dress of the darkest crepe.

"I promise that the funeral will be exemplary." Despite her fatigue, Carolyn mustered the energy to remain in motion, fastening the stays at the back of Stella's dress. "No member of the peerage will be able to find fault. We'll prove that we're as distinguished as *they* are."

Carolyn's left knee buckled. She regained her balance and put a mourning cap on Stella's head, then lowered the dark veil over Stella's pale, radiant features.

"Always hate them," Carolyn said. "Never weaken. It's in their nature to look down on us, but apart from the accident of their breeding, they aren't any better than *we* are. Hate will give us the strength to raise ourselves until only the queen and the prince will dare to look down on us."

Again, Carolyn's left leg faltered.

"You're exhausted," Stella told her. "You ought to rest."

"You haven't rested either."

"But I'm not in my sixties."

"We'll rest when we reach Park Lane this afternoon. Meanwhile, my telegram should have arrived there. Edward will waste no time informing Harold's creditors that I'll no longer pay his debts. By day's end, wagons will arrive to seize every stick of furniture in this house and every implement in the barns and the fields. Harold will learn what it feels like to be penniless."

"Truly, you ought to sit down."

Carolyn considered Stella's mourning costume and shook her head. "It will do only until we reach Park Lane. Lord Cavendale's friends in the peerage will criticize you for wearing a bereavement dress that they recognize from Jennifer's funeral two years ago. I'll send for the best dressmaker in London. He'll arrive in the darkest of coaches with the blackest of horses. None of your neighbors will be able to complain that the proper observances weren't made. Your bereavement costume will be the most remarkable that anyone in the peerage has ever seen, because none of them has the resources to afford it."

A knock on the door distracted her. "Yes? What is it?"

"Little Jeremy has wakened," a servant's voice informed them.

Stella quickly opened the door.

The servant did her best not to react to the gloom of Stella's dress.

"Is he ill?" Stella asked. "Is he coughing? Does he have a fever? Last night's storm nearly killed him."

"No, Lady Cavendale. Little Jeremy wakened in the finest of health."

"Did he accept the wet nurse?"

"Yes, my lady."

Carolyn watched Stella disappear along the hallway. Only then did she allow herself to move toward a chair near a window. Beyond the glass, she saw the bleak smoke hovering over the remnants of the water-cure clinic. It was a serious setback, but she reminded herself that her life had been filled with setbacks. They made her only more determined.

Before she could sit, a male servant arrived. "The local undertaker is here, Mrs. Richmond. He brought his best coffin. He's in the parlor."

Carolyn nodded and left the room. *His best?* she thought. *I'll purchase it to transport Lord Cavendale's body to London. But for the funeral, I'll buy the most expensive coffin from the most respected undertaker in the entire city. No—in the entire nation.*

The servant followed her down the staircase, adding, "And there's someone here to speak with Lady Cavendale."

"Who?"

"Someone from the water-cure clinic."

"Dr. Wainwright?"

"No, madam. I've never seen him before."

"Tell the undertaker I'll speak with him in a moment."

"Very good, Mrs. Richmond."

As the servant walked toward the parlor, Carolyn proceeded to the entrance hall and did her best to keep her left leg steady.

She told the footman at the door, "You may go to the kitchen and take some refreshment."

"Thank you, madam."

When the footman was no longer visible, Carolyn opened the door.

The man who stood there wore the white trousers and coat of a medical attendant. "I need to speak to you and Stella."

"You're insane to have come here."

"It's my only chance."

"Midnight," Carolyn said. "At the Bloomsbury house."

"THIRD CLASS?" HAROLD asked.

"Be glad I'm not making you walk," Ryan said.

Harold gasped when he peered into the third-class train carriage, which didn't have compartments but was instead a large open area that resembled a livestock enclosure.

Normally, only laborers stood in it, but this morning, so many guests from the clinic wanted to return to London that, after the first- and second-class compartments had been taken, the numerous remaining passengers grudgingly shared these close quarters, enduring the gross indignity of touching one another.

They might have grumbled less if they'd been allowed to receive newspapers at the clinic. Then they'd have known about Daniel Harcourt's murder and the other incidents involving trains. They'd have perhaps decided that they weren't so eager to board a train after all. Rather than fear for their lives twice in so short a time, they might gladly have paid for wagons to take them where they wished to go.

Becker stood next to Ryan, scanning the crowd.

He watched a coffin being loaded onto the freight carriage. Presumably one of the Russians watched it also.

Becker turned his attention toward the many passengers boarding the second-class carriages. Because he knew what to look for, he noticed a stooped, elderly woman wearing a veil. She needed assistance climbing into a compartment.

The man who was kind enough to help her wore a shapeless trades-man's coat and a plain hat. Without his silvery mustache and his aloof manner, Wainwright was difficult to identify.

Becker again looked at Ryan. "There's room in the commissioner's compartment."

"I wouldn't dream of making Emily sit near the man who whipped her," Ryan said.

"The *police* commissioner?" Harold brightened. "Take me to him. He'll insist that you remove these handcuffs."

"Get on the blasted train, Harold."

As Ryan shoved him into the congestion of the third-class carriage, Becker walked toward the front of the train. He entered a compartment where Emily, her father, and Commissioner Mayne waited. Despite the demand for seats, the commissioner had used his authority to make certain that no one else joined them.

"All of you look exhausted. After everything you've been through, I won't be offended if you sleep on the way to London," Mayne said.

"We have too much to discuss," De Quincey told him, fingering his laudanum bottle. "Emily, did you remain in the telegraph office and make certain that the operator sent all our messages?"

"When have I ever not been thorough, Father?"

"Good. Responses ought to arrive at Lord Palmerston's house by this evening. Commissioner, I need the help of a half a dozen constables who wear street clothes instead of uniforms."

"Street clothes?"

"And Sergeant Becker, I need you to tell me about the fire on the train Saturday night," De Quincey said.

* * *

Lᴏʀᴅ Pᴀʟᴍᴇʀsᴛᴏɴ sᴀᴛ at his breakfast table and considered the tea, toast, butter, marmalade, bacon, and soft-boiled egg before him.

"My lord, is the preparation of the food not acceptable?" a servant asked.

"I don't seem to have an appetite," he replied. He attempted a sip of tea but had difficulty swallowing.

"Perhaps some porridge would be more to your liking," the servant suggested.

"No. Please take everything away."

Another servant entered. "My lord, the person you sent for has arrived."

Finally, Lord Palmerston thought.

He set his embroidered napkin on the table, waited for the servant to pull back his chair, and stood. He straightened his shoulders and expanded his chest, trying to give the impression of youth.

But when he walked along a corridor and reached the entrance hall, he found only Edward Richmond waiting for him, not Carolyn. Richmond's suit, goatee, and walking stick looked as elegant as usual.

But Edward didn't offer his customary winning smile. "Good morning, Prime Minister."

"Richmond?" Lord Palmerston tried not to sound disappointed. "I thought that perhaps Carolyn would join you."

"She has yet to return from Sedwick Hill. In fact, she sent me a telegram with unfortunate news."

Lord Palmerston braced himself. After the near explosion of the railway trestle the previous night, the last thing he needed was additional bad news.

"I regret to say that Lord Cavendale was murdered last night," Edward said.

"Murdered?"

"By his son."

Lord Palmerston felt as though he'd been struck. He hadn't been close to Lord Cavendale, but that didn't matter. The death of any peer was a blow to every other peer, a reminder that despite the lofty position with which God had provided them, all were finally indeed mortal.

"Surely I didn't hear you correctly. His *son* killed him?"

"To inherit his father's estate and pay his gambling debts," Edward replied. "I'm afraid that Carolyn sent another piece of unhappy news."

"Another?"

"Dr. Wainwright's hydropathy clinic was destroyed in a fire last night."

Lord Palmerston tried to retain the appearance of steadiness. *Dr. Mandt,* he thought. *What happened to Dr. Mandt?*

"My lord, do you feel ill?" Edward asked.

"Over the weekend, the war required me to attend many late-night strategy meetings."

"I'm certain that your responsibilities are extremely stressful. If you'll kindly explain why you sent for me, I'll leave you to your demanding schedule."

"Let's talk upstairs."

As they climbed, Edward said, "Your messenger indicated that there were important reasons for me to enter your house through the servants' door at the back. I confess that I'm curious about the motive for the subterfuge."

"Given the damage to the economy because of the attacks on the railways, I didn't think it wise for you to be seen visiting me publicly here or at Downing Street or for me to be seen visiting you in Park Lane. The world might wonder why I'm consulting a financial expert who isn't associated with the government when my chancellor of the Exchequer is readily available. It might suggest a lack of confidence in him."

"The person to consult about financial matters is indeed your chancellor of the Exchequer," Edward noted.

"Unless the financial matters I wish to discuss aren't related to the government."

They reached the next level. Opposite the ballroom, the library beckoned. After Lord Palmerston closed the door behind them, they sat, facing each other.

"Please tell me the problem," Edward said.

"Although the Stock Exchange hasn't yet opened this morning, I'm curious whether you've heard any predictions about the railway shares," Lord Palmerston began.

"The consensus is that there'll be a further twenty percent decline in prices. Not only for railway stocks but for those in related areas such as mining, manufacturing, and shipping."

Lord Palmerston wasn't able to speak.

"It was inevitable," Edward said. "These are new conditions. The market needs time to adjust."

"How long will that take?"

"There's no way to anticipate, but I assure you the market *will* absorb the recent shocks. It always does. If anything, this is an opportunity."

"I don't understand."

"To buy," Edward explained.

"My intention was the opposite."

Edward frowned. "Are you telling me you have financial pressures that require you to sell stocks?"

"After the uncommonly harsh winter in Ireland, the farmers on my properties there aren't able to pay their rents. Without that income…"

"How urgent are your debts?"

"A mortgage payment for this house is due in three days. Normally that wouldn't be a problem, even without the rents. But the social duties of being prime minister are greater than I anticipated. The past six weeks, since I assumed office, have drained my reserves. Today, I planned to sell some of my railway stocks, but I made that plan before everything happened. With the value of the stocks sharply reduced…"

"I can't recommend selling those stocks."

"But I don't have an alternative."

"A short-term loan is a better solution," Edward told him. "When the railway stocks rebound, as they certainly will, you can sell them without penalizing yourself. The interest on the loan would be considerably less than the pain you would feel if you sold your stocks for a fraction of their value. What is the size of your obligations?"

"Ten thousand pounds."

Edward paused at the gravity of the amount. "If I go immediately to the City, I can make arrangements for the loan by the end of the day."

"But the lenders can't know who receives the money," Lord Palmerston warned. "If rumors spread that the prime minister has financial difficulties, the Stock Exchange will interpret that as a further sign the nation is in peril."

"I can process the loan so that no one knows who requires the money," Edward assured him. "But the financiers will ask for collateral."

"Do you think they'd consider accepting my railway stocks as collateral?"

"Because those stocks have lost considerable value, the financiers will probably require your mining, manufacturing, and shipping stocks as additional collateral. Perhaps..."

"What are you thinking?"

"To prevent anyone from knowing about this, I'll finance the loan myself."

At Whitehall's police station, the grizzled jailer listened with great interest as Ryan removed Harold's handcuffs and explained the charges against him.

"Smothered your father, did ya?" the wizened man asked. "Whipped your father's widow and then the widow's mother, just to be thorough?"

"All right, I admit to whipping them," Harold conceded, "but I had nothing to do with—"

"He also whipped a good friend of mine," Ryan said. "Cut her face."

"Thorough indeed," the jailer declared.

"This is lunacy! Wait until the home secretary hears what you've done to me!" Harold protested.

"I'll make certain that Sir George knows," Ryan said. "He'll be interested to learn about your brother also."

"My brother?"

"Two years ago, you and he went on holiday to a casino in the German States, but only you came back, I've been told. You claimed that your brother died from typhoid fever, but you didn't have a death certificate."

"The death certificate was in a travel bag that someone stole from a lodging house where I stayed!" Harold responded.

"Well, I'm certain that a telegram to the German police will confirm the cause of death," Ryan said. "But in case it doesn't, a jury might conclude that you killed your older brother so that you could replace him as the heir to your father's estate. Last night, after two years of waiting, you lost patience and killed your father also. Why don't you ease your conscience and admit it, Harold?"

"Stop calling me Harold! I'm Lord Cavendale!"

The jailer grinned, revealing gaps in his teeth. "We're not accustomed to peers visitin' us. My lord, I have a special cell for you. Step this way. Down at the end on the right. What makes it special is it don't have any drafts."

"No drafts?" Harold asked.

"Because it don't have a window. If you ask me, it's better to sit in the dark than in a draft."

"I want to see my lawyer!"

"Your lawyer's dead," Ryan pointed out.

"Then send for someone in his firm!"

The jailer scratched his hairless scalp. "Do you see any messengers here waitin' to be sent on errands?"

"Never mind. *I'll* send a messenger," Becker said. He'd been standing in the background, listening to the conversation.

Ryan turned to him in surprise.

Becker shrugged, explaining, "If we give him every advantage, the evidence will look even stronger."

"Evidence he admits he tampered with," Ryan said.

"Tampered with evidence, did ya, my lord?" the jailer asked Harold, leading him along a corridor of cells. "Busy, busy."

NUMBER 10 DOWNING Street dated back to the 1600s, when Sir Richard Downing built a row of town houses near Parliament. Three of the houses had been combined into a warren of one hundred rooms that formed the prime minister's offices and living quarters, but prime ministers seldom lived there because the ground was so soft that the floors sank, the walls tilted, and the fireplaces buckled.

Sitting dismally behind his desk, Lord Palmerston stared at a crack in the wainscoting across from him, a crack that seemed to have widened since he'd become prime minister.

Someone knocked on the door.

"Enter," he said wearily.

An assistant stepped inside. "Prime Minister, two police detectives are here to see you. They say you're expecting them."

"Show them in," Lord Palmerston said.

"Two other people are with them, my lord."

"Two others?"

"A short elderly man and a woman wearing what appear to be trousers under her skirt."

Lord Palmerston groaned. "Show them in also."

"Begging your pardon, Prime Minister, but the little man says that it would be better if he first spoke with you alone."

Lord Palmerston looked again at the crack in the wainscoting, which now seemed even wider.

He sighed and nodded.

De Quincey entered, clutching his laudanum bottle as if it were a talisman. "My lord, thank you for—"

Something next to Lord Palmerston's desk made De Quincey stop talking. The little man approached the wall.

"What's wrong?" Lord Palmerston asked.

"This painting. It's slightly askew."

De Quincey straightened it.

"But *this* painting is askew also. And *this* one, and *this* one."

De Quincey proceeded along the wall and straightened all the paintings.

"It won't do any good," Lord Palmerston said. "The soft earth beneath this building causes a shift in the walls. I myself have straightened those paintings several times since I became prime minister."

"With all the paintings tilted, my brain might make me believe that *I* was the one tilted," De Quincey concluded. "Not realizing, I might start to lean sideways so that the paintings and I were in agreement."

"Yes, yes. What did you wish to discuss?"

"My lord, there's a German doctor who became famous for saving the life of a field-worker."

"I'm sure that's fascinating, but please get to the—"

"In the middle of the afternoon, the field-worker felt tired and lay down in the grass to have a nap. A defect in his nostrils required him to breathe through his mouth. While he slept with his mouth open, an adder slithered into it. As several of his friends approached to waken him, they witnessed the serpent's tail disappearing into the field-worker's mouth and down his throat."

Lord Palmerston tried not to show how troubled the story made him, although not because of the snake.

"Naturally, there was a great outcry," De Quincey continued. "The other field-workers ran into town, shouting to everyone they met about the terrible calamity that had seized their friend. They dreaded what would happen when the adder realized that it was trapped in the field-worker's stomach. No doubt it would try to go back the way it had come, only to realize that some sort of obstacle—a stomach valve, but the serpent couldn't know that—blocked it. Anger or fear would compel it to thrust its fangs into the resisting object. Surely the field-worker's life could be measured only in minutes."

Lord Palmerston inwardly squirmed, aware of the story's direction.

"This happened in one of the German States. As fate would have it, a doctor was visiting the village. He hurried to an apothecary and then to the field-worker, who was by now awake, sweating in terror. The friends who'd remained with him kept warning him not to move in the slightest, lest he alarm the serpent coiled within his stomach. He lay rigidly, straining to keep his chest tight when he breathed. He felt the serpent shifting within him, tickling his stomach. His lips and mouth were dry with panic, but he didn't dare drink anything to slake his terrible thirst.

"The doctor amazed everyone by saying, 'That is exactly what you *must* do. Drink.' He opened a bottle that he'd obtained from the apothecary and made the victim swallow from it several times.

"'What's in it?' someone asked.

"'Laudanum,' the doctor replied.

"'What? But the amount you forced him to drink will kill him!' the victim's friends objected.

"'Or else it will kill the snake,' the doctor responded.

"He forced the victim to lift his head and drink from the bottle several more times. Finally, the field-worker moaned, lowered his head to the grass, and lost consciousness. When his body became still and breathless, his friends concluded that he was dead. They wept. They bemoaned the fact that God had created a world in which serpents existed. The allegory of Satan as a serpent wasn't ignored. The doctor wasn't ignored either. The crowd threatened to beat him or worse for killing their friend, but the doctor urged them to have faith. The sun sank. Darkness gathered. They covered the field-worker with a blanket, built a fire, and sat around him.

"'Trust my skills,' the doctor told them.

"The sun rose. The field-worker remained motionless. 'Send to the next village for the minister. Bring the undertaker,' the field-worker's wife told his friends, weeping. But suddenly the field-worker moaned again. His fingers twitched. His eyelids fluttered. His chest moved, and he drew a deep, anguished breath.

"'It's a miracle!' the wife exclaimed.

"'Yes, of medicine,' the doctor told her.

"The victim wasn't able to work in the fields for the next two days. His wife prepared his favorite stew and tried to make him eat some of it, but he complained of a terrible fullness of the sort that follows a banquet. It was the dead adder, of course, which he evacuated from his bowels at the end of the second day."

De Quincey sipped from his laudanum bottle.

"I see no point to your story unless you're telling me that you believe your opium habit makes you immune to adders," Lord Palmerston said.

"The doctor's name was Martin Wilhelm von Mandt," De Quincey noted.

"Mandt?" Lord Palmerston pretended to search his memory. "I don't think I've ever heard of—"

"The incident made Dr. Mandt so famous in the German States that it was printed in many newspapers, several of which I was in the habit of reading when I lived in Edinburgh and I mingled with a small German enclave there as a way to retain my fluency in German."

"I really don't have the time for this," Lord Palmerston said, standing.

"Indulge me a moment longer, my lord. The relevance will soon be obvious. The incident also made Dr. Mandt famous *outside* Germany, especially in Russia, where Czar Nicholas became so fascinated that he invited Mandt to his court at St. Petersburg and asked him to become his personal physician."

At the mention of Czar Nicholas, Lord Palmerston felt that the floor of his office was tilting.

"Last night, at the water-cure clinic in Sedwick Hill, Emily and I encountered a German doctor," De Quincey said.

Lord Palmerston sank back into his chair.

"So did Inspector Ryan and Sergeant Becker. The German doctor was terrified. Two Russians were searching for him—*hunting* him, in fact."

"Russians," Lord Palmerston murmured.

"A third Russian had also been searching for him, but the doctor later told me that when the Russian discovered him hiding in the clinic's attic, the doctor stabbed him."

Lord Palmerston felt ill.

"In the process, a lantern broke, and a fire started," De Quincey added.

Lord Palmerston now felt that he too had swallowed a serpent. "I know about the fire."

"The doctor spoke only German," De Quincey emphasized. "In the company of Emily, Inspector Ryan, and Sergeant Becker, I was the only person with whom he could communicate. He told me something that I didn't translate to the others."

"What was that?"

"His name."

Lord Palmerston let out a long breath.

"Emily, Inspector Ryan, and Sergeant Becker don't know who he is. They have no idea that he'd been the principal physician to Czar Nicholas until the czar died two weeks ago. I can think of only one reason why angry Russians would pursue him all the way to England and make him frightened enough to hide. But it's not something that I dare say aloud, even in the privacy of this office."

Lord Palmerston worked to keep his voice calm. "And where is Dr. Mandt now?"

"To stop the Russians from hunting him, Inspector Ryan and Sergeant Becker made it seem that Mandt died in the fire. Ryan arranged for a coffin to be brought to what remained of the clinic. The coffin was then taken to the local undertaker's shop, from which other coffins were soon dispatched, one to a train leaving for London, another to Lord Cavendale's house. Alive or dead, Mandt had gone in so many possible directions that the Russians were powerless to pursue all of them. Meanwhile, Wainwright and Dr. Mandt assumed disguises and escaped."

"You refer to *Dr.* Wainwright?"

"Wainwright is no more a doctor than the boy selling newspapers on the street corner. But he evidently has other skills. Mandt said at one point that if he survived the night, Wainwright would know where to take him."

Lord Palmerston hesitated, finally saying, "That is true."

"My lord, I came here to assure you that neither I nor Emily nor Inspector Ryan nor Sergeant Becker will ever reveal our suspicions about what happened at the water-cure clinic last night. In fact, Ryan and Becker helped your intentions by speeding Dr. Mandt on his way. Commissioner Mayne is totally ignorant about all of this. He believes that the coffin contains the corpse of an unidentified beggar who took shelter in the clinic during last night's storm and accidentally set the place on fire. Your secret is safe. In turn, I hope that my daughter and the others are safe."

"You think I'd harm any of them in order to protect—"

"My lord, like the paintings on your walls, the universe has tilted."

Lord Palmerston looked again at the crack in the wainscoting. "You have my word—no harm will come to them."

"Thank you, my lord. If I may be so bold as to inquire, was your tactic successful?"

"You are fearless."

"I fear only for my daughter and my friends, Prime Minister. As for me, I told you six weeks ago that I'm the only man you know who has so little regard for himself that he'll speak with you honestly."

Lord Palmerston stared at him for a long time.

Finally he nodded. "The new czar doesn't have the appetite for the war that his father did. There are signs that he cares less about the Crimea and more about the growing rebellion among his people because of food shortages caused by the war. We're planning a new offensive. I predict that hostilities will conclude by this time next year."

"But you don't sound jubilant, my lord."

"I'm reminded of something else you told me six weeks ago."

"And what was that?"

"Absolute power is an absolute burden."

"Daniel Harcourt was your attorney, my lord. When you refused to allow the police to have access to the documents in his office, was it to conceal that Harcourt helped you with projects you didn't wish anyone in the government to know about?"

"I can't answer that."

"Then perhaps you can answer *this*. Was your motive for wanting Inspector Ryan and Sergeant Becker to stay away from the water-cure clinic motivated only by your need to prevent them from learning about Dr. Mandt?"

"What other possible motive could I have had?"

"Perhaps you suspect who killed Daniel Harcourt and you want to protect his murderer."

"Protect his…Good heavens, Daniel was a friend! It pained me to interfere in the investigation."

"Then you'll no longer interfere now that Dr. Mandt is on his way to safety?" De Quincey asked. "Are Inspector Ryan, Sergeant Becker, Emily, and I at liberty to use all our skills to hunt the killer?"

"If you catch whoever did it, I myself would be tempted to act as the hangman."

HAROLD SAW NOT one but two lawyers approaching along the shadowy corridor—a solicitor *and* a barrister. He stood up excitedly from the cot in his cell.

"Skiffington and Lavery, thank you for coming!" Harold knew them not only as attorneys but as gambling companions and felt free to address them as friends. "I was beginning to despair!"

"Your legal difficulties have been explained to us," the handsomer of the two men said.

"Then you know how preposterous it all is. Prepare whatever documents you need. Get me out of this horrid place."

Both men regarded him uncomfortably.

"We decided to give you the courtesy of coming here in person," the thinner man said.

"Of course you're here in person. I can see that! Just do what's necessary to get me out of here!"

"Well," one of them said, "there's a problem."

"What do you mean?"

"Someone hired us *not* to represent you."

"*Not* to represent me?"

"Normally we wouldn't divulge a client's name, but in this case, we were specifically instructed to tell you that the person who hired us is Mrs. Edward Richmond."

"What?"

"We're not the only attorneys Mrs. Richmond hired not to represent you," the barrister said. "But leaving that aside, I don't see how any respectable solicitor and barrister would take your case. They know they'd be laughed at if they tried to defend you."

"Laughed at?"

"Consider the facts as though we're in front of a jury," the barrister suggested.

"Yes! You'll see that it's all a mistake!"

"You blame your stepmother for your father's murder."

"Don't call her my stepmother. I hate that word."

"Obviously you loathe her because she took the place of your dead mother. Logically, she's the one you'd try to cast blame upon. You have massive gambling debts, is that not correct?" the barrister continued.

"You know I have gambling debts. Some of them are owed to *you*."

"You admit to having interfered with evidence that made you look guilty."

"I didn't want anyone to think I'd—"

"Harold, keep looking at this from a jury's point of view. With your older brother in the grave—a suspicious death that I'm sure the prosecutor will explore—by right of male succession, you're the next person in line to inherit your father's estate. The widow has no rights. She always depends on the good graces of the male who inherits, and you demonstrated your new power over her by throwing her out of the house into

a hailstorm. So, tell me, Harold. What possible motive would your stepmother have had to kill your father? She had nothing to gain."

"Her motive? Well, I...if you'll give me a moment to..."

"The only person who had anything to gain from your father's death
was *you*."

A BELL RANG AS De Quincey and Emily entered the shop. An athletic-
looking man glanced up from arranging a display of pistols. Firearms
of every type—long and short, with cylinders and without—were everywhere, their gleaming metal and polished wood almost as luminous as the
offerings in a jewelry store.

The clerk assessed their nondescript clothes and the trousers beneath
Emily's skirt. He pointed to the two stitches on Emily's cheek. "Does your
injury give you pain, miss?"

"Less than it did."

"I'm pleased to hear it." The clerk put his hands on the counter. "May
I help either of you? If you'll forgive me for saying, you don't appear to be
the type to buy gentlemen's sporting firearms."

"Would you be so kind as to read this?" De Quincey asked, removing
a letter from his coat pocket.

The clerk frowned at the prominent government seal at the top of the
page. "This appears to be from the prime minister."

"That is the case. As you see, the letter asks you to give us every assistance in a police matter with which we're helping."

"My father and I have been visiting gentlemen's firearms shops,"
Emily added. "But only the best ones, which we've been told are the two
in Regent Street and this one in Oxford Street."

"There are plenty of firearms shops in London, of course," the clerk
told her, "but if anyone wants the best instead of barrels that blow up with
the slightest miscalculation of a gunpowder charge, this shop and the two
others you mentioned are the only reliable places to visit."

"We're particularly interested in the gunpowder to which you referred," Emily said.

The clerk regarded her with wonder. "I don't believe I've ever had a conversation with a woman about gunpowder."

"It's poured into the firearm and then a ball and wadding are added, is that correct?" Emily asked.

"Yes," the clerk answered in surprise.

"In what form do you sell the gunpowder?" she asked.

"A ten-pound wooden keg, such as this one." The clerk opened a cabinet door and lifted a keg from a shelf. "It's far superior to the gunpowder sold in lesser shops. They add additional powdered charcoal and multiply two kegs into three. All the diluted gunpowder does is fizzle."

Thinking of the bomb that had exploded in Waterloo Station, De Quincey rejoined the conversation. "Did a constable visit you and ask if anyone purchased gunpowder here on Friday afternoon or Saturday morning?"

"Yes. I told the constable that several people had indeed bought gunpowder from me."

"How did he react to this information?"

"He didn't seem to think it was useful."

"Oh? Why not?" Emily wondered.

"Well, what he asked was whether the wrong sort had purchased gunpowder. I assured him that the wrong sort weren't welcome in my shop. This is Mayfair, after all."

"Quite so," Emily agreed. "But of the purchases made by the *right* sort, was there anything unusual about any of them?"

"Most of the gentlemen arrived with their gamekeepers, needing advice about new firearms they intended to purchase. Sometimes the gentlemen came alone, merely to look at the firearms and then order gunpowder and ammunition. In each instance, they arranged for their purchases to be delivered to their country estates."

The clerk paused.

"Yes?" Emily asked. "Do you remember something?"

"On Friday afternoon, there was a gamekeeper who came alone. He said that his master, Lord Ashley, was interested in buying a new rifled musket for shooting stag in Scotland. The gamekeeper inspected several items and indicated that he'd pass his recommendation on to His Lordship. Meanwhile he purchased ammunition and a keg of gunpowder. He asked to have the items wrapped so that he could carry them. He was returning to Lord Ashley's country house, he said. Because I couldn't guarantee delivery until Monday, he took the gunpowder with him so that Lord Ashley wouldn't be idle over the weekend."

"How do you know the man was a gamekeeper?" De Quincey asked.

"His rustic clothes and hat, of course, and his weathered complexion."

"Do you have his name?" De Quincey asked.

"Because the keg wasn't being delivered, I didn't need his name any more than I needed Lord Ashley's address."

"Perhaps you remember more details about his appearance," Emily said.

BECKER STOOD AT the clamorous nexus of the six streets that Ryan had told him were the center of the world. He studied the immensity of the Bank of England and the eight columns of the massive Royal Exchange. Feeling overwhelmed, he assumed that the Royal Exchange was the place he needed to visit, but when he entered, he learned that its occupants were actually insurance companies. He stopped a doomed-looking man who hugged a document case to his chest and asked, "Can you tell me where stocks are bought and sold?"

"Around the corner, but God help you if you go inside."

Becker veered past carriages whose occupants appeared ready to slit their throats. He entered another columned temple, within which he encountered hundreds of desperate men shouting names, amounts, and prices.

Madness, Becker thought.

He stopped another doomed-looking man and needed to raise his voice above the din to ask, "Who do I speak to about railway stocks?"

"Heaven help you if you need to sell."

"But who do I talk to?"

"There. Over there." The pallid man stumbled out of the building.

Becker proceeded toward where the unfortunate soul had pointed, jostling his way through the agitated crowd.

A large-chested, round-faced man stood to the side, leaning against a wall, watching the spectacle with disgust.

Becker showed his badge long enough for the man to see that he was a detective but not long enough for the man to realize that the badge was for the police force of metropolitan London and not this independent district, where he didn't have jurisdiction.

"I want to talk about railway stocks," Becker said.

"Never heard of a policeman who could afford to own stocks."

"Or who was stupid enough to."

The man gave Becker a second look and laughed. "That's the first time I laughed all day. What do you want?"

"Is there any place that's quiet in here?"

"Down this hall. Here's my office."

The man led him inside, closed the door, and gestured toward a chair. "What do the police care about railway stocks?"

"Did the price go down today?"

"Like a stone in a pond. As did the prices for shipping, mining, and manufacturing stocks. Many lives were ruined. The Russians found a way to defeat us."

"Well, maybe it's not the Russians."

"What are you talking about?"

"Tell me how all of this works."

The man shrugged. "Someone wants to start a company. But he doesn't have enough money, so he sells shares to people who want to own just a part of it. If the company makes a profit, the shareholders get a percentage of it. But when all the shares are sold, other people might want to own part of the company, so they buy shares from the people who already have them. If there's enough demand, the share owners ask for more money than they paid. The Stock Exchange is a way for buyers and sellers to get together. The man who brokers the buying and selling gets a commission."

"Sounds like the man in the middle has the advantage."

The large-chested man laughed again. "What's your name?"

"Sergeant Becker."

"I'm Stephen Corey."

They shook hands.

"Just to make certain I grasp this, if something bad happens to the company, people lose their nerve and sell," Becker said. "The price goes down because hardly anybody wants to risk buying stock in a company that might fail."

"You grasp it exactly. Maybe you're in the wrong line of work. If you're interested, I could talk to someone about getting you a job here," Corey said.

"I see enough suffering as it is."

Corey laughed yet again. "I wish you'd come here three hours ago."

"So the people who buy a falling stock are betting that the company's problem will go away and the price will rise to where it was."

"That's the essence of it."

"How do I find out who's buying the railway stocks?"

THE WINDOW OF the Regent Street office displayed drawings of expensive-looking properties for sale in Mayfair. When Ryan opened the front door, a man peered up from a desk, decided that Ryan wasn't a potential client, and returned his gaze to a document on his desk.

Ryan showed his badge. "May I trouble you to answer a few questions?"

Now the man gave Ryan his full attention. "We always wish to be on good terms with the police."

"I need some information about a property."

When Ryan supplied the address, the man said, "They don't come much better."

"I could search through various public records, but I'm hoping you can save me time. Can you tell me who purchased that property and when?"

DE QUINCEY AND Emily opened the door of another shop. An elderly man with a bare pate and white whiskers stopped pouring a blue powder onto a set of scales and regarded them through his spectacles. "Good day. May I help you?"

"My daughter and I have been visiting various Mayfair chemists," De Quincey explained. "We assume that the items you and your fellow apothecaries sell are purer and safer here than in other areas of the city."

"Without question. Our competitors in Soho and farther east adulterate their products until you receive no benefit and might even be poisoning yourself."

De Quincey looked around, curious about something. "Was this shop always at this location? A little more than fifty years ago, I seem to remember coming to this very spot in Oxford Street to make my first purchase of laudanum because of a toothache."

The elderly man smiled. "My father owned this shop at that time. Laudanum, did you say? Is that what you wish to purchase?"

With a tone of defeat, De Quincey said, "Yes." He made an effort not to look at Emily. As the chemist took a bottle from a shelf, De Quincey drank the final drops from the bottle in his possession.

"Sixpence," the chemist said, frowning at the empty bottle that De Quincey set on the counter.

De Quincey put the new bottle in his coat pocket.

With a sigh, Emily pulled a silver coin from a skirt pocket and set it on the counter.

"Would you please look at this letter?" De Quincey asked.

The chemist considered the elaborate government seal. "Lord Palmerston, eh? I don't know why anyone in his borough ever voted for him."

"But you'll obey his wishes and help us?" Emily asked.

"Certainly. Can I give you something for the injury on your cheek, miss? It looks painful."

"Perhaps white vitriol would cause the swelling to shrink."

"Actually a dab of what I gave your companion would be more effective, at least for the pain."

"I believe that white vitriol is safer."

The chemist gave her a small bottle of the liquid. "No cost. It's a shame to see so pretty a woman have a blemish."

"Thank you. If the white vitriol does its work and contracts the tissue, perhaps there won't be one," Emily said.

"I hope so, miss. What is the information that Lord Palmerston asks me to give to you?"

"Did a constable come here asking if the wrong sort of person had bought red food dye from you?" De Quincey asked.

"That's exactly how he asked the question. 'The wrong sort.' I couldn't imagine why the Metropolitan Police would be interested in red food dye. At any rate, I told him that nobody who was suspicious-looking bought red dye or anything else from me."

Thinking of the man who'd vomited red liquid at Waterloo Station to distract people while he left a travel bag containing a bomb, De Quincey said, "But you did sell red food dye on Friday afternoon or Saturday morning."

"It's a popular item. Bakers use it to make their confections vivid."

The mention of baked goods caused Emily's stomach to grumble.

The elderly man pretended not to notice.

De Quincey looked around the shop and pointed at a substance in a jar of water. "Did a person who bought red food dye also buy some of *that*?"

"As a matter of fact, yes. The two hardly go together. It was an odd combination of purchases."

"But the buyer didn't look suspicious?"

"To the contrary."

"What do you mean?"

"He wore the white collar of a clergyman."

THIRTEEN

THE HOUSE IN BLOOMSBURY

A HALF HOUR BEFORE midnight, a closed carriage arrived at a fog-shrouded address in Park Lane. A man and two women, one of the latter dressed in the deepest mourning, the other needing a cane to steady her walk, departed from the mansion and climbed into the vehicle.

The driver proceeded north, turned east into deserted Oxford Street, then north along Tottenham Court Road, and then east along Francis Street. Amid Bloomsbury's numerous squares, the carriage arrived at one of the few detached houses in the area, lanes separating it from the usual array of terraced dwellings. The two-story structure was distinctive in another way: its corners were rounded, resembling squat towers.

The curtains were closed, although a gap in them revealed the light from several lamps.

"He arrived early," Edward Richmond said.

"We'll see what he wants *this* time," Carolyn said.

"For the *final* time," Stella said.

As much as they could tell from the fog-hazed streetlights, all the other windows along the street were dark.

"Come back in an hour," Edward told the driver.

They stepped from the carriage, opened a gate, passed leafless shrubs on each side of a walkway, and climbed wooden steps to the darkness of a covered porch.

Carolyn removed a key from her purse, but it wasn't necessary. She discovered that the front door was already unlocked.

After they entered, Carolyn bolted the door. The shadowy entrance hall had a table with a vase on it, but no flowers. Although the house was furnished, it had the empty feeling and the musty smell of a residence that was seldom occupied.

They turned to the left, toward the open door of a drawing room.

A tall, thin young man stood from an upholstered chair next to the hearth as coal burned and crackled in the fireplace. He no longer wore the white uniform of a medical attendant at the hydropathy clinic. Instead, his garments were those of a gentleman, clothes that the three new arrivals knew came from a wardrobe in a bedroom upstairs.

"The house was cold," he said. "I didn't see any point in having a discussion while we shivered."

But the expressions of the three people facing him were beyond cold. They were icy.

"Rick, this is the last time we'll meet," Edward said.

"I don't believe that is so," the young man replied.

"We paid you well for both your services and your silence," Carolyn said. "The contract is now complete. But we're prepared to pay you a bonus to compensate for the loss of your occupation at the clinic."

"Yes, it's only fair," Edward agreed. "You served us well by informing us about investment opportunities you heard the clinic's guests discussing. As a parting gesture, we'll pay you a bonus."

"I was promised more than money," Rick said.

"*More* than money?" Carolyn asked. "Whatever are you talking about?"

"From her." Rick pointed to Stella.

"*I* don't know what he's talking about either," Stella said from behind her widow's veil. "My husband's been murdered. Don't you have any decency? Leave me to mourn."

"We had an understanding," Rick said.

"Truly, I don't know what—"

"That we'd be married."

"Married?" Stella asked in astonishment. "I gave you no reason to—"

"Isn't siring two children with you enough reason?"

Although this wasn't a topic that could ever be discussed in polite society, neither Carolyn nor Edward was shocked—or even surprised—by the statement.

"Rick," Carolyn said, "we made you a straightforward business proposition, and you accepted. Why, after two years, are you demanding a renegotiation?"

"Because circumstances have changed. Now that Lord Cavendale is dead, Stella is free to marry. Mind you, I don't expect it to be soon. Stella's year of being sequestered in mourning needs to be observed."

"I won't marry again," Stella told him.

"Why don't we discuss this alone?" Rick pointed toward the other half of the drawing room.

"I won't allow you to be *anywhere* with me alone."

"You didn't say that when you needed my help. We were certainly alone *then*."

"Stella, perhaps the two of you could speak more freely without Edward and me in your presence," Carolyn said.

"I've spoken as freely as I intend to," Stella replied. "Are you actually suggesting that I should agree to marry him in order to buy his silence?"

"That's a crude way to put it," Rick said, "but it might give you peace of mind to know that you'd never need to fear anyone finding out that little Jeremy isn't Lord Cavendale's son."

"And if I refuse?"

"Suppose I told the newspapers. Suppose I waited outside the Parliament buildings and told every peer who emerged from the House of Lords. What would be the harm to me? Mere embarrassment. But you," he said to Stella, "and *you*," he said to Carolyn, "would lose your chance to have a family member who's a peer and who can pass his title to his oldest son. When Harold is hanged for killing his father, little Jeremy will become the next Lord Cavendale. Isn't that the success you wanted, Carolyn? To rise so high that no one can look down on you. To know that Stella's male descendants will be lords. What a triumph. But if you don't agree to my terms, I can take it all away from you just when you're on the verge of grasping it."

"We'll give you fifty thousand pounds," Edward said.

It was an immense amount, but all Rick did was shake his head. "When I marry Stella, I'll have both her *and* access to the fifty thousand pounds. In fact, to more than that. Why are you reluctant? Are you afraid that I'll embarrass you? Don't you agree that I look respectable in the fine clothes you provided for me? When I come to London, I enjoy the best theaters and restaurants and no one is the wiser that I'm not as proper as any of them. The waiters even call me sir. When I marry Stella, I too will belong to a family in the peerage—a stepfather to a lord, although of course I'm his actual father."

The coals sparked in the fireplace.

"Stella, I think your mother's suggestion is a good one. Let's discuss this alone," Rick said. Again, he pointed toward the other half of the drawing room.

Stella looked at Carolyn and then at Rick.

"Very well," she said. "We shall settle this once and for all."

As she stepped into the back part of the room, Rick struck a match and lit a gas lamp. Partitions were recessed into the wall on each side of the entrance. He drew them shut.

"STELLA, AM I so repugnant to you?" Rick asked when they were alone. "You didn't act this way when we shared a bed upstairs on numerous occasions."

Stella shuddered. "I needed to make you happy."

"You succeeded. And as my wife, you'll continue to do so, I'm certain."

"This is not a topic for decent conversation."

"Suddenly you're shy after what we experienced many times?" Rick asked.

"My mother told me that a child conceived when a male is in full passion will be stronger and healthier."

"You make it sound like two animals being matched for breeding purposes," Rick objected. "It was more than that. I proved that I'm worthy to be your husband. You have no idea what I've done to save you."

When Rick tried to grasp her hand, she stepped back, asking sharply, "What do you mean that you proved you're worthy?"

"Last week, you came to me in this house," Rick said.

"You left me no choice. When I brought my husband for therapy at the clinic, you acted so blatantly familiar with me that, to make you stop, I was forced to promise to come here."

"After you did, as you departed in your carriage, I looked out the window and noticed a man watching you from the shadows," Rick said. "The man was solidly built. His ordinary clothes suggested that he didn't belong in this neighborhood. Even though he was a stranger, I suddenly realized that I'd seen him before. At the hydropathy clinic and at train stations and in London streets. He was following you or me or both of us. I shut off the lamps, stepped from the house, and locked it. Then I walked south past the quiet of the British Museum, hearing him behind me in the darkness. I was raised in the streets. I know every dodge there is. When we reached the distraction of the noise and traffic in Oxford Street, I turned a corner, veered into a lane, ran to the end of it, and returned to the street that I'd just left, but now I was behind the man, not in front of him. Now *I* was the one doing the following.

"When he realized that I'd evaded him, he tried to find me as best he could and finally gave up. I continued to follow him until he arrived at what I discovered was his lodging in Southwark. I found a public house that could rent me a room for the night, one that had a window with a view of the street where the man's lodging was located. In the morning when he reemerged, I continued to follow him. That evening, he led me to Lombard Street. At that hour, the area was almost deserted. Because

I wore a gentleman's clothes, a constable didn't even ask me what I was doing there. I mounted the stairs that the stranger had used. I listened outside an office door and heard the stranger address someone as Mr. Harcourt. I got the impression that the office belonged to a solicitor."

"Daniel Harcourt?" Stella pressed her hands against the mourning veil that covered her face.

"I heard the stranger tell Harcourt everything about us. The stranger was a private-inquiry agent, I learned. He referred to a sketch that he'd hired a street artist to make of me. As they ended their meeting, I crept back down the stairs to the dark street. Soon the stranger departed. Soon also, the man who I assumed was Harcourt came down the stairs and hurried toward a cabstand. He clutched a document case as though its contents were precious. I followed him to Euston Station. When he bought a first-class ticket to Sedwick Hill, I could reach no other conclusion than that he was on his way to your husband's country house, where he planned to show your stepson the proof of your infidelity to his father. The lawyer was alone in a compartment when I joined him."

"*You* murdered Daniel Harcourt?" Stella asked in shock.

"There were many other times when I proved that I'm worthy. The private-inquiry agent knew about your infidelity, of course, as did his wife, who'd prepared the documents that he gave to Harcourt."

"You killed them too?"

"And a cabdriver and a turnpike gatekeeper, both of whom could have identified me."

"Good God, *all* of them?"

"Stella, why do you sound surprised? Do you think I doubt for a moment that you're the one who killed your husband? Harold doesn't have the imagination to plan a murder."

"I had nothing to do with it! Harold owes huge gambling debts! He wearied of waiting to inherit his father's estate!"

"I'm sure the police believe the story I heard you tell them at the water-cure clinic, but don't insult me by expecting *me* to believe it. You stole some of Harold's snuff and placed it on your husband's chest after you smothered him, making it seem that Harold was the one who'd leaned over him with a pillow."

"No!"

"You depended on the Opium-Eater to confirm the discovery of the snuff and agree with your accusation that Harold had killed him."

"You're wrong!"

"It was a risk to involve the Opium-Eater and his daughter, but your daring appears to have succeeded. Those two detectives respect their opinions. After Harold is hanged, your son will become the next Lord Cavendale. It's brilliant. You found a way for a hangman to commit murder for you just as surely as you murdered your husband. You might not be steeped in death to the extent that *I* am, but it's a difference only in numbers. You and I are two of a kind, Stella. We deserve to be together."

"Don't you dare to compare us!" she said. "You're nothing more than a common—"

"*You* risked doing whatever was necessary to achieve what you dreamed of, and *I* risked doing what was necessary to help you. Oh yes, we're alike. Could anyone else possibly love you more than *I* do?"

Again he reached for her hand.

"Don't."

"You never objected when I touched you before."

"I didn't have a choice."

"And you don't have a choice *now*."

"Stop. Truly. I can't bear this. You—"

"I what?"

"Disgust me. If it hadn't been absolutely necessary, do you think I'd ever have allowed you to paw me the way I saw men pawing my mother when I was a child?"

"I don't understand."

Stella pushed him away. "You're as loathsome as every other man! I hated every instant I endured beneath you, feeling your weight crush the breath from my lungs, feeling you press into me."

"What you really mean is that you were disgusted with *yourself*," Rick said.

"I have no idea what you're—"

"Raise your veil. Let me see your eyes. Look at me directly and tell me that in making *me* happy, as you put it a moment ago, you didn't make *yourself* happy. In spite of yourself, you enjoyed it. *That's* why you're disgusted."

"This is *not* a proper topic."

"Do you think I'm so naive that I can't tell the difference between a woman who enjoys my affections and one who only pretends to?" Rick demanded.

"Well, I certainly tricked *you*. You were an animal engaged to perform a breeding service. Now take the money you were offered and go!"

"Yes."

"What? You actually agree?"

"I'll take the money and leave." Rick paused. "On one condition."

"What's the condition?" she asked suspiciously.

"Raise your veil."

"So you can see my eyes? That's what you wanted a moment ago."

"No. So that I may kiss you. Prove to me that you don't enjoy it."

When he stepped toward her, Stella again moved away. But then she bumped against a table and couldn't put any more space between them.

"Convince me," Rick said. "Prove that all those afternoons and evenings we spent upstairs were only to make certain that you conceived a male heir. When you came here a week ago, it wasn't to produce a child."

"I told you it was because you threatened to cause a public scandal if I didn't comply."

"Make me believe that was your motive. Let me kiss you. Prove that you don't enjoy it. If I'm wrong, I'll walk away, and you'll never see me again."

Stella seemed paralyzed.

Rick stepped closer. He touched her veil. Slowly he pulled it above her face and set it on her black bonnet, exposing her lustrous green eyes.

"So lovely."

With his right hand, he stroked her exquisite cheek.

"Don't hate yourself for what you're feeling," he said.

She shuddered.

"It's the most natural thing in the world," he assured her.

He put his left hand on her other cheek, gently framing her face. He leaned forward and touched his lips ever so softly against hers, the kiss of a butterfly.

He leaned back and admired her.

Again he kissed her, again softly, barely brushing her lips, feeling a tingle come from her to him.

"So lovely," he said again.

The next time he kissed her, he felt her lips part.

Whimpering, she leaned into him.

THE SCREAM WAS so loud, so filled with pain and terror, that Carolyn flinched as she and Edward listened at the partition. Accompanied by muffled, pounding sounds, the scream became so agonized that Carolyn and Edward hurriedly slid the doors aside.

Rick lay on the floor, Stella crouched over him, thrusting a jagged shard of something repeatedly into his mangled face. Pieces of an object lay around him. One of the fragments had a ceramic handle, and Carolyn abruptly realized that it was a broken vase, the other handle of which Stella clutched as she continued to drive the spiked remnant into the crimson pulp of Rick's features.

"Stella!" Carolyn shouted.

"Stop!" Edward yelled, reaching for her arm.

Stella swung with the weapon, forcing Edward to lurch back, but not soon enough. His outstretched hand erupted with blood.

Groaning, he stumbled against a chair, lost his balance, and fell.

"Don't touch me!" Stella screamed. "I won't let a man touch me again! Ever!"

Her veil hung to the side of her head. It was splattered with blood. So were her cheeks. So was her black crepe mourning dress.

"I won't let a man paw me the way you let men paw *you!*" she shrieked at Carolyn.

Something walloped against the front door. As Carolyn whirled toward the drawing room's entrance and the hallway beyond it, the front door shuddered.

It crashed open. Two men charged inside. As they rushed toward the lamplight of the drawing room, Carolyn recognized the two detectives she'd met at the clinic. Two other figures hurried behind them.

"Thomas! Emily!"

From the Journal of Emily De Quincey

On the train to London, Father had asked Commissioner Mayne to make six constables dressed in street clothes available to us. In shifts, they'd watched Carolyn's Park Lane address. After a day of asking questions at various shops, Father and I had finally rested at Lord Palmerston's house, along with Sean and Joseph, who joined us after their own long day of asking questions.

We waited for something that Father said he was certain would happen—that at least one member of Carolyn's house would depart after nightfall. By half past eleven, we'd begun to doubt him. But indeed one of the constables, having run the short distance around the corner from Park Lane to Piccadilly, suddenly pounded on Lord Palmerston's door, alerting us that not one but three people from the Park Lane address had gotten into a carriage.

A police van waited in Lord Palmerston's driveway. We hurried north along Park Lane to the other watcher, who shouted, "The carriage turned right into Oxford Street!" In the fog of London's half a million chimneys, we sped after it as best we could. A vehicle traveling at so late an hour was unusual, attracting the notice of patrolling constables, who directed us farther along Oxford Street until other constables shouted that the carriage had gone north along Tottenham Court Road and then eastward along Francis Street. In the darkness, the passing carriage had been the only thing of interest for the constables to observe.

While we *had a reason to rush, the carriage's occupants apparently did not. In Francis Street, we caught up to it, hearing its clatter. But there was considerably less chance of our quarry hearing us, because Father had recommended a highwayman's tactic that he'd written about in one of his murder essays: the hooves of our horses were muffled with padded burlap bags.*

When the carriage made the sounds of stopping, our driver stopped also. We descended into the cold fog, and as the carriage ahead of us resumed its clatter, we walked quietly along the street, finally discovering the only lit windows in the area, behind the draperies of a detached house that had a squat tower on each corner.

We separated and listened at various windows in front and back.

After the horrid scream sent Sean and Joseph crashing into the house, we encountered a frenzy that I shall never be able to purge from my memory. The combined effect was overwhelming: the pulped face of the motionless man on the floor, the crimson on Stella's black bereavement dress, the blood that dripped from the shattered vase that she clutched, the blood that gushed from Edward's slashed hand, and the look of terror on Carolyn's face.

Sean moved toward Stella, reaching for her weapon.

"Keep away! Don't touch me!"

Sean said something so softly that I couldn't hear it.

"Speak up!" Stella said.

"Be calm," Sean whispered.

I realized that he wanted her to strain to hear him, to lean forward, giving him a chance to yank the jagged vase from her grasp.

But when he took a further step, she swung at him. Sean jerked back a moment before his hand would have been gashed as Edward's had been.

I never removed my gaze from Stella's gleaming eyes while I shifted toward Edward and tore off his cravat. "Press it on your wound. Press it firmly," I told him. All the while, I focused on Stella's shockingly contorted features.

"This is all her fault," Stella said, pointing hatefully at Carolyn.

"Be calm," Sean repeated in a soothing voice.

Joseph shifted slowly to the side, obviously hoping to grab her while Sean distracted her.

"She made me do it," Stella said.

"Your mother made you do what?" Father asked, moving forward.

"Stay away!" Stella yelled to Joseph.

"I need to find out if the man on the floor is alive," Joseph said. "Let me go past you so that I can try to help him."

"He's in hell. Nobody can help him."

"Stella, what did your mother make you do?" Father repeated.

"Don't," Carolyn begged. "Please."

"She made me allow this man to paw me, just as she allowed so many men to put their filthy hands on her," Stella said.

"Enough," I told everyone. "This poor woman is the one who needs help."

Stella looked at me with desperation.

I stepped toward her.

"Will you let a woman touch you?" I asked.

Her expression changed to bafflement.

"These men can't possibly understand," I said. "Let me help."

"Never understand," Stella murmured.

I took another step. She jabbed at me with the porcelain fragment, but it didn't quite reach me, and I didn't retreat.

"There's a sofa against the front window," I said. "You're tired. Come with me and rest."

Another step brought me to her. Slowly I reached out and touched the arm that didn't hold the broken shard.

"Come with me," I said, leading her toward the front part of the drawing room.

"You cut yourself," I said. I eased her onto the sofa and sat next to her.

"Cut?"

"Look at your other hand. Give me the remnant of the vase. No one will hurt you."

As softly as I could, I took it away. Her knuckles were gashed. I pulled an embroidered cover from the arm of a nearby chair and put it on the injury. Then I moved Stella's other hand and pressed it onto the cloth.

While I did this, Sean and Joseph went to the back part of the drawing room and knelt beside the man on the floor, checking to see if he was alive.

Their expressions made it clear that nothing could be done for him.

"At the back window, I heard him confess to murdering Daniel Harcourt and the others on Thursday night," Joseph said. "But who was he?"

The damage to the man's face was so severe that even if he'd been one of our closest friends, we wouldn't have been able to recognize him.

"He worked at the clinic," Carolyn said wearily. "He noticed Stella when she brought her husband there several times a week for treatments. Over time, he developed an unhealthy attraction to her."

"She's lying!" Stella said with sudden fury. "She hired him to touch me! She hired him to…" Stella began wringing her blood-covered hands. "Don't touch me. Worst thing to be is a woman. Pawing, pawing."

"My daughter managed to survive a brutal attack tonight," Carolyn said. "She was forced to fight for her life. Clearly she's so distraught that she doesn't know what she's saying."

"What were all of you doing here at midnight?" Joseph asked.

"Worst thing to be is a woman," Stella kept saying. "Pawing, pawing. Could never have allowed…"

"Allowed?" I asked in confusion.

"Sweet little Jennifer."

"Yes, your baby daughter," I said.

"Could never have…"

Despite the burning coals in the fireplace, the house suddenly acquired a heavy chill.

"…allowed her to grow up. To be pawed. Sweet little…she sleeps peacefully. Never to be…"

The house felt even colder, but that wasn't why I shivered.

Carolyn moaned—the most profoundly despairing sound I've ever heard. "Stella, what have you done?"

Carolyn tried to step toward her, but something went wrong with her left leg. It buckled, causing her to grip the side of a chair.

"You wanted a male heir!" Stella said in a rage. "You told me it was the only thing that mattered! A male heir who would be a lord so that no one would ever look down on us again!"

Stella's fury made the sinews in her neck stand out. "But you didn't tell me how on earth little Jeremy was going to become a lord as long as Harold was alive! Did you hope Harold would drink so much that he'd fall down the marble stairs and break his neck before my husband died from his own injuries? No, you didn't tell me what to do, but I knew what you thought was necessary!"

Carolyn sobbed, tears streaming down her face, her lips quivering. "What have you done? What have you done?"

I stroked Stella's arm. "It's finished. You're safe now. No man will ever touch you again."

Stella kept clutching and unclutching her bloody hands. "Pawing, pawing. Sweet little Jennifer won't ever need to..."

"'The horrors that madden the grief that gnaws at the heart,'" Father said, quoting a passage in one of his essays.

"She's insane," Joseph murmured.

"But in the eyes of the law, only partially," Father noted. "To avoid the gallows, a judge and jury will require proof that she didn't know what she was doing and that she didn't know it was wrong when she murdered her infant daughter and her husband. She obviously knew what she was doing, but she didn't believe it was wrong. This will be a difficult case."

"She won't be able to bear the horrors of Newgate Prison while waiting for her trial," Joseph said. "Perhaps a judge will allow her to stay in Bedlam before she stands in front of a jury."

"I'll hire the best lawyers," Carolyn vowed.

"Unfortunately, you'll have more than one use for the lawyers," Sean told her. He turned to the entrance to the drawing room and the shattered front door beyond it. "Constable, please bring them in."

Sean and Joseph weren't the only people who'd waited with us at Lord Palmerston's house. The clerks from the firearms shop and the chemist shop had been with us also.

When they saw the carnage on the floor, they turned away in horror.

Sean closed the partition at the back of the room, hiding the body.

"I know this is difficult," he told them, "but it's important that you do your duty. Did anyone here come to either of your shops on Friday and Saturday?"

"That man." The clerk from the firearms shop pointed at Edward. "He bought a ten-pound keg of gunpowder. He wore the rustic clothes of a gamekeeper. He had a weathered face. But I recognize him."

"This is preposterous," Edward said.

"And you?" Ryan asked the chemist.

"He wore a clergyman's collar when he bought red food dye and phosphorus from me."

"I've never seen you in my life," Edward protested.

"Red food dye? Phosphorus?" Carolyn asked. "I don't understand."

"The man who detonated the bomb in Waterloo Station vomited red liquid on the railway platform," Father told her. "Travelers were so shocked that they didn't notice he left his bag on the platform before he departed to see a doctor. The bag contained the bomb, which had a slow-burning fuse, giving him enough time to escape before the gunpowder exploded."

"I had nothing to do with any of that!" Edward insisted.

"Phosphorus?" Carolyn repeated in greater confusion.

"The fire on a train out of Paddington Station occurred five minutes after the train departed on Saturday night," Father explained. "Someone left a travel bag on the luggage rack of a compartment but never boarded the train. Sergeant Becker told me that he and Inspector Ryan were baffled about how even a slow-burning fuse could last that long. It occurred to me that a fuse and gunpowder didn't cause that fire."

Father turned to Edward. "When you and I met for the first time on Sunday morning, we had a discussion about phosphorus and a product you were testing that included phosphorus in a paste that glowed in the dark. As you acknowledged, the recipe for that paste came from me. It was a rat poison that I gave to Carolyn. I might not have remembered our discussion if you hadn't told me that, should the product ever be sold in shops, you'd try to arrange a small royalty for me. Despite your pose of friendliness, I detected condescension in your voice, the smugness of someone who thought he had gotten away with something.

"Phosphorus, of course, bursts into flames when exposed to air," Father continued. "It's safe when diluted in the paste, but normally it's stored in a jar of water. All you needed to do was put a jar of phosphorus and water into a travel bag. At the railway station, just before the train departed, you visited the station's privy, where you poured the water from the jar and dumped the exposed phosphorus into the bag. After putting the bag onto the luggage rack of a compartment, you used sickness as an excuse to walk past the guards and leave the station. Having tested how long the remaining water would take to evaporate from the phosphorus, you knew that the train would be well on its way before the fire occurred."

"These are the opium suppositions of a drug-addled brain!" Edward objected.

Sean turned to the chemist. "Are you absolutely certain that this man bought phosphorus from you?"

"Yes."

"He's mistaken—"

"Mr. Richmond, I spent the day at London's Stock Exchange," Joseph interrupted.

"What?"

"Because of the war, everyone said that the Russians were the cause of the attacks on the railway system," Joseph explained. "But with Mr. De Quincey as my guide, I wondered if there was another reality. What if

someone was using the attacks to lower the price of railway shares? After the attacks stopped, the shares would rise to their original price or even higher. Whoever bought the shares at the reduced price would make an enormous profit."

"That's the principle of the stock market! Buy low and sell high!" Edward insisted. "I advised many people to buy as the price of the shares declined!"

"And you certainly took your own advice," Joseph said.

"What the devil do you mean?"

"The devil indeed." Joseph removed a piece of paper from a pocket and consulted a list. "The largest blocks of shares were purchased by Railway Investment Partners, Consolidated Financiers, and Amalgamated Holdings. When I investigated who owned these businesses, I discovered they were all controlled by a firm called United Capital." Joseph pointed at the list. "There are six members on that company's board of directors. Five of them don't exist. The sixth member is you. Edward Richmond, you're under arrest."

"This is outrageous! When the prime minister hears about this—Carolyn, contact our attorneys! Go to Lord Palmerston! These idiots deserve to lose their jobs!"

But Carolyn just stared at him. Her expression of bewilderment was one that I would expect to see on somebody who was lost in a dark forest, without any compass bearings. She seemed to have even more strands of gray in her hair.

"What have you done?" she murmured to Edward and then to Stella. "What have both of you done?"

"Inspector, a carriage has arrived outside," the constable said.

"It's for Mother, Edward, and me," Stella said, apparently oblivious to the blood on her face and hands and black bereavement dress. She kept clenching and unclenching her crimson fists. "May we go back to Park Lane now?"

Gently, I helped her to stand. "You and I will leave in the carriage," I told her.

I leaned toward Sean and whispered, "Shall I take her to Bedlam?" I referred, of course, to London's mental institution, which had a wing for the criminally insane.

He nodded sadly.

"I'll go with you," Joseph said.

"No!" *Stella exclaimed as he stepped toward her.* "Keep away! I won't be pawed! Won't be pawed!"

"I'll be safe with her," *I assured Joseph.*

"Constable," *Sean said,* "to the west along this street, you'll find a police van waiting for us. We'll transport Edward Richmond to the Whitehall police station."

"I'm warning you! When the prime minister hears about this—"

"Shut up, Edward," *Sean told him.*

"And what about..." *The constable nodded toward Carolyn.*

"My long-ago friend and I shall wait for someone to bring a vehicle back for us," *Father said.* "We have much to discuss."

"CAROLYN, THIS PLACE is almost as cold as Lord Cavendale's country house," De Quincey told her after everyone had left. "Please sit with me in front of the fire."

He motioned toward a thickly upholstered chair across from him. As he eased down on his own chair, he noticed that she faltered when she sat.

"What's wrong with your leg?" he asked.

"I'm not certain. This morning, it began to fail me."

"We should ask Dr. Snow to examine it."

"Yes."

"You look weary."

"Yes."

De Quincey drank from his laudanum bottle. His legs were too short for his boots to reach the dusty rug on the floor.

"Carolyn, this morning, I sent telegrams to various places in Bristol. To the police, the principal newspaper, and the courthouse."

She looked at him with defeated eyes, her once-vivid cinnamon-colored hair now lifeless.

"I asked for information about events that occurred around 1802 or 1803, at approximately the time you and Brunell disappeared from London. My inquiries were related to the narrative you gave me about what subsequently happened to you. I asked about a prosperous dock merchant whose partner was killed in an accident and who himself was killed in an accident shortly thereafter, with the consequence that his estate was thrown into confusion. About a cousin who inherited the business but gave generous considerations to the merchant's widow. About a long-banished son returning with a ten-year-old child whom the widow learned to cherish."

Carolyn turned her gaze toward the burning coals.

"The answers to my telegrams indicated that there's no record of any of those events having occurred," De Quincey said. "Nor is there a record of an Edward Richmond doing business in Bristol or a record of your marriage to him there, as you implied to me."

Staring at the fireplace, Carolyn murmured again, "Stella and Edward. What have they done?"

"It was all a fiction—am I correct?" De Quincey asked.

Carolyn seemed to try to muster the strength for an explanation, but in the end, she only shrugged.

"Today, Inspector Ryan made inquiries about your purchase of Park Lane," De Quincey said. "That occurred seven years ago, in 1848. No one had any idea where you came from, but everyone was impressed by the ability of you and your husband to purchase a house in that exclusive street."

"It was indeed an impressive thing to be able to purchase that house," Carolyn said in a wistful tone.

De Quincey studied his laudanum bottle, deciphering the secrets of the universe from the dosage instructions on the label.

"Most people remember 1848 as the Year of Revolution, when numerous nations in Europe erupted into flames because of mobs that toppled monarchs," he said. "England itself almost erupted into flames when a hundred and fifty thousand laborers marched on London, demanding rights from Parliament. Only because of terrible weather and an overwhelming police presence did the crisis end. Was it a coincidence that you came to London in that year?"

Carolyn stared at the burning coals, shivered, and didn't reply.

"Did you escape from one of the endangered European capitals?" De Quincey asked.

"I could tell you another fiction, but I suspect that you're so dogged, you'll learn the truth eventually," Carolyn replied in exhaustion. "Yes, I escaped from Europe before the revolutionaries could steal my assets."

"Is that where you and Brunell fled in 1803, to Europe, not Bristol, during the week I was away from London?"

Carolyn nodded despondently.

"Why did the two of you flee?"

"You know Brunell was always afraid and never slept in the same building twice in a row."

"His fear was palpable," De Quincey agreed.

"Whomever he feared finally came too close. One day, while you were away in Eton, he rushed into that dismal house in Greek Street and told me we were leaving."

"He never acknowledged you as his daughter," De Quincey said. "Why would he take you with him when he was in so great a hurry?"

"Did you hear something?" Carolyn shifted her gaze toward the closed partition that concealed the corpse in the back half of the drawing room.

"It's only the contraction of the house in this cold," De Quincey answered.

"Yes, in this cold." Carolyn hugged herself.

"To where did the two of you flee?"

"To Paris."

"Why did Brunell take you with him?" De Quincey repeated.

Carolyn shivered. "Since he didn't have the authority to act as a lawyer in the French courts, he resorted to other measures to earn a living."

"Other measures?"

"He took refuge in a Paris brothel. He earned money by offering me to its patrons."

De Quincey couldn't speak for a moment. "My heart breaks for you, Carolyn."

She made a brushing-away gesture with her hands, showing contempt for her past, disposing of it.

"Brunell was a fool. Without imagination. As I wept each morning after yet another unspeakable night, I tried desperately to think of a way to save myself. At last, I realized how he could earn far more money than by offering me to…" Carolyn shuddered. "It required the help of another man, a strong, hateful-looking man, and it required us to look presentable. With the last of his money, Brunell and I went to the public baths. It had more water than I ever imagined I could be immersed in. He bought better clothes for us. He took me to the sort of taverns where so-called respectable men seek diversion. He offered me to them, but as soon as I was in a rented room with one of them, the hateful-looking man would charge inside and demand to know what the gentleman was doing with his daughter. The intruder carried a cudgel and told the man the choice was his: he could receive a thorough beating or he could hand over a generous sum to compensate for the insult to his daughter.

"Some nights, we earned as much as the equivalent of a hundred pounds. We were able to afford better clothes and attract wealthier gentlemen searching for the kind of entertainment of which their wives and children would not approve. Eventually we needed to leave Paris for French cities where we wouldn't be recognized. Then we went to Spain and Portugal and the Italian states, wherever wealthy English gentlemen traveled for secret diversions."

Carolyn again turned toward the partition that separated her and De Quincey from the corpse in the next room. "Are you certain that you don't hear anything back there?"

"Only the contraction of the house," De Quincey assured her.

"You don't hear rats? I should have brought saucers filled with the phosphorus paste. I should have placed them in each room."

"Tell me about Europe, Carolyn."

Slowly she removed her gaze from the partition. "Eventually I grew too old to play the role of a young, innocent girl. Our scheme changed and I became a virginal sister whom Brunell had supposedly abducted from a family in Kent. The hateful-looking man became a brother who claimed to be searching for me. This worked well, but it didn't produce the degree of shame in our victims—and the commensurate amount of money—that the original scheme did.

"Soon I thought of a better plan. After Brunell rented me to a gentleman and we went to a room, the angry-looking man burst through the door, this time claiming to be my husband and holding a crying baby. He thrust the baby into my arms and threatened to beat the gentleman to within an inch of his life for despoiling the baby's mother. We earned considerable money with that particular dodge. But the babies didn't know how to be actors. They cried when we didn't want them to, and when we did want them to cry, they often remained exasperatingly silent, so in time we went back to a version of the original scheme and arranged for gentlemen to be alone with girls of six, eight, and ten years when they were interrupted by the hateful-looking man with a cudgel. As I said, we earned considerable money. Brunell and the various assistants whom we employed gambled and drank their money away. But I saved mine." Carolyn nodded proudly.

"How did you meet Edward?"

"Brunell died from typhus. Edward—that's not his actual name—was one of Brunell's acquaintances. Edward was a sometime actor. He had a gift for assuming genteel airs, and I decided that he'd be perfect for the role of the man who offered the young girls to gentlemen. He looked like someone whom the gentlemen he approached could trust."

"Eventually you married him."

"After what I just told you? Heaven help me, I would never submit myself to marriage," Carolyn replied in horror.

"Then who is Stella's father?"

"I haven't the faintest idea. She was one of the babies I used in my various schemes. Unlike the rest of the babies, somehow Stella knew how to play her role. I told her that I was her mother. I raised her. I trained her. Sometimes the role required her to be in a cradle behind a curtain when the gentlemen visited me and the angry man burst into the room, claiming to be my husband. Stella was perfect. She always wailed on cue, further surprising the gentlemen."

"That's how she saw men pawing you."

Yet again Carolyn looked toward the partition that hid the corpse.

"Truly, I don't hear anything behind there," De Quincey said. "Tell me about 1848."

Carolyn sighed in exhaustion. "By then, I lived in wonderful houses on splendid estates in the various cities where Edward and I and Stella worked our schemes. But it was obvious to me that the wealthy displayed such arrogance that the poor would soon revolt. Before Europe exploded, I sold everything I owned. The prices I offered were so tempting that I had no difficulty enticing fools to buy my houses and estates. Three months later, those properties were in flames. But by then, Edward and I and Stella were in London, posing as a respectable family who'd managed to escape the chaos. I thought that the name I invented—Richmond—was brilliant, combining the concept of wealth with the French word for 'world.' London was so fearful over the possibility of a revolution that no one questioned our story. Even if someone *had* suspected that our story wasn't true, he couldn't have investigated us, given the chaos that had seized the Continent. Edward opened an office in the business district, at first as a lender and then as an investment adviser. Owning a house in Park Lane establishes immense credibility. An increasing number of people trusted us, including the prime minister and various cabinet members. All the business decisions were mine, of course. Edward might seem elegant, but he isn't very clever. Even so, I needed him because investors won't trust a woman the way they do a man."

"Wainwright told me that you and he were in league together and that you owned the hydropathy clinic."

Carolyn hesitated. "Everything's ruined now. Why not tell you? Wainwright was another of my associates in Europe. It took me a while to find a use for him. Wainwright listened as the wealthy clients at the clinic talked among themselves about investment opportunities, and then he reported their conversations to us."

"Lord Palmerston told me he trusted you so much that he enlisted your help in clandestine government matters. You arranged for Dr. Mandt to hide at the clinic, for example."

Carolyn gave De Quincey a mournful look. "So you asked questions of the prime minister also?"

"He and I have an unusual relationship."

"I thought that *my* relationship with him was unusual too. But no longer." Yet again, Carolyn turned toward the partition that hid the corpse. "I spent a lifetime clawing my way to an unimaginable status. I almost rose even higher. Having a grandson who's a lord—can there be anything more wonderful than that? And I lost it all in one night."

They heard the rattle of a vehicle approaching along the street; it stopped in front of the house.

"That's our transportation," De Quincey said. "I'll escort you back to Park Lane."

"Thomas, what made you distrust me?"

"From the start, I was bothered by your sudden appearance at Lord Palmerston's house on Saturday morning. You'd followed my career and knew all the books that I'd published. You knew many of the details of my life, which you'd gleaned from reading my work. But you'd never bothered to contact me, even though it would not have been difficult to send inquiries to the magazines for which I wrote and to the publishers who released my books."

De Quincey studied his laudanum bottle. "You see, I care so little about myself that I don't expect anyone to care for me either. Emily's devotion to me at the expense of her own happiness astonishes me. So I couldn't help wondering about your sudden determination to see me face to face. Did you want something? I wondered."

With hollow-sounding footsteps, a constable walked through the house and stopped at the drawing-room door. "The carriage is ready whenever you are, Mr. De Quincey."

"In a moment," De Quincey told him. "Could you please wait outside?"

"Of course."

"Carolyn, what did you want from me?" De Quincey asked.

"As you noted, Dr. Mandt was hiding at the hydropathy clinic. Daniel Harcourt's murder while he was en route to Sedwick Hill attracted the attention of the newspapers and the police—and perhaps the Russians. I thought that if I took you to the clinic, the presence of so famous a personality would provide a distraction so that Dr. Mandt would be able to get away unnoticed."

"In the end, your plan succeeded. Wainwright is escorting him to safety. Carolyn, are you certain that you didn't wish me to go with you to Sedwick Hill so that I could be present when Stella killed her husband and so that I could acknowledge the evidence that made it seem Harold had killed his father?"

"I knew nothing about any of it."

De Quincey considered this reply, nodded, and stood. "Allow me to escort you to the carriage. Please lean on me to compensate for your weak leg."

She accepted his offered hand and rose from the chair with the aid of her cane. She was so tall that he felt even smaller. Nonetheless, he was able to support her.

"Thomas, on Saturday, you asked me if there was any moment in my life that I wish I could change."

"Yes, a moment when if something hadn't happened or if something else *had* happened, our lives might have taken a different course. Perhaps a better one."

Carolyn leaned harder on him. "I wish you'd never gone to Eton to visit the family friend who had the power to save you from being a beggar. I wish you'd stayed with me in that terrible house in Greek Street. When

Brunell rushed inside and announced fearfully that he and I had to hurry away, you could have told him I wasn't going with him and that you intended to take care of me."

"Yes. We could have been a family. You and I and Ann," De Quincey said.

With De Quincey's support and that of her cane, Carolyn limped toward the door. "How different things could have been," she said.

"*Too* different. I wouldn't have had Emily," De Quincey told her.

As Ryan tugged Edward Richmond along the murky jail corridor, Harold stood from the cot in his cell.

"Edward!" he exclaimed. "Thank heaven, you've come to get me out of here!"

"He's taking your place," Ryan said.

"What?"

Keys jangling, the grizzled jailer unlocked the barred door, saying, "Busy, busy. Out, out. Make room for your cell's new guest."

"But I don't understand," Harold said, exiting the cell.

Ryan removed the handcuffs from Edward and pushed him into the cell.

"It's the best we have," the jailer told Edward, twisting the key. "No drafts 'cause there ain't a window. I hope you're not afraid of the dark."

"I won't be here for long! Carolyn will soon bring lawyers!" Edward shouted.

"You'll need many of them!" Ryan called over his shoulder as he took Harold along the corridor.

Outside in the cold fog of Whitehall, Harold hugged his arms around his chest. "What's this all about?" he asked.

"Lord Cavendale, you're free to go."

"You're using my title?" The lamp above the jail's entrance revealed Harold's look of surprise. "You're no longer accusing me of killing my father?"

"We know who did it. I apologize for arresting you, my lord."

"You're actually addressing me as *my lord?* Who are you accusing now?" Harold sounded astonished.

"Your stepmother."

"I kept telling you she did it!"

"Yes, but all the evidence was against you."

"What in blazes changed?"

"We heard her admit to it."

The reference to *we* included Becker, who stood in the background.

"Admit to it?" Harold repeated, stunned.

"My lord, as I indicated, you're free to go."

"To where? I don't have the money for a cab, let alone a room."

"I'm sure the jailer will let you sleep in an unlocked cell until morning."

"Sleep in a cell? I've seen more than enough of that place!" Harold walked toward a streetlamp. "Perhaps my club will let me stay there, even though I haven't paid my dues."

"Lord Cavendale?" Ryan called to him.

Harold turned. "What is it?"

"If I ever hear that you struck another woman…"

Harold considered him for several seconds. "I understand. You have my word that I never shall."

Harold disappeared into the fog.

Ryan turned to Becker. "You weren't as certain about his guilt as *I* was. That's why you sent someone to contact lawyers on his behalf."

"The evidence was definitely against him."

"Then what was your difficulty?" Ryan asked.

"Because of what he did to Emily, we were rushing him to the gallows," Becker replied. "In fact, you nearly killed him the night we arrested him."

"Again, I thank you for stopping me."

"It's for a judge and jury to decide if he should hang," Becker said. "If you hadn't been furious about what he did to Emily, you might have seen the evidence in a different way."

Ryan considered what Becker had said. After several seconds, he peered down at the cobblestones and nodded. "It could be that I've taught you as much as I can."

THE CARRIAGE EMERGED from the fog and arrived at Carolyn's Park Lane house. De Quincey stepped down and escorted her through the darkness up the stone steps to the large double doors.

"Tomorrow, you need to ask Dr. Snow about your limp," he advised.

"He'll probably tell me I should rest."

"An excellent idea," De Quincey said. "I hope that you manage to sleep. In the morning, I'll come back and see if there's anything I can do to help."

"Help?" Carolyn seemed to find the concept incomprehensible. "Thank you, Thomas." She leaned down and kissed him on the cheek. "If only we'd never parted."

She watched him go back to the street and tell the carriage driver to proceed without him. He turned to the left, the fog enveloping him. She heard the sound of his footsteps diminish as he walked toward Piccadilly and Lord Palmerston's house.

She withdrew a key from a pocket and freed the lock. After she limped into the entrance hall and bolted the door behind her, the echoes seemed more reverberant than usual. She noted that the servants had, as always, placed a saucer of the phosphorus paste at the bottom of the curved staircase.

She moved to an ornate side table, where she struck a match and applied it to the wick in a silver lamp. The entrance hall had never seemed vaster, its crystal chandelier never more elegant, its black-and-white marble squares never more grand, its paintings, pedestals, and ancient Roman sculptures never more sublime.

How far I have come from that horror of a rat-and-ghost-filled house in Greek Street, she thought.

Holding the lamp, she limped past the green-glowing paste. After tucking her walking stick under a sash on her dress, she used her free hand to grip the polished brass railing of the staircase and climbed, although *pulled herself upward* might have been a more accurate description. She admired the railing's outward curve, designed to provide space for the widest of hoop dresses. She thought of the many glorious dinners and receptions that had awaited guests at the top of the staircase.

There, another green-glowing saucer lit the way. Carolyn entered the large room on the left and set the lamp on the long table where, only a few days earlier, exotic teas and confections had been arranged for one of her twice-monthly whist parties, invitations to which were coveted by the wives of the rich and powerful, all of them eager for her opinions about the latest trends and investment opportunities.

She made her way across the deep reds and greens in the intricate pattern of the much-admired Persian rug. She reached the French doors that led to the enormous balcony outside. While most households kept their draperies closed so that outsiders couldn't see the private activities within, Carolyn told her servants not to shield the windows, proud of the luxurious life she'd attained, happy for anyone in the lesser world to see it.

Tonight, as usual, the fog prevented her from seeing Hyde Park across the way, the trees and horseback-riding trails that created the illusion of the countryside. But staring toward the fog, she had no difficulty imagining the incomparable vista that the night concealed. When she was a starving ten-year-old in Greek Street, if a fortune-teller had told her that this would be her destiny, she would have assumed that the fortune-teller was not only a charlatan but also a lunatic.

The lamp revealed Carolyn's reflection on one of the glass doors. For a moment, she tensed, not recognizing the wan woman in front of her. Then it seemed to her that the figure was a ghost, one that was all too familiar.

She thrust her apprehension aside and turned to scan the room where the very best of English society had delighted in her company. She heard her guests saying, *Oh, Mrs. Richmond, how clever of you. Oh, Mrs.*

Richmond, where on earth did you find that lovely dress? Oh, Mrs. Richmond, who designed this remarkable set of china? Oh, Mrs. Richmond. Mrs. Richmond.

Then she heard Thomas asking if there had ever been a moment in her life that she'd wished she could change.

Scrittle-scrattle.

She raised her walking stick, ready to defend herself against the rats.

Where are they? Not on the floor, Carolyn decided. *The carpet won't allow their claws to make that sharp sound.*

They're in the walls.

She listened harder, but now all she heard was the ticking of the clock in the entrance hall, so huge and lonely did the house seem.

She picked up the lamp, limped into the corridor, and reached another green-glowing saucer of paste, this one on the next tier of the staircase. Again she put her walking stick under the sash of her dress, gripped the railing, and pulled herself up the steps.

She reached a door next to her bedroom and opened it. Curtains encircled a child's bed. When she parted them, she saw little Jeremy sleeping between the metal bars that prevented him from falling out.

A figure rose from the shadows.

Carolyn raised the walking stick, preparing to strike at the ghost.

"Who's there?" the figure murmured sleepily. "Oh, it's you, Mrs. Richmond."

Carolyn lowered the walking stick.

"I'm just checking on little Jeremy," she whispered to the servant.

She tilted her head to indicate that they should retreat to the corridor.

Outside, the servant frowned. "Forgive me for asking, Mrs. Richmond, but are you ill? You look pale."

"Merely tired. But thank you for your concern, Marybeth. Did little Jeremy accept the wet nurse I sent for?"

"He was very hungry," Marybeth replied with a smile.

"Good. We want him to grow up to be big and strong."

"Indeed, ma'am."

"Do you enjoy attending to infants? It may be that his mother needs to take a journey."

"A journey, ma'am?"

"Yes, a very long one. Are you comfortable with an infant?"

"I cared for my baby brother when I was only ten and my baby sister when I was fourteen," Marybeth answered with another smile.

"Then at nineteen, you shouldn't have any difficulty."

"Not at all, Mrs. Richmond. Why is Jeremy's mother taking a long journey?"

"You'll know soon enough. Go back to sleep. I want you to feel rested. From now on, little Jeremy will be your sole duty."

"I feel honored. Thank you for trusting me."

Scrittle-scrattle.

Carolyn whirled.

"What's wrong, Mrs. Richmond?"

"Did you hear that?"

"Hear what?"

Scrittle-scrattle.

"They're under the floor."

"They, Mrs. Richmond?"

"Rats. Don't you hear them?"

Scrittle-scrattle.

"No, ma'am. I don't hear anything."

Scrittle-scrattle.

Carolyn pounded her walking stick against the carpet on the floor.

"Go away, damn you! Go away!"

She struck the floor harder.

In the bedroom, little Jeremy whimpered.

"Please, Mrs. Richmond. You're scaring him."

"What?"

"You're scaring little Jeremy."

"Scaring…" Carolyn raised the walking stick in her hand and stared at it. She directed her attention toward the half-open bedroom door, beyond which Jeremy whimpered.

The noises stopped.

"Well, we can't have that. We don't want him frightened," Carolyn agreed.

She lowered the walking stick. The candles of two servants appeared on the staircase that led down from the topmost level.

"Is everything all right, Mrs. Richmond?" a footman asked.

"You need to put out more saucers of the paste," she said.

"Yes, madam. At once."

Carolyn turned to Marybeth. "Please go back to Jeremy." She started to walk away.

"Mrs. Richmond, you're limping. Are you certain you're all right?"

"Tired. I'm only tired."

Once more, Carolyn put the walking stick under the sash on her dress. She held the lamp in one hand, clutched the brass railing with the other, and hobbled down the staircase.

At the bottom, she entered the library, where she set the lamp on the desk and made her way to the cabinet of shelves where all of the books had the same author's name. She opened the door and removed a volume that, because of innumerable readings, parted automatically to the passage she wished to read yet again.

She sank onto a chair, drew a breath, and returned to when seventeen-year-old Thomas had arrived at the house in Greek Street.

Again, she heard Thomas's young voice.

...a large unoccupied house. Unoccupied, I call it, for there wasn't any furniture. But I found that the house already contained one single inmate, a poor friendless child, apparently ten years old. I learned that she had lived there alone for some time, and great joy the poor creature expressed when she found that I was to be her companion through the hours of darkness. From the want of furniture, the noise of the rats made a prodigious echoing on the spacious staircase, and amidst the fleshly ills of cold and

hunger, the forsaken child suffered still more from the self-created one of ghosts. We lay upon the floor, with no other covering than a horseman's cloak. The poor child crept close to me for warmth and security against her ghostly enemies. I took her into my arms.

From repeated readings, the pages opened to another passage as though with a will of their own.

Again, Thomas's young voice filled her mind, but this time he spoke about the night he'd left the house in Greek Street, intending to journey to a family friend who might be able to redeem him from the life of a beggar. He'd promised to return in five days.

I set off, accompanied by Ann, toward Piccadilly, for it was my intention to go on the Bristol mail-coach en route to Eton. Our course lay through a part of London which has now all disappeared, Swallow-street, I think it was called. Having time enough, we sat down, not wishing to part in the tumult and blaze of Piccadilly. I had told Ann of my plans, and I now assured her again that she would share in my good fortune, if I met with any, and that I would never forsake her. I loved her. I was full of hope. She, on the contrary, was overcome by sorrow, so that when I kissed her at our farewell, she put her arms around my neck and wept without speaking a word.

Carolyn went to the desk, took a sheet of paper from a drawer, dipped a copper pen into a crystal inkwell, and wrote hastily.

Scrittle-scrattle.

She stopped and peered around the room.

When the noise wasn't repeated, she resumed writing.

Scrittle-scrattle.

Again, she stopped and listened to the silence of the house.

It's the sound of the nib on the paper, she thought.

Trying to make herself believe that explanation, she rushed on despite the ever-louder *scrittle-scrattle,* never again pausing, the words having accumulated pressure in her mind over a lifetime.

She completed the document, blotted it, folded it, and sealed it with wax. She wrote *Thomas* next to the wax. Then she composed another document, and this she left on the desk for anyone to read.

She tugged at a bookshelf that swung out and revealed a fireproof safe, the lock of which was the most sophisticated available. After withdrawing a key from a concealed pocket in her dress, she opened the safe, removed an object, and set it on the desk.

FOURTEEN

THE DISCONNECTED HEART

"MRS. RICHMOND IS not at home," a footman said when he opened the door the next morning. His face should have expressed the satisfaction of a servant at one of the very best addresses in London, but instead he looked confused and even fearful.

"She might not be at home to anyone else," De Quincey said. "But she's expecting us. Please tell her that Thomas and Emily are at the door."

"She put a sealed message on her desk and addressed it to Thomas. Perhaps it's for you. But truly, Mrs. Richmond isn't at home."

"You look as if something has happened," Emily said. "What's wrong?"

"When the church bells rang at five o'clock this morning, the cook found Mrs. Richmond downstairs in the kitchen. Mrs. Richmond had heated the stove. It didn't make sense. Mrs. Richmond knows that if she's hungry, all she needs to do is waken the cook. Mrs. Richmond was dressed to go out. She was limping and supported herself with a walking stick. As if all of that weren't unusual enough, she left a troubling note and an immense amount of money on her desk."

Without waiting for an invitation, De Quincey stepped inside. "Show us."

Relieved that someone was taking charge, the footman led the way to the library's entrance.

De Quincey and Emily hurried toward the desk and a large stack of Bank of England twenty-pound notes.

Emily ran her thumb along them, trying to estimate how many there were. "At least ten thousand pounds," she said in amazement.

The footman pointed at a piece of paper. "Even though Mrs. Richmond's message says that she wants this money to be divided among the servants, I swear that none of us touched any of it. We're afraid we'll be accused of theft."

De Quincey read what was on the paper. "It's an amendment to Carolyn's will," he told Emily in surprise. "She wants the servants to share this money. She wants a maid named Marybeth to take care of her grandson. The infant inherits everything except for whatever money will be required to defend Stella in court and maintain her if she's put in a madhouse. The only thing she gives to Edward is her contempt."

"Look, Father." Emily pointed to a copy of his *Confessions* lying open on the desk.

De Quincey scanned the passage. "It's about the night I departed for Eton and said good-bye to Ann."

He picked up the message that was addressed to Thomas. His hand trembled as he broke the wax seal. The more he read, the more the rushing of his heart made him feel dizzy.

"What does it say, Father?"

"There's no time." He turned to the footman. "Take us to the kitchen."

On the bottom level of the house, the kitchen was appointed with the largest cast-iron stove that De Quincey had ever seen.

"You found Mrs. Richmond here before dawn?" De Quincey asked the cook.

The round-faced woman nodded in bewilderment. "She'd stoked the fire in the stove until it was as hot as when I prepare dinner."

"What was she doing?" Emily asked.

"Making biscuits."

"Biscuits?" De Quincey repeated. The word sounded like a moan.

"The strangest biscuits I ever heard of," the cook said. "Brandy, lard, sugar, flour, and—"

"And a big chunk of something that she took out of a jar of water," De Quincey said.

The cook nodded. "Whatever it is, another servant uses it to make the green-glowing paste that's in the saucers on the stairs. I didn't know you could eat it."

"And then she departed from the house?" De Quincey asked hurriedly. "That's what the footman told us."

"I did my best to advise her not to," the cook insisted. "Her left leg didn't have any strength. Her left arm looked weak also. But she wouldn't listen. She's my mistress. How could I stop her? She put the biscuits in her coat pocket, braced herself on her walking stick, and went away."

"Did she tell you where she was going?" Emily asked.

"No. All she said was 'Thank you for your years of help. There's something for you and the other servants on my desk in the library.' What in the name of heaven is going on?"

"It's not in the name of heaven," De Quincey said. "Emily, we need to hurry. We might already be too late."

As they ran from the front door, Ryan and Becker came through the gate.

"At Lord Palmerston's house, a servant told us where to find you," Ryan said. "We thought you'd like to be present when we ask Edward Richmond more—"

De Quincey interrupted. "We need to find Carolyn as soon as possible."

They hurried to the nearby cabstand on Hyde Park Corner. All day, drivers came and went, but the same water boy remained, attending to the horses and helping passengers get into the vehicles.

"When did you start working this morning?" Becker asked him.

"Five o'clock."

"Did a woman with a limp hire a cab around that time?"

"She also 'ad trouble with one of her arms. She gave me this when I 'elped her climb inside." Amazed by his good fortune, the boy showed them a twenty-pound bank note. It was more than he could earn in a year.

"Do you remember where she told the driver to take her?" Ryan asked.

"Yes, to—"

De Quincey supplied the answer. "Greek Street near Soho Square."

"That's right. How did you know?" the boy asked.

"It couldn't be anywhere else."

De Quincey climbed quickly into a four-seat cab. Emily, Ryan, and Becker joined him.

As the driver did his best to hurry through the clamor of dense traffic, De Quincey showed them the message that Carolyn had left for him.

Reading it, Emily wept. When she managed to regain her voice, she repeated something that De Quincey had said during Stella's revelations the previous night. "'The horrors that madden the grief that gnaws at the heart.'"

The cab reached Greek Street and proceeded toward Soho Square.

"Which house?" the driver called down.

"The gap between buildings," De Quincey replied.

People were gathered at the wooden barrier, pointing in alarm at something below them.

"We didn't get here in time," De Quincey moaned.

He jumped from the cab before it stopped. Emily, Ryan, and Becker followed, pushing through the crowd.

De Quincey was so short that he needed to stand on his toes to peer over the barrier and glimpse the stone floor of what had once been the kitchen on the bottom level.

Carolyn lay facedown on one of the slabs.

Ryan and Becker moved a section of the barrier, revealing steps that descended to the bottom level. They rushed down. Despite his short legs, De Quincey reached Carolyn before anyone else did.

She wasn't moving. When he gently turned her onto her back, he whimpered. She had aged alarmingly. Her formerly radiant smooth skin was now the color of pewter and etched with wrinkles. Her hair seemed coated with dust.

"Emily, do anything you can to help her," De Quincey begged.

Emily pointed. "There's a remnant of a biscuit in her hand. And there are crumbs at the corner of her mouth."

She felt for a pulse. She opened Carolyn's eyelids and studied her eyes. She performed all the other tests, finally gripping Carolyn's ankles.

"Cold. So cold. The poison was too powerful. Father, she's gone."

De Quincey sank to his knees. The message Carolyn had left for him was clutched in his hand. He could never forget the words on it.

Dearest Thomas,

Memories are indeed like the stars, which disappear during the day but come back in the darkness…along with ghosts and nightmares.

One ghost in particular.

The night you left me alone while you went to Eton to try to persuade a family friend to lift you from poverty, I couldn't bear to be without you. I followed you. I saw you meet Ann, where she waited for you farther along Greek Street.

I didn't understand why you wouldn't let me go with you. If you let Ann walk with you to the mail coach, why couldn't you have included me? I followed you both to Swallow Street, where you sat on a bench. The two of you were obviously making plans. I watched as she put her arms around you. I watched you kiss her.

After you left, I went to Ann on the bench. She was weeping. When she noticed that I too was weeping, we hugged. I asked her to come back with me to that wretched house so that we could console each other.

I told Ann that you'd given me a recipe for biscuits. The coals from which you and I had built a fire still glowed in the hearth. I blew on them, creating flames to which I added the rest of the coal that you'd brought. I found an old pan in one of the dusty cupboards. I cooked biscuits.

Thomas, I used to fantasize that you and Ann were my father and mother and that I was your child and that you'd always take care of me. Sometimes I fantasized that instead of being my father, you were my husband. When I saw you making plans with Ann, not including me...when I saw you kiss her...

At the chophouse on Saturday, you told me that when you'd returned to the house five days later, the stench was dreadful. I explained that it came from the many rats your poison had killed.

But the stench was from something else. That's why Brunell fled with me. He was afraid that his enemy would discover what I'd done and blame it on him. After hiding what he could, he forced me to run away with him. In the end, I had done it all for nothing.

Is there anything about my life that I wish I could change? I wish that I hadn't followed you that night. I wish that I hadn't brought Ann back to the house. I wish that I hadn't...

Perhaps the three of us could have been a family, the two of you taking care of me. How wonderful it is to imagine. But then, as you said, you wouldn't have had Emily.

Yours forever,
Carolyn

De Quincey slumped beside Carolyn and wept.

"Inspector Ryan," he finally said.

"Yes?"

"Please do me a favor."

"Certainly."

"I noticed some workmen farther along the street. Would you ask if they have a pole that you can use to pry at something?"

Ryan looked puzzled but said, "Of course."

"Father, I..." Unable to find the words, Emily knelt beside him, putting an arm around him.

"Sergeant Becker?" De Quincey asked.

"Yes?"

"Please help me to move Carolyn's body."

Emily helped also. Gently, they shifted her toward the steps.

When Ryan returned with a pole, De Quincey pointed toward the stone slab upon which Carolyn had lain facedown.

"Please lift that," he said.

Ryan stuck the end of the pole into a gap between the slab and an adjacent one. He pulled down on the pole. As the slab rose, Becker pushed it aside, the sound of its impact booming off the walls.

In the dirt beneath the slab, a skeleton was arranged with its hands over its breastbone.

"Ann," De Quincey said, his voice breaking. "I finally found you."

"Is there nothing I can do to persuade you to change your mind?" Lord Palmerston asked. He, Commissioner Mayne, Becker, and Ryan were seeing Emily and De Quincey off, and the train to Manchester was making impatient chugging sounds. "I complained about your midnight pacing. But all of a sudden I realize that I'll miss the company of the only man in England who cares so little about himself that he'll always tell me the truth."

"My lord, it's been an honor to share your hospitality and admire your greatness," De Quincey said.

Lord Palmerston smiled. "And I shall even miss your sarcasm."

"The memories here are too strong," De Quincey explained. "In December, I was lured to London from Edinburgh because someone promised to reveal to me what had happened to Ann. That promise turned out to be a cruel hoax. But now at last I have learned what happened to Ann, and my purpose in coming to London has been achieved. If I stay any longer, I fear that I shall dwindle even more than I already am, crushed by the memories that Oxford Street and Soho Square and Greek Street evoke. While there's no such thing as forgetting, that doesn't mean I should torture myself by allowing my memories to be vivid. Away from those memories, I'll attempt once more to reduce my laudanum intake."

"I wish you good luck in your efforts," Commissioner Mayne said. "Where will you and Emily go?"

"To Grasmere, in the Lake District," De Quincey answered. "I spent many happy years there in my youth. Emily and I intend to complete the journey that we began on Thursday night. Perhaps some of my books survived the auction."

"I don't know if London can manage without you," the commissioner said. "The next time there's an inexplicable murder—"

"Inspector Ryan and Sergeant Becker are more than capable," De Quincey told him, smiling, "as long as they follow the principles of Immanuel Kant."

The commissioner chuckled.

"We're pleased to have studied the fine art of murder with you," Becker said.

Travelers passed them and climbed into train compartments. In the days since the funerals for Ann and Carolyn, the latter in unhallowed ground because she was a suicide, the newspapers had published numerous reports assuring readers that the person responsible for the attacks on the trains had been apprehended and that there was no longer a reason to fear the railways. Each day, more people boarded the trains.

"The queen and the prince are at Windsor Castle," Lord Palmerston said. "The news of your departure reached them too late for them to return to London and offer their good-byes. They told me to say they will miss you. And, Emily, they wish you the greatest success in your medical endeavors, if that is what you decide to pursue. They asked me to give the two of you some financial assistance for your upcoming travels. Perhaps it will help relieve the pressure from your bill collectors."

Lord Palmerston gave De Quincey some bank notes that were secured in a bright blue band.

"There must be three hundred pounds here," De Quincey said in astonishment. "I can't accept this."

"Actually, Father, you *can*." Emily took the bank notes from him and put them in her pocket.

Now De Quincey shook hands with Ryan and Becker. "Thank you for your friendship," he said.

The train's whistle shrieked.

"We're departing," a railway guard said to De Quincey. "You need to climb aboard."

"Thank you. I'll leave Emily to bid farewell."

After the little man disappeared into a compartment, Emily kissed Lord Palmerston on the cheek.

"Can you actually be blushing, Prime Minister?" she asked.

He deflected the question by pointing at the healing injury on her face. "The swelling and the redness have disappeared. I predict there won't be a scar."

"You know exactly what to tell a woman," Emily said.

She proceeded to Commissioner Mayne and kissed *him* on the cheek. "I shall miss having adventures with you."

"The past three months have been a rare experience," he said, blushing as Lord Palmerston had.

She kissed Becker on the cheek and then Ryan. "And I shall certainly miss the two of you. I don't wish to leave, but Father would die without me."

"Perhaps one day you'll return to London," Becker said. "You know that we would welcome you back."

"Yes, perhaps one day," she said, wishing.

The train's whistle reverberated shrilly beneath the iron-and-glass ceiling.

"I shall write to you," Emily said.

Wiping away a tear, she stepped into the compartment.

The guard locked the door and waved to the driver. As the engine made labored sounds, the train moved forward.

"Commissioner Mayne, I have two items for you," Ryan said.

He tugged the Benson chronometer from his pocket. Its gold had been dulled by the water on the night of the fire.

"It no longer keeps time. But perhaps Mr. Benson can set it right. As for the second item…"

Ryan pulled out his badge and gave it to the commissioner.

"Sean, what are you doing?" Becker asked.

"Because of my regard for Emily, I nearly killed a man who'd cut her face," Ryan said. "And then I nearly allowed a hangman to kill him for me."

"Sometimes emotions get the better of us," Becker tried to assure him.

"Us? Were *you* tempted to kill for Emily?"

"I…no."

"Tell me what you want from her."

"Want?" Becker hesitated, self-conscious about having this conversation in the presence of Lord Palmerston and Commissioner Mayne. "To marry her and have children with her."

"For a time, that's what I wanted also. But now all I want is to be in her presence and keep her safe."

Ryan walked toward the departing train.

"I'm fifteen years older than you," he told Becker, turning his head. "Only a few times have I felt like this. In each case, I let the chance slip away. But I won't let *this* chance slip away."

He walked faster toward the departing carriage.

"Commissioner, I recommend my friend as my replacement!" he shouted over his shoulder. "There might be a few things that I didn't teach him, but I can't imagine what they are!"

He broke into a run.

"All the compartments are locked!" a train guard yelled. "You need to wait for the next train!"

"And maybe never find her? No!"

Ryan leaped and grabbed the bars on a compartment window. Dangling, he felt gravel scrape past the bottom of his boots. He strained to pull himself higher and managed to brace his feet on the metal step outside the door.

Perhaps the driver will look back and notice me clinging to the side of the train, he thought. As air pushed against him, his newsboy's cap blew away, exposing his red hair. *Perhaps the driver will stop.*

But even if the driver didn't see him, Ryan was prepared to cling to the bars until the train reached the next station, no matter how far it was.

Or cling to the bars forever.

Through the window, he saw Emily react with surprise to his sudden, impossible appearance. She put a hand on the glass.

She smiled.

ACKNOWLEDGMENTS

For seven years, while writing *Ruler of the Night* along with its predecessors, *Murder as a Fine Art* and *Inspector of the Dead,* I felt like a time traveler. Several people made the journey possible. I'm deeply grateful to Robert Morrison, author of *The English Opium-Eater: A Biography of Thomas De Quincey,* and to Grevel Lindop, author of *The Opium-Eater: A Life of Thomas De Quincey,* for their friendship and support.

Victorian scholar Judith Flanders became a friend also. Her *The Victorian City, Inside the Victorian Home,* and *The Invention of Murder: How the Victorians Reveled in Death and Detection and Created Modern Crime* occupy a prominent place on my research shelves. Judith also authored a series of addictive mysteries (*A Murder of Magpies, A Bed of Scorpions,* and *A Cast of Vultures*), the amateur detective of which is a London book editor whose sense of humor sounds suspiciously like that of Judith herself.

The first murder on an English train occurred in 1864, not 1855, but its details are essentially as I describe them. I use those details for my own purposes. In life, the historical plot went in a different direction; Kate Colquhoun describes it in *Murder in the First-Class Carriage: The First Victorian Railway Killing.*

That murder struck a blow to the heart of what made Britain great, intensifying an anxiety that had festered since the railway era propelled the nation from traveling at a few miles an hour to moving at an unimaginable fifty. Newspapers wrote fearfully about "the annihilation of time and space." Wolfgang Schivelbusch's *The Railway Journey: The Industrialization of Time and Space in the Nineteenth Century* analyzes the trepidation with which passengers sat in small locked compartments, seeing little of the landscape they hurtled through, fearing for their safety while they did their best not to look at the strangers with whom they traveled.

The hydropathy craze of the mid-1800s began when Vincenz Priessnitz, the son of a farmer and a man with no medical training whatsoever, established a water-cure clinic in the town of Gräfenberg, located on an Austrian mountain that's now part of the Czech Republic. The clinic became so popular that British doctors replicated it in the town of Malvern Hills in the West Midlands of England. My Sedwick Hill is a version of Malvern Hills, but for plot reasons, I moved the location near London. I didn't invent or exaggerate the wet-sheet method with which Dr. Wainwright attempts to cure De Quincey of his opium addition. The shoulder and upward douche treatments as well as the plunge bath were all widely used. No less a literary personage than Edward Bulwer-Lytton (renowned for his often-parodied sentence that begins "It was a dark and stormy night...") became a hydropathy addict and wrote a magazine article called "Confessions of a Water-Patient," its title echoing De Quincey's *Confessions of an English Opium-Eater.* For more about this mania, read Kate Summerscale's *Mrs. Robinson's Disgrace: The Private Diary of a Victorian Lady* and E. S. Turner's *Taking the Cure.*

Dr. Mandt and the suspicions about him aren't invented. I first learned about him in Orlando Figes's definitive history *The Crimean War.* The story that De Quincey tells about the field-worker and the adder is part of Mandt's legend.

Emily's medical knowledge (the benefit of inhaling the steam from pine resin boiled in water, for example) is taken from *Enquire Within Upon Everything,* a popular Victorian "how things work" volume that was published in 1856. My descriptions of London's streets, particularly

Ludgate Hill, are based on Gustave Doré's vivid illustrations of the city's daily life published in *London: A Pilgrimage* (1872).

Wyld's Monster Globe, with its mountains and oceans turned inward, attracted millions of London tourists in the 1850s, but after a dispute about its Leicester Square lease, the building was destroyed in 1862. Lord Palmerston's Cambridge House still exists, however. One of the few set-back-from-the-roadway properties on Piccadilly, the dramatic structure is located across from Green Park, just down the street from Park Lane. In the twentieth century, it was the site of the Army and Navy Club, popularly known as the In-and-Out Club because of signs on the two gates giving entrance and exit directions to drivers, but the club members departed years ago, and two Russian investors now own it, with hopes of converting it into the most expensive private residence in London. On the *Ruler of the Night* page of my website, www.davidmorrell.net, you'll find photo essays about the Monster Globe, Cambridge House, Euston Station, and the Malvern Hills hydropathy clinic. You'll also find an 1855 sketch of what De Quincey and Emily looked like.

Commissioner Mayne existed, as did J. W. Benson and his fabulous gold chronometers. They are some of the fascinating figures that I encountered in the following books: Peter Ackroyd's *London: The Biography,* Peter Ackroyd's *Wilkie Collins,* Richard D. Altick's *Victorian People and Ideas,* Anne-Marie Beller's *Mary Elizabeth Braddon: A Companion to the Mystery Fiction,* Alfred Rosling Bennett's *London and Londoners in the 1850s and 1860s* (a memoir), Jan Bondeson's *Queen Victoria's Stalker: The Strange Case of the Boy Jones,* Mark Bostridge's *Florence Nightingale,* David Brown's *Palmerston: A Biography,* Jennifer Carnell's *The Literary Lives of Mary Elizabeth Braddon,* Belton Cobb's *The First Detectives and the Early Career of Richard Mayne, Police Commissioner,* Tim Pat Coogan's *The Famine Plot: England's Role in Ireland's Greatest Tragedy,* Heather Creaton's *Victorian Diaries: The Daily Lives of Victorian Men and Women,* Rosalind Crone's *Violent Victorians,* Alison Gernsheim's *Victorian and Edwardian Fashion: A Photographic Survey,* Horace Ainsworth Eaton's *Thomas De Quincey,* Judith Flanders's *Consuming Passions: Leisure and Pleasure in Victorian Britain,*

Gillian Gill's *We Two: Victoria and Albert, Rulers, Partners, Rivals,* Ruth Goodman's *How to Be a Victorian,* Kate Hubbard's *Serving Victoria: Life in the Royal Household,* Winifred Hughes's *The Maniac in the Cellar: Sensation Novels of the 1860s,* Steven Johnson's *The Ghost Map: The Story of London's Most Terrifying Epidemic,* Petrus de Jon's *De Quincey's Loved Ones,* Henry Mayhew's *London Labor and the London Poor* (a contemporary account published in 1861 and 1862), Sally Mitchell's *Daily Life in Victorian England,* Paul Thomas Murphy's *Shooting Victoria: Madness, Mayhem, and the Rebirth of the British Monarchy,* Catherine Peters's *The King of Inventors: A Life of Wilkie Collins,* Liza Picard's *Victorian London,* Daniel Pool's *What Jane Austen Ate and Charles Dickens Knew,* Edward Sackville-West's *Thomas De Quincey,* Charles Manby Smith's *Curiosities of London* (an 1853 account), Lytton Strachey's *Eminent Victorians,* Lytton Strachey's *Queen Victoria,* Judith Summers's *Soho: A History of London's Most Colorful Neighborhood,* Kate Summerscale's *The Suspicions of Mr. Whicher: A Shocking Murder and the Undoing of a Great Victorian Detective,* Matthew Sweet's *Inventing the Victorians,* F. M. L. Thompson's *The Rise of Respectable Society: A Social History of Victorian Britain, 1830–1900,* J. J. Tobias's *Crime and Police in England, 1700–1900,* Tamara S. Wagner's *Financial Speculation in Victorian Fiction: Plotting Money and the Novel Genre, 1815–1901,* Yvonne M. Ward's *Censoring Queen Victoria: How Two Gentlemen Edited a Queen and Created an Icon,* A. N. Wilson's *Eminent Victorians,* A. N. Wilson's *Victoria,* and A. N. Wilson's *The Victorians.*

Many of De Quincey's principal works are included in the following collections: *On Murder, Confessions of an English Opium-Eater and Other Writings,* and *Thomas De Quincey: Twenty-First-Century Oxford Authors,* all of them edited by Robert Morrison. To immerse yourself totally, go to the complete *Works of Thomas De Quincey* in twenty-one volumes, for which Grevel Lindop acted as general editor. (Somehow Grevel also found time to write about another fascinating author in his *Charles Williams: The Third Inkling.*) *Walladmor* isn't usually included in De Quincey's collected works, but he did indeed write that fraudulent Sir Walter Scott novel under the comedic circumstances that I describe.

About the title *Ruler of the Night:* When American essayist Ralph Waldo Emerson traveled to Britain in 1848, one of the authors he most wanted to see was Thomas De Quincey. They met in Edinburgh on four occasions, for one of which De Quincey walked ten miles in the rain (getting robbed by two children en route). Emerson gave a lecture about Transcendentalism and was so delighted by De Quincey's presence that he couldn't restrain himself in a journal entry: "To my lecture! De Q at my lecture!" The two spoke about De Quincey's opium addiction and how his nightmares led him to conclude that the human mind is composed of "chasms and sunless abysses, depths below depths." De Quincey later said that Emerson, referring to those opium nightmares, called him the "ruler of the night."

The mysterious Brunell, the rat-filled house on Greek Street, the haunted ten-year-old girl with whom seventeen-year-old De Quincey shared a horseman's blanket, and beloved Ann, the fifteen-year-old street-walker who saved his life—these are the most vivid parts of *Confessions of an English Opium-Eater.* De Quincey never stopped searching for the little girl, just as he never stopped searching for Ann. In fiction, he has now found both of them.

I'm grateful for the friendship and guidance of Jane Dystel and Miriam Goderich along with the other good folks at Dystel and Goderich Literary Management, especially Lauren E. Abramo, Mike Hoogland, Sharon Pelletier, and Amy Bishop.

I'm also indebted to the splendid team at Mulholland Books/Little, Brown/Hachette, particularly (in alphabetical order) Pamela Brown, Josh Kendall, Michael Noon, Tracy Roe, Ruth Tross, and Wes Miller.

My wife, Donna, gave her usual excellent advice as my first reader. It takes a special person to be married to a writer. She understands the tyranny of deadlines and loves narrative as much as *I* do. Her decades of companionship and wisdom have filled my life.

ABOUT DAVID MORRELL

David Morrell was born in Kitchener, Ontario, Canada. As a teenager, he became a fan of the classic television series *Route 66,* about two young men in a Corvette convertible driving across the country in search of themselves. The scripts by Stirling Silliphant so impressed Morrell that he decided to become a writer.

The work of another writer, Hemingway scholar Philip Young, prompted Morrell to move to the United States, where he studied with Young at the Pennsylvania State University and received his MA and PhD. There, he also met the esteemed science-fiction author William Tenn (real name Philip Klass), who taught Morrell the basics of fiction writing. The result was *First Blood,* a groundbreaking novel about a returned Vietnam veteran suffering from post-traumatic stress disorder who comes into conflict with a small-town police chief and fights his own version of the Vietnam War.

That "father" of modern action novels was published in 1972 while Morrell was a professor in the English department at the University of Iowa. He taught there from 1970 to 1986, simultaneously writing other novels, many of which became international bestsellers. They include the classic spy trilogy *The Brotherhood of the Rose* (the basis for the only television miniseries to be broadcast after a Super Bowl), *The Fraternity of the Stone,* and *The League of Night and Fog.*

Eventually wearying of two professions, Morrell gave up his academic tenure in order to write full-time. Shortly afterward, his fifteen-year-old son, Matthew, was diagnosed with a rare form of bone cancer and died in 1987, a loss that haunts not only Morrell's life but his work, as in his memoir about Matthew, *Fireflies,* and his novel *Desperate Measures,* whose main character lost a son.

"The mild-mannered professor with the bloody-minded visions," as one reviewer called him, Morrell is the author of more than thirty books, including *Murder as a Fine Art, Creepers,* and *Extreme Denial* (set in Santa Fe, New Mexico, where he lives). An Edgar finalist and a recipient of the Anthony, Inkpot, Macavity, and Nero awards, Morrell is also a three-time winner of the distinguished Bram Stoker Award. The International Thriller Writers organization gave him its prestigious Thriller Master Award.

With eighteen million copies of his books in print, his work has been translated into thirty languages. His writing book, *The Successful Novelist,* analyzes what he's learned during his more than four decades as an author. Please visit him at www.davidmorrell.net, where the page for *Ruler of the Night* features pictorial essays about some of the Victorian locations in this novel.